NOW YOU SEE IT

NOW YOU SEE IT

And now you don't

An aviation mystery
by

Tony Blackman

This book is entirely a work of fiction. All characters, companies, organizations and agencies in this novel are either the product of the author's imagination or, if real, used factiously without any intent to describe their actual conduct. Description of certain aircraft electronics have been altered to protect proprietary information. Mention of real aircraft incidents are all in the public domain.

Now you see it ISBN 978-0-9553856-7-4, 0-9553856-7-9
First Published 2009

Blackman Associates
24 Crowsport
Hamble
Southampton SO31 4HG

Previous books by the same Author

Fiction:-

A Flight Too Far
ISBN 978-0-9553856-3-6, 0-9553856-3-6
Published Blackman Associates

The Final Flight
ISBN 978-0-9553856-0-5, 0-9553856-0-1
Published Blackman Associates

The Right Choice
ISBN 978-0-9553856-2-9, 0-9553856-2-8
Published Blackman Associates

Flight to St Antony ISBN 978-0-9553856-6-7, 0-9553856-6-0
First Published 2008
Published Blackman Associates

Non Fiction :-

Flight Testing to Win (Autobiography paperback)
ISBN 978-0-9553856-4-3, 0-9553856-4-4
Published Blackman Associates September 2005

Vulcan Test Pilot
ISBN 1-904943-888 hardback
ISBN 978-1-906502-30-0 paperback
Published Grub Street June 2007/2009

Tony Blackman Test pilot (Autobiography hardback)
ISBN 978-1-906502-36-2
Published Grub Street June 2009

To Margaret, my long suffering wife, who once again has helped me in constructing this book, providing first class ideas, giving me continuous encouragement and providing painstaking editing. Without her support this book would never have seen the light of day.

Acknowledgements

This book could not have been completed without the help of specialist advisers, Melvyn Hiscock, Richard James, Georgia and Josh Hindle, Charles Masefield, Oliver Masefield, David Mason, Chris Payne, Rogers Smith, Kathryn Tuma and many others who have helped me in different ways.

Despite all the help I have received, there will inevitably be inaccuracies, errors and omissions for which I must be held entirely responsible, particularly as the technology in this book is at the edge of the possible now but, hopefully, will become commonplace in the years ahead.

Anthony L Blackman OBE, M.A., F.R.Ae.S

About the Author

Tony Blackman was educated at Oundle School and Trinity College Cambridge, where he obtained an honours degree in Physics. After joining the Royal Air Force, he learnt to fly, trained as a test pilot and then joined A.V.Roe and Co.Ltd where he became Chief Test Pilot.

Tony was an expert in aviation electronics and was invited by Smiths Industries to join their Aerospace Board, initially as Technical Operations Director. He helped develop the then new large electronic displays and Flight Management Systems.

After leaving Smiths Industries, he was invited to join the Board of the UK Civil Aviation Authority as Technical Member.

Tony is a Fellow of the American Society of Experimental Test Pilots, a Fellow of the Royal Institute of Navigation and a Liveryman of the Guild of Air Pilots and Air Navigators.

He now lives in Hamble writing books, giving talks and designing and maintaining databases on the internet.

DRAMATIS PERSONAE

Given Name	Family Name	Description
Peter	**Talbert**	**Aviation Insurance Investigator, Narrator of Book**
Adrian	Wallace	Chief Test Pilot, Murray Aerospace
Alice	Browning	Taipei Embassy official
Anne	Moncrieff	Surveyor, SRG
Arthur	Broderick	Marshall's salesman
Augustus	Tull	Boeing Test Pilot
Barbara	Maitland	First Officer, VP-BEV
Bill	Castleford	CEO, Castle Harbour Airlines
Bob	Furness	Head of AAIB, UK
Bruce	Shiu Liao	Senior Accident Investigator, CAAC
Cedric	Yao Xueqiang	Police, Hong Kong
Charles	Hendrick	Chief Pilot, Worldwide Airlines
Charles	Simon	Director General, UK Department of Transport, responsible for Safety
Charlie	Simpson	Art Insurance Expert
Chris	Henderson	MD Total Avionics, Basingstoke
Chuck	Steventon	Chief Test Pilot, Vision Unlimited
Derek	Finborough	Hull Claims Insurance
Eddie	Gonzales	Airlines Servicing, Newark
Fabio	Costello	NTSB Inspector
Elizabeth	Dunston	Worldwide Airlines, Purser
Frank	Daly	Worldwide Airlines Manager, Melbourne
Fred	Xie Tingxi	CEO, West Orient Airlines
George	Straker	Murray Aerospace sales
Harry	Foster	CEO, Vision Unlimited
Helen	Partridge	Talbert's Fiancée
Henry	Denis	Department of Transport
Jane	Roberts	FAA Safety Inspector
Jean	Spenser	Test Pilot, Vision Unlimited

Jimmy	Brown	Chief Engineer, EVS Total Avionics
John	Corrigan	Professor, New York State University
John	Luscombe	Minister of State for Transport
John	Southern	Hull Claims Insurance Executive
Jon	Larsen	Air Traffic Controller, Kulusuk
Jonathan	Stable	Chief Engineer, CHA
Ludwig	Teifel	Chief Test Pilot, European Aerospace
Margaret	Rogerson	Chair, British Board Film Censors
Martin	Spencer	Chief Pilot, CHA
Mary	Foster	Head hunter, Senior Placement Ltd
Mary	Turner	Charles Hendrick's secretary
Matt	Watkins	CEO, Total Avionics
Michael	Noble	Seattle Editor of Aviation Week
Mike	Mansell	Insurance Executive, Australia
Monty	Rushmore	EASA Test Pilot based at Gatwick
Olav	Pedersen	Kulusuk doctor
Oscar	Yang Jianli	Head of Maintenance, West Orient Airlines
Pat	Miles	Harry Foster's secretary
Patrick	Williams	Chief engineer VU
Philip,Sir	Brown	Permanent Secretary for Transport
Pietro	Greco	Chief Engineer, West Shore Airlines
Ricardo	Gemelli	Station manager, CHA Kennedy
Richard	Haycroft	CEO, Hull Claims Insurance
Roger	Chesterfield	Head hunter, Senior Placements Ltd
Roger	O'Kane	ITAC Avionics engineer
Ted	Gaillard	General Manager, Safety Management Air Services Australia
Thomas	Huai Tiantian	Hong Kong Air Traffic
Tommy	Tucker	Total Avionics project director, Vision Unlimited
Trevor	Smithson	Captain VP-BEV
Vince	Masella	General Manager, Air Transport Operating Group CASA
William	Roscoff	Avionics Support, Total Avionics
Winston	Tuan Feng	CAAC Avionics expert

ACRONYMS AND DEFINITIONS

Acronym or Expression	In full or explanation
AAIB	Air Accidents Investigation Branch
ABC	Australian Broadcasting Corporation
ATC	Air Traffic Control
ATIS	Automatic Terminal Information Service
ATSB	Australian Transport Safety Bureau
CAA	UK Civil Aviation Authority
CASA	Civil Air Safety Agency, Australia
CEO	Chief Executive Officer
C of A	Certificate of Airworthiness
DfT	Department of Transport
DOT	Department of Transportation, United States
EASA	European Aviation Safety Agency
EPIRBS	Emergency Position Indicating Radio Beacons
EVS	Enhanced Visual System
FAA	Federal Aviation Agency
FDR	Flight Data Recorder
FMS	Flight Management System
GAPAN	Guild of Air Pilots and Air Navigators
GPS	Global Positioning System
HUD	Head-up Display
ICAO	International Civil Aviation Organisation
ILS	Instrument Landing System
NTSB	National Transportation Safety Board
NWIA	New World International Airlines
PA	Aircraft Public Address System
PPL	Private Pilot Licence
SRG	Safety Regulation Group, CAA, Gatwick
TCAS	Traffic Collision Avoidance System
BOOK	**SPECIAL ACRONYMS**
CHA	Castle Harbour Airlines
ITAC	Independant Transport Aircraft Company
VU	Vision Unlimited
TA	Total Avionics

Author's Note – for the less technically minded

Examination of aircraft accident statistics in the real world shows that most accidents occur during the approach and landing phase of a flight. Furthermore, a contributory factor to these landing accidents is the state of the weather, despite the fact that there are definite weather minima and rules to which airlines and pilots have to adhere.

Landing weather minima are divided into three categories I, II and III with Category III minima covering landings in fog. Basically, a landing in Category III weather conditions at the present time requires the aircraft autopilot to make the landing instead of the pilot and in the very worst conditions, when the visibility falls below 200ft, the regulation authorities have to be satisfied that the autopilot will not fail or, if it does, the human pilot is able to complete the landing using a so called 'head-up display', usually situated in the flight deck roof. The pilot can pull down the glass of the display so that he or she is able to look through both the glass of the display and the windscreen and see computer generated visual cues in the display to help land the aircraft if the runway itself cannot be seen.

Currently, a Cat III landing may only be made on an airfield which has an Instrument Landing System installed; an ILS consists of two radio beams, one lining the aircraft up directionally with the runway and the other ensuring that it is on the correct descent path to the touchdown point. Furthermore, to be able to land in really bad weather the runway has to have very bright lighting installed on the final approach and also lights set into the runway itself.

Of course there are many airfields in the world that are not suitable for automatic landings due the surrounding terrain or because they do not have the necessary lighting or ILS to which the autopilot can be coupled. However, market forces make some of these airfields very important to airline operators and so they are always looking for ways of ensuring that their aircraft can land at these lesser equipped airfields regardless of weather. Consequently, aircraft and avionic equipment manufacturers are developing ways of showing the pilot the airfield and runway ahead by displaying the information on the head-up display, even when the runway is not immediately visible due to poor weather.

There are basically two types of simulated runway pictures that can be displayed on the head-up display during an approach, which the pilot can look at until the real runway can be seen through the windscreen. First there is the computer generated display of the runway from information based on worldwide airfield information held in a database; the second type uses real time active information from infra red sensors with, possibly, the addition of active aircraft based microwave radar. The computer generated picture on a head-up display is called synthetic vision and it relies on satellite global positioning systems to ensure that the computer generated runway lines up with the real one. However, a head-up display driven by real time information from infra red sensors and radar, an Enhanced Visual System, EVS, is a far more accurate system and will include extra information, such as showing if there are any aircraft or obstructions on the runway.

At the time of writing, the head-up displays which are described in this book and the information they display are slightly ahead of what is currently possible on commercial airliners. However, technology is advancing all the time and the pictures displayed on head-up displays will become better and better in the years ahead as new more capable sensors are introduced. The permitted weather minima when the pilot is landing an aircraft manually using an EVS on a commercial airliner in bad weather is a very important issue, as is the relationship between EVS and the autopilot when landing in Cat III conditions. It is vital that the introduction of these new systems, while giving greater capability, do not lower the overall safety standard of the operation.

Nevertheless, regardless of new technology, what does not change is human behaviour and this book is about the people who make, regulate and use the new systems.

ALB October 2009

INDEX	PAGE
Prologue	14
Chapter 1	18
Chapter 2	38
Chapter 3	67
Chapter 4	89
Chapter 5	115
Chapter 6	136
Chapter 7	153
Chapter 8	172
Chapter 9	188
Chapter 10	204
Chapter 11	223
Chapter 12	253
Chapter 13	286
Chapter 14	309
Epilogue	328

Prologue

"Trevor, go around, you're not lined up, we're much too fast," Barbara, all formality forgotten, yelled at the Captain, "go around, for God's sake Trevor, overshoot."

Barbara Maitland, first officer of a European 630 of Castle Harbour Airlines making an approach in fog on runway 22 Left at Kennedy airport, yelled again at the Captain. The aircraft was below one hundred feet above the ground but instead of the engine throttles being opened to maximum power, to her horror she saw they were still descending. She heard the radio altimeter automatically announce 'fifty feet' and suddenly Barbara saw the runway appear out of the murk to her left with the aircraft banked steeply to the left, impossibly trying to recover the centre line. There was a sickening lurch to the left as the left wing tip hit the ground and then the aircraft hit the runway very heavily, levelling off as both sets of main wheels impacted the ground. The aircraft carried on moving left leaving the runway and Barbara could see that they had touched down far too far down the runway to have any chance of stopping. Trevor had selected reverse thrust but the aircraft was not slowing down quickly enough as it careered across the airport, seemingly completely out of control and heading for the River Hudson at the far end of the airfield. She could see that disaster was inevitable and she stopped both engines and operated the fire extinguishers as the aircraft crossed runway 31 and careered down the bank into the water, finally coming to rest half submerged in the water. The flight was over.

***

The weather had been fine when they had left Bermuda at seven o'clock, just over an hour before, but the forecast at New York was for fog. As they had approached Long Island Barbara had heard the New York's Kennedy Airport broadcast weather information, ATIS, giving thick fog on runway 22 Left, the one they were going to have to use for landing. Barbara knew the fog would soon burn off but not in time for their landing.

Air Traffic had told them to approach the airport using the published 'Kennebunk Four' standard arrival air traffic procedure. Then the radar had taken over giving them directions so that they were taken a long way to the east of the airport in order that there was greater separation than normal between the aircraft landing in the fog. They had been cleared down to 10,000ft and looking ahead she had seen the low cloud.

As they had got nearer to the airport she could see the Manhattan skyscrapers sticking up through the cloud on her right so Barbara had known that the fog could not be very thick but as she listened to the airport weather it was clear that the cloud was going right down to the ground. Trevor Smithson, the Captain of the Castle Harbour airliner, had reduced speed as they were cleared down to 3,000ft and Barbara had selected the first flap setting for landing. As they got closer to the airport, approach radar had given them headings to line the aircraft up with the runway and then they had been cleared to start the approach. She had selected the landing gear down and set the flap for landing. Trevor had coupled the autopilot to the ILS and set the final approach speed on the auto throttle. Then, after making the final landing checks and getting clearance from air traffic control, Barbara saw that Trevor had selected the autopilot to make an automatic landing.

At 700ft they had gone into the fog. Everything on the electronic displays had looked perfect as the aircraft descended on the glide path. She had checked that the ILS showed that they were lined up with the runway, on the correct glide slope and that the speed of the aircraft was being accurately controlled by the automatic throttle.

As they had descended to 400 feet above the ground Barbara heard the runway visibility on the ATIS weather suddenly drop to 100 feet which was below their permitted landing minima.

She had called out "Captain, the visibility has just dropped to 100 feet."

Barbara had heard the warning horn as the autopilot was disconnected and out of the corner of her eye she saw the throttles start to open. Then to her amazement the throttles did not open any more and she realised with some alarm that Trevor was not going to carry out a missed approach but was going to try to land. She briefly looked ahead and for a moment she saw the approach lights immediately underneath them but then they were in fog again. She looked back at her instrument displays and saw that the aircraft was descending but going to the right of the centre line. In addition the airspeed was increasing above the correct approach speed.

"Trevor, you're going right, you're too high and you're too fast. Go around."

The radio altimeter had announced "One hundred feet" and Barbara yelled again at Trevor to abandon the landing. She saw that they were so high on the glide slope that they could never touch down in time. But Trevor seemed not to hear and everything from then on had seemed to happen in slow motion as she could see disaster was inevitable. Neither the reverse thrust nor the wheel brakes seemed able to stop the aircraft quickly enough and she stopped the engines as they raced across the airfield just before they went into the river.

Now, with the aircraft completely in the water she heard Trevor announcing over the cabin address system. "Evacuate the aircraft into the liferafts. There is no danger."

As she looked out of the windows the aircraft seemed to be sinking steadily and she yelled again at Trevor, this time to move, but he did not seem to hear. She unstrapped herself and as she opened the cockpit door freezing cold water poured in. She rushed back and put her lifejacket on and saw to her relief that Trevor was getting his out from underneath his seat. Looking down the cabin she could see it was half full of water. The cabin staff had opened the emergency exits and nearly all the passengers had left, clambering into the escape chutes which had inflated automatically as liferafts when the doors were opened. However the water was rising fast and by the time Barbara reached the front exit the icy water level was up to the top of her legs. As she forced herself out of the exit she was able to haul herself up into the liferaft where the rescued passengers looked very frightened, very wet and completely shattered. She turned round to see the cabin purser starting to follow her into the liferaft but she couldn't see Trevor. She tried to stop the girl getting in and yelled "Trevor, Trevor" but he did not appear and the girl pushed her away into the liferaft and cut the securing line. The liferaft was now drifting away from the aircraft; there were lots of boats coming to rescue them and all the other liferafts filled with the passengers and crew.

She shouted as a boat came alongside saying that Trevor was still in the aircraft but nobody seemed to be listening.

Chapter 1

The phone rang. “Peter Talbert?” I agreed. “This is Bill Castleford. I’m the CEO of Castle Harbour Airlines. I wonder whether you can help us?” I didn’t say anything but made a murmuring noise and he carried on. “Peter, one of our aircraft had an accident at Kennedy yesterday and slid into the water.”

“Bill, that’s terrible. When did it happen? I haven’t seen the papers to-day.”

“It was the first flight of the morning and apparently there was a shallow layer of fog. The aircraft was landing on 22 Left and something went wrong. It touched down but then veered off to the left, and went into the river at the far end of the airport. The cabin crew were magnificent and got all the passengers out.”

“Thank goodness for that. We should get a first hand account of what happened from the crew.”

“Yes and no. Very sadly the Captain died but the first officer is OK.”

“What happened to the Captain?”

“We don’t know. According to the first officer he should have been able to get out without any difficulties.”

“What aircraft type was it”

“It was a European Aerospace 630. Almost brand new in fact. We’d only had it a month. We’ve got five others but they are quite a bit older.”

“Well Bill, it should be a fairly open and shut case. The National Transportation Safety Board will have the crash recorders and they will be able to talk to the first officer. They should be able to get a report out very quickly. I assume the aircraft is a write off.”

“Yes, Peter. But we want you out here to help us. We’re worried about the insurance. Unfortunately it seems that how the accident happened may be relevant.”

“Who is insuring you?”

“Airplane Protection Inc based in Seattle. I’m worried that they will try to wriggle out of paying.”

“They won’t be able to do that, surely, even if the pilot did make a mistake?”

"They might try and say the aircraft was not properly maintained."

"Excuse my asking, but was it?"

"Absolutely. Costs us a bomb as we can't do it all on the island. We use Airlines Servicing at Newark."

"Anyway even if it wasn't, surely it can't matter should the accident be judged to be pilot error?"

"I'm not sure but these insurance companies can be very difficult, you know that."

"Yes, Bill, I am aware of that. When do you want me to come out. I'm tied up next week."

"I had hoped you would come out straightaway."

"Sorry, Bill. Can't make it. Anyway, by the middle of next week the NTSB will have analysed the crash recorders and there should be a lot more details of the accident available. To be frank, it will save you wasting your money paying me when I can't do anything."

"Now you mention it, what are your fees?"

"Daily fee plus itemised expenses including business travel."

"That sounds fair. Please send me an email confirming that so it's on record."

"I'll do that. I've been thinking, why don't I come out to Bermuda on Sunday, not this one but the next one and have a chat. I can then go on to New York on the Monday or the Tuesday?"

"Alright. I'll go along with that. Let me know your flight number. We'll meet you and book a hotel."

He hung up.

"That sounds as if you've got some more work, my love. Where was the accident?"

I looked at Helen, my partner, who had just come in with the *Daily Telegraph.* She looked great in a close fitting jumper, shortish skirt with long legs to match, but then she always did. We'd been together now for about a year since we had first met when I was working for Hull Claims Insurance, protecting their interests. They had been insuring a twin engined ITAC 831 of Worldwide Airways from Gatwick which ditched at night just off the coast of St Antony in the Caribbean. Helen was a cabin attendant at the back of the aircraft and, with another girl, saved the lives of over forty passengers as the rest of the aircraft sank with the loss of over two hundred passengers and crew.[1] She was now a First Class purser for the airline.

I explained the situation to her and the need for me to go to New York.

"Peter, that sounds as if I'd better try to bid for the East Coast routes then next month."

"Wait a minute. Don't jump the gun. I shall only be out there a day or so. It looks as if the pilot clearly made a mistake. Anyway I don't like flying with you when you're working. You look at me as if you've never seen me before, especially if I'm flying first class."

"But we enjoy layovers."

I looked at her. "I'm not sure that's a good description of the situation. You are understandably exhausted and invariably you have to go back the next day."

"Alright, I'll take time off and we can travel together."

"That will cost a fortune. You won't be being paid."

"All you can think about is money and, occasionally, sex. I get discounted travel and anyway, in the States, you only pay for the room, even if it's a ménage a trois." I could see her thinking. "What happened to that girl in New York?"

"I've no idea but she won't be joining us. Two's company, three's a crowd, certainly in bed they tell me."

We sat down to have lunch together.

"Peter, you've been looking frustrated for the last day or so."

I nodded. "It's all very well for you. Every few days you go off seeing the world. I have to sit here reading all sorts of requests from airlines to advise them on some incident and to tell them why they shouldn't be found to blame if someone has made a mistake."

"You've got a nerve. You've been to Australia, the Caribbean, the States, Bermuda and the Philippines doing goodness knows what. Always coming up smelling of perfume." I couldn't help smiling. "What are you grinning about? It's not a grinning matter."

"I knew a girl once who said the same thing."

---

[1] ***Flight to St Antony*** by same author

"You'd better keep her out of it." Helen looked at me. "You're very successful and you've got quite a few important airlines asking you for advice and getting you to talk to them. When anything goes wrong they're knocking at your door. Look, you know I'm right; that airline with the crashed aircraft has just phoned you. I rest my case."

"But I'm only consulted when things are going wrong. I don't feel I'm contributing to airline safety. Preventing things happening.

"Nonsense, every time you discover what has happened you are preventing something similar occurring again. Get over it, move on and eat your lunch. You can take me to that Chagall exhibition at the Royal Academy. It closes on Friday, that's to-morrow."

"So that's why you are all dressed up."

"I am not all dressed up. I look like this everyday and just you remember that. But you look as if you've just got out of bed and kept your pyjamas on."

"But I don't wear pyjamas in bed."

She grinned. "You'll have to go and change the moment we've finished eating."

"But my work."

"Bother your work. You'll do better when you've had some culture."

I acquiesced, took the paper and scanned the headlines.

"Peter."

There was something in Helen's voice that made me look up and pay attention. She was looking at the *Telegraph* pink pages which advertised the jobs vacant, mostly government jobs with very high salaries and often with no obvious responsibility to match the salary.

"Have you seen this?"

I looked at the page she was showing me. The Department of Transport was advertising a new post, Chairman Transport Safety Board, who would in effect be the Chief Accident Inspector. Apparently the intention was to unify the Marine Accident Investigation Board, MAIB, the Air Accidents Investigation Board, AAIB and the Rail Accident Investigation Board, RAIB.

"Do you think Bob Furness is going to apply?" Suddenly a look of comprehension appeared. "You bastard. You knew about it.

You might have told me. You're thinking of applying. That's why you've been going around all twisted."

"My parents wouldn't like to hear you talking like that, especially as it's not true." I considered the situation. "Well actually some civil servant rang me a couple of days ago. I would have told you but I was trying to put the whole thing out of my mind."

"Peter Talbert, you really are the ruddy limit. We're meant to be working as a team. You're so secretive."

She looked at me.

"Alright you're not twisted but it's as I said, you've got that frustrated look. You're wondering whether to apply for the job. Did he ask you to?"

"It doesn't work like that. He just wanted to make sure I knew of the impending change."

She looked at me as if she wasn't convinced.

"What did Bob say?" Bob Furness was the head of the Air Accidents Investigation Branch; she had never met him but she had heard me talking to him so often that she felt she knew him.

"How do you know I rang him?"

She raised her eyes as if I was mad. "Does a duck swim? Is he going to apply?"

"No and he's not too worried about having a new boss as he's leaving in another six months."

"Isn't there an obvious candidate?"

"Probably. I didn't like to ask."

"Presumably Bob guessed someone had told you?"

"I had a sort of feeling that he might have been talking to the Department himself."

"That's great. It will be shoe-in. When are you going to apply?

"Now wait a minute. I don't think I'd be a very good civil servant. Anyway, the advertised base salary doesn't seem very high for the importance of the job though apparently it will be based on experience. It certainly won't be a shoe-in. It should be a very demanding and prestigious job and there will be lots of applicants. The bosses of RAIB and MAIB for a start I should imagine."

"At least it's regular and it's pensionable as well."

"You've got a real point there. My pension is costing me a bomb. And these days I'm not sure if it's a safe investment. At least as Chairman I'd get a secure pension, it would be index linked too and I could retire at sixty."

I put the paper down and drank some coffee.

"Gorgeous, what time are we leaving?"

She look pleased. "Don't try that on. Are you going to apply?"

"Wait a moment. The advert has only just appeared."

"But you've been thinking about nothing else for the last day or so. Admit it."

I nodded. "I don't know what to do."

"Why don't you go and see Bob?"

"To-morrow, two o'clock."

"That settles it. It's two o'clock to-day for us as well, so get a shove on."

I went upstairs thinking about what I should do. The job was obviously a very responsible one but, even if I got it, I wasn't convinced that I would be a good choice. I was not really a team player as I liked to follow my own ideas and not have to get permission for everything I did. If I was running a department there would need to be rules which in my view tended to spoil initiative. And I would need to keep the Department of Transport civil servants up to speed.

"Are you coming down? Stop agonising and get some clothes on." Helen's voice penetrated up the stairs.

I smiled to myself. Helen understood me very well. I grabbed a blazer and tie, a suit would have been over the top, and went downstairs. We locked up and walked to the station. Forty minutes later we were in the Friends room of the Royal Academy having coffee and biscuits.

The exhibition was on the first floor and the rooms were packed, presumably because it was finishing the next day. It was very difficult to see the pictures and we both decided after an hour that enough was enough.

"I'm not sure I like his paintings all that much. You can take me to Tudeley on Monday to see his stained glass windows in the church there. I'm off to San Francisco to-morrow week."

"You always seem to be going to LA or San Francisco."

"They're our best routes."

"I'd go mad in the hotel waiting to fly back."

"That's why it's just as well you had to give up being an airline pilot. I find things to do. You sit on your computer reading about aviation. I love going to the theatre, the cinema, driving around. The Getty Centre is one of my favourites while I'm in LA."

"I've only been once. I loved the impressionist room."

"I love it all. Fantastic."

"Wait a moment. It's 23rd July and I'm at Farnborough at the beginning of next week at the Air Show. Then I'll have to go to Bermuda. Your glass gazing will have to wait."

"I thought the accident was in New York?"

"It was but I need to see the airline first."

"I haven't been to Bermuda."

"You wouldn't like it."

"Come on, don't try that one on me. You'd better suss out the hotels to find one I'd like in case you need to go back again."

We walked along Piccadilly to the Royal Air Force Club and then down to the Running Horse for an early supper. I handed Helen a menu and she put it down without looking at it.

"So what have you decided? "

I understood what she meant but I wasn't ready to make a decision, certainly not until I'd spoken to Bob.

"Fish and chips." I knew the menu by heart.

She looked at me and smiled. She knew I knew what she meant but decided not to respond.

"Good idea. Two fish, one chips, one salad and a coffee."

I gave the order with two coffees and returned to the table, right in the corner hidden from the bar and most of the room. Helen had got hold of an Evening Standard.

"Have you seen this?" She passed me the paper. A Murray Aerospace LightJet 100 had just been certified by the Federal Aviation Agency and was going to fly at Farnborough. "Peter, I'm confused. There seem to be so many new small jets. How many does that make?"

"Not sure. At least five. But the LightJet is different from most of them as it is single engined and aimed at the trainer rather than the business or utility market. It's not as fast, its performance is not as good but because its circuit speeds are much slower its more akin to the propeller trainers."

"I thought VLJs were taking over from the bigger business jets because they were more efficient and less costly?"

"It's not like that. There are two types really. The bigger versions have two engines for fast local flights like Southampton-Edinburgh and can be used commercially. The ones with just one engine are mostly fantastic sporty machines aimed at the guy who wants to feel like a fighter pilot."

"Sounds great, I want to feel like a fighter pilot but I'm not a guy or hadn't you noticed?"

"I've noticed alright and stop fishing for compliments. You're interrupting me but I've started so I'll finish. I think the new single engine ones, like the LightJet 100 have a great future, particularly if they have a reasonable range. They are getting very efficient and can take-off and land in quite a short distance, ideal trainer aircraft."

"Why don't we get one? I can learn to fly and you can learn to fly again."

"I love the idea of your learning to fly. Super idea. However, my love, I'm not anticipating having to learn to fly again. I can't help feeling that in my case 'getting current again' is a better description of what would be required."

"Don't bet on it, big head."

"Actually it's funny you should mention the LightJet. I was thinking of checking whether I can get a Private Pilot Licence in spite of my heart murmur. In fact I've arranged a medical on the Friday you're off to San Francisco. Mind you, we can't afford an aircraft of our own. Better to rent one when we need it."

"I thought you could share a plane these days."

"Yes, but I'm not sure if you can with VVLJs yet."

"Did you make up that acronym."

"Not sure, but you know what I mean. The ones with two engines or large single engines are called VLJs so the small ones which can be used for flight training need a different name."

Our food arrived and we went home after we had finished our coffees.

***

I was at the AAIB at Aldershot in plenty of time for my appointment with Bob. He came down to reception to meet me and we went up to his office.

"So Henry Denis rang you? I thought he might."

"No Bob. It was Charles Simon, whoever he is. He sounded like a real 'smoothie' talking about some of the investigations I'd done and buttering me up. He finally got round to mentioning the policy change and that the UK were going to copy the NTSB and have just one accident investigation organisation. I asked him why the change and he reckoned it would avoid duplication now that the boats and trains were going to carry sophisticated recorders. I didn't question him further but I did wonder whether the EU are about to pass yet another regulation to make it mandatory to have centralised accident investigation and then try to take it all over. Mind you the French would never agree unless the boss was always French."

"You may be right but you do realise that you got the Director General on the Transport Board responsible for safety calling you. You must be on the short list."

"That's ridiculous. I hadn't heard of the proposal until he called me and the more I think about it the more I have doubts whether I'm the right sort of person for that job. I don't think I'm going to apply."

"You must, Peter. You understand that accidents are invariably associated with human failings while so many people are hypnotised by the technology, which they don't really understand."

"But I don't think I'd make a good civil servant. I say what I think."

"Don't give me that. That's the last thing you do. You're like Hercule Poirot, you keep everything to yourself until the denouement. You're problem will be that you do what you want without consulting anybody."

"Well that's really what I meant, Bob. I don't like to wait for a decision from a committee."

"Simon must have checked you out or he wouldn't have called you. You must apply. I'll gladly sponsor you."

"Thanks very much. I really do appreciate that. However, it's a big decision."

"You can't keep travelling round the world every time there's an accident. You've got to let other people do it and report back. I know you like travelling and meeting people but you're getting too senior for that sort of thing."

"I'm not sure about any of that, Bob, but maybe I should settle down a little. Anyway the chances of being selected must be very slim. Remind me when the applications have to be in by."

"You've got another two weeks and then there will be an interview if you're short listed. They should tell you in a couple of weeks after that."

"OK. I'll think about it."

"Let me know what you're doing." Bob looked at some papers on his desk and passed me a newspaper cutting. "What do you think happened there?"

I looked at the Daily Mail which he passed me. Tucked away on page four was a small paragraph. 'Airliner slides off runway into water in New York.'

"Yes, Bob. I did know. It happened on Wednesday. I'm going out there next week. Castle Harbour Airlines. Will you be involved at all?"

"No. NTSB will be doing the investigation. Bermuda use the FAA for certification even though it is a British Overseas territory. It was a European 630 wasn't it?"

"Yes it was. They've got several I believe. All the passengers escaped except the Captain. The First Officer was OK. Don't know the details except it was foggy."

"Sounds like another lucky escape from the river Hudson."

"Well, yes. But this aircraft wasn't flying. Are you thinking of the one which had a double engine failure due to striking a flock of birds? The crew there did a fantastic job."

"Peter, the cabin crew must have done a great job in this one by the sound of it as well. As for not flying, the aircraft must have been going far too fast." He thought for moment. "Wonder what happened to the Captain?"

"I'll call you when I get back and let you know but I expect you'll already have heard from the NTSB."

"Possibly. In fact, what we hear and get from NTSB depends a bit on what happened and, sometimes, on the politics of the aircraft and its equipment. The reason for the accident is normally spot on but the recommended remedial action is sometimes debatable. You know, was it US built or was it Airbus and EU funded? Sometimes in the reports you feel as if some pressure has been applied. You must have read that recent one on the Rolls Royce engine."

"Have you seen this?" I pointed to the bottom of the page he had shown me. "I see FAA have certificated the Murray Aerospace LightJet. What puzzles me, Bob, is why didn't EASA do it at the same time?"

"It's funny you should say that. I noticed that as well and I've no idea why. Apparently the people in Cologne were dithering on how to classify the aircraft."

"How do you mean?"

"Whether to make it a trainer or just a normal jet requiring a type rating. Anyway I believe they've now decided to certificate it but a type rating will be required. Why are you interested?"

"I was wondering whether to try to get current again and maybe have a go flying it. I rather like the look of the aircraft."

Bob made no comment and we went down to the lobby and made our farewells.

"Peter, let me know when you apply and use me as a sponsor if you want to."

***

Over the week-end I had a look at Castle Harbour Airlines on the internet. They had some Boeing 737s and European 630s. and flew to most of the cities on the United States East Coast from Bermuda. Then I looked for the accident news items. The BBC news page mentioned the incident but did not give any useful details. I booked the flight to Bermuda for the following Sunday with open segments to Kennedy and back to Heathrow and then sent an email to Bill in Bermuda to let him know my arrival details.

On Monday I made my first visit to the Air Show, looked at the flying display aircraft, wandered round the stands and then met one or two contacts. I wasn't sure I liked Farnborough and the Air Display any more. It was so huge and tried to cater for everyone, not like the early days after the Second World War when there were lots of prototypes and people came to look at the planes. I had given up taking my car and trying to find somewhere to park years ago and relied on the train and buses.

On the Tuesday, as I had already been round the aircraft and the exhibition halls, I decided to go straight to Hull Claims Insurance where John Southern, a senior executive I knew well, had invited me for lunch; the firm didn't have a stand in the exhibition halls but had a small chalet on the third row overlooking the runway. As I made my way through the crowds of people looking at the exhibits in the halls, I saw there was a newspaper stand selling the *Evening Standard* with banner headlines 'Chinese airliner crashes in Hong Kong.' I grabbed a paper but hadn't had time to read it by the time I reached the chalet. John Southern saw me come in and came over.

"Great to see you, Peter, and for once there are no problems." He checked. "I mean none that affect you. For a change you're not rushing round on our behalf. Come and meet my new boss Richard Haycroft, he's the CEO."

Haycroft was clearly positioned to meet all the arriving guests; he looked very smart and professional wearing a grey suit, white shirt and plain blue tie. He was nearly six foot tall, stood very upright and looked very fit.

"Mr Talbert. I'm very glad to meet you. As you might expect, since I've taken over I've been looking through the recent accounts and it's clear you've helped us a lot. That ditching[2] last year could have bankrupted the firm."

"Call me Peter, please." I hesitated but decided to continue. "Yes, we were lucky to find out what had happened. To be frank, even though I tend to work for insurance firms, what always worries me is the total effect on the survivors and the dependents of these terrible accidents. Quite apart from losing their loved ones, some of them very understandably get into terrible financial straits." Haycroft nodded in agreement but I wasn't sure where his sympathies lay. "It always takes a long time for the final settlement

---

[2] ***Flight to St Antony*** by same author

and there seems to be no way of hastening things up." I looked at him. "By the way, who did pick up the insurance on the ditching in the end?"

Not surprisingly Haycroft was instantly ready with his answer. "The aircraft was actually on a long lease and the firm leasing it had a back-up insurance to cover situations like the Worldwide accident. It cost the airline a bit but most of the money came from the lessor. Insuring aircraft is such a challenging business even though they are getting safer all the time."

I nodded. "Yes, you're right, aircraft are incredibly safe these days. But despite all the design safeguards things still seem to go wrong. One never knows what is going to happen next."

Haycroft nodded his head vigorously. "You're right there. Did you see that yesterday morning a Chinese aircraft had a problem landing in Hong Kong and, unfortunately, we're insuring it."

"Not until just now. I haven't had a chance to read it yet." I showed him the paper I had just bought.

"It was a CC21 manufactured by Shenzhen Aircraft and operated by West Orient Airlines out of Taipei. Apparently it was foggy and it will almost certainly be a write off."

"Anyone killed?"

"No, thank goodness. The wings almost came off the fuselage and the fuselage itself is very crumpled apparently. Nothing we can do even though it looks as if the pilot made a mistake."

"Is it usual for your firm to insure a Chinese aircraft?"

"Good point. No, it's most unusual. However we insure the rest of the airline's fleet which are Airbus aircraft and so we were rather forced to take it on."

"It? How many have they got?"

"Just the one at the moment. It was brand new. Hope they don't get any more."

"Do you know what happened? What was the problem?"

"Don't know. We are completely frustrated because the pilots were taken away by the Hong Kong police so it has been impossible to talk to them. The Chinese investigators, CAAC, have the recorders. We'll probably have to pay up I'm afraid. Just as well no-one was hurt." A secretary came up to Haycroft. "If you'll excuse me. I'm sure John knows how to contact you if we need you." We shook hands and he went over to someone who looked as if he might have come from the Middle East.

John got me a half of Carlsberg and we sat down for lunch.

"I don't think you're very keen on our new Chief Executive."

"I think you're overstating the situation, John. As I said, even though I do a lot of work for you and other insurance companies, you know how I hate the way claimants have to wait while the insurers battle amongst themselves and the solicitors pick up fat fees. It all seems so unfair. It's bad enough to have an accident but the associated human problems are enormous, like losing your bread winner, for example." I paused and we watched the latest European Aerospace aircraft being towed away from the aircraft display park. "You told me there were no problems when I came in."

"None for you, I meant. There are always problems for us somewhere in the world. It's the nature of the business."

"What really happened at Hong Kong?"

"I've no idea. Richard has engaged a new young guy, Derek Finborough, from one of our competing firms, Aircraft Assured, and given him the job. I think Richard thinks I'm past it, and I'm sure Derek does for that matter. Maybe it is time I retired."

"Absolute nonsense. They clearly don't understand the business." A waiter brought us the menu. "I'm not looking for work but surely you need to be represented?"

"I think I would probably agree but it's not my call. Anyway at least Derek is there."

"Will you really have to pay? "

"No idea. Richard clearly thinks so. If the aircraft was doing a routine automatic landing then I can't see how we can avoid picking up the tab. Goodness knows what happened."

"John, apparently it was almost a brand new aircraft. Were they operating correctly? What equipment do their other aircraft have? Do you have any caveats in your insurance?"

"You bet we do. The aircraft has to be properly maintained and it has to be operated within the regulations. Very important of course for a Category III landing where the crew have to be correctly trained. "

"There could be a lot of arguments over those caveats."

"You're right, but it's not a take it or leave it situation. We always have to pay fifty percent but not the full amount if, for example, the software is not up to the latest standard and it is relevant to the accident."

"So your man Derek will obviously be checking everything out?"

"He should be but, I told you, Richard is supervising him, not me."

John clearly didn't look too pleased with the situation. I suspect he would have had me out there straight away if he'd been responsible.

"John, it's strange but you must have seen that accident the other day at Kennedy when the plane went off the runway into the Hudson?" He nodded. "That's two fog accidents in a week."

"Not all that strange, Peter. Most aircraft accidents occur during landings and normally due to bad weather. Are you involved?"

"Yes, Castle Harbour airlines want me to look after their interests. I gather it's insured with Airplane Protection. Not sure I agree with you about the accidents. I think it's very strange, John, because I believe both aircraft were on Cat III approaches."

"Well you'll soon know when you get out there."

The lunch took some time so by the time our coffee arrived the flying display was starting. I looked at the flying programme which had been inserted in the exhibitors catalogue.

"Peter, what are you looking at?" He smiled. "Not the aircraft, surely? I'd have thought you've been to these shows so often you wouldn't bother."

"I'm curious about the very very light jets as I call them. Not the ones with two engines but the small single engined ones."

"We've had a few requests to insure VLJs and we've decided to keep clear of the ones with just one engine. We're not going to take them on. The fast ones with high performance are liable to get the private pilot into trouble. The slow ones are probably safer but we think a new pilot is better off with a propeller than a jet when learning to fly; they fly more slowly and there is a real advantage to having the slipstream over the wing and elevator controls. The field lengths required tend to be longer with a jet engine because the take-off and landing speeds are usually higher which makes flying it more demanding for a student, especially the emergency landing."

"But the engines are more reliable and they are much simpler for the pilot to control than a conventional piston engined/propeller combination."

"You may be right but the response time for the thrust to build up when the throttle is opened from idling power is much greater for a jet engine. At the moment we are just watching and letting the statistics build up. Airlines and commercial airplane manufacturers are our specialty and it keeps the numbers of our clients down. VVLJs as you call them will be very numerous and there will be too many customers for us to deal with. Anyway why are you so interested?"

"I'm thinking of getting my pilot licence back again if the doctors will let me."

"That's great. When will you know?"

"I'm going to Gatwick next Friday to the CAA down there. The whole thing is a bit ridiculous. I've got an FAA Airline Transport Rating and assuming I pass my medical all I have to do in the States is to get checked out again and pass current air law. Over here because I haven't flown for a long time my previous experience is quite likely to be ignored. I may have to start again to get a private pilots licence."

"But the medical requirements, are they the same in both countries?"

"I believe so."

"Do the rules permit ab initio training on a jet aircraft and not a propeller?"

"A very good question. Don't see why not but I'm not an expert. It's so confusing these days with EASA; they are a typical European organisation making rules and regulations as fast as they can which we slavishly follow and the French find ways to interpret differently if it suits them. All your questions are ones I've got to sort out in the next few weeks."

We watched the aircraft flying. There were about four small single engined jets, Embraer, Cessna and Cirrus had their latest models but the Murray Aerospace LightJet 100 was the one that got my attention. The plane was by far the smallest of VVLJs with only 1,100 lb of thrust from the jet engine, which was placed at the back of the aircraft. The tailplane was divided into two and cranked in a V shape with an elevator behind the two sections so that the jet exhaust went over the top. There were twin rudders fixed to the ends of the tailplane. It reminded me of a very old design, the Miles Student, which had been proposed to the Royal Air Force as an ab initio jet trainer. The thing that attracted me to this arrangement was that there was no butterfly tail which instinctively I did not like, though quite clearly the VVLJs with butterfly tails were much cleaner in design with lower drag. However, the LightJet take-off and landing performance was superb though it wasn't quite as fast or as sporty as the other VVLJs. It was a lot lighter and significantly cheaper than the high performance single engined aircraft and clearly was going to make great inroads into the ab initio market. With the low speed performance it was demonstrating, there didn't seem to be any point in flying a propeller aircraft at all since it would be able to take-off and land from almost any farm field. The one problem that I could see was the cost of fuel since it would use more than a propeller aircraft; the jet engine was not as efficient as the piston engine so despite the small size and good economics of the LightJet engine it was always going to be more expensive on which to train. However, the life of the small jet engine should be better than the piston engine which would tend to compensate for the extra fuel burnt per flying hour.

"That's the one for me, John. If I'm allowed to fly again it will be the LightJet."

"It looks pretty Mickey Mouse to me, Peter. The rear end looks very different from the others."

"Yes, you're right, that's what I like about it. Not sure about butterfly tails. And the good news is that it has just been certificated by the FAA. Its performance looks good for short fields. If it can displace the propeller I think it will be a winner."

"Rather you than me. How many seats has it got? You may need more than two seats one day."

I looked at John and wondered if he was clairvoyant. I too had been thinking that Helen might decide that we should start a family and I wondered if I would be the last or the first to know. I supposed I could hardly complain since I sometimes omitted to tell her everything I knew or had discovered.

"Well I think it has room for two close together up front and two small seats behind and, because of its strange rear fuselage, there is quite a lot of room in a compartment over the engine."

"You've been looking."

"You bet."

We chatted some more and then I walked to the bus stop on the airfield as the aircraft carried on their demonstrations. Luckily there were some other people seated in the bus so we did not have to wait long before it left for Farnborough Main station. Two changes and one hour ten minutes later I got back to Kingston and walked home.

Helen was waiting for me, looking at her watch. "Good. I was just about to ring you. You've got twenty minutes to change and then we're off to the Dunstons. Elizabeth is a First Class purser like me on Worldwide Airlines and Tom is a Captain with BA." She looked at me. "You look a mess, can't think what you've been doing at Farnborough, I'll drive. They've got a house on the Thames."

There was no point in answering or arguing so I didn't and after a quick change we were on our way. The traffic was not too bad and an hour later we were seated outside the house, having a drink looking at all manner of boats going by. The Dunston's had two children at primary school and I noticed that they were reading and not watching television which impressed me. Tom clearly knew all about the Worldwide Airlines ITAC 831 night ditching at St Antony a year earlier where I had been involved and had met Helen. He started asking me about the electrical failure the aircraft had had.

"Actually Tom we were very lucky to find out exactly what went wrong. The aircraft had the latest crash recorders so that the voice recorder lasted the whole flight instead of just the last two hours being available. Had it only met the old operating requirement of two hours we might not have heard the failures occurring on the recorder."

"Peter, did you read about that European 630 that landed and ran off the runway into the Hudson?" I nodded. "I wonder what happened there. Apparently it was thick fog when he landed."

“Yes, I did know about it. The airline have asked me to act for them. I’m going out on Sunday.”

“I saw a headline on the *Evening Standard* to-day. It looks as if there’s been another one in Chek Lap Kok. Won’t be good for airline accident statistics this year.” He looked at me. “I suppose you’re involved with that as well?”

“Actually no, but I was with the insurers to-day so I was aware of it.”

“Don’t they want you to go out and find out what happened?”

“They think they’re going to be liable and they don’t want to incur any extra expense by sending me out.”

“Sounds unlikely. I thought insurance companies never gave up.” I nodded and felt he had a point. We finished our drinks and went inside where Elizabeth and Helen had prepared a buffet meal. It occurred to me as I started eating the rather splendid buffet that having trained airline pursers as partners wasn’t all bad.

“Elizabeth, how on earth do you manage to carry on flying with two kids?”

“With difficulty, but I have a great friend who lives close by and is always delighted to live in. Tom and I try to bid for flights so we are not both away at the same time. To be blunt we need the money. The kids are at a private school which is a hell of a drain.”

I nodded but didn’t comment. If Helen had any children I wondered if she would want to carry on flying; her parents lived near Portsmouth and mine were in Cheshire so if we lived near London we wouldn’t have a parent option. I wasn’t sure that I would make a good baby minder and, anyway, I was always liable to be called away. I glanced at Helen who looked as if she was thinking of something else but it occurred to me that if I were to get the accident supremo job it would help a bit. Knowing her, she had probably already worked that one out.

We didn’t stay very late and, as I had had only a slimline tonic, Helen gave me the car keys. When we got back I realised from the way she started to take her clothes off in the living room that it was just as well she had given me the keys, not that I was complaining, quite the reverse. However as we lay in bed, the evening still had not finally finished. My mobile was ringing.

"Peter, Derek Finborough of Hull Claims. I'm in Hong Kong looking at that CC21. I need you out here to discuss Cat III operation with the Chinese people. Can you get a flight out to-morrow morning?"

There was something about his voice which put my back up. Maybe he thought I was a full time employee with Hull Claims.

"Mr Finborough, it's one o'clock in the morning here and I don't have my diary in bed with me. I'm fairly busy at the moment. I'm not sure I'll be able to help you. Let's talk in the morning."

I could hear that my answer hadn't gone down well but I wasn't prepared to get involved so late at night with an accident that could be investigated at leisure. We exchanged a few unhelpful remarks and I rang off.

"What on earth was all that about? You didn't sound too cooperative."

"I haven't had time to tell you but Hull Claims have got a new guy on the block who has a lot to learn, like good manners. He's in Hong Kong dealing with that aircraft that left the runway at Chek Lap Kok."

"I noticed that accident but I didn't know you were involved."

"I'm not really. I only heard the news when we were having lunch to-day."

"It's a Hull Claims insurance job then?"

"Yes it is but in fact it's nothing to do with me at the moment and I'm not sure I want it to be. I'll probably turn the job down if it comes my way; I need to think about it."

"Well turn your phone off and come back over here, I want to make sure."

"Make sure of what?"

"Never you mind. I'll tell you later."

Chapter 2

It was Wednesday but there didn't seem to be a need to rush and get up in a hurry. Helen wasn't going anywhere and subconsciously I was trying to avoid dealing with the Hong Kong problem, but the phone rang.

"Peter, John Southern here." I wasn't surprised but I definitely wasn't delighted. "Derek Finborough is upset because you wouldn't agree to go to Hong Kong."

"John, does he think I work for Hull Claims? He called me after midnight and told me he wanted me to travel to-day, this morning, to Hong Kong. As you know I've got a few things on at the moment like going to New York and anyway there doesn't seem to be any urgency. Presumably the Chinese are looking at the Flight Data Recorders. They've got the two pilots so they should be able to find out exactly what occurred and they will be getting statements from Air Traffic. If your man needs help why doesn't he get a local guy who can speak the language and understand the politics of the situation? In my view the solving of this accident could be more than just a technical issue."

"That's what I told him and I think that's what he's going to do. Incidentally you weren't the only one to get a call after midnight. He rang me after you'd read his fortune."

"I thought I was very polite in the circumstances. Do you know what his problem is?"

"Not really. I think he doesn't understand the way the aircraft systems work and the way Chinese accident investigations are carried out."

"Well in that case he's in the wrong business. Anyway he doesn't need me for that. Would you mind telling him I'm not available?"

"I'll do that."

We got dressed slowly and I got the paper in before I sat down at the kitchen table."

"When's your medical?"

"Friday. It's written on the calendar."

"That's convenient, I'm off to San Francisco then."

"Should you be going in your condition?"

Helen looked at me and shrugged her shoulders. "I should have known I'd not get away with it. However if I am pregnant I intend to fly until I'm eight months."

"I don't think that's allowed and you'd frighten all the passengers."

"Anyway what makes you think I'm enceinte, as they say? One swallow doesn't make a summer."

"I think you're getting your metaphors mixed up and anyway I made it two, but then I was on slimline tonic and you clearly weren't."

"We could make it three to be on the safe side."

"I'm having breakfast."

"So it was true after all."

"What was?"

"Never to believe the saying 'Of course I'll still love you in the morning.'"

"But I do and I'd still love you even if you didn't look like you do now, absolutely fabulous."

Helen looked at me, clearly deciding whether to let me finish my piece of toast.

"What time is it?"

"Half past nine. What's the rush, we've got all day?"

"No, when is it?"

"When is what?"

"Your medical. It is at Gatwick isn't it? You could take me or we could go by train."

"1400."

"Good. I've got to report by 1100 for my San Francisco flight. We can go together and you can have lunch there or meet one of your girl friends in SRG."

I wouldn't have put Anne Moncrieff[3] in that category but in fact I had been thinking of trying to contact her. "I'll take the car to

---

[3] ***Flight Too Far*** by same author

save you carrying your bag and you can travel in uniform. However, I probably won't be able to meet you when you come back. When's that by the way?"

"Tuesday 1000."

Helen absentmindedly got herself some cereal and I tried to read the paper.

"Are you serious about starting to fly again?"

"Are you serious about learning to fly?"

"Why not? I'd get more pay as a pilot than a purser."

"It might take bit longer than you think."

"Well I could start. But how about you?"

"Well I rather fancy flying that Murray Aerospace LightJet, but a lot has got to happen first. Like my medical for a start."

"There's nothing wrong with you my love that I've noticed and I do tests that you don't get at any medical that I know of."

"But I don't get an electrocardiogram at the same time."

"Just as well as it would be most uncomfortable. And I hate that grease to ensure a good electrical contact." I could see her thinking. "Can we afford it? Are you going to buy the plane or just rent one?"

"Can't answer any of those questions and not going to try until I know if they are going to let me fly."

I went in to my office and tried to catch up with my work. I tried calling Anne Moncrieff at home and to my surprise she was in.

"What are you doing on Friday? Will you be at Gatwick and how about a quick lunch?"

Her French accent was still there. "Yes I'll be there. What do you want? I take it this is not a social call."

"I want to know who to talk to about aircrew licensing."

"Not sure, but I can find out. Why do you need to know?"

"I'm thinking of flying again. I'll explain when I see you. Can you manage twelve o'clock?"

She agreed and I decided that at the very least I'd better download the application form for the Chairman, Transport Safety Board. I went on to the Department of Transport web site and found the advertisement for the post. I noticed that the Government was using a recruitment agency which I knew was standard practice but I felt was probably unnecessary and a waste of money since the

Department were going to have their own team to choose the Chairman. Furthermore the agency, in order to try to demonstrate how thoroughly they were doing the job, had made the application form unbelievably long, twelve A4 sheets. I printed the form out and tried to work out what was really required. I came to the conclusion that all I needed were two referees, an explanation of why I felt I would be the right person for the job and an account of my work history including relevant accomplishments.

There was no way that this information, except for the referees, could fit neatly on to the downloaded form pages; clearly I would have to write it all up and attach the information to the form. Bob had agreed to be one referee and John Southern was my other obvious choice. I downloaded another copy of the form and started making a draft. After I had waded through all the sheets and decided how I would reply, I started on the serious work of analysing why I was considering applying for the job and why I felt I could do it.

I felt a tap on my shoulder. Helen had crept in and was looking at what I was doing. “So you’ve decided to apply?”

“I suppose so. I’m still not sure it’s me but I think I’d like to have a go.”

“Well I think that what you lack in diplomacy you will make up in intelligence.”

“That’s a very back handed compliment, and I’m not sure you’re right. These days a lot of people are very suspicious of cleverness. They’re afraid of it. They want ‘mensa’ to be what the Romans intended, a wooden table, not a society of the intelligentsia. Anyway it doesn’t matter what you and I think, it’s what those civil servants in Whitehall think that’s going to decide who gets the job.”

“Don’t the politicians have a say?”

“Not if the civil servants can help it.”

“Peter, far be it for me to argue with you but I’m not sure you’re right. On these quangos, I’ve noticed that the people who get these very highly rewarded jobs often don’t seem to have any particular qualification except being in the right political party and maybe related in some way to a politician.”

“I’m not saying your wrong, darling, but you’d better be careful where you are when come out with remarks like that or I definitely won't get the job. Anyway I would hardly call this new Safety Board a quango. If it is I don't want to be associated with it."

"If it is a quango you do want to be associated with it since what it does doesn't matter." I shook my head since a Board without real purpose and effectiveness would be of absolutely no interest to me. "Anyway you had better get on and don't forget I want to read it before it goes out. It's got to be checked for spelling, punctuation and tact."

She went out and I started trying to list why I was the ideal person to get the job. It wasn't easy since, though I had proved to be a good investigator, it didn't follow that I would be good at supervising not one but three investigation departments, in very different environments, air, rail and sea. However, I noticed that the new job didn't have 'accident' in its title which I felt was good because it was always much better to try to prevent an accident than investigate why one had occurred.

The equipment required to be fitted on all types of vehicles, such as recorders and GPS position transmission via satellites, was rapidly becoming very similar though the information they recorded was very different; nevertheless the analysis of the data in recorders with the positional information was going to be very similar. Another aspect that occurred to me was that all forms of transport were becoming a lot safer so I wondered whether it might be more efficient to have fewer inspectors but have them capable of dealing with any type of accident, though specialists would always be required for consultation. In addition I had noticed that the American NTSB covered roads and all types of disasters such as oil pipeline failures, which I rather favoured, but I wasn't convinced that the UK was ready for such a big change. If I got the job then I'd reassess the situation since accident avoidance was the real driver. I smiled to myself thinking I was already re-writing the mission statement; perhaps I could do the job after all.

I decided to ring John Southern and tell him what I was doing. "You're not serious, Peter? I always think of you as a doer, not as an office manager. Surely if a catastrophe happened you'd want to be there, not twiddling your thumbs wondering what was going on and thinking how you would be doing the investigation."

"Possibly John. But these days if something goes wrong it's necessary to get help. Remember how we prevailed on the UK and St Antony governments to fund recovering that aircraft that was in the water?[4] Then there was the need to search for that aircraft near Bermuda[5], we needed government help for that as well. You told me yourself the other day that I should stop travelling all over the world."

"Touché, Peter. By the way I'd be absolutely delighted to be a referee if you need one. I know you'll be absolutely first class in the job. Incidentally I think you'll be splendid on TV as well. You hate giving out information.

"Thanks a lot. Let's hope if I get the job I won't be invited to appear or talk on the media."

"If there are any serious accidents, my friend, you will be pushed to the front by the DfT and the politicians."

I hung up and tried to do some more work but decided that I had had enough. Helen closed the book she was reading and we went out to the Red Lion for supper. We had had to cancel our visit to Helen's parents on Saturday since she was going to be away. It was a pity as I knew they were clearly bemused that Helen was living with me but there was no talk of marriage. What I hadn't told them was that I too felt that the situation was rapidly becoming unsustainable and I was wondering when to choose my moment.

On Thursday morning I got up and prepared a full English breakfast downstairs. Helen came down and clearly approved. She sat down and poured some coffee. "Well what are we going to do to-day?"

I looked at her. "Well, I thought I'd start by asking you to marry me."

She looked at me, clearly not knowing whether to be pleased or cross. Then she came over and embraced me. "You really are impossible. What a way to propose."

---

[4] ***Flight to St Antony*** by the same author

[5] ***The Final Flight*** by the same author

"You're quite right I need practice. You ought to be flattered that you're getting my first attempt."

"Rubbish. It may be your first with me but definitely not your first attempt since presumably you proposed to your ex-wife and goodness knows how many other girls you've proposed to.

I tried not to flinch as she hit me. "Anyway you haven't answered my question."

"You'll have to be a lot more romantic than that to get an answer."

"Not sure I can. We'll just have to wait until February 29th and see how you feel then."

"But that was only a few months back. He'll be illegitimate by the next one."

"No she won't because we'll be married."

"Don't bet on it. I might take a fancy to a young airline Captain."

"But he won't want a ready made daughter."

"Son. And he'll be delighted."

"Why don't you just say 'yes' and I'll buy you lunch."

"You're going to buy me lunch anyway and I might let you know then."

The phone rang.

"Peter Talbert?" I nodded and agreed. "This is Harry Foster. I'm the CEO of Vision Unlimited, we're based in Palmdale CA. We make Enhanced Visual Systems." I knew of the firm vaguely but I wasn't very sure of what they did exactly. "Are you still there, Peter?"

"Yes, Harry. I can hear you fine."

"I expect you know we're very much in the aviation electronics business. In the last few years we've been developing enhanced visual systems to make sure the pilot can see to land whatever the weather, using head-up displays, HUDs. The pilot looks through the HUD glass and can see the runway displayed using special forward looking sensors on the glass even if the weather is so bad he can't see the real runway through the windscreen. Ours is an enhanced enhanced visual system if you like. We've had the airplane companies looking at our products and they are very enthusiastic but I thought I'd like to have someone who is completely independent flying with us and telling us what he thinks. I've followed one or two of the accidents you've been involved with, Peter, and I have been very impressed with your approach. How would you like to come out and visit us and let us show you what we've been doing?"

"Harry, I'd like that very much. However, if I may enquire, what makes your system better than the opposition?"

"Well, as you know on head-up displays you can have several levels of displays. The most elementary display on a HUD is a command bar calculated from the autopilot computer which, if the pilot follows it, enables him or her to land manually. Normally there is additional symbology as well on the display such as the radio altimeter, aircraft speed and deviations from the desired flight path so the pilot doesn't have to look down to get this supporting information."

"But that's not called synthetic vision is it?"

"No, it's not. I was just coming to that, Peter. As you may know, the next level of display on the HUD is for the aircraft to carry a worldwide database of airfields and runways so that on the approach a computer calculates where the runway is and what the airfield looks like and shows the computed runway. That's called synthetic vision but it relies for accuracy on global positioning systems like GPS and Galileo. On a bad weather approach when the real runway appears, the synthetic runway will only lie over the real runway if the aircraft calculated position and heading are correct."

"So what does your system do?"

"Well the next level of HUD display uses passive infra red sensing. The infra red sees the runway and it displays it on the HUD. The quality of the runway display depends on the weather between the aircraft and the airfield. However, the runway will always overlay the real runway when it appears out of the fog, rain, snow or dust. Nevertheless, despite what you see advertised we don't believe that the display is good enough in all weathers and so we have pioneered the introduction of microwave radar which paints a picture of the runway on the HUD."

"Can you use just the radar by itself?"

"Not in our system. The radar really is a supplement to the infra red. Our EVS mixes the displays of the infra red and the radar making the display less dependent on the ground database and the calculated position information."

"That sounds fantastic Harry. I've believed for some time that all large commercial jets should have EVS for the airfields that are not equipped with Cat III ILS so that the pilot can 'see' the runway whatever the weather conditions. Of course it would probably be safer if all approaches and landings of these large aircraft were by autopilot getting the very fallible human pilot out of the loop. Unfortunately this is not always possible because in some cases the airfield has geographical features which prevent a Cat III ILS system being fitted but marketing pressures still make the airlines want to land at these airfields, so EVS that really works seems a good substitute."

"Well we're agreed about that and we feel that our EVS is the answer and it really does work superbly with the added radar." There was a pause. "Peter, excuse me asking but do you have a commercial licence?"

"I've got an ATR but I don't have a current medical at the moment though hopefully I'll have one by the time I come out. I'll need to do some flying before I'm current again."

"No problem. You can do some flying on our Raytheon 800. When can you come out?"

"Not sure exactly but in the next few days."

"Yes, that'll be fine. We will start you off in the simulator of course to save wasting flying time."

"How do I contact you?"

"Have a look at our web site. It's all there and you can see the system working. I'm in New York at the moment."

"What will be the financial terms?"

"We'll pay business class travel, allowable expenses like hotel rooms and of course your daily consultant fee."

"OK. That's a deal."

I put the phone down. Helen had been listening intently to the conversation. "Who on earth was that?" I explained about Vision Unlimited. "But my love, why do they need you?"

"I'm not really sure. The CEO obviously thinks it will be a good idea. He has followed some of the accidents that I've been involved in. It will be interesting to hear what he is looking for when we meet."

"Where is it?"

"On the West Coast, Palmdale."

"That's great, you can come out on one of my flights. We should be able to have at least one night together."

"You're jumping the gun. I don't know when I'm going and you've got your schedule to keep."

We went out to the Withies in Compton. It was very busy outside so we sat near the bar.

Helen leant over. "I've decided to accept your offer." I kissed her on the hand, produced a ring from my pocket and put it on her ring finger on her left hand. "You're lovely but you're so sneaky." She examined the solitaire diamond ring. "How did you know I would like the ring?" She had another look. "I don't like to say this and give you an even bigger head than you have at the moment but you were quite right. It's lovely." She thought for a moment. "And you're so lucky because the ring fits perfectly."

"That wasn't exactly luck. I took that aquamarine you sometimes wear on your other hand along to the jeweller."

"It's just as well I don't trust you. You may kiss me." I obliged but as she offered her lips she breathed in and suddenly leant back. "That beef smells great. I'm hungry. I'll have a warm roast beef sandwich on white."

"That's not a terribly romantic prelude to the start of an engagement and a wedding breakfast."

"It's an engagement lunch. You'd better save up for the breakfast."

We went straight back after we had eaten and Helen suggested that I'd better work out when I was going to Vision Unlimited but I knew I could not do that since I had no idea how long I would be in New York. I was about to explain that to Helen when the phone rang again.

"Mr Peter Talbert?" I nodded and made an agreed sound. "My name is Fred Xie Tingxi. I'm the CEO of West Orient Airlines. I wonder whether you can help us?" I didn't say anything but made a murmuring noise and he carried on. "Mr Talbert, did you see that one of our aircraft, a CC21, had an accident at Chek Lap Kok and went off the runway?"

"Yes, Mr Tingxi, I noticed that. It was a Cat III landing wasn't it?"

"Right. Well Hong Kong authorities are saying that the crew hazarded the lives of the people in the aircraft and the police have got hold of the two pilots." I didn't say anything. "Are you there, Mr Talbert?"

"Yes, Mr Tingxi. I'm here but I'm not sure what you're telling me. Are you saying the police have imprisoned the crew? That's vindictive. What are they up to?"

"Our solicitor says the airport authorities are encouraging the police to hold the pilots as the accident caused a severe disruption of traffic flow. I think they are being particularly difficult because we are a Taiwanese airline. I called you because I know your track record. We need your help. Apart from anything else we want to make sure the insurance company pays us as soon as possible and doesn't try to wriggle out of their commitment. You know them, Hull Claims."

"Yes, Mr Tingxi. I know them very well. They don't like paying out if they can avoid it."

"Most insurance companies are like that."

"Yes, but I think they are tighter than most. I've done some jobs for them."

"So I have noticed. You must have saved them a lot of money. That's why I'm asking you to act for us. You are good."

"Mr Tingxi, you're very kind but you would be wasting your money. By chance I've already discussed the case with Hull Claims. They've got a man in Hong Kong. I got the feeling they were resigned to paying out."

"When did you speak to them? Did they know that the Chinese Authorities are holding the crew? They may decide that there may be a way of avoiding paying the full amount if we can be blamed. And anyway it will be a first class excuse to delay paying us."

"You could be right, Mr Tingxi." I thought for a moment. "Unfortunately I'm off to the States on Sunday for a few days. Anyway, I couldn't take the job on until I've spoken to Hull Claims bearing in mind I've already discussed the accident with them and they've got a man with you. And another thing, nothing much is going to happen before the Chinese accident authorities, CAAC, have examined the recorders and made a statement. Hull Claims will never pay you until the Chinese have said something."

There was a pause as Fred was clearly thinking the situation through. "Alright, Mr Talbert. I'm very disappointed that you can't come straight out. If you change your mind please let me know straightaway. I'll send you an email so you'll know how to contact me."

I put the phone down. Helen had been listening intently to the conversation. "Was that the Chinese airline?" I nodded. "John Southern isn't going to be pleased."

"Why? I didn't agree to help him. Anyway it's not up to him. He's being sidelined. It's my decision."

"Hadn't you better talk to John just in case? He's a much bigger client of yours than the airline. We'll need all the money we can get for school fees."

"Are you telling me something?"

"No, but I'm sure we can't do without Hull Claims. Call him now. I know it's Sunday but airplanes don't know what day of the week it is."

"It's not really that urgent. As I told Mr Tingxi, the Chinese have got a lot of work to do to analyse the records. It's not as if something was time dependent. And Derek, or whatever his name is, is already out there. "

"Peter, just do it."

I couldn't help grinning. I'd heard the phrase before! But it wasn't worth arguing about.

John answered the phone.

"I've had Mr Tingxi on the phone."

John butted in. "West Orient Airlines CEO?"

"Yes, do you know him?"

"Yes, I did the insurance with him. What did he want?"

"He wants to retain me to look after their interests in that Hong Kong accident we were talking about." There was a long silence. "John, are you there?"

"Yes, Peter. I'm here. I don't know what to say. You know perfectly well if I'd been running this investigation you'd be in

Hong Kong right now working for us. However, I'm not and you're a free agent. You've got your living to earn. You must do whatever comes up."

"John, you're a key client of mine. I can't afford to upset you. However, if you don't need me and I'm offered a job I've got to take it."

"I can't argue with that. Tell you what. Why not wait and see how things develop before committing yourself with West Orient Airlines? I know you will always try to find out exactly what happened regardless of who's paying you."

As the conversation finished Helen chipped in. "Well I suppose that's good."

"What do you mean?"

"More trips together."

"I haven't agreed to help him or Hull Claims for that matter. It's almost certainly pilot error. Besides your schedule will probably prevent you joining me."

"I'll have started my maternity leave by then."

"You have to be pregnant first. Anyway you said you'd be flying until you were eight months."

"I may have to retire to get pregnant. It'll be fun trying."

"You are impossible and furthermore we can't afford it. My consultancy fees don't cover a partner permanently in attendance."

"It'll be a wife by then."

"Maybe but my fees are not related to my marital status or to how many children I have for that matter."

"We have. Unless you've got some other children I don't know about."

We stopped our exchanges and my mind went to Hong Kong. The situation at Chek Lap Kok really puzzled me. I didn't know what the Chinese might do or when they would release the pilots. Even though I had not taken on the job, I logged on to their web site and tried to find the name of the chief pilot and chief engineer but all I could find was their routes from Taiwan and how to book a flight.

"Did you find anything?"

"Nothing of any interest."

"How long are you going to be away in New York?"

"Only for a few days. There won't be time for you to come out."

"You mustn't be there long. There's the accident supremo job."

"Only if I'm short listed and unfortunately the clowns in the DfT have hired a recruitment agency."

"Peter, stop a minute. Do you know what you've just said?"

I thought for a moment and then smiled ruefully. "I just wanted to make sure you were on your toes. Alright, I shouldn't have said that. Let me try again 'The DfT regard the job as being so important that they have hired a recruitment agency to ensure that they get as wide a list of applicants as possible.' Not sure what their brief will be; probably to narrow applicants to three or four I guess."

"If you are selected you don't have to take the job, do you?"

"I wouldn't do that to them. If I apply and then get selected I'd have to take the job. Anyway there's a lot got to happen before then."

"Look it's not too late. Why don't you have another go at the forms now?"

"I've done quite a bit. I'll print it out."

I found the forms on my computer, printed them and gave them to Helen. She came back after about an hour while I was dealing with some outstanding mail.

"Not a bad first effort except there appears to be a fault with the key that types commas. And don't you think you may have been a bit modest on the accident at Heathrow? It was very tricky technically and AAIB were shouting you down. Goodness knows how you found out what really happened."

I did wonder if Helen was embarking on a fishing expedition and trying to learn about the girl who put me on the right track, amongst the other things she did, like sewing, but I decided not to try to find out. "It was just fortunate really meeting that servicing guy in Sydney. However I suppose I could jazz it up a bit. Anything else?"

"That Bermuda triangle aircraft that was lost. Didn't you recover all the pictures? You don't mention that. I've always wondered how you managed it. Did that art expert help?"

Helen looked very concerned but then I often thought she must have had a course on acting. I wasn't about to discuss Charlie, she was something else. "It wasn't relevant, darling. It was the aircraft that mattered. Accident investigators don't care about the financial implications. If that's all, let me have another go."

She wandered off and I went right though my response again trying to make it all as relevant as possible. Helen had another look through and pronounced that it was fine. We packed it all up ready for posting in the morning.

"Good, my love. You'll be hearing from them shortly."

"Possibly, darling, with a 'don't call us, we'll call you' message.'"

"Nonsense. You are perfect for that job. I bet you that you'll be on the short list."

"How much?"

"A holiday in St Antony."

"But I thought we were going to Sydney? St Antony won't be a holiday. The whole world to choose from and you choose a place where people know us."

"I like it there. Wonderful beaches, people are nice, food is good, hotels are lovely."

"I expect you'll want to stay at the airline hotel and talk to all your girl friends?"

"Why didn't I think of that. Is it a deal?"

"If short listed, yes. If selected, the world."

"You'll be far too busy if you're selected. We'll do St Antony if you're short listed and see that lovely policeman and his wife."

***

In the morning we got organised and left for Gatwick soon after nine, fighting the traffic every inch of the way. I dropped Helen off at the South Terminal and then drove round to the Safety Regulation Group. There was a man sitting in the reception area wearing a smart blue pin striped suit, white shirt and multicoloured tie; he got up and came towards me as I went over to the desk to ask for Anne Moncrieff.

"I'm Roger Moncrieff. I thought I recognised you from that accident at Heathrow some years ago when Anne and you gave evidence at that Inquiry and you explained to the Court what had really happened. I hope you don't mind but I've invited myself to join you for lunch."

"Anne mentioned to me that you work with an airline here."

"Well remembered. I currently manage their short haul fleet."

Anne appeared and we went into the cafe on the ground floor. We stood in line, chose some sandwiches and found a table.

"Peter, what are you up to? Why did you really call me? Is it the aircraft that went off the runway at Chek Lap Kok?"

"Anne, believe me I called you because I need to know about getting myself a PPL again."

"So you're not involved with that CC21?"

"Not really but I might be. I don't know anything about it and I certainly didn't know I might be involved when I called you. The airline in Taiwan want me to go out and help them but I haven't agreed as I've got a lot on and they would probably be wasting their money. Not sure why they need me. Hull Claims are expecting to have to pay for it all anyway and they've got a man out there already. It was a standard Cat III landing but something obviously went wrong." I looked at her. "Did you find out who I should talk to about licensing?"

"Franz Hoffman is the person you want. He's in charge of licensing and I warned him to expect some awkward questions."

"Not sure I like the introduction but thanks." I paused and went on. "Am I right that we don't have any CC21s on the UK register?"

She smiled. "I thought you couldn't resist probing on that accident. Yes, you're right. There are no CC21s on the UK register. However we've had a look at the aircraft on behalf of EASA. A beautiful flight deck the pilots tell me. Certainly it has all the latest systems. Total Avionics supply the equipment and are responsible for the whole installation."

Roger joined in. "Peter, we're considering buying the aircraft. It's very efficient from a fuel burn viewpoint. They learnt a lot from building that production line for the Airbus A320. Naturally the flight ops people are very keen as you would expect since it has a shiny new flight deck, and the aircraft comes fully equipped for operating in bad weather. And most important for us, it is very very competitive pricewise compared with the Airbus and Boeing aircraft."

"The equipment didn't seem to work very well in Hong Kong."

"Too early to say, Peter. You know that. Let's wait and see what the flight recorders say."

"I hope we find out. Not sure how forthcoming the Chinese accident people will be now that the Hong Kong police are involved. It all seems very political which is what has concerned me from the start."

"Strange there should be another Cat III accident. You must have seen the one at Kennedy?"

"Yes Roger. That also had a Total Avionics system. Not sure yet if it was exactly the same though."

Anne smiled. "You're involved with that as well? I might have known it."

"Yes. I'm going out on Sunday."

Anne asked me if I was going to try to see Hoffman but I explained I was booked for a medical.

"What do you need a medical for?"

"I thought I might fly again if the doctors will let me."

Anne looked at me carefully. "Surely you've done flying. You've got a tick in that box. You're now a worldwide expert on airplane safety and accidents. Why go backwards? You should be applying for that new Safety Board job." She looked at me. "Are you?"

"Well flying and the Safety Board are not mutually exclusive, are they?"

She smiled. "So you are applying. That's very sensible. You will be the ideal Chairman."

"Nice of you to say. Not sure the selection committee will think so. They will probably want an organisation man. However since you've mentioned it, would you do me a favour? I'd like to get the application off to-day and the post offices will be shut by the time I finish here."

She looked at the envelope and smiled. "It won't even need a stamp as it is official mail. I really hope you get the job and stop all this talk of flying."

"I can still fly if I get the job. In my view it would be a definite bonus for the Chairman to fly and I rather fancy flying a small single engined jet."

"So that's why you want to talk to the licensing people as well as having a medical?"

"Yes. I'm wondering if I would be allowed to fly in the UK. I have an FAA ATR and ATRs don't expire; providing you are checked out and comply with the regulations you can exercise the privileges of a private pilot. But over here if your ATPL expires by over five years I'm not sure what happens. The rules don't seem too friendly and I need advice. I would have to get a PPL but I'm not clear what that will entail. EASA are involved. Reading their documents I'm reminded of something one of my bosses once said to his line manager when they brought out some heavy bit of administration 'you're trying to make flying as difficult as you find it!'"

She smiled. "Doesn't sound very tactful."

"No. I think he stopped being a management pilot very shortly afterwards. Luckily the aircraft I am considering flying is made in the States so I won't need a UK PPL initially, assuming I'm allowed to fly at all. Just as well as, at the moment, I believe you have to go solo on a propeller aircraft to get your PPL; they won't give you a licence just because you can fly a jet aircraft."

Anne shook her head. "You'd better talk to Franz, but in a way I hope the doctors won't let you fly again. I don't think the small jet aircraft are all that reliable and they're not as easy to force land as a propeller aircraft."

"The Murray Aerospace LightJet has got a very clever energy management system if the engine does fail to get to the nearest suitable airfield."

"Well if it were me I'd only fly if the weather was perfect and I'd go as high as possible."

We said good-bye and I made my way to the medical centre. There was a long form to be completed and then I had to go through a whole variety of checks, blood tests, urine samples, cholesterol checks, X-Rays and many others, all done by nurses. Finally, after a long wait I was examined by a doctor who started by giving me an electrocardiogram.

"Well you've still got your systolic murmur."

"How did you know I had one?"

"The system found your old records. I've actually read the reports and I'm surprised they wouldn't let you carry on flying. Why didn't you fight a bit harder? You could have gone to appeal."

"I know but to be honest I was getting bored with line flying and I preferred to get the loss of licence insurance and do something else."

The doctor looked at me and nodded. "You were involved with that terrible accident at Heathrow some years ago, weren't you? I examined quite a few of the passengers as part of a research into stress and the effect of accidents. In fact I'm still interviewing some of the survivors. You did a great job sorting things out."

"It was an amazing accident technically. I was very lucky finding the cause."

"Bit more than luck I think." He looked at the traces again. "How are you physically. Do you get short of breath?" I shook my head. He started to examine me carefully with a stethoscope and then told me to put my gown on again and sit down.

"I see absolutely no reason why you shouldn't fly again if you want to. As you are probably aware, because of the tendency to globalise medical standards and because there is a much larger database than we had a few years ago, the requirements have been relaxed a little."

"Will I have any limitations? Will this medical help me to get an FAA medical? I have an American ATR airline pilots licence and if I can get my FAA medical back then I can use my licence for private flying."

"Did you ask for me specially to examine you?"

"No, not at all. Why?"

"Well I happen to be an FAA approved medical examiner but you will have to fill in their paperwork." He got up from his examination desk, went over to a large filing cabinet and extracted some papers. "If you go back and explain to the desk that I am going to give you an FAA airman's medical certificate later on there won't be a problem. Fill in all these sheets and when you've finished ask to see me again. You'll have to wait a bit as I'm pretty busy but it shouldn't be too late. I'll keep all these reports here and transfer the results to the FAA papers." He smiled. "It will cost you.

You can write me a cheque. By the way you could be an airline pilot again if you wanted to."

"I've done that, thank you. It's the small jet aircraft I'm thinking of having a go at."

I went out of the consulting room and gradually worked through the forms. When I had finished I decided to call Franz Hoffman. His secretary answered and asked me to come up to his office. I told medical reception where I was going and asked them to call me when the doctor was ready for me.

Hoffman was a German and he had been head of UK licensing for about eighteen months. He looked very athletic and was wearing a yellow open necked shirt and light brown trousers.

"Anne told me you wanted to ask me some questions Mr Talbert." His English was perfect but I kept on expecting him to say 'Herr Talbert'. "What can I do for you?"

"I've got two questions. As an ex ALTP holder and an FAA ATR, now that I have my medical back will I have to start all over again to get my PPL? The other question is can I get my PPL back by flying one of the new small jet aircraft."

Hoffman considered my questions for a moment or two. "Let me answer your second question first. Currently a jet aircraft, irrespective of size, is regarded as a high performance aircraft and cannot be used to obtain a PPL; you need to get a type rating for all jets. You will have to fly a propeller aircraft to get checked out for your PPL. Then you can fly a jet aircraft."

I decided to be diplomatic. "Is that a UK rule or a European rule? It doesn't sound very sensible."

"The UK can't make it's own rules any more. This is a EASA ruling."

Clearly it was no use trying to argue. Hoffman could see nothing wrong with the rules but then I always suspected it was the German element of EASA that loved formulating the rules. I got the feeling that he thought that it was applying the rules that mattered, not whether the rules made sense.

"What about the PPL?"

"You will need to have a PPL to fly a UK registered aircraft. You must write to us giving us your exact licensing history and your flying experience and we will then let you know what exams and tests you will need to do get your PPL back."

Luckily, as I was musing over my reply and trying to be pleasant Hoffman's secretary appeared and said that the doctor was ready for me. I thanked Hoffman for his help and wondered to myself if I could get a junior member of his licensing team to help me. Back in medical reception I was soon back with the doctor who did my medical; he started his paper work using his notes and the forms I had filled in. It did not take him long and, as agreed, we exchanged a medical certificate for a cheque. I found my car and drove home feeling pleased with the doctor but not pleased with the licensing situation.

The house seemed empty without Helen but it was probably a bit too early to try to contact her. I sent her a text message "Fully fit to fly anything. Have UK and FAA medical certificates. Off to New York Sunday."

Saturday seemed to go slowly. I decided I could manage with one carry-on bag and my netbook computer. I made sure I had its charger and also the ones for my phone and razor. At 2pm the phone rang. "My love, we had a long flight with a strong headwind. Was I glad to get to San Francisco last night and the hotel. I had a very early bird special and went to bed."

"Well you've woken up early, 6 o'clock."

"I think that's quite good."

"If you're not travelling back until Monday what on earth are you going to do?"

"We're taking a car and going wine tasting up the Napa valley for a couple of nights."

"Sounds great. Don't drink and drive. Who's we?"

"Don't worry. We'll have a great time."

***

On Sunday morning I caught the train to Gatwick and checked in with British Airways in plenty of time for a 1500 departure. We arrived on schedule at 1830, seven and a half hours later after a four hour time change. I was soon through customs and immigration and I saw a driver holding up a board with my name on it. We drove straight to Hamilton which overlooked the harbour and I got the impression it was very much a ships' terminal and business district. The car stopped at the Pompano Beach club and I discovered that a room had been booked for me for two nights by Castle Harbour Airlines. There was a message from Bill Castleford 'Will have dinner with you 1930, see you in the bar.'

My room was on the second floor of the main building and it had a good view of the spectacular harbour. I was half expecting to see some cruise ships but there were none in sight. I showered and got changed into a lightweight shirt and trousers, then checked if I could go on-line with my computer without having to pay a ransom to connect.

I called Helen on her mobile. "Where are you?"

"I'm in Calistoga and we've been tasting wines. Bought a couple to bring home. We're staying the night in Dr Wilkinson's Hot Springs resort and we've just had a mud bath."

"Sounds horrible. How was it? And I'm still waiting to find out who was with you."

"The baths were a bit smelly. However I think it washes off. You'd better get me some perfume just in case there is a problem."

"Good idea. Can't wait. You still haven't told me who you were with."

"I think you're jealous. No need to be. It was Elizabeth, you met the other night."

"You'd better not be late getting back to the airport."

"Plenty of time. We are not going until to-morrow and we don't have to be there until 1400 hours. What are you doing, my love?"

"I've just arrived at the hotel in Bermuda. I've got a working dinner."

"Well I think it's a shame that we are not together when we are both overseas. You must be tired. Be careful you don't fall asleep over the meal. It might create a bad impression."

Down in the gloomy bar I found a small table at the side of the room and ordered a beer. It was possible to see people entering the room and I soon spotted Castleford, dressed in a smart blue suit and tie but carrying his jacket. He looked over, saw me getting up and came straight over. We introduced ourselves and the ever attentive girl at the bar brought him what looked like a scotch as he sat down.

"Bill, you didn't tell me you're a ventriloquist."

He grinned. "This isn't the first time I've been in this bar, Peter. She'd have taken it away if I'd wanted something else. How was your flight?"

"OK but very boring. Just as well I had some journals and papers to read. What's happening in New York?"

"We've had a statement from the NTSB saying that at about 300ft the autopilot was disconnected, the throttles started to open and then closed again, the aircraft continued to lose height and the left wing hit the ground. It veered off the runway heading left down the airfield going very fast, initially at 140 knots, and then went into the river at the far end."

"What did they say about the crew?"

"Apparently shortly after the autopilot was disconnected the first officer told the captain that the aircraft was to the right of the runway and it was."

"Did they say if the pilot took the autopilot out or whether it just disconnected?"

"They didn't say."

"What happened next?"

"The aircraft banked steeply to the left, presumably to regain the runway centre line. The wing scraped the ground, the wings levelled as the aircraft landed but it then carried on going into the river."

"The report goes on to describe the rescue praising the cabin crew and as you know everybody was saved except for the captain, Trevor Smithson."

"Where did they find him?"

"Still sitting in his seat. The accident was at low water and the aircraft was over half full of water when it came to rest. It was a spring tide so that a few hours later it was almost completely submerged."

"That's terrible. Was he married?"

"No, he was divorced. He had a lovely home in St George overlooking Castle Harbour. They didn't have any children. The wife left him and I think she went off with some guy she'd met on the golf course."

"Well at least he didn't leave any dependents."

"Yes, there is that to be thankful for. Still we shall miss him. He was a very good pilot and great supporter of the airline." Bill looked very upset. We sat for a bit not saying anything and sipping our drinks.

"Well Peter, obviously the aircraft is a write off. I'm chasing Airplane Protection Inc for the money. However the New York Port Authority is claiming that the pilots behaved irresponsibly and have named the first officer as well as us in a legal case and are trying to sue. I'm very worried that the insurance company might not pay us because they might try and claim poor maintenance. If nothing else, they'll try and delay payment. I'm sure you know that, you've worked for insurance companies often enough. They've got a new CEO who has a reputation of being bad news"

"Bill, let me tell you something. You must understand I don't care who retains me. I just want to find out what happened." I looked straight at Bill. "What do you think did happen? It seems such an elementary mistake not to execute a missed approach and go round again."

"I've no idea. Wish I knew. The weather was foggy and the landing went wrong."

"What about your Flight Operations. What are they saying?"

"They are not saying anything at the moment."

"How many aircraft have you got? Can you carry on your services?"

"We've now only got five 630s but European Aerospace are arranging a lease for us until we can get a replacement; however we need to sort out Echo Victor's insurance."

"Well what I propose is that I should talk to your head of engineering and your Chief Pilot and then go to New York to see if I can talk to anyone there. I'd like to speak to the first officer as well if I may."

"That will be alright. I'll call Jonathan Stable, our director of maintenance, and see how he's placed to-morrow."

Bill got his phone out and spoke to Stable. When he'd finished he turned to me. "That's OK then, he's working here to-morrow.

When you get to the airfield in the morning go to the first class check in and Jonathan will get someone to collect you. Now I'll try Martin Spencer, our chief pilot."

"Martin, I'm with Peter Talbert at the Pompano Beach; he's helping us try to find out what happened with Echo Victor and getting the money from Airplane Protection." I raised my eyebrows slightly but Bill signalled me not to react. "Are you free to-morrow, he'd like to come and talk to you?" Bill listened for a moment. "OK. I'll ask Jonathan to get him to you when he's finished talking to him."

We went into the restaurant which didn't seem to be very busy; maybe the occupancy depended on the passenger cruise ships which was said to be a flourishing business. Bill told me how he started the airline with a few old Boeing 737s and then, encouraged by the Government, he went to European Aerospace who arranged the finance for the brand new 630s which suited the airline very well. The island was a tax haven for many overseas firms and there was a continual flow of people travelling to and from the States on company business. However the business was very dependent on the world's financial health so the airline's results tended to vary from year to year.

Bill left declining to have dessert or coffee which suited me as it was already three-thirty in the morning UK time.

***

I woke up at six o'clock, ten o'clock UK time, and decided it was time to get up. There was a light breeze from the west and I went down to have a look at the harbour. There were a few fishing boats going out and then I saw a cruise liner coming in. I watched as the tugs manoeuvred the ship alongside the quay which was clearly a tight fit. Back in the hotel I had some fruit and toast for breakfast and then got the front cab from the line outside the hotel to take me down to Kindley Field. As I went into the airport I could see, judging by the check-in lines, that there was a Castle Harbour flight just leaving so I went to the ticket desk and asked for Jonathan Stable.

A girl, Rosie, came down who proved to be Jonathan's secretary and she led me upstairs through a security door to a small office area and eventually into his office. He was on the phone and he waved for me to sit down. Jonathan was wearing smart blue shorts and an open necked blue shirt. There was a mountain of papers in various folders in front of him. He seemed to be discussing some servicing problem with someone in the States. It went on a bit and he was clearly getting frustrated but finally it sounded as if he had managed to make his point.

He stood up and we shook hands. "Sorry about all that. It's difficult to maintain a fleet of aircraft which are serviced in New Jersey but there's no other way as we don't have enough room here."

"How do you manage?"

"Well we keep the master records here and tell Airlines Servicing in Newark what needs to be done. They send us the results of all their work. We try to arrange the schedules with the aircraft so that the ones that need servicing finish up at Newark so there's no wasted flying."

"How many aircraft do you maintain at Newark?"

"We do the 630s there. We've just lost Victor Papa Bravo Echo Victor so we've got five left, Foxtrot Alfa to Foxtrot Echo. Airlines Servicing do the 737s for us at Philadelphia."

"What's your experience with the 630s? Do you like them?"

"They're great mechanically. The avionics are the least reliable system. We seem to get problems with the displays and the Flight Management System."

"What sort of problems?"

"Mainly software faults. The actual displays and the FMS computers are OK but the pilots report operating faults which are difficult to reproduce on the ground. We keep complaining to Total Avionics who make both the displays and the FMS and to be fair they are supporting us well, both here and at Newark. However it is a critical item for us and they always seem to be upgrading their software."

"That must be very difficult to do if you do your maintenance in New Jersey."

"We are able to do software upgrades and computer changes here. Otherwise we couldn't manage. You need to talk to Martin who will give you a better run down on the situation."

"What about Echo Victor? Any special defects?"

"No, Echo Victor was our newest aircraft and had very few problems. Even the avionics seemed very reliable."

Jonathan showed me the records for Echo Victor and the other aircraft. There was nothing of any interest as far as I was concerned and so I made my farewells and Rosie took me to Martin Spencer's office. He got up to greet me, offered me a chair on the far side of his desk and then returned to his chair. He was quite short, five foot eight I guessed and he was wearing an open necked white shirt; I saw his jacket and tie on a hangar near the door.

"This is a fine mess, Peter. Trevor drowned, an aircraft destroyed and the New York Port Authority is charging us and the crew with hazardous flying."

"Where is the first officer?"

"Barbara Maitland, she's still in New York. Her passport has been taken away. Absolutely ridiculous."

"Why do New York think it's hazardous flying? What were the exact words of the NTSB?"

" They said it was pilot error because the aircraft did not do a go-around. I must say I'd love to know why Trevor didn't do a missed approach. As to why the Port Authority is chasing us I'm not sure. I think the aircraft did quite a lot of damage to their lighting and ground equipment. They're trying to get their money back. Maybe their insurance company has told them to sue. They lost quite a few flights and revenue as well while they repaired the runway and the lighting. Took two or three days before they could use the runway again and as bad luck would have it the wind strengthened from the South West so they were left with only one runway."

"What was the weather like when they were landing?"

"Oh it was definitely Cat III with less than 100 feet reported visibility when the autopilot disconnected. Barbara told me that in fact the fog was not very thick as they could see the tops of skyscrapers before they went into the cloud. Apparently the fog thickened as they were making the final approach."

"How do you keep your crews trained for Cat III landings? It must be quite expensive."

"Flight Safety International has a 630 simulator at Newark and my operations manager keeps a careful check of the pilots and when they need to go on it. That way it doesn't cost too much to keep the crews current and it's well worthwhile. We've got a great reputation for reliability. However the autopilot is not 'fail operational', we're not allowed to land if the visibility is less than 200 feet."

"Jonathan told me the aircraft was your latest."

"Yes, that's right. Echo Victor was up to the latest mod standard. We'd only being flying it for two or three weeks. In fact I think it was Trevor's first trip in it since we collected it, though he'd been in the European simulator."

"Do you have an aircraft on the ground? Could I have a look on the flight deck? I've never been on a 630."

"No problem. We've got one on maintenance until this afternoon. Why don't we go now?"

"Great, but do you think you could do something else for me? I'd like to go to Kennedy when I've finished here. Could you ask your secretary to book me a seat this evening or to-morrow morning?"

"Do you have a licence?"

"Actually I do, an ATR. And a current medical certificate."

"Alright. you can be supernumerary crew on the jump seat to-morrow first flight. I'm taking it myself so there won't be a problem."

"That's great, Martin. I really appreciate that."

"Right. Let's go and look at the Flight Deck."

He led me down some back stairs and then outside finally finishing at a hangar door. He punched the numbers in on the key pad, waved to an engineer working on the landing gear and climbed up some steps at the rear door. We walked through the cabin which was being cleaned and reached the front.

The flight deck was like most modern aircraft with six flat panel TV like displays but was more akin to a Boeing Aircraft than an Airbus as there was a central wheel rather than a side stick controller. There was power on the aircraft and the flight deck displays were running but no flight plan had been loaded into the Flight Management Computer so that the situation display just showed compass heading.

We walked round the outside of the aircraft and then went back to Martin's office. "Peter, to-morrow morning be at first class check-in at 0745 and I'll arrange for you to join us in operations before we go out to the aircraft."

I got a cab back to the hotel and had a swim. Then I called the NTSB in Virginia. I asked for the inspector dealing with the accident at Kennedy and was put through to the information desk. I explained my interest in the accident and the lady at the other end of the phone took down my details and said she would get someone to call me; she was very polite and courteous but somehow I wasn't convinced that I'd get a call back. However she did give me the general email number of the office so I composed a request to meet the inspector and sent it off.

My next call was to FAA Flight Standards Office near Kennedy. Again I was put through to the information desk but this time was forwarded to a very helpful girl and I explained my interest.

"My name's Jane Roberts and I've just got the NTSB report. You're very welcome to come to the Office sometime but you may be wasting your time at the moment." I thanked her and said I would be along to see her in a day or so.

I logged on and booked to stay at the Courtyard Marriott on 40th Street. There was nothing more I could do that evening and went to bed early.

Chapter 3

I was at the airport in plenty of time and went to the first class desk to check my bag. I filled in the customs and visa forms and then the check-in clerk called Operations. A dispatcher appeared and I followed him to the flight briefing desk. Martin was already there with his first officer, Jimmy Walters. "The good news is that we've got a full load and the weather is fine. Shall we go?"

He led the way through the United States customs and immigration inspection points and then out to the gate. There were already a lot of passengers waiting as he unlocked the door and we walked down the finger to the aircraft, VP-BFC. The cabin crew were there checking everything was in order and we went through the flight deck door. We stowed our small bags in the stowages provided and I sat in the jump seat after Martin and Jimmy had strapped in. Jimmy checked that the flight plan had been loaded in the Flight Management Computers and they started going through the check list. The aircraft started to rock slightly as the passengers entered the cabin and then a few minutes later the dispatcher came onto the flight deck to give the final loading to Martin for signature. The door automatically locked as the dispatcher closed it and a few minutes later the chief steward informed Martin that the cabin was ready. Jimmy got the clearance from air traffic as Martin started the engines and we were soon on our way to the take-off point.

"Peter, that's the nice thing about Bermuda, very little traffic. No waiting in line to take-off. What a contrast with Kennedy."

We had to wait a few minutes at the holding point for take-off due to a delay from New York Oceanic air traffic control and then we were off. Immediately after getting airborne Martin engaged the autopilot and autothrottle; in fact he never touched the wheel again until after we had landed. When the aircraft was on the approach he primed the system for autoland. The aircraft touched down very smoothly but firmly under autopilot control and then Martin selected reverse thrust after lowering the nose wheels. The worst part of the flight was following the ground controller instructions to the gate, threading our way through all the other aircraft.

After the passengers had disembarked I walked with Martin and Jimmy to immigration. We had to wait in line at the crew immigration gate. "By the way Peter, I've told our manager Ricardo Gemelli, that you are here and probably will be contacting him. Keep in touch and let me know if you find out anything interesting."

"Thanks and I'd appreciate your keeping me up to date. You've got my number. I need to talk to Barbara Maitland."

"I don't see why not. Get Ricardo to fix a meeting. Here's my card with the station number on it. Hope you manage to see NTSB."

There was only a short line for a cab and using the mid-town tunnel I was soon at the hotel. They managed to find a room for me straightaway even though I was a bit early for regular check-in; I told the girl that I would be with them for a week. Up in my room, which was more like an apartment, I started off by calling Ricardo Gemelli at the airport.

"Martin told me you would be calling. You'd like to talk to Barbara I believe?"

"If that's possible. I gather she's had her passport removed."

"Yes, she doesn't have her passport but as she's a US citizen it's not a big deal."

"But doesn't that mean she's out of a job with you?"

"As it turns out, not at all. She just has to keep in the immigration and customs area at Kindley."

"Of course." I realised that she could be at Kindley without actually being in Bermuda by staying in the United States immigration area. "That's very fortunate. So where is she now?"

"I'm not sure. She's flying out and back on our last flight to-night. If you give me your mobile number I'll see if she's prepared to phone you."

I started to unpack hoping that Barbara would call and in fact the phone rang before I had finished.

"Peter Talbert?" I acknowledged. "I'm on Broadway right now. I gather you'd like to have a chat. Where are you staying?" I told her. "That's convenient. I'll call you from the lobby in a few minutes"

She was as good as her word and we arranged to meet in the lobby. She was wearing uniform so I spotted her straightaway. She had brown hair, quite tall about 5ft 10 inches, with a trim figure, not overweight. I guessed she was probably just on the wrong side of fifty.

"Let's go to the bar. I can't drink but it's less conspicuous than talking in the lobby."

She settled for a diet coke and I ordered a slimline tonic.

"It's very good of you to meet me, Barbara. You must be fed up with questioning."

"Yes I am. I told the NTSB man exactly what happened and the next thing I knew was that I was served a notice by the Port of New York and New Jersey claiming that I flew dangerously and was hazarding the lives of the passengers. They named me as a co-defendant with Castle Harbour airlines."

"Barbara, if you can bear it, why don't you tell me what occurred."

She looked at me and clearly was trying to decide where to start. "There's very little to tell really. The weather flying over from Bermuda was fine but there was fog at Kennedy. We could see it was only very shallow as the skyscrapers were visible as we manoeuvred to line up for an approach to 22 Left.

"Trevor primed the autopilot for an automatic landing and we went into cloud at about 700 feet. At about 400 feet I heard the ATIS information change and it said that the visibility had dropped to 100ft. I told Trevor and I heard the autopilot disconnect. I thought Trevor was going to go around for a missed approach because of the reduced visibility but the fog suddenly cleared and he must have decided he could land. Then we went into the fog again and the next thing I knew was the ILS indicator showing we were slightly right of the centre line and the airspeed was far too high. I warned him and Trevor closed the throttles and then he banked the aircraft to correct.

"The radio altimeter called out the height at one hundred feet and I yelled at him to go around for a missed approach as we were still not lined up, far too high and going too fast. The radio altimeter called the height at fifty feet and the throttles started to open. I looked out and I saw the ground very close. However we were over the edge of the runway with left bank on and there was a terrible crashing noise which I think must have been the left wing tip hitting the ground. The aircraft rolled level hitting the ground hard and then went left leaving the runway going very fast down the airfield into the water at the far end. It did slow down a bit but not nearly quickly enough. I shut both engines down and operated the fire extinguishers."

"Didn't Trevor say anything?"

"He made an evacuation announcement on the public address system but that was all. He seemed mesmerised. Motionless."

"Why on earth didn't he go round?"

"I don't know. As I said, shortly after the autopilot came out we caught a glimpse of the approach lights. He must have thought he could land. However things went wrong, we went right, he banked left and, as I said, when we hit the ground we were going far too fast to stop."

"So why have you been charged?"

"I've no idea. Perhaps they think I should have ordered him to go around. I don't know what their problem is."

"Perhaps they are trying to get someone to pay for the repairs on the runway?"

She considered my suggestion for a moment or two and sipped her drink. "You could be right. But isn't that FAA's responsibility? Anyway I've got no money and the company insures us. I've never heard of anything like it. The whole thing is ridiculous."

"Maybe, but it's strange Trevor didn't go around."

"I know, Peter. But it was nothing to do with me."

"Well the crash recorders have clearly confirmed everything you've told me. I think the summons was rushed through to please their insurer." I looked at her. "May I ask you one more question?"

"Try me."

"Why did Trevor lose his life? Was it difficult getting out of the aircraft?"

Barbara looked troubled. "That's been worrying me. As I said Trevor lost control as he tried to touch down and the aircraft left the runway at quite an angle going quite fast. We had just got past the intersection of 13 when we went across the grass and down the slope right into the water. When I opened the cabin door icy cold water rushed in and I had to dash back to get my life jacket.

“There was water well above my knees. It was freezing. When I left it was getting quite difficult wading to the door but Trevor shouldn’t have had any problem. I saw him bending down to get his life jacket as I was leaving and I thought he was following me out into the liferaft but when I looked round he wasn’t there. I told the purser in charge of the raft that Trevor was still in the aircraft but she wouldn’t let me go back when I realised he hadn’t followed me. Then she followed me into the liferaft and cut the line attaching it to the aircraft so that we drifted away. A boat came alongside and we all climbed onto it. I felt terrible and pleaded with the guy who seemed to be in charge of the rescue to go in and find Trevor.”

“Did anyone go in to have a look?”

“I don’t know. The tide was rising I think and the aircraft was almost submerged. Maybe it was moving or settling in the mud. The guy in charge of the boat could see everyone was frozen and scared and he decided to get everyone ashore as quickly as possible.” She paused, obviously recalling the scene. “I tell you what. Trevor looked absolutely shattered. Perhaps he didn’t leave his seat. The water was above his knees and remember it was icy cold.”

She stopped and I judged it was time for me to stop questioning her. We shook hands and then she left to go to the airport. Initially I was surprised she was flying but on reflection it was probably the sensible thing to do instead of moping around reliving the accident.

Up in my room I called Helen at my house. “You’re home. How’s everything? Did you have a good trip?”

“Peter, it’s work. Subconsciously you think I’m a passenger. It’s bloody hard work and the first class passengers are worse than economy, especially the ones that pay their own money. I’m knackered.”

“That’s not fair. I know how hard you work. When do you go away next? I could be back the day after to-morrow.”

“That’s great. I’m home for a day or two. Meet you at the airport, Heathrow I assume.”

***

In the morning I decided to ring the FAA Flight Standards Office and Jane Roberts was in. "You can come round now if you like. I've had a good look at the NTSB report. Have you seen it? It's on the web."

I took a waiting cab to the FAA Office on Stewart Avenue in Garden City. I signed in and the man behind the desk telephoned Jane Roberts. She came down and led me up in the elevator to her office. She was dressed in a grey trouser suit and I guessed she was in her forties.

She looked at me and asked me for a card. "I thought your name sounded familiar. Weren't you involved in that terrible accident at Heathrow some years ago?" I nodded. "That was also a Cat III landing."

"Yes but there was a technical explanation for that accident. In this case it just looks like pilot error and I hate accidents like that when the pilot is not there to answer the questions. What does the NTSB report say? I haven't had a chance to read it yet."

"It says the aircraft was doing a normal approach and then at about 300ft the autopilot was disconnected. The aircraft continued descending going right of the runway, then banked left, started correcting and then the left wing hit the ground."

"How did they know that?"

"Looking at the report it infers that the wing hit the ground from the radio altimeters, the accelerometers and also the loss of various sensors as the aircraft hit the ground. The report goes on to discuss the plane going into the Hudson and the emergency procedures carried out by the crew. However, in the discussion it blames the pilot for not executing a missed approach when the autopilot disconnected." Jane pushed the report towards me. "Have a read. It won't take you too long and there are one or two things I need to do. You'll be alright over there."

I sat down and read the report. It was quite lengthy and took me the best part of an hour by the time I had finished making notes. It read like a final report though no doubt there would be another report later. Pilot error was stamped all over it.

"Jane, it's clearly pilot error though why he did not go around beats me."

"I suppose they were doing an ILS approach and not a GPS one?"

"The report makes it clear it was definitely ILS."

"Have you spoken to the first officer, Peter?"

"Yes I have. She told me that for a moment the fog cleared and they were lined up with the runway and then they went back into the fog as the autopilot came out."

"The report doesn't make that very clear, does it?"

"No Jane but I expect it will do in the final version."

"Did you ask the first officer how the captain was drowned?"

I decided it wouldn't help discussing what Barbara had told me. "Not really. She assumed the captain was following her."

"He had plenty of time, didn't he?"

" Believe so but apparently there was quite a lot of icy water in the cabin and the tide was coming in."

I left her and went back to the hotel and rang Bill Castleford.

"Bill, it certainly looks like a clear cut case of pilot error. The autopilot came out. Trevor didn't go around for some reason. Presumably he thought he could land the aircraft when the fog cleared for a moment. Barbara says they were lined up. The fog came back, the aircraft went right, and both the speed and the aircraft were too high, Trevor banked left and the wing hit the ground. I'm not happy since Trevor's actions don't make sense. However I can't see what else to do."

"Alright Peter. Airplane Protection are not being difficult so from the airline's viewpoint we may be able to survive."

"Bill, there's not a lot more I can do here. I think Trevor took the autopilot out deliberately because the visibility had got worse and dropped below 100ft but then for some reason he decided to try to land instead of executing a missed approach. I'll send you my report in the next day or so. If anything happens that I ought to know about give me a call. I'm going back to UK, probably to-night. "

I logged on, decided to catch the later BA flight to London and told the hotel I wanted a late check out and texted Helen. The flight took off on time, we got in at 10 o'clock and she was waiting for me. We found the car and were soon home.

"Where are we going and when?"

"Well why don't you go and freshen up and we can have a debrief on what you've been doing. Then we'll go out later and have an early meal. I won't come up with you now while you're changing as it might delay things."

"Aren't you going to change?"

"I don't need to. I've changed already in case you hadn't noticed and if I come upstairs again I'll need to change again."

"So?"

"Get on with it. You're tired after a long trip, remember. Oh by the way, Roger Chesterfield from Senior Placements rang. I'd got your message so I said you'd probably call him later to-day."

"That'll be the Safety Board people. I'd better ring him now."

Helen had written down the number on my desk and it clearly was a direct line.

"Roger Chesterfield?" He agreed. "Peter Talbert here. You asked me to call."

"Thanks, Peter. As you know we're acting on behalf of the Department of Transport to produce a short list for the new post of Chairman, Transport Safety Board. We've received your application and we'd like to meet up and have a chat."

"No problem. Where shall we do it?"

"Well we like to make things informal at this stage. How about if I come round with a colleague to your office?"

"I have an office I rent in Farringdon Street but it might be easier if you came round to my office at my house in Kingston if you have no objection."

"Fine. When can we come round?"

"Can you manage to-morrow afternoon or would you prefer to wait until next week?"

"Yes, to-morrow would be fine. Two thirty would suit us."

I explained where we lived and hung up. It was clearly going to be an important interview however informal they might pretend it was going to be. I needed to rehearse in my mind why I wanted the job and why I was the ideal candidate.

"That sounded good. Off you go and change."

I spent the rest of the day trying to catch up. I got out the paperwork I had sent in with my application and read through it again to get my mind up to speed.

Helen made some sandwiches for lunch. "I've decided to go out to-morrow when these people come round."

"My love, there's no need. You would be very welcome."

"Maybe but I think you should concentrate fully without having to think of anything else. You needn't worry. I'm only going shopping with a friend to Fenwicks and then Fortnums."

"What makes you think I won't be worrying if you're shopping in Bond Street and Piccadilly?"

"You should be delighted if I buy a little something."

"In my experience I've found that little somethings very often cost more than big somethings."

"That only applies to short dresses and lingerie."

"Exactly."

"You should be very excited if I buy new lingerie."

I grinned. "We'll just have to see."

I did a bit more work but started to get tired. We left early and went to a new French restaurant in the High Street, had a quick meal and went straight to bed when we got home.

Helen left soon after breakfast. "Give it your best shot, my darling. The job's made for you. A marriage made in heaven."

"Possibly. Actually, on balance I'm beginning to think you could be right. Wish me luck."

"You don't need luck. Go for it."

Helen's words cheered me up and I made significant progress with my work. I found that I was impatiently awaiting the team's arrival. In fact they turned up a few minutes early. Roger was just under six feet, late forties, and looked a real professional, smartly dressed in a grey suit and plain blue tie; he clearly couldn't wait to get started. His colleague, Mary Foster, was a bit younger than him, oozing efficiency and very smartly dressed in a dark suit with a skirt that was perhaps longer than the current fashion, certainly considerably longer than Helen's skirts. I had arranged some chairs round a small table in my office but after looking round they preferred the living room with its sofa and two easy chairs.

Roger didn't waste any time on socializing. He got some notes out of his briefcase and took a pen out of his jacket pocket. "We just want to run through some of the points you made in your response applying for the job." I nodded. "Your record in accident investigation is outstanding, superb. It must have been a huge change after being an airline pilot?"

"Yes, you're right. But you know it didn't happen by chance. I was trained as an electrical engineer and while I was in the airline I became very interested in cockpit and aircraft system design. It seemed to me that insufficient time was being spent on considering the interface with the pilot. I decided there was a job to be done in the airlines talking to pilots and discussing some of the issues, in particular when systems malfunctioned. But it was a struggle persuading airlines to spend the money and getting them to organize their pilots for my talks. Then I had a stroke of luck. An insurance company asked for help rebutting an insurance claim where an engine had been severely damaged and the crew were being blamed. My advice saved the company over a million pounds and they were very grateful."

Mary Foster chipped in. "How did that help?"

Her question was unnecessary as I was about to explain but in fact I welcomed the interruption. "You remember that terrible accident at Heathrow when over 300 people were killed? Well CrossRisk Insurance, the firm that employed me before, asked me to look after their interests during the investigation."

"Why would they do that, Peter?" I was a bit surprised at the question but I suppose the whole accident scene was outside their expertise.

"Well Roger, accident investigators are only interested in why accidents happen. Who pays is not their worry. Consequently, firms and people who might be adversely involved and blamed want their interests represented. Anyway, by flying to Sydney where the aircraft had come from I found that it had had a fault which had not been repaired correctly and, through poor aircraft design, this maintenance error was the prime cause of the accident. As a result of the Public Inquiry I suddenly found that my name had become well known and I started getting retained by other insurance firms and airlines."

Mary asked a fair question. "What were your relations like with the official accident investigators?"

"You mean AAIB?" She nodded. "If I may say so, a very interesting question. In fact, the chief inspector was in some trouble because of his failure to monitor the senior inspector who was investigating the accident but he didn't blame me and in fact we now have a very good relationship. I'm sure you must have met him, Bob Furness. In my opinion he would be an excellent Chairman but he is nearing retirement and he tells me he is not going to apply. I don't think I would have applied if he had wanted the job."

"Peter, you're obviously very successful in the work you are doing. However, I must ask you the obvious question. You are really a one man band, brilliant but a loner. Being chairman of a government administered board is something entirely different. You would be a team player overseeing several accident boards. Why do you think you would be effective in this new post?"

"I spent a lot of time thinking about that question before I applied, Roger. I think the key is that it is a new post. The Chairman will be able to discuss with the accident boards the way that they operate and how they envisage carrying out effective accident investigation in the future bearing in mind the unstoppable advance of technology. The world is always changing and no organisation can stand still."

I felt that I had scored a point but Mary chipped in. "That's very true but you will be subject to government policy and responsible to the director responsible for safety."

"In my judgement governments don't like interfering too much with safety investigation. Accident Boards have to be completely impartial. It is often a very harrowing job dealing with fatalities in full view of the media and the public."

"What is your view of the media in these matters?"

"They have a job to do and it is very important to make certain that they are kept as fully informed as possible in the particular circumstances, so that they don't start inventing possible scenarios. Media conjecture will always be a problem but they have some very good well balanced technical experts."

"Doesn't the Financial Times retain you?"

I looked at Mary and then Roger, choosing my words carefully. "No it doesn't, though I have done the occasional article for them. No-one has an exclusive call on my services and, furthermore, it doesn't matter who is employing me on a problem; I am only ever interested in finding out what actually occurred and why it happened. Like the accident boards, I don't get involved with financial settlements though I am well aware that there may be financial repercussions as a result of my discovering what happened. If I am appointed Chairman of the Safety Board then there will be absolutely no change in my attitude to these matters."

"But the government may be involved. There may be some faulty legislation or some legislation they failed to put in place. They may have a view on the way an accident report is written."

"Roger, I will support the chief inspector of the boards in the presentation of their reports. I'm sure the Government will want to see the reports before they are issued but only, in my view, to prepare their spokesmen who have to deal with the media. I would be most unhappy to be told that a particular report needed to be rewritten."

"That Heathrow accident, the government got involved there."

"Yes, Mary, they did and it delayed the discovery of what actually happened. They claimed it was in the interest of national security and of course there will always be problems in this area, but such excuses must not be used to cover incompetence. In fact, the actual report when it came out told the whole facts including the way the government had interfered."

"Let's leave that aspect for the moment; bearing in mind the way you have investigated other accidents, won't you find it difficult as Chairman to avoid telling the investigators what they should be doing?"

"No, Roger. Not at all. Anyway I won't be directly involved with individual accidents, however serious they might be. Obviously I will discuss progress with the head of each board on a routine basis but that is all. I will be interested in organisation, equipment and how much commonality there will be in the future in the facilities of the boards. Vehicles are becoming safer and safer thanks to technology and accident rates are declining. Routine position reporting for example is becoming commonplace on ships, aircraft and even trains. Accident recorders are not just confined to aircraft these days. These recorders need analyzing. Should there be a common centre dealing with recorders? Should accident investigators be confined just to one type of vehicle? Inevitably we are all driven by budgets and if there are fewer accidents should we be spending less on investigation? What about the EU? What is their view of the future? Do they want a European Transportation Board? What is the Government view? You can see that the Chairman will have a lot more to do than getting concerned with an individual accident."

I could see both of them scribbling away. Perhaps I was the right person after all to be the first Chairman. I didn't have an axe to grind or a private agenda and I went on to explain that very clearly. We went on to discuss some of the other work I had been doing but before leaving they broached a new subject.

"Peter, your personal life. Is there anything that you have done that we should know about? There have been some cases recently when the government appoints somebody and then gets egg on its face when the person concerned has been in prison for fraud, has committed bigamy or some other unfortunate happening which the media have got hold of straightaway. Our firm always likes to make sure that the people they recommend don't have some hidden secret which will appear immediately they are appointed."

I smiled appreciatively. "Good point. I don't think I've done anything that would excite the press. I've been married, now divorced, had girl friends in the past and I'm about to get married again. I don't have any children as far as I know."

They left at about five o'clock without making any observations. Not that I expected any. They were in the learning mode. I didn't bother to ask when I might hear if I was going to be short listed or not. It did occur to me that I might well be, if for no other reason than that the Director General on the Transport Board responsible for safety had called me to make certain I knew about the job.

It was a bit of an anti-climax after they left but Helen's return soon sorted that out. "How did you get on?"

"Pretty well I think."

"Do you want to see what I've bought?"

"Depends what it is."

She showed me some gloves and some stockings.

"Anything else?"

"Yes, but I need to try them on. Are you coming up to see?"

"Do I need to?"

"Not necessarily. I'll come down but make sure the central heating is turned up."

I followed instructions even though it was not cold and decided that it might be better if I went into the living room. It was a good decision as Helen reappeared wearing a thin housecoat.

"Surely that housecoat isn't new. I remember taking it off you the first time you slept here."

"Well you can take it off again but then, this time, you'll have to admire my new lingerie, first."

***

In the morning we sorted out our diaries. I needed to go to Vision Unlimited in Palmdale and Helen was scheduled to go to LA the following day, Sunday. "That's great, my love. Give your man a ring and let's see if we can't go on the same flight. Then I can come with you to Palmdale."

"When do you go back?"

"On the Tuesday."

"Good. We can have two nights in Palmdale but you'll need to catch an early bus to the airport. What time do you have to check in by?"

"Not sure. We can work that out later. My trip is set up. Yours isn't. Get phoning to your man in Palmdale!"

"Too early. I'm going into my office in Farringdon Street to collect some papers; it'll be empty but it won't matter. I'll phone him when I get home. What are you going to do?"

"How about the washing if we're setting out on Sunday?"

At four o'clock I called Harry Foster. "Peter, glad you can make it. By all means come out to-morrow but, to be frank, Wednesday will be better for meeting the team and going in the simulator."

"No worries, Harry, we'll probably go up to Mojave and visit Murray Aerospace."

"Great. Let's have breakfast in your hotel at 7.30 Wednesday."

Helen had been listening and put her arms round me.

"So there's another saying that's true. The luck of the Devil. You didn't mention that Murray Aerospace was so close. How very convenient for you."

"You're right. It seems rude not to go and see them."

"Alright then. Don't sit there. Where are we staying? What about a car?"

"I'll do a deal. You unhand me and get me a seat on your flight and then I can let Hertz know the flight and the time."

"Not as simple as that, my love. You have to book the flight and then I'll try to upgrade you. Your man is paying anyway. When we're married it will be different as I might be able to get a discount but they're all sub-load, which won't do for this trip."

"Well at least find out what time you have to check-in by."

I booked the flight with Worldwide and sorted out the car with Hertz. Then I called Murray Aerospace, explained that I was visiting Vision Unlimited and asked if I could visit them on the Monday and look at a LightJet 100. The guy I spoke to, George Straker, agreed straightaway and I explained that I'd be with him at about 9 o'clock. The yellow pages didn't have too many hotels in Mojave and I chose the Best Western for the Sunday and the Monday. I followed that up by booking at the Hampton Inn in Palmdale from the Tuesday night and emailed Harry to let him know.

Helen came in, still holding her mobile. "I've got to check in by 1030 and you can check-in then as well. I've left a note for the dispatcher who's going to be on duty to-morrow asking for you to be upgraded. As I'm in charge of the first class and I know the dispatcher you may be in luck. It all depends on the load."

We packed our things and I was going to have to check Helen's bag as well as my own. I put my netbook in my cabin bag.

In the morning we went in Helen's car to Gatwick as she got a special rate in staff parking. The bus picked us up and took us to the South Terminal and I found my way to the passenger entrance where I showed my boarding pass, which I had printed the night before, dropped off the bags and went to the business class lounge. The girl there looked at my boarding pass and I was pleased to see that she swapped it for a new first class one and then directed me to the first class lounge which was through another door.

We boarded on time and Helen led me to my seat. “Can I take your coat and hang it up, Sir.” She inspected it. “It’s rather old and it needs cleaning, Sir.” I could see horror on the cabin attendant’s face close-by.

“Well you’d better see to it, my love.” The attendant’s face cleared and grinned. I looked at her. “Didn’t she tell you?” She shook her head.

“No fraternising with the staff, please Sir.”

“Is that a company rule?”

“No. It’s my rule and just you watch it. What sort of water would you like?”

Luckily the other first class passengers were coming on to the aircraft so Helen was forced to concentrate on their arrival. One or two of the faces seemed familiar but I couldn’t give names to any of them. I guessed there would be a lot of well known people travelling the route frequently.

Helen wasn’t looking after me but supervising all the passengers. The attendant who hadn’t been briefed by Helen on our relationship was clearly assigned to my seat and to a few others near-by. I thought she was being very attentive and, looking at Helen’s face, so did she. I managed a couple of hours sleep before our arrival at LA.

Helen was waiting for me outside the customs hall and we caught the Hertz courtesy bus to their facility on Airport Boulevard. We got a car very quickly and in no time were on the ramp for 405 going north. However, it was Sunday afternoon and there was a lot of traffic. It seemed to take forever to get onto the freeway and then drive another thirty miles to exit on to 14. After that, as we climbed up into the desert things seemed to improve but there was still a lot of traffic going to Palmdale and Lancaster. We finally made the Best Western in Mojave after two and a half hours at 7pm.

Luckily Helen was not too worried as she had gone straight to sleep as we left Hertz and only started coming round as we went by Palmdale.

“Peter, that didn’t take long.” She looked at her watch. “Just in time for a drink. I’ll stay here while you find out where our room is.”

Chapter 3

I checked in and then drove the car round close to our room which was on the first floor, British definition. We carried our bags up and Helen got out of her uniform and had a shower. I watched her getting dressed. "That's some more new underwear I haven't seen. Very smart. How much did you get the other day? It looks great and very expensive."

"I don't wear underwear, you do. I wear lingerie."

"You didn't answer my question."

"Get a move on, I need a drink."

As usual in most American bars it was very dark but we found a table. There was waitress service and I ordered two gin and tonics. Looking at them when they arrived, I was glad I hadn't ordered doubles.

"I'm ravenous. Let's go straight to the restaurant, we can take our drinks in with us. You won't want anything after all that food and drink that girl kept on giving you."

"Do you mean Lorna? You trained her very well. The service was excellent."

"So I saw." She grinned. "Alright. I'll let you off with a caution and you can order me a fillet steak medium rare with french fries and a side salad."

"But you haven't looked at the menu yet."

"I didn't want to be confused. What are you having?"

"Am I allowed to look at the menu?"

"If you must."

I settled for a bowl of mushroom soup and watched Helen tucking in. We went to bed the moment we had finished and slept until about five in the morning and then dozed until 6.30. I opened the curtains and the sun was already heating up the desert.

"Helen, my love, why don't we go for a swim?"

There was a long silence and then a slightly reluctant "Alright. Off you go and I might join you."

There was a gate to the pool at the bottom of the stairs. I collected a towel, chose a couple of chairs, and then entered the pool. The water was warm and I had managed a couple of lengths when Helen arrived in a brief swimsuit. "You look terrific."

"Well I don't feel it. I think I will try a width in the shallow end. You'd better watch me."

We stayed in the pool for about ten minutes and then dressed and went down to the coffee shop. "What time is my bus to-morrow morning?"

"What time do you have to report by? The choice at LAX is 11,1.30 or 4.30 and it takes two hours."

"11 will be perfect."

"Fine. I'll drive you down to Lancaster to catch it."

We got our things and I drove to the Mojave airport. We saw the sign for Murray Aerospace as we approached the entrance. After driving around for a few minutes I managed to find a visitors parking slot and went into reception.

The building seemed very new and I didn't have long to wait before George Straker arrived. We introduced ourselves and then he took us straight into a hangar where there were two nearly completed LightJets and a complete one with two engineers working on the engine. Helen left us, walked round the hangar and found a seat.

"Peter, the first production aircraft is on its way back from Farnborough and this one is our prototype which we used to obtain certification. I'm afraid the flight deck is not representative."

George opened the left hand door for me and it was very easy to step up and get into the pilot's seat. The instrument display was a standard Bendix flat panel director horizon with the situation display underneath, in front of each pilot. The control was a stick and not a wheel so that there was a good view of the panels. "Does it have the energy management system as standard?"

"Not on this one, of course, but it is standard on the production aircraft. There are twin GPS/Galileo receivers and their outputs feed into the flight management box which has the engine fail/nearest airfield facility."

"What about an autopilot?"

"That's optional. You can save a bit of weight and money by not having one. We think most people will want to fly the aircraft themselves. However the aircraft with its very economical engine can stay up over three hours with full fuel flying for range, over 1,000 nautical miles with reserves."

"When can I have a flight?"

"When the Farnborough aircraft gets back."

"George, when's that? How is the Farnborough aircraft getting back?"

"The same way it went. Flying across the North Atlantic."

I looked at him with some surprise. "Surely it hasn't got enough range for that?"

George smiled. "Oh yes it has. We fitted a small extra tank behind the pilots, just in here." He pointed to the two rather cramped seats behind where we were sitting. "The aircraft can make Reykjavik in Iceland from Stornoway. Then Sondrestrom/Kangerlussuaq, or whatever it is called these days, in Western Greenland, Frobisher Bay in Nunavut Canada, Wabush in Labrador, Montreal in Quebec and so on. I've got a table here of distances to Cambridge where Marshalls, our European sales agent is located."

He passed me a sheet to look at.[6]

Airfield	ICAO Ident	Dist. nm	Web Details
Mojave, CA,USA	KMHV		http://gc.kls2.com/airport/KMHV
		805	
Gillette,WY,USA	KGCC		http://gc.kls2.com/airport/KGCC
		772	
Milwaukee,WI,USA	KMKE		http://gc.kls2.com/airport/KMKE
		628	
Montreal,QB,CA	CYUL		http://gc.kls2.com/airport/CYUL
		522	
Wabush,NL,CA	CYWK		http://gc.kls2.com/airport/CYWK
		654	
Iqaluit, Frobisher Bay,NW,CA	CYFB		http://gc.kls2.com/airport/CYFB
		487	
Kangerlussuaq, Greenland	BGSF		http://gc.kls2.com/airport/BGSF
		718	
Reykjavik, Iceland	BIKF		http://gc.kls2.com/airport/BIKF
		585	
Stornoway, UK	EGPO		http://gc.kls2.com/airport/EGPO
		424	
Cambridge, UK	EGSC		http://gc.kls2.com/airport/EGSC
	TOTAL	5595	Great circle distance 4667

[6] Great circle data and links courtesy Karl Swartz <karl@kls2.com>

"That's fantastic. What a great trip."

"Well if you buy one you can ferry it to UK."

"You know it's almost worth buying one just to make the crossing. Mind you it's downwind to England. Isn't the range a bit short the other way?"

"You're right. The critical leg on the North Atlantic is Reykjavik to Sondrestrom. The only alternate is Kulusuk on an island of Eastern Greenland. The landing strip there is just under 4,000 feet gravel but it's safe to use in the summer when there's no ice or snow though the weather has to be perfect."

"So when is the aircraft coming back?"

"In a week or so. We're demonstrating it in Europe as well as the UK before it sets course. It certainly will be a critical ferry as it will be at max weight carrying two pilots, extra fuel and all the survival gear, dinghy and EPIRBS. The pilots may have to wait a few days to get a favourable wind and good weather." George looked at me. "How serious are you as a customer? We get lots of people who want to fly but have no chance of buying one. "

"I'm not sure. It would take all my savings to buy one but I'm thinking of trying to share one."

"That's what a lot of people are saying. What we are doing at the moment is taking details of people like yourself and then putting you in touch with other possible buyers."

"That seems very sensible. Count me in. Now that the aircraft has FAA certification you should be getting a lot of interest."

"We are and we aren't. Problem is that money is very tight at the moment though of course the interest rates are low if you can get a loan. We'd like flying schools to buy the aircraft but they won't commit until they know what rules the FAA and EASA are going to make."

"What about the cost of training, George? The fuel usage is significantly higher per hour."

"Yes that's right but the overhaul costs of the engine will be less with the LightJet engine. Of course the insurance companies aren't helping by charging very high premiums." He paused. "You work for an insurance company don't you? What's their view?"

"Actually I don't work for an insurance company but they do employ me occasionally. But VVLJs are not for the large insurance companies I deal with. It's not their scene. They insure commercial aircraft and they don't want to get involved."

George showed me all round the aircraft in detail and I was very impressed. The design had been optimised on simplicity, reliability and minimising maintenance costs without penalising the performance. As we were leaving the hangar I noticed one of the two aircraft being completed had a UK registration, G-MRAY.

"Whose bought that one, George?"

"Marshalls of Cambridge, I told you they are our sales agents. We did a deal with them. It's going to be their demonstrator. Mind you it's got to be certificated first. We've had the EASA handling pilots here but they're not completely satisfied yet. Not sure when it'll be leaving."

I called Helen over and she sat in the left hand seat. "It's great. Can I learn to fly on it?"

"Of course. Not sure about the licence."

The three of us went over to the restaurant at the Best Western for a quick lunch. I explained my licence situation and George told me that there was no flying school at the airport, probably because it was under the military complex area called R-2508 covering the flying from Edwards Air Force Base and the Naval Air Weapons Center at China Lake. He reckoned my best bet therefore would be to go to the General William J Fox airfield near Lancaster. There was a relatively new school there, the Desert Flying School, and they would almost certainly be able to get me current again. We exchanged contact details and George left us.

We went back to the car, drove down highway 58 and found the flying school about 45 minutes later. I explained my situation to the office and showed them my ATR and medical certificate. The girl there, who seemed very switched on, asked me to come back in the morning as I needed to fly with their chief instructor and he was away flying. I booked 12.30pm and she gave me the latest FARs and the legislation for someone like myself who was getting current again. We drove back up to the hotel and I waded through the paperwork while Helen rested. When the sun was on its way down we went back to the pool.

"Peter, it's a pity you can't come with me on all my trips. I'm really enjoying this. Come on, let's have an early meal and go to bed. I've got a very long day and night to-morrow."

We had a leisurely breakfast and then Helen packed her things. "I'll put on my uniform at the airport. We've got facilities there. Let's go."

We got into the car and I drove round to check out. Then we went south the twenty six miles to the Lancaster bus station. We bought a ticket and the driver put Helen's bags in the boot. We said our goodbyes. "Darling, I've really enjoyed it. Keep in touch and come home as quickly as you can."

Chapter 4

I waved to Helen as the coach pulled out and very conveniently I was in the flying school at General Fox in a very few minutes. Franco Martelli, the chief instructor appeared and he listened as I explained what I wanted. In no time at all I was in a Piper Cadet doing stalls, spins, and circuits. Time rushed by. Two flights and $600 later I had a certificate saying I could fly the plane and had done a couple of circuits by myself.

I drove back through Lancaster to Palmdale and checked in at the Hampton Inn. It was lonely without Helen; I turned on the television but there was nothing I felt like watching. I started trying to sort out my emails which never seemed to stop coming, which on reflection was just as well as I needed clients to pay my bills. To my surprise the phone rang and a very efficient lady, Pat, who turned out to be Harry's secretary came on the line and checked everything was fine. She said Harry would come in and look for me in the coffee shop at 0730. I was wondering what Harry looked like and as I started trying to find out with my computer an email arrived from Pat with an attached picture of Harry who, at the time the picture was taken, was clean shaven, blue eyes, brown hair but of indeterminate height since the picture cut him off just below the knot of a red tie on a white shirt. I was still out of phase with the eight hour time change from UK but I forced myself to stay awake until nine o'clock when I gave up the unequal struggle and went to bed. In fact I slept quite well and wasn't fully awake until six thirty. As it got light I consulted the hotel guide and found the pool opened at six so I swam for about twenty minutes and then got dressed slowly. At seven fifteen I was at the news stand buying the Los Angeles Times and at seven twenty I was being seated at a side table in the coffee shop.

I scanned the arrivals and saw Harry, true to his picture, arriving with his red tie, white shirt and brown trousers and not carrying a jacket. He was five foot ten, slightly tanned and looked very athletic. I got up to meet him and we introduced ourselves.

"Did Pat tell you to wear the red tie and the white shirt, Harry? I'd have managed without."

Harry reacted instantly and smiled. “Pat Foster is the best secretary I’ve ever had. Even my wife approved before she left me. How’s the hotel? I was in two minds which to recommend.”

“It’s fine and it’s great to be here. I’m really looking forward to seeing what you people have been up to.”

“We’re looking forward to showing you. It’s been a long and expensive struggle but I think we’ve finally got a system that works in all weathers and which we can certificate. So many of the competing systems only work in certain weather conditions but my aim was to have a system that would always work regardless of weather, fog, rain, sandstorm or snow. The other problem, of course, was getting patents that would prevent firms from copying and using our technology. Until we’d done that we didn’t dare show people our system.”

“How did you get into this business, Harry?”

“I was working at Total Avionics on flight management systems but obviously I was aware of their work on synthetic vision, showing the forward view on the approach even though the runway was not in sight. They were also looking at trying to interface passive infra red sensing with their synthetic vision but not doing too well. It seemed to me that the system was great for a lot of the weather conditions but it just wasn’t good enough from a weather viewpoint for the pilots to depend on it. It really only worked reliably at night. However, I realised that the concept had a great future but, in my view, what was needed to make the system completely reliable was an active microwave radar interfacing with the infra red and the synthetic vision. I decided to start my own EVS business. So I left and after a worrying couple of months I managed to find a venture capitalist firm which was prepared to back me. I recruited one or two key engineers I knew and off we went.”

“How long ago, Harry?”

“About four years and luckily as the Government were very interested in my work I was able to operate from Palmdale, in fact they gave me some launch funding. Of course it has been all spend, spend, spend. Now we need to cash in and get the airlines to commit. We’ve had the technical pilots from some of the main airlines flying with us and also test pilots from the manufacturers.

I've asked you to come out because I think you may approach things from a different perspective. I don't like surprises."

"When can we start?"

"As I mentioned, you need to start in our simulator and then go flying."

We finished our breakfast and I followed Harry to the facility which was quite close to the airport. He introduced me to Chuck Steventon, the chief pilot. He had been a test pilot with Boeing and, when business took a turn for the worse, he saw the chief pilot job at Vision Unlimited being advertised and Harry took him on.

We went to the simulator and Chuck explained the set-up. "As you can see the simulator is fixed base, there was no point in buying a very expensive moving base machine because what we are demonstrating here is the avionic installation on the flight deck and in particular the head-up displays. I believe Harry has explained to you that basically our system on the display side consists of three completely different sub-systems; there is an infra red passive system, an active microwave radar and a synthetic display of the outside world based on a world database. All systems output information to the head-up displays and also down on to the normal head down vertical situation displays if the pilot makes the necessary selections. What makes our system outstanding is the great progress we have made in integrating the three sub-systems so the pilot is not aware of the integration. All the pilot sees on the HUD is a fantastically realistic display of the airfield ahead which exactly correlates with the real world which the pilot sees through the windscreen."

"Chuck, it's synthetic vision isn't it?"

"Peter, I know what you mean. But it's more than synthetic since it uses real time information that the infra red and the radar actually 'sees'."

Harry who had been listening carefully joined in. "It's in the area of integration and the microwave radar, Peter, that we have been lodging a lot of patents. We've invested a lot of money developing this product so we've got to stop our competitors free loading at our expense."

Chuck started showing me the installation. "Here are the two head-up displays for the pilots; the pilot pulls the glass down from the stowage position and as the display locks down it shows whatever the captain has selected; in the normal switch position the display shows the blend of infra red, radar and synthetic world. However there is another switch for selecting what is being shown on the HUD down onto the vertical display."

"So the pilots can select the forward looking information on both HUDs and both vertical displays at the same time?"

"Yes, that's quite right."

I could see Harry looking at me but I made no further comment as I needed time to think. He got up and went away.

Chuck carried on. "So are you ready to have a go?" I nodded. "For the first run we'll have the HUD working from take-off to touch down. After that we'll use the reset button on the simulator so that the aircraft can be positioned at the start of the approach which prevents a lot of time being wasted after each landing flying the simulated aircraft round for another approach."

I settled myself in the seat and from force of habit strapped myself in even though there was no motion on the simulator. Chuck had set the real world for a night approach and I pulled the HUD down and could see what looked like the runway overlaid on the real runway lighting. I opened the throttles and the runway slid past as the aircraft accelerated. Chuck said 'rotate' and then 'V_2' and we were airborne. As the aircraft climbed and then levelled off at 1,500ft it was strange seeing the outside world being painted on the HUD correlating with the real world, but the effect was really an outline rather than a camera shot. However there could be no argument that the display was very accurate and realistic.

The aircraft went round the circuit and as I turned in on finals I could see the runway and the airport buildings standing out clearly on the HUD while all I could see through the windscreen were the runway lights. It felt strange flying again after a gap of about six years but I managed a reasonable touch down. Chuck froze the simulator.

"That was very good, Peter. When did you fly last?"

"I flew for the first time for six years in a Piper Cadet yesterday. However, I think the aircraft you have on the simulator is very easy to fly."

"You're right but you still did a good job. You forget I've seen other pilots having a go who are in practice. But don't worry, we'll try one with a faster approach speed in a moment but first let's do some approaches with simulated bad weather."

Chuck repositioned the aircraft for eight miles on finals and as we captured the ILS localiser and glide slope I could make out the runway and airport on the HUD but could not see anything through the windscreens. Finally, at about three hundred feet above the ground the real approach lights began to appear followed by the runway lights as I flared the aircraft for touch-down.

"How did that feel, Peter?"

"Very impressive. What was the simulated visibility?"

"About 2000 feet in mist. Shall we do some more?

I agreed and we did about ten more, simulating snow, rain and then torrential rain. Not surprisingly the view through the HUD was not as good in heavy rain but otherwise the runway appeared on the HUD and head down displays well before it was possible to see it through the windscreens.

"Chuck, if the aircraft is anything like the simulation you really have got something to sell. Can we try a more representative aircraft with a faster approach speed?"

"OK. What aircraft do you fancy? A Concorde?"

"That would be unrealistic. How about a 787 at maximum landing weight?"

"Fine by me. Let's try an approach in Cat III conditions. I'll turn the radio altimeter voice on."

Chuck made some adjustments at his control panel and I started down the approach. Incredibly, at about two miles I could see the runway on the HUD and I was able to make a reasonable flare and touch down following the radio altimeter calling out the heights.

"OK, Peter, lets finish up with some heavier snow."

"Chuck, I'd like to try a sandstorm as well or the equivalent."

He looked at me. "You know more about EVS than you said. OK we'll do snow and then sandstorm."

To my surprise I was still able to flare the aircraft successfully on both approaches when the 'real' runway came into view at the last moment though I was able to see the runway rather earlier in snow than in the sandstorm simulation. Chuck was clearly delighted.

"Peter, I'm really pleased since though you hadn't flown for some time, you managed splendidly."

"I'm rather pleased myself. I thought it was going to be much harder. Mind you, starting on a slow aircraft was very sensible. It made things a lot easier."

Chuck looked at his watch. "I've got to go and fly right now. Harry wants to have lunch with you and we're planning for you to fly in a real aircraft to-morrow; the problem is that unless a miracle happens out here in the desert it is most unlikely that there's going to be any fog." He took me back to Harry and we went to the Olive Garden Italian restaurant not far from the airport.

"Peter, I gather you had a good session with Chuck. What do you think of the equipment?"

"Well the simulation of what the HUD sees in bad weather is fine but then I've seen a lot of simulations from firms using infra red only which claim to be as good in any weather but clearly aren't. Your addition of the microwave radar seems to have solved that problem. I'm looking forward to flying, though of course we won't have poor visibility unfortunately. How are you going to convince the airlines? They'll want to see flying in bad weather as well."

"Yes that's a real problem. We don't want to wait until the winter as we need orders right now. We're wondering about Seattle or Portland. As you know it isn't just getting the bad weather. We've got to get the key airline technical pilots at the same time."

"What about the FAA certification pilots?"

Harry looked at me thoughtfully. "Chuck thought that could come later after we've got some orders."

"Possibly, but if it were me I'd try to get the FAA pilots to look at what you've got and make comments. The last thing you need after you've got orders is to have to redesign the thing."

"But if it works, then it works, surely."

"Not really, Harry. The pilot interfaces with all the equipment, not just the EVS."

The waiter came over and we both ordered small margaritas. There was a long silence as Harry considered the impact of my remarks.

"You know I had a feeling we might be missing something. That's why I asked you to come out. Chuck has arranged for you to fly to-morrow. Unfortunately it won't be with him but with Jean Spenser, his deputy. Chuck has a medical arranged he can't change."

"Can I talk to your chief design engineer this afternoon?"

"That's Patrick Williams. By all means. He's been with us right from the beginning. I persuaded him to leave Boeing the moment I got the project funded."

The food arrived and we started talking generally about the impact that electronics had made on the aviation industry. There seemed to be no limit to the new devices that were appearing to help the pilot and therefore to increase safety.

"Peter, that's a benefit of EVS I haven't mentioned. On the ground in poor weather it is easy to spot other aircraft on the taxiway. Of course it's only an add-on, if you like. It won't make an airline buy the EVS. You can also see aircraft on the runway during the approach."

"Yes, Harry, that's obviously useful but I'm not sure whether the certification authorities will allow the EVS on during a CAT III approach."

"Why on earth not? It must help."

"The FAA and EASA will have to be satisfied that having the display on won't distract the pilot. It should be alright but a decision is required. That's why I recommended to you that you get the FAA pilots to fly with you."

Harry took me over to Patrick Williams, did the introductions and explained the reason for my visit. "Don't be afraid to answer his questions, he's not working for Total Avionics. He was an airline pilot and has a degree in electronics."

"But it was a long time ago, Patrick. I work free lance for airlines or insurance companies now, if there are problems or accidents."

"I know you do, Peter. I was still with Boeing when that aircraft crashed at Heathrow in freezing fog. We tightened up our modification procedures after you'd explained what had happened."

"I've been chatting to Harry. Have you run what you've been doing past the FAA?"

"You bet. We've agreed with them the software certification standard we need."

We spent the afternoon discussing the installation of the HUD. I went back to the hotel and wrote up the details of the day and then went down to the coffee shop and watched golf being shown on the TV for a bit before going to bed.

In the morning I logged on and there was a message from John Southern. The Chinese accident investigation department, CAAC, had been on to him asking for help. They knew Hull Claims were insuring the aircraft and they wanted to discuss the accident. Would I ring him? I looked at my watch, John would still be up and I gave him a call.

"John, what's going on. How did they contact you?"

"A man from their embassy in London called. How he knew to contact me I don't know."

"Do you know what they want? Why don't they contact Derek?"

"No, I've no idea what they want. Derek is back and says it's a clear case of pilot error and we'll have to pay up. He reckons they are trying to save face because the police have still got the pilots and they want an excuse to justify having taken them plus a reason for releasing them."

"But they are the accident investigators aren't they? Why can't they get them released?"

"Derek says it's the Hong Kong police who have got the pilots because the Chinese asked them to and now they have got to have a good story when they release them because they are bound to talk."

"Didn't Derek see the pilots?"

"No. The police said it was up to the accident investigators and the people at CAAC said it was up to the police."

"Well send Derek back out again if they want someone. He seems to know what's going on."

"That's what I recommended to Richard. Oh, Derek is very happy to go out again but for some reason Richard suggested you might like to go. Did you agree to work for the airline?"

"No, John, I didn't. Of course, Derek did ask me to go out, you remember but I said no! Surely it's a bit late for me to go out now?"

"Not at all. You may see something Derek missed."

"This will now be the third invitation I've had, first Derek, then Fred Xie Tingxi and now the Chinese accident people through you. To tell you the truth I'm not particularly enthusiastic. What have you told them?"

"I said we would let them know. They seemed very keen. How are you placed in New York? When could you go to Hong Kong?"

"Wait a moment. I haven't agreed to go and to be honest I'm not sure when I can go. I'm at Palmdale at the moment looking at EVS and I'm not sure when I can get away. Let me think about it overnight and I'll call you to-morrow. By the way did they give you a contact name, number or email?"

"Yes to all three. I'll send you an email." There was silence for moment. "Peter, I'd rather like you to go out there. We need to know what's going on. As I told you Derek has said that everything is in order and we'll have to pay up but there's a lot of money at stake. We want to be sure."

"Presumably Derek went to Taipei to check things there?"

"Of course."

"Then it all looks cut and dried to me."

"Peter, I've been at this game a lot longer than you. I don't feel comfortable."

"John, forgive me for saying so but you're almost certainly biased."

"Maybe. Let me know as soon as you can."

After a quick breakfast I went to the airport and met Jean Spencer. I suppose I had been expecting Gene Spencer and not a very smart well shaped forty year old wearing a white blouse with her bra showing through and a tight pair of slacks. I got the feeling she knew she was easy on the eye and didn't like to hide it.

"Hi, Peter. The aircraft is ready over there but first let's talk about what we're going to do."

I looked over to where she had indicated and saw a twin engined Raytheon 800 which was based on the original de Havilland 125. We went into what I took to be the operations room. She looked at me in what I thought was a slightly condescending way but maybe I was too sensitive.

"Peter, I gather you're not a practising pilot." I made no comment. "Perhaps it would be best if I flew the aircraft while you look through the head-up display on your side. I thought we would do an approach first with the HUD displaying just the key parameters like ILS displacement, height, speed, command bar only; then I'll switch the infrared and radar on and you can see the difference."

"Where are we going to do the approaches, Jean?"

She looked surprised. "Here at Palmdale. We don't want to waste flying time." Again I made no comment. I was there to learn and I always included the people as well as the equipment.

Jean checked the weather. There was no wind and the visibility was unrestricted which I thought was rather a pity. We went out to the aircraft and she clearly expected me to get into the right hand seat. She started up the engines from the batteries.

"Pull the HUD down and I'll put the display in the ground mode so that the sensors will display other aircraft when we taxi out."

I lowered my HUD and could see the hangars, terminals and a parked aircraft ahead of us.

"Peter, I'm going to test the symbology but you won't need it in until take-off."

The HUD filled momentarily with all the symbology necessary to define a flight path and then disappeared leaving just the infrared and radar display. Jean taxied out, switched the symbology back on and we took off with everything working well. We went round for a circuit and did an ILS approach with Jean flying manually following the vertical and horizontal command bars. After touch-down we did a roller and then Jean told me to switch on the infrared and radar. We did another approach and this time I could see not only the display generated from the infra red and the radar but also the computer generated runway based on the GPS, ground database and the aircraft altitude. Not surprisingly the computer generated runway looked at through the head-up display was positioned exactly on the real world runway looking out through the windscreen though being daylight it was hard to see. After landing Jean taxied off the runway and round for another take-off.

"What shall we do now, Peter?"

"May I have a go?"

Jean looked surprised. "Do you think you'll be able to manage? It's quite complicated, not as simple as it looks."

"I used to fly. I could try."

Jean got permission for us to take-off and do a wide circuit. I didn't bother with the HUD for take-off but downwind I pulled the glass down and switched on the symbology. "Is there a small airfield we can go to so I can get a better idea of how good the equipment is? Little Buttes Antique Airfield?"

Jean began to look unsure of herself. "Well I suppose we could go there but it's very short."

"It's only about 20 miles or so north of here near Lancaster and we don't have to touch down. Tell you what. I'll do a run here and then perhaps we could go there."

She looked definitely uncertain. Things clearly weren't going as she expected. "OK. Let's try a circuit."

Air traffic gave us permission to go and I took off in the Raytheon 800. The moment we got airborne I could feel what a nice aircraft it was. I knew I was still very rusty but the time in the simulator had certainly improved my flying. Jean got permission from air traffic to do an ILS followed by an overshoot.

"Jean, I'll do this first approach without the sensors please."

"But that's why we're flying."

"But I can't assess it on an airfield like Palmdale, my dear." I shouldn't have called her that but I wanted to put her in her place. "That's why I want to go Little Buttes where there is no help except from the sensors. Obviously I need to do some night flying to make a realistic assessment but Little Buttes will be a start."

We did an ILS approach using the head-up display symbology which was great and then we set course for Little Buttes keeping low level away from the military traffic. It was a short 3,000 ft grass strip and there was no air traffic. We broadcast our intention of doing two or three circuits and Jean called our position as we did the approaches. I asked her to switch the sensors on as we started our first approach and I was very impressed as the display showed the airfield despite only being earth and not concrete. I did three approaches and then we went back to Palmdale and taxied in.

Jean shut the engines down and looked at me "I thought you said you couldn't fly?"

"No, my dear. You assumed I couldn't because I didn't have a licence and you clearly felt you were wasting your time." She started to colour up in her cheeks. "It's alright. No hard feelings as far as I'm concerned. I am out of practice but I'm getting better every time I fly and I'm very impressed with your EVS. However I need to fly at night to make a realistic assessment."

She scowled, clearly very put out. "Peter, that decision is beyond my pay bracket. You'll have to ask Chuck or Harry."

"Will Chuck be back to-day?"

"He's probably back now. Let's go and see.'

A much more thoughtful Jean led me back into the building and into Chuck's office but he wasn't there so she took me up to Harry. He was busy so she said good-bye and left me with Pat.

"Is everything OK, Mr Talbert? Jean looked a bit concerned."

"Call me Peter, Pat. Everything's fine. I think my flying might have upset her."

Harry finished dealing with some of his papers and came out. "How did you get on?"

"Great thank you. Couldn't really see how good the system was at Palmdale so we went to Little Buttes."

Harry went pale and led me into his office. "Is the aircraft OK? Surely it's not long enough and it's turf. Jean shouldn't have gone there."

"Harry, relax. We just did approaches and overshoots. I wanted to see what the airfield looked like using your EVS and amazingly I could make out the landing strip. Very impressive."

"Was that your idea?"

"Absolutely. Jean went pale but to be fair she agreed that we could go there. By the way, when we started she hadn't realised I used to be a pilot."

"Chuck says you're very good."

"Thank you but I think all he told Jean was that I didn't have a licence so she started off in the 'let me show you how good it is' mode. Anyway as it turned out it didn't matter but Harry, can I have a go at night? It would be much easier to assess how good the system is."

"Of course. I should have realised that's what you would want. Unfortunately Chuck has rung me and won't be in until lunch time to-morrow. Will Jean be alright?"

"She'll be fine if she's free."

Harry phoned her and he sat there obviously listening to a long message from Jean. Every so often he said 'yes' and then finally he managed to get a word in. "OK, Jean, we'll talk about it but some other time, not just now. I was going to ask you if you were free this evening to go flying with Peter but perhaps we should wait until Chuck comes back."

There was another burst from the other end. "Jean, I understand. We'll wait for Chuck to come back."

He put the phone down and looked at me quizzically. "You certainly made a great impression with her, Peter."

"Harry, I blame Chuck for not briefing her properly and then she felt a fool when I suddenly took over and clearly was not having any difficulties."

"My problem, Peter, is that I'm paying you on at a daily rate and Chuck isn't here until to-morrow."

"That's fine. Pay me for one more day starting to-morrow afternoon. I'll have to spend time writing a report for you."

I went back to the hotel and went through my notes, had a meal and went to bed.

In the morning I looked at the flights to Hong Kong and the earliest I could get away seemed to be Saturday late. I would have liked to travel after flying with Chuck but there wouldn't be enough time. I called John Southern at home.

"I'll go to Hong Kong but on one condition only. I want to talk to the pilots. If I can't do that I'll fly straight out again."

"Peter, I can't check now. The time change is all wrong."

"Well I can go to-morrow, Saturday arriving Monday at dawn as long as you'll cover my costs even if they won't let me talk to the pilots."

"Peter, that'll be fine."

"John, there's another problem. I hadn't reckoned on going on to China. I haven't got enough clothes. You're going to have to buy me some trousers, shirts, underwear and maybe a case to put them in."

John agreed and so I booked the flight and sent an email to him asking him to let me know how to contact CAAC. As usual I had to guess a hotel and chose the Marriott near the airport, thinking it would probably be more convenient than being in Kowloon or Hong Kong.

I called Helen to tell her about Hong Kong. She didn't sound over the moon.

"Well when shall I see you? It's lonely being stuck here on my own."

"I should be back at the end of the week."

"That's nice. While you're enjoying the flesh pots of China I'm working like a slave. I'm off to LA again next Saturday, back on the Tuesday and then a San Francisco on the Friday back on the Monday. That's followed by a ten day trip to Australia and then, thank goodness, three weeks off which I shall need."

"I'm not sure I'll see anything but offices in Hong Kong. Anyway I wouldn't know a flesh pot if I saw one. With any luck we'll be together next Saturday or Sunday."

"Alright, my love. Really looking forward to seeing you. Don't work too hard or get into trouble."

The weather was completely clear so I went back to the Desert Flying School at General Fox and rented a Piper Cadet. The sun was hot at eleven and as I got airborne it was quite turbulent until I had climbed 3,000 feet above the desert. The visibility was good and I enjoyed flying over brown landscape and looking at the hills close-by. I flew north and kept well clear of the dry lake by Edwards Air Force Base before returning. I drove back to Palmdale and was back in the hotel by two o'clock and then went to Vision Unlimited.

Chuck had returned. "Sorry you had a problem with Jean yesterday. She thinks you should have told her that you were a pilot and not just an engineer."

"Chuck, she obviously didn't listen to your briefing."

"Actually it was probably my fault because I went away and left her a note which clearly didn't explain the situation very well. Anyway, hopefully we'll be all set to fly this evening. Sunset is 8.09 so we need to be here at 7.30. Why don't we have something to eat first? Where are you staying?" I told him I was in the Hampton Inn. "OK. We can have an early bird special. See you at six."

Chuck was clearly busy. I went in to see Pat, told her I was planning to leave in the morning and suggested Harry should have breakfast with me.

Back in the hotel there was a message light on; Harry was going to join me for breakfast.

Chuck arrived promptly and we went into the restaurant.

"It's strange about Jean, Peter. She really seems to have taken a dislike to you."

"I don't know why but it seems so. What is her background? Was she a test pilot?"

"Interestingly she was and I wasn't. She was in the Army flying helicopters and did the course in the UK, the Empire Test Pilots School. When she left the Army she got an ATR and started flying out of San Francisco with Air Alaska and, as you know, they did a lot of pioneering work on using HUDs in bad weather. She had had a lot of experience with night goggles so when she read about Harry launching Vision Unlimited she applied for a job. Her background was absolutely perfect for what we were doing and I hired her straightaway. She is very good indeed."

"If I may ask why did Harry recruit you?"

"Well I had a degree in avionics and Boeing were employing me as a test pilot even though I hadn't done the course. They used me on avionic system development and in fact we were developing an early EVS on our business 737s in competition with the Gulfstream G4s and 5s. The Boeing chief pilot gave me a very good write up; I think Boeing realised they needed a better EVS so in a way it was an opportunity to have an inside track on what was happening. Their test pilots have flown with me quite a lot and are very supportive."

"That's great. What about the FAA pilots?"

"I knew you were going to ask that. Harry mentioned your concern and I've just invited them down. You were quite right. I thought their visit could wait until we had sold something but on reflection it's just as well to let them look."

We left in plenty of time and I slowly got settled in the left hand seat, checking the HUD for the normal symbology from the flight instrumentation. Chuck showed me how to switch on the infrared and radar and full EVS interface and it all looked good. The sky was completely clear as we taxied out and the stars were just beginning to appear. By chance it was only three days after the new moon so we were not going to get any help from the moonlight.

I took off and we decided to go to Mojave as there would be less traffic and less illumination from the ground. We went low level and the EVS was superb, showing the terrain very clearly. As we turned final the airport and the runway stood out and it was a delight to make the approach. As we got really close the command bar of the symbology on the head-up display indicated when to flare but I had already started flaring maybe a second earlier as I always liked to touch down fairly slowly.

As I opened the throttles after touch down Chuck re-trimmed the elevator and selected the flaps to the take-off position. We did several approaches with and without the sensors; out of the corner of my eye I could see Chuck getting very nervous approaching the runway when I didn't have the sensors on and relying just on the symbology.

"Would you like to try an approach at Edwards on the dry lake?"

"Chuck, will they allow that?"

"It'll be OK if they're not busy. We were able to get special permission because we've got some military funding. The controllers get bored and they know the aircraft and what we're doing. We filled in all the forms and so got permission."

He called Edwards and they told us to proceed VFR to the north east of the airfield. We had UHF on the aircraft and Chuck switched to their approach frequency as I marvelled at the display from the EVS. We were vectored onto finals for 22L runway and the lake was very clear as we approached touchdown just beyond it.

Chuck then asked for permission to land on the lake bed runway. The controller gave us permission but warned us that there would be no lights.

I took the plane on an extended downwind and watched the main runway disappearing past on our left. The Edwards radar positioned us for finals on the lake bed and the EVS showed the terrain but no obvious runway. However it didn't matter because as we approached the ground I used the aircraft instrument symbology and we touched down safely if rather firmly. Chuck took over and did another roller on the lake bed with a rather superior touch down and then instead of flying straight back to Mojave he got permission to do an approach at California City municipal airport so we could see the hills on our right. Then after touch down he flew towards and then over the hills so that they were clearly visible on the HUD. Finally he gave the aircraft back to me and I landed on runway 30 pointing right at the hills with the best touch down of the evening.

Chuck looked at me as the engines ran down. "Peter, your flying improved throughout the trip. Jean's an examiner on the 800. I'm sure you'd be able to get a type rating."

"Chuck, you're very kind but I don't need a rating on this airplane. I came here to look at the EVS and that's what I've been able to do. Obviously I'd like to fly in bad weather so if you do decide to position the aircraft in Seattle please let me know straightaway so I can be on stand-by for the weather going bad. Mind you if the weather is bad I hope British Airways will be able to land at Seattle and not divert to Portland."

"Perhaps they'll need to buy our EVS."

"Possibly."

I could have said a lot more but decided that ten o'clock in the evening was not the right time to start talking about certification issues. Chuck came back with me for a quick drink. I was planning to see Harry in the morning but Chuck was not going to be around so we said farewell.

"Don't forget I want to fly with you in fog, rain, snow and in a dust storm."

Chuck grinned. "Don't worry, I've got the message. See you soon."

Harry arrived at 7.45. “So how did you get on last night, Peter? Did it all work?”

“Yes, it was fine. No problems in performance at all. Chuck tells me that you’ve already spoken to him and he is going to get the FAA pilots to look at your setup. I’ve asked him to let me know if he positions the aircraft looking for fog on the West Coast in Seattle or Portland and I’ll come back over if you’d like me to.”

“That would be very useful, I think, but check with me first before you start incurring expenses, in case something has changed.”

“I’ll be sending you my report in the next couple of days, Harry. How are your sales going?”

“We’ve got two serious customers so far, both with a lot of aircraft.”

“Well be careful with any contract you sign with an airline. FAA may want changes which might be costly. They may be restrictive in the use of the equipment.”

“What do you mean?”

“I mentioned the problem the other day. A lot depends on the other equipment on the aircraft when using EVS. For example if the aircraft has an autoland autopilot the FAA may not allow the EVS to be switched on. It could be dangerous for a pilot to take over in a Cat III situation with the autopilot flying the aircraft. It is alright of course for the basic aircraft symbology to be there but in my view adding an EVS system, however good it is, may not necessarily be a benefit. The two systems have to agree perfectly. You would have to convince the FAA that EVS wouldn’t be a distraction on a Cat III autopilot approach.”

“Peter, though I don’t accept that having our system on during an autoland could make the operation less safe, I do understand that FAA may feel more comfortable not having to justify leaving it on. But that situation is only true for airfields equipped with autolanding lighting and ILS. There are many other airfields where EVS is a real godsend making it much safer for the pilot when coming in to land, particularly if he or she doesn’t know the place well.”

"Harry, I do know that, but the airline has to make up its mind if EVS is worth the money for the reliability of operations and extra safety it brings going into non-autoland airfields."

I thought for a moment. "Harry, have you ever fitted your system on a commercial airliner which has a full suite of avionics including a Cat III autopilot.?"

"Certainly not. Why do you ask?"

"It would have avoided any surprises during certification."

We carried on the discussion for a bit longer, then we said goodbye. I got into my car drove down to LA on 405 and stopped off at the Getty Museum which I had really liked on my previous visit, particularly the paintings. I left at seven as it was getting dark and checked the car in at the airport. I had plenty of time and went to the business class lounge prior to boarding.

***

We took off at midnight and looking at the map all I could see was water. The Pacific seemed to stretch for ever and we finally reached Chek Lap Kok fifteen hours after we had taken-off from Los Angeles. I managed to eat a little, sleep a little and watch some old movies but I didn't feel all that sharp as I got out of the aircraft.

When the door was opened there were some announcements and I heard my name being called. I couldn't understand what was being said so as I left I asked the girl who was clearly ground staff for the message. She pointed to a smart middle aged Chinese man close to the entrance and we shook hands. He spoke perfect English. "Mr Talbert, welcome to China and to Hong Kong. My name is Shiu Liao but please call me Bruce."

I guessed Bruce was from the CAAC. He led the way, asked for my passport and we by-passed the immigration line and arrived at the baggage carousel. My business class bag appeared promptly and again we went straight through customs. "You are staying in the Marriott here, Mr Talbert?" I nodded. There was a car waiting for us and it took us the short distance to the hotel. A porter took my bags and I checked in while Shiu Liao waited behind me.

"We would like to talk about the accident to B33057. We will collect you at ten o'clock to-morrow morning."

I clearly wasn't required to respond. He bowed towards me and went back to the car. I wondered whether I should have raised the subject of the pilots but on reflection I was in no great shape to do anything constructive. I dozed a bit on the bed and then, looking at my watch, realised it was only 2pm so I decided to buy some clothes. I took a cab to Kowloon where there was no shortage of shops. It only took me half an hour to get what I wanted and I was soon back in the hotel. My room on the tenth floor looked out over the water. It had everything I required but lacked inspiration in the design. I might have been anywhere but as I switched on the television there was no doubt I was in China. There were hundreds of channels, in English as well as Chinese, but nothing I wanted to watch. I gave up, switched on my netbook and looked at all my emails.

Later I went up to the bar and restaurant on the top floor and had a beer, watching the aircraft coming in to land. I marvelled at the huge airport built on a man made piece of land recovered from the sea. Why the UK couldn't build a new airport on the banks of the Thames in England was beyond me after seeing what the Chinese had achieved on a site where there hadn't been any land at all when they started.

I was completely confused about where Helen might be and our time difference so I sent her a text message 'Love You, Peter' and got one back 'Luv u 2 H' which didn't tell me anything new.

Back in my room I slept fitfully until seven o'clock when I went for a swim in the indoor pool; I didn't stay long as it already had too many swimmers for my taste so I could not get any real exercise swimming lengths.

Breakfast likewise was not very enjoyable as it seemed as if all the guests were there at the same time, though in truth it probably could have been a lot worse. I came to the conclusion that I wasn't very sociable and was very glad when ten o'clock arrived and I was whisked away back to the airport where we entered an administration building, up two floors in an elevator and into a small meeting room. There were already two more Chinese officials there, Tuan Feng who I soon learnt was an avionics expert and was called Winston, and Huai Tiantian from air traffic control who asked to be known as Thomas. Bruce seemed to be the inspector in charge of the investigation of the mishap to the CC21.

"Mr Talbert," Bruce started the meeting the moment we sat down "Thank you for coming out here so quickly. The accident looks as if the pilots made an error landing in fog but Tuan Feng thinks the aircraft may have had a fault. West Orient Airlines and your Derek are blaming the pilots. CAAC wants to make certain that the true facts are known."

"Bruce, if may ask, what do the pilots say? Where are they?"

His face went blank. "They are with the police because air traffic think that the accident was due to lack of skill and that they should be punished." Huai Tiantian nodded but in my view he looked uncomfortable and certainly not inscrutable.

"Well what do they say? I'm sure John Southern of Hull Claims told you that I must talk to them. "

"The police are waiting for instructions from Hong Kong administration. They are not sure whether to release them."

"Have you spoken to them?"

"Not yet."

"Is there a problem because the plane comes from Taiwan?"

Bruce smiled. "It is not helping."

"Did Derek talk to them?"

"No, Mr Talbert."

"Well I must."

"We think the police might now let you talk to the pilots but you must speak to them first."

Clearly politics was a big issue and it looked as if CAAC were hoping that a third party might 'unlock' the prisoners.

"Mr Talbert, would you like to talk to the chief policeman?

"I'd be delighted."

Bruce dialled a number and started a conversation. He took the phone in his hand and put his hand over the mouthpiece. "Mr Talbert this is Yao Xueqiang; he is known as Cedric."

"Mr Talbert, how can I help you?"

It was a long and awkward conversation but finally it was agreed that if I went into Hong Kong I could talk to the pilots. I handed the phone back to Bruce who made some notes before closing the conversation. "Mr Talbert, we need to go to the Tung Tau Correctional Institution in Stanley on Hong Kong Island."

We left the meeting and drove into the city and took the tunnel to the island. We threaded our way to Stanley through a lot of buses and taxis. The building looked quite old and was guarded by two armed policeman. We went to a desk in the entrance room and Yao Xueqiang appeared. He led the way to a small empty room and made it clear that we should sit down. After a wait of about ten minutes the two pilots appeared guarded by a policeman. They were still wearing uniform which looked far from fresh. I smiled at them and the older one, known as Norman, looked at me carefully. It was made clear I could start to talk to them.

It was difficult at first because they were very suspicious and had no idea why I was there. I told them I was from the insurance company and tried to explain that I just wanted to know what had happened. Norman's English was excellent but the other pilot known as Robert clearly found the conversation difficult to follow. Apparently they had made an instrument approach using the autopilot. It was very foggy so they primed the equipment for an automatic landing. At about seventy feet while they were still in fog the autopilot unexpectedly cut out and Norman opened the throttles to go around but only the starboard engine opened up. He was not able to control the aircraft and make it climb away so he throttled back and tried to follow the flight director. The rate of descent built up and when the runway appeared he couldn't flare in time and the aircraft crash landed. It hit the ground very hard and veered off to the right. The undercarriage collapsed, the pilots stopped both engines, operated the fire extinguishers and the aircraft came to an abrupt halt.

Clearly it should have been possible to have kept flying on one engine but the fact that the engine failed at a critical moment meant that it would have taken a pilot of considerable skill and in full flying practice in Cat III landings to have rescued the situation in cloud, no autopilot and the aircraft descending very close to the ground. In the event he had done well not to lose control and decide to try to land. What was exercising my mind was why the autopilot came out. Clearly I was in the middle of a tricky political situation with a Chinese manufactured aircraft, US avionics, Chinese engine and a Taiwanese airline with a Taiwanese crew.

I asked Norman where they did their Category III training procedures. Despite his good English it took a lot of questions before he understood what I said and then he told me that he had had training at the Shenzhen Aircraft facility. I tried to find out if there was a regular refresher training procedure anywhere but Norman couldn't understand my questions. I gave up and asked if I could make some enquiries and come back later. Bruce looked surprised but I needed to talk to him. I suggested we went to the Marriott for a sandwich. We agreed and went to the coffee shop.

"Bruce, does the pilots' account match up with the crash recorder?"

"Yes, Mr Talbert."

"What is the problem then? Why keep the pilots in prison?"

"The aircraft manufacturer is afraid that the aircraft will be criticized because it has Chinese WQ-14 engines. So they are trying to blame the pilots and delay their release."

"Who makes the autopilot? A Chinese firm?"

"No, Total Avionics."

"Did one of the pilots disconnect the autopilot?"

"No, it was an autopilot fault."

"Have you asked Total Avionics if they have any ideas why the autopilot cut-out?"

"Yes I did but they haven't replied."

I got my phone out and operated the browser. I tried text only after 'googling' Total Avionics and after a struggle found a telephone number for support. It seemed to be located in New Jersey and the time was probably midnight but I got a crisp voice answering. I explained the situation and asked for someone who was dealing with the matter to call me. To my surprise my phone rang ten minutes later. It was a William Roscoff and I explained where I fitted in.

"Peter, are you sure the autopilot had the latest modification? The aircraft shouldn't have carried out automatic landings unless it had modifications up to 156 installed."

"I've no idea, William. You seem very up to speed with the problem. Don't you have a man in Taipei who knows the answer?"

"The airline does the software upgrades and any hardware changes. They get regular bulletins from us."

"Well what did they say?"

"They said all the modifications were incorporated."

"Well then there's not much more to be done. Please give me your email and telephone numbers."

We rang off. Bruce had been listening very carefully.

"Mr Talbert, I've tried to find out from Taipei about the modification state of the autopilot but there have been no answers."

"Did you follow my conversation? The airline said all the modifications were up to date."

He nodded. "Mr Talbert, I've also tried to establish their training procedures for Category III and have not been successful."

I began to realize that Bruce had a very clear understanding of the whole situation but was also mindful of the politics.

"Did you know about modification 156 being critical?" He shook his head. "Well we must get an answer to the modification state."

I suspected that he was hoping I could help unlock the situation but I decided I needed help. We went back to the airport and I asked for a telephone. He showed me into a small room and I rang the Consul General's office. The exchange put me through to his secretary who was very helpful. There wasn't a specialist in aviation on the staff apparently but I explained I needed political advice. There was a pause and the Consul General himself came on line. I explained the problem that the UK interest was because the insurer of the crashed aircraft was a UK firm. The Consul General, Jim Fortescue, knew about the aircraft crash but had not realised that there was a UK agenda.

"Mr Talbert, clearly the Chinese aircraft manufacturer is very concerned and has approached the Hong Kong authorities and CAAC for help. I think you should tell CAAC that you are leaving because there is nothing you can do while the pilots are in prison. If they are released then you would go back with them to Taipei to look at their training records. They won't want you to leave without something being settled."

"That sounds like good advice. I'll try it on. In fact, I definitely will go if they won't be sensible."

"Good. Come and see me for a coffee sometime. I like to meet people from the real world occasionally."

I turned to Bruce and explained that I couldn't help any more. I needed the pilots to be released and to come back with me to Taipei or I was going back to England. Bruce left me and I started looking at flights to Taipei. After about three quarters of an hour he reappeared and told me that it had been agreed that the pilots could be released providing they went straight back to Taipei. I guessed the Chinese didn't want the pilots to be interviewed by the media in Hong Kong. He said that there was a mid-morning West Orient flight the following day and Norman with his co-pilot would be on-board.

Bruce asked me to send my report to him directly after seeing West Orient Airlines and he gave me his email and postal address. We went back to the hotel and said good-bye.

Up in my room I booked a seat on the same flight as the one planned for Norman and his co-pilot and then booked a room at the Marriot. I sent an email to John Southern so he would know what was happening. Then I called Fred Xie Tingxi but apparently he was not available. I decided to send him an email with my travel and hotel details. I went down to the coffee shop and on my return there was message from Fred.

'Please delay your arrival for some weeks until I return. Regards Fred Xie Tingxi'

The message put me in some difficulty but reluctantly I decided to accede to the request. I cancelled my Taipei flight and instead booked Qantas direct to Heathrow. The flight left at 0730 the following morning so I hurriedly packed up, sent Helen a text message with my ETA Monday and went to bed.

On the way back to Heathrow I tried to draft out my report on the accident at Chek Lap Kok. The aircraft had clearly crashed because the pilot had not been able to execute a missed approach when the autopilot cut-out and one engine surged, leaving only one engine operating at full power. However I had been unable to find out why the autopilot had cut-out and I felt that somehow this was important. To finish my investigation someone obviously needed to go to Taipei to have a closer look at the paperwork and modifications.

I called John Southern and told him what hadn't happened in Hong Kong.

"Peter, make sure you chase Fred and go to Taipei. I want to make certain that the aircraft had been maintained properly."

"John, does it matter? Surely you'll have to pay up? The pilots might have managed to prevent the aircraft hitting the ground but it must have been very difficult when one of the engines failed right at the critical moment."

"Peter, if the avionics had not been maintained properly it could affect the insurance claim."

"Did Derek mention the mod state of the autopilot? It is clearly critical."

"I don't know" was the very unsatisfactory answer.

Chapter 5

Helen was waiting at Heathrow looking as lovely as ever. "Peter, you've arrived early for a change. I thought I'd have left before you got back."

"Well in fact I would have been several days later as I should have gone to Taipei but the airline boss apparently was away and didn't want me to go there. I'm not sure I believed him but it's John Southern's problem." I looked at her carefully.

"You look really great, my darling."

"So will you when I've washed you down."

"That sounds a splendid idea."

"Well don't think about it and let's get to my car."

We started walking through the car park dragging both my bags. "How did it all go? Did you get paid?"

"I gave Vision Unlimited my invoice."

"That won't buy us a cruise from London to Sydney."

"Who is going to Sydney?"

"We are. You can take a holiday any time and I shall have to resign shortly when he becomes uncomfortable."

"Are you telling me something?"

"Yes. You can drive."

"No, thanks. I'm too tired."

"I'm not sure I should drive in my condition."

"Why not? You drove here. I thought you looked blooming."

"I'm not sure I want to look blooming. Actually I persuaded the doctor that I needed a blood test and the result said I was expecting. Look out. Concentrate or we'll be run over or there'll be a miscarriage or worse."

"Darling, that's great. When will she be due?"

"You should be able to work out when he's due. When did we see the Dunstons?"

"Over three weeks ago I think. But Kingston isn't a very nice name for a girl."

"Or a boy. We'll have to do some research."

With Helen driving we got home a lot quicker than if I had been at the wheel. “How many points have you got on your licence?”

“None, thank you Peter. How about you?”

“Three. I can’t believe you haven’t got any. It’s not fair. You went past three cameras well above the limit.”

“The speedometer over reads.”

“Not by ten miles an hour.”

“They’re set for seven miles over the limit. Stop complaining.”

She carried my flight bag into my study and then came over towards me. She had taken off her jacket and there was a definite smell of the perfume she knew I liked. “Would you like breakfast or go to bed? You must be tired.”

I looked at her to try to work out the right answer and came to the conclusion that it was a no brainer. “Are they mutually exclusive?” It was definitely the correct reply.

“No, but they have to be consecutive.” From the way she stood in front of me and then kissed me I managed to work out the right order.

“Wait a moment. I thought I was the one getting ready for bed.”

When we got back downstairs there was message to call Monty Rushmore. The number looked familiar but the name wasn’t. Helen looked at the number. “That’s a Gatwick area number, one of the new exchanges, isn’t it.”

“Alright, know all. Well done. It must be a guy from SRG at Gatwick.”

I called the number and Monty Rushmore answered. He was a test pilot for EASA, based at Gatwick.

“Peter, I gather that you are interested in the Murray Aerospace LightJet?”

“How on earth do you know that?”

“By chance I was over at Farnborough with the AAIB talking about Cat III and GPS. Bob Furness was there and your name came up and he mentioned the LightJet. It so happens that I’m ferrying one to Cambridge next week from Mojave and I need a another pilot. Are you current?”

"I've got an ATR, a full medical certificate and I've just been checked out as a private pilot."

"That'll be fine. I've got to air test the aircraft in Mojave before we can leave."

"Monty, I saw the aircraft the other day when I visited Mojave, G-MRAY. Are you taking the extra fuel?"

"You bet. I know it's downwind so there shouldn't be a problem but better too much than too little. We should have lots of fuel in hand. We'll have to wear survival gear over the water in case we lose the engine. Why don't we fly out together next Tuesday and you can get yourself up to speed on the aircraft and the emergencies? We're flying to LA and they're sending a car to meet us."

"Sounds great. Tell me, why should I be so lucky?"

"Because Marshall's are busy and asked me to collect it and the wife of the German pilot from EASA who was coming with me is about to give birth. The aircraft only really needs one pilot but for the ferry it is much safer to have two and Marshalls are going to pay expenses, you'll be glad to know. By the way we've done most of the certification testing at Mojave on one of their prototypes but we need to do one or two checks on a production aircraft. This is the first one on the UK register."

"Are we going business class or World Traveller Plus?"

"British Airways business class. Apart from anything else I've got a lot of kit to take so please keep your bags as small and soft as you can. Sixty kilograms between us should be OK and there's not a lot of room on the plane, as you know. If the BA flight is full when you make the booking let me know. I'm sure we will be able to use another airline."

Helen as usual had been listening. "It's alright for some. Leaving me here on my own."

I opened a file. "Your schedule says you're going to be away on Saturday, back Tuesday, and then away Friday back the following Monday. That will fit in nicely with when I'm away."

She had the grace to smile. "You're not meant to be looking at that. I can't trust you with anything."

I decided that booking on the net wasn't going to solve our seating requirement so I called BA and managed to get an aisle seat opposite Monty.

***

The days rushed by. Helen left on Saturday for Los Angeles and it seemed a very a long week-end without her.

On the Tuesday my taxi was at Heathrow in plenty of time. I had agreed with Monty that we would meet and check-in at the same time so that we could pool our total baggage allowance. I had not met him before but there was no problem recognising him since he had two large trolleys laden with his own kit, the cold weather survival clothing for both of us and the EPIRBS beacon. He was about my height, five foot ten, but slightly overweight which surprised me because pilots tend to be careful with their weight and anyway the doctors start being difficult on medical renewals.

We managed to avoid having to pay excess baggage and then we went up to the business class lounge.

"What are doing about a dinghy, Monty?"

"Good point. Murray Aerospace are lending us the one that the Farnborough demonstrator used. The aircraft is back so they don't have an immediate need for it." He stopped for a moment. "Why are you so interested in the aircraft? I'm sure you could do a deal with Marshalls as a part time demonstration pilot. Their test pilots always seem to be pretty busy."

"Great idea but really I only want to fly as a hobby."

He nodded. "I've brought a DVD of the LightJet's pilots notes which I thought you might want to look at on the plane. I've got the book as well if you would prefer it."

He showed me the book and I was pleased to see it was not too big. "I'd like to copy the DVD if I may but I'll read the book on the plane."

Luckily I had an old rewritable DVD with me so I reformatted it and copied Monty's DVD while we were still in the lounge. In fact there was no hurry as the flight was delayed for some reason and we left an hour late. Eleven hours thirty minutes later we landed in LA by which time I knew a lot more about the LightJet's systems than I had before we took-off. We got through immigration quite quickly but I was a bit shattered by the size of the bags. "Can we get all that gear in a car, let alone an aircraft, Monty?"

"I've asked for a van and then we'll see what we can get into the aircraft."

Customs were very curious but raised no objection after Monty explained the reason for the gear. Everything went like clockwork and there was a van to meet us; we went to the airfield first, dropped off the bags, survival suits etc and then went to the Days Inn.

We relaxed in the bar with some beer. "What's the aircraft like? Did you have any problems certificating it?"

"Not really. As you know it's not a high performance aircraft. It's aimed at the trainer market but nevertheless it's got quite a good range."

"When are we leaving?"

"Well first we'll have to check the aircraft out very carefully on Marshall's behalf. Then we can do some flying. We should be able to leave Friday if we're lucky."

In the morning we took a cab to Murray Aerospace and had a look at the aircraft, G-MRAY. It was all white with Murray LightJet written in red on both sides. George appeared.

"Do you like it, Monty?" He stopped when he saw me. "You've organised that ferry very quickly."

"I was lucky. Monty called me and offered me the ride."

"Well this one has got all the bells and whistles."

"How about a loo?"

"You know damn well there isn't one. It's not necessary for normal flying."

"We're ferrying it across the Atlantic."

"Alright, you'd better take a bottle then."

We looked inside first and Monty examined the small pair of seats behind the pilots. The extra fuel tank was already in position. "The back of the rear seats will go almost flat so that we should be able to stuff our bags in the space behind. Then we'll put the dinghy on your side next to the tank with the EPIRBS next to it but tied on. When we're not wearing the immersion suits we can cram them in on the side there; they don't take up all that much room. Let's climb in and look at the panels."

The flight deck was superb, though there wasn't a lot of spare room round the pilots' seats. The flight and performance manuals were stowed in special pockets by the pilot's shoulders which just left room next to the pilots for maps and navigation material.

"It's a bit cramped for flight planning material and books to read, Monty."

"It will all be on the horizontal display so you won't need maps."

"What if it goes wrong?"

"There are two flight management computers and four displays so it isn't going to happen. And there is a stand-by horizon if there is an electrical problem."

"What about stand-by electrics?"

"There are two generators and batteries for thirty minutes on essential supplies. It is a trainer after all so it shouldn't get too far away from an airfield."

"If you say so."

We got out and checked when the aircraft would be ready for flight and agreed 1330. Monty phoned air traffic to get permission for us to be able enter the R-2508 controlled airspace above the military operating establishments like Edwards Air Force Base, and then we had a sandwich before went out to fly. There was no weather, just a cloudless blue sky with good visibility.

We strapped in, did the checks and then started the engine from the batteries. There was not much noise, particularly as we were using headsets though the aircraft was fitted with speakers and hand mikes. Monty waved the chocks away and we were off. The view was great through the bubble canopy and the glass windscreens as we taxied out. There was very little activity but Monty told me to keep a very good look-out for military traffic and unmanned aircraft being tested. We were soon off, he selected the code we had been pre-assigned, requested cover from Joshua FAA radar in R-2508 and then we climbed up to 30,000 ft. We hadn't put any track into the FMCs and our displays just showed a map of our position and the position of other aircraft with any possible conflicts. I kept a sharp eye on the TCAS display as well as looking outside for conflicting aircraft.

Monty started checking all the systems for correct functioning, pressurisation, fuel, electrics, hydraulics, pneumatics and the radios.

"Do we have a satellite radio?"

"Yes, we have to have one as we don't have HF and we must be able to talk to the Oceanic centres. I'm just going to check it out now."

Monty called Oakland Oceanic for a check and we got an immediate response.

"Well that's about it. You fly it for a bit and we'll go back to the field."

I took hold of the stick. The forces were light and the aircraft was very responsive. I tried flying at constant speed and height and it seemed straightforward. Monty indicated it was time to go back and I throttled back and dived towards the airport. I positioned the aircraft downwind after getting permission for a visual circuit and turned finals. The approach speed was only 70 knots and the threshold speed with full flap was an amazingly low 45 knots. I was a bit fast crossing the threshold and we floated more than we should have done before we touched down. Monty took over, applied full power, re-trimmed the elevator and we took off again. However he gave me the aircraft back again almost immediately the flaps were up and I tried another landing.

"Go around again after touch down. I'll select the flap up and re-trim the elevator. Try not to pump the throttles on the approach."

The next approach was much smoother as was the touch down and then I opened the throttles and took off again. Monty took over and did the final landing touching down very slowly so we needed very little braking. We stopped the engines and turned everything off.

"When did you say you flew last?"

"Last week. I've been flying a Raytheon 800."

"That explains it. You're obviously back in full flying practice. By the time we reach UK I should be able to give you a type rating."

"That would be great. I must say that the airplane felt fine. But then it was nice and slow on the approach and landing. How do they manage to balance the controls?"

"They use spring tabs on the ailerons and just geared tabs on the elevator and rudder. It saves a lot of complication, weight and expense."

"That's impressive. I suppose I thought jets had to have powered controls."

"Not at all. Some of the post second world war fighters had controls just like this. The Venom for example could do .86 mach and fly well over 40,000 ft whereas the LightJet only goes up to .78 mach and 35,000 ft. The cabin's pressurised of course."

Monty went round the outside of the aircraft very carefully and then we went into the hangar and he listed a few defects to the supervisor at the desk. "We'll fly it again to-morrow and then leave on Friday. We'd better go over to air traffic to get our clearances."

He took his navigation bag to the tower and we sat down in the briefing room. I could see he had worked out each leg very carefully.

"This is our itinerary. It's the same one that they used for the ferry to Marshalls and the SBAC show. Assuming we leave Friday we should be in Milwaukee that evening. I've allowed plenty of time on the Saturday in order to clear customs so that we'll just have one leg to do to Montreal. Customs shouldn't be bad there as we are just passing through. Hopefully we'll arrive early as it's a nice place to stop. On Sunday night we should be at Frobisher Bay, Monday night Reykjavik and arrive Marshalls Tuesday. I've asked Marshalls to talk to the customs at Stornoway to make sure there are no problems importing the aircraft into the UK. We might just be able to cut out Stornoway depending on the weather. Anyway I'll get air traffic to send out our intended plan right now, there shouldn't be any problems. I've made FMS input files for each leg to save fiddling around entering the route by hand into the computer. Then I've got maps with our route plotted on and route cards which we can fill in as we go along to double check our fuel usage as well as our navigation."

I was very impressed and said so.

"Thank you Peter. As you well know 'time spent in navigation is seldom wasted'."

We did another flight on the Thursday and then, on the Friday, we arrived at 0700. The aircraft was outside all ready with the dinghy and the extra fuel tank filling most of the space on the rear seats. The survival suits were tied on top of the dinghy. Monty had already filed the flight plan from his room and had managed to print the weather on the hotel's business computer system. The forecast was completely clear on our first leg with an expected tail wind of 30 knots. George appeared to see us off which we appreciated. He came out with us carrying the EPIRBS. We managed to get our bags into the space behind the seats and the beacon we forced in next to the extra fuel tank. We checked round the aircraft, said goodbye to George and got into our seats. With the battery power switched on we loaded the first leg route to Gillette into the FMS and started the engines.

Though I had flown airliners round the world I found this a very exciting moment, since somehow I felt much closer to the airplane because it was so small. The other point I realised was that we were in charge of what was happening whereas in an airline one was just a cog in the whole system.

Monty was flying this first leg and I was doing the communications. I copied down the airways clearance to Gillette as we taxied out and after a brief hold we were on our way at 0825. Our clearance was to flight level 290 where we levelled off at .55 mach. We had a 30 knot tail wind so we landed at 1115 local time, one hour fifty minutes later and taxied to Fliteline to be refuelled.

Monty went in to the office to file the flight plan while I supervised the refuelling, done the old fashioned way over the wing. I was concerned that the extra tank wouldn't be filled but it had been very neatly installed with its vent going outside the cabin; it had it's own refuelling cock which I opened and there was no problem. The engine lubrication system was a 'total loss' one instead of the oil being re-circulated, so it was necessary to add a can of oil through a hole in the side of the fuselage after every flight and this was clearly going to be my job. The aircraft attracted a lot of attention from the pilots and ground crew who were close by and I had my work cut out trying to work and talk at the same time.

Now you see it

I joined Monty in the Fliteline crew room for a sandwich and some coffee.

"Peter, you can do the next leg. I got the weather when I filed the flight plan and we shall be landing at Milwaukee just after a cold front has gone through so there will be 25kt north westerly wind. I imagine we'll be landing on runway 33."

"Should be exciting with our slow approach speed and all the airlines using the one runway."

"I know. I wanted to go to the general aviation airfield but there were no customs there so I thought it would be better to go to the main airport."

We walked out, checked all round again and this time I was in the left hand seat. We got our clearance almost immediately and with now a 40kt tail wind we were in the traffic pattern at Milwaukee two hours and fifteen minutes later. However it took another twenty minutes before we were allowed to make our approach and we had to fly at high speed on the approach and then clear the runway almost immediately.

We taxied slowly to the Signature fixed base operation and shut down. After refuelling, plugging the static vents and pitot tubes, putting chocks in place and locking the controls we got a courtesy car to take us to the Holiday Inn close by.

Our ferry proceeded uneventfully, the aircraft behaving beautifully. We were in Montreal after clearing customs at Milwaukee by 1300 local time and after refuelling at Skyservice we went to see the Canadian customs to make sure there were not going to be any problems.

On the Sunday we decided we had better put on our survival suits so that we felt rather uncomfortable strapping ourselves in. We made Frobisher Bay after a Wabush refuelling and, though it was still early August, the weather felt distinctly nippy. Touchdown did the refuelling and we stayed in the Frobisher Inn.

"Monty, it all feels very leisurely. We could almost do three legs a day."

"I know. But it would then be a rush and there would be no provision for things going wrong. Going downwind like this I feel we could have done longer legs than just 800 nautical miles but there wasn't anything convenient in the Hudson Bay area so I just settled for this. However there's no flexibility on the next two legs."

"What about Narsarsuaq, Bluie West One, in southern Greenland?"

"Well that was a distinct possibility. Actually it was very attractive as it's only 676 miles from Goose Bay to Narsarsuaq and a further 652 miles to Reykjavik. Problem is that the weather has got to be perfect and its opening hours are restricted. Maybe we should have gone that way. Next time!"

In the morning the weather had deteriorated and Monty had some decisions to make. Amazingly even though it was only late August it had started to snow at Frobisher and more was forecast with very poor visibility. We checked the weather at Kangerlussuaq and the cloud base was forecast as overcast 2,500ft with visibility 4 miles which was within limits. Monty was wondering whether we should wait for a day or so until the snow stopped at Frobisher but there was a strong following wind forecast at altitude of 50 knots and he reckoned we could make Iceland where the weather was good if we were really stretched. We put on our survival gear again and set course to Greenland.

As we approached the coast the Kangerlussuaq control tower told us that the weather had deteriorated and the cloud base was now on the minima of 2,000ft with 2 miles visibility. I had a distinct feeling that this was not our day. Monty, who was in the right hand seat, decided we would make one approach and if we couldn't land then we had enough fuel to make Keflavik, the military base in Iceland which was twenty miles closer than Reykjavik.

I suggested he should take over flying the aircraft but I noticed he didn't look at all well. In fact he was very busy entering data into the flight management system and calculating our fuel reserves but was clearly struggling. The approach chart showed that we would have to do a radio beacon approach to runway 09 with a 10 knot following wind which was not ideal but the USAF Ground Control Approach radar had long since gone. As we descended to 5,000 ft the tower told us that fog was rolling in and I realised that fuel was now going to be critical. Monty looked terrible but indicated that we should climb immediately. It didn't seem wise to go back to

Frobisher Bay as the weather was clamping so the only thing we could do was to head for Iceland and Keflavik. Monty had told me that there was a strong following wind forecast at 30,000 ft so I climbed straight up on track since there didn't seem to be any traffic and requested a new clearance which came through soon after I had levelled out at 29,000 ft.

I looked at Monty and clearly he wasn't going to be much help as he was being sick, poor fellow. He croaked "Peter I've got a hell of pain in my stomach. Must have been something I've eaten. Keep an eye on the fuel for Keflavik."

He really looked ill but there was nothing I could do. Luckily the autopilot was working well keeping us on track to Iceland and holding us at 29,000 feet, our cleared altitude. As things had worked out I hadn't had a full briefing on the Flight Management Computer but fortunately I had been using it on the previous legs. However I had only really been using it for navigation and had not bothered with the fuel state because there just hadn't been a problem. I took another look at Monty and clearly he was not going to be able to help me navigate the hundreds of different pages on the computer. Sensibly, at each waypoint the fuel available was stated and a quick check at Keflavik showed that despite the forecast wind we would be very marginal on fuel. Whether Monty had made a mistake working out the fuel approaching Kangerlussuaq I just didn't know but we clearly had a serious problem.

I pressed the alternate key and looked at the listed options and the only place listed was Kulusuk on the east coast of Greenland but the good news was that apparently we would have plenty of fuel if we landed there. Years ago when I used to go direct to Canada on this route from the UK I remembered that I had often noticed that there was a very strong radio beacon at Kulusuk with the morse identifier KK, not that we ever had to use it because we had GPS. Luckily I remembered George Straker telling me there was an airfield that was usable if the weather was right. I looked again at Monty and decided that we needed to land as soon as possible.

Somewhere I knew in the FMC there was a way of getting details of all the airfields on track but I didn't want to waste time searching through myriads of pages in the database. Luckily I knew that very sensibly Monty had brought a Jeppeson folder with him which was in the pocket by his right knee. He looked very sick and unable to help. I shouted 'Jeppesons' at him and to my relief he nodded and just managed to lift the rather heavy book out of its stowage though it was no longer in mint condition despite Monty using a sick bag. I opened the page at Kulusuk and my heart dropped when I saw that the airfield was only a gravel strip 4,000 feet long, not that the length or the surface would be a worry for the LightJet. It was the lack of facilities that worried me.

The weather at the field was going to be crucial because the Jeppeson airfield chart made it very clear that the strip was on an island close to the steep hills of the ice cap. In addition it was clearly necessary to approach from the east up a fjord. I called Shanwick Oceanic and asked for the Kulusuk weather, explaining we might have to divert there. There was a five minute delay which seemed like half an hour before the controller told me that the weather was clear, visibility unlimited. I looked at Monty who had clearly heard the message and he managed a grimace which I took to be a combination of a nod and a smile. I asked Shanwick to check with Kulusuk that we could land and to get me a clearance to the field.

While I was waiting for a reply the cloud below miraculously seemed to clear and we could see the old United States Distance Early Warning radar station which was used in the cold war in the 1960s and had long since ceased to be operational. I remembered how well it used to show up on our weather radar when I was flying the route commercially, a splendid fix not that we needed it with GPS. Shanwick came through with the clearance but I elected to maintain altitude until I could see Greenland's magnificent icy mountains, still a dramatic sight to behold from nearly five miles high despite global warming.

I called Kulusuk approach, re-programmed the FMC for Kulusuk as the destination, re-checked the weather and started to let down. At the same time I requested a doctor to meet the aircraft though I did wonder as I passed the message what facilities would be available. I spotted the airfield and the approach fjord and made a visual approach to the strip. I switched to the tower frequency and the same voice with a Scandinavian accent cleared me to land.

There was no wind and I landed towards the west with the mountains ahead. I could see that Monty was watching though obviously in great discomfort. I tried to touch down as slowly as possible because of the gravel since I didn't want the fuselage to be scratched by more flying stones than was absolutely necessary. I was torn between using full flap and approach flap, again because with full flap the stones were more likely to damage the paint; in the event I decided I'd better use full flap because of the relatively short length of the strip though the LightJet landed so slowly it probably wouldn't have mattered if I had used less flap.

In fact we didn't use much of the strip when I landed and I kept the nosewheel in the air as long as possible, again to minimise flying stones. Instead of having to brake I had to open up the engine to taxi to the terminal which was at the far end of the airfield next to the strip itself. There was an Icelandair DHC7 on the apron and I parked the LightJet right at the edge of the small apron to keep well clear of any commercial traffic. As I shut the engine down a car came over and two men got out. I extricated myself from the aircraft still wearing my survival clothing and went round to open Monty's door. One of the men introduced himself, Olav Pedersen, the doctor who lived on the island and he had a friend with him who was there to help. Pedersen had a look at Monty who was obviously in great discomfort. The two of them somehow got him into the car and drove off to the village leaving me to wonder what to do next.

I did everything I could think of to make sure the aircraft was secure and managed to find some chocks for the wheels. I kept the jacket of my survival suit on to keep warm and then with both our bags I walked over to the terminal. The passengers had loaded and the DHC7 was starting up so by the time I got to the terminal there was just one girl tidying up some papers. She pointed to a man wearing a uniform who was walking over towards me. He turned out to be the government official in charge of customs and immigration and I explained why we were in Kulusuk. I only had my passport but he seemed to know about Monty; I guessed in a small island like Kulusuk there were very few secrets. He suggested I went up to the control tower situated above the terminal and he showed me the door leading to the stairs.

I climbed up to the control room and met Jon Larsen, the duty controller, who couldn't have been more helpful. He telephoned the hotel to make sure they had a room and then gave me the telephone number of the fuel man. I asked where Monty was and he said there was a house in the village where people who were not well were taken. The doctor apparently was employed by the Greenland Government as was Jon himself, though his contract ended in a few months and he told me he was going back to Denmark.

Jon explained that it was a forty minute walk to the hotel and even further to the village but as no more aircraft were expected he drove me to the village and I noticed the hotel on the way. We stopped at a house which I knew was the correct one as I recognised the car outside the building as the one that had come to the aircraft. We went inside and I saw Pedersen sitting at a desk.

"Well Mr Talbert, your Mr Rushmore is going to be alright. He has some sort of infection in his stomach but I have given him medication and it should work in a day or so."

"That's wonderful. I thought he was having a heart attack in the aircraft. What happens next?"

"He can stay here until he feels strong enough and then he can go into the hotel. There is always someone on duty here." He gave me a card with his number and the number of the house. "Mr Rushmore is asleep at the moment as I gave him a pill to calm him down. He was very worried about the aircraft but I assured him that everything was alright and that you were looking after it."

"How do we pay you for all your help?"

"Don't worry about it. All you will have to pay is for the use of this place. My services are courtesy of the Greenland Government. Why don't we all go to the hotel, relax and have a beer?"

Jon took me to the hotel, I checked in and then we got some Tuborg lager which was very welcome. He left after one beer and Olav said he would collect me and take me to see Monty at 8pm. I went up to my room and started to sort out what needed to be done. There was wifi in the hotel which amazed me though they told me it was slow when having conversations because it was all done by satellite. I started by logging on, finding Marshalls number in Cambridge and giving them a call using SkypeOut. I got the security guard and asked him to get the chief test pilot to call me at the hotel. I reckoned Helen was in transit across the Atlantic so there wasn't much more I could do.

After about half an hour the chief test pilot called me and I explained the situation. He gave me his contact numbers and I promised to keep him informed. He was undecided what to do to help since his pilots hadn't been checked out on the aircraft and of course neither had I. We decided to wait for a few days and see how Monty got on.

I ate in the hotel and then went with the doctor to see Monty who was awake and feeling sorry for himself but obviously over the worst. I left his bag with him and told him I'd come and see him in the morning. When we left I asked Pedersen if there was a taxi I could use to get backwards and forwards but apparently this was not possible. He told me he was not too busy and was only too happy to help.

In the morning he collected me and we went to see Monty. He looked a lot better and started to apologise but I cut him off and told him not to be stupid. Pedersen reckoned Monty would be able to go to the hotel the next day. Back in the hotel I called Helen at home.

"About time. Where are you, Peter."

I explained the situation to her.

"But when am I going to see you? I'm off to Australia on Monday."

"I'm not sure my love. Hopefully we'll get away in about three days if Monty continues to recover."

"Well I think it's rotten. Can't you leave?"

"Not unless there's going to be a really long delay."

"Well darling, I know you'll do your best. All my love."

After I had spoken to the fuel man I managed to get the hotel to use their van to take me to the airport. We refuelled the aircraft but I didn't bother with the extra tank as we only had to get to Reykjavik. I put in the oil and cleaned the right hand seat area where Monty had been sitting as best I could. I inspected the underside of the aircraft and was very relieved that there were no scratches from the gravel, not even on the flaps. A flight had just come in and I took the opportunity to get on the bus taking the passengers, all tourists, to the hotel.

The day went very slowly watching old films on the local hotel TV. In the morning I got the hotel van to take me to Monty and brought him back to check in. He looked a bit weak but mad keen to get away.

"Why can't we go to-morrow, Peter?"

"Are you sure you're going to be fit enough?"

"Well the aircraft only requires one pilot and you're terrific. Even though I felt I was dying I watched you come in here and I wasn't worried."

"Thank you for that but I don't have a UK PPL and I've not been checked out on the aircraft, even on my ATR."

"But I'm checked out so we'll be legal, even if I do nothing."

"Alright I'll file the flight plan for a 0930 departure and we can always cancel if you don't feel up to it."

In the morning the van took us to the terminal. Monty was still weak and I carried his bag as well as mine to the aircraft. We agreed that survival suits would not be needed, particularly as his had not been improved by his being sick on it. I went up to the tower to thank Jon and then we were on our way.

We were airborne by 0945 and landed at Reykjavik one hour and thirty minutes later. I checked the weather which was good and Monty agreed we could file for Cambridge and regard Stornoway as an en-route alternate. It was over 1,000 nautical miles but a 25 knot following wind was forecast and hopefully, this time, the wind would not disappear. I filed the flight plan and went back out to the aircraft.

I switched my phone on when I had finished refuelling and saw that Helen had been calling. It rang a few minutes later. "Where are you, my darling."

"Who is that?"

"How many darlings do you have?"

"You sound strange."

"It's probably my mobile. My car battery is flat and I'm waiting for the AA man to arrive. Anyway where are you?"

"We're in Reykjavik about to fly to Cambridge, hopefully."

"That's great. Will you be home to-night?"

"Should be if we get away on time and don't have to refuel on the way at Stornoway."

"How's Monty?"

"He's much better but not a hundred per cent."

"But is it safe to fly the aircraft if he's not well?"

"There is another pilot."

"Touché , I put my foot in it. How was the rest of the trip?"

"Great. Looking forward to doing it again with you someday. How were your trips?"

"Same as usual. Hard work and boring. The sooner I stop the better."

"Rubbish. You will be much more bored sitting at home."

"He'll keep me busy."

"She you mean."

"We'll see."

Monty came out slowly from the terminal and we got into the aircraft but delayed starting until we had our clearance, in order to save fuel. Three hours and twenty five minutes later we landed at Cambridge and handed all the papers over to Marshalls after customs had had a good look round the aircraft. The chief test pilot came over and we had a chat and agreed that Monty's rapid improvement solved what might have been a difficult aircraft recovery situation.

Monty was very relieved that we had arrived safely and was effusive in his thanks. A car appeared and took me to the station. I was home by half past six and Helen was waiting for me.

"John Southern has been on the phone. Wants you to ring him back."

"That wasn't the welcome I was expecting."

"How about 'I've called the registry office in Kingston to see how much notice we have to give to get married?'"

"How about 'I'm exhausted from the ferry and need to go to bed?'"

"I think you're looking for a quick leg over. You men are all the same."

"How do you know? And are you complaining?"

I was in two minds to call John Southern but looking at Helen carrying my things upstairs I decided he would have to wait. Some time later I left Helen and called John.

"Peter, glad you called. Thought you might like to know we've decided to wait before we pay West Orient."

"I think that's probably very sensible if you can. Did you find out if Derek knew about mod 156?"

"Yes I did. I checked with my boss and apparently he hadn't discovered its importance, which didn't please Richard. All he did was to check with the airline that all the paperwork was in order and that all the mods were up to date."

"Well if I was in your position, or rather your boss's, I'd send Derek back to Taipei to have a closer look."

"That's the conclusion I've come to."

"By the way the Chinese CAAC man, Bruce, is very sharp but it's going to take a long time for a detailed report to be produced. Who took the decision to delay payment, Richard?" John agreed and I wasn't surprised. "Thanks for letting me know. I've no desire to go out again. Of course basically it must be pilot error I'm afraid. I asked for the pilot Category III training procedures and there's been no response. Having an autopilot disconnect at the critical height, only one engine spooling up and not having had any training would be a very difficult situation. Are they getting a replacement machine?"

"Yes, I believe so. Fred Xie Tingxi told me that Chinese Aerospace are painting an unallocated one for delivery to them right now. I know this because we've agreed to insure it, though we're now making them pay the first 15% of any claim and raising the premiums by 10%."

"That will make their eyes water."

"I know but we're not a philanthropic institution. As you know we have to secure our commitments and the cost is rising all the time."

Helen came into the room. "Do I gather you are not about to rush to Hong Kong again? Has Hull Claims settled?"

"You are right. I'm not going to Hong Kong again or Taipei for that matter. It would be pointless. However, I'm not very happy with the situation. Hull Claims should send Derek out again to have a closer check since he missed the obvious re modifications. I've explained to John that, in the event, the pilots were faced with a very difficult situation, autopilot disconnect and only one engine accelerating. However I'm sure there's something we don't know."

"You do like to cross every i and dot every t."

I grinned. "Something like that, anyway. I like to give every stone a good stir. You know, there is a question mark over what happened and I really hate that."

"Alright. Where are you taking me? You have to feed an expectant bride."

"Expensive bride, more like." I avoided the blow. "It's rather late. How about that French restaurant again in the High Street? Will it be open? We didn't give it a fair test the other day. You can tell me what you've been up to."

We managed to get a reservation and being lazy and in a hurry I drove and parked in a side street. "Are you sure you want a registry wedding, my love? Can't we do it properly? How about in Portsmouth near your parents?"

"I'm definitely undecided. The problem is that you could be called away at any time and then there are the interviews and the new job you're going to get." I shook my head. "Don't interrupt. I want us to be married before the baby is born. I don't like the marriages when the children come along as well. It would be nice to have a formal wedding with all the trimmings but we're both very busy and it will be difficult to organise properly. On balance I favour a registry office and then having a splash when you get the new job."

"Well I'm definitely undecided as well. Your analysis assumes I'm going to get the job, which I keep telling you is most unlikely. The civil servants will be more comfortable with someone they know, like the head of one of the existing accident boards. Of course I'm sure our parents would prefer the whole bit given a choice but on the other hand they will be relieved when we are safely married."

"I don't want to be safely married. I want some excitement."

"You should have thought about that earlier. Why can't we do the deed and then have a celebratory party sometime later?"

"That's what I thought we'd decide so I've booked Friday in three weeks time at 1200 at the registry office in the Kings Road and a room in the RAF Club for lunch."

I looked at her and couldn't help smiling.

"You're a gambler. I might have wanted a church wedding."

"No worries. I'd have cancelled the arrangements."

"Who are we asking?"

"Just family."

"Great. We'll spread ourselves later. When are you off next? Are things getting uncomfortable?"

"So far I'm OK and I'm not advertising my condition. Monday I'm off to Australia, Melbourne this time."

"Won't you have to tell Worldwide that you're married, next-of-kin and all that?"

"I've already told them you're my partner so the fact we're married won't be all that important."

"When do you tell them you're expecting?"

"In a few weeks. It can wait. After we're married."

Chapter 6

I took Helen to Gatwick on the Monday for her flight and then went back home to catch up with my work. The place felt empty again and I found it hard to concentrate. I had a job to do in Copenhagen and it took two days longer than I was expecting. Helen called me from Melbourne soon after I arrived in Denmark and said she expected that it would be two complete days before she started back. When I got back home and realized that I had not heard from her I called her mobile but there was no reply. I sent a text message and an email and went to bed.

The next morning, when I still hadn't heard, I was beginning to get worried and called Worldwide. They put me on to the scheduling department and the girl there said she should have reported for the flight back that night, Sydney time, but she and another purser, Beryl Simpson, were missing. I logged on to *The Australian* and saw to my horror that fires had broken out in north eastern Victoria. For some reason I began to get a sinking feeling in my stomach. It was unlike Helen not to be on time and not to communicate and I felt powerless to do anything. The airline said they had informed the police and would call me back the moment they had some news.

I logged on to Melbourne's paper, *The Age*, and saw that the fires were being driven by a northerly wind. The situation seemed very serious. Apparently it was unheard of to have fires so early in the year and clearly the fire fighters were at full stretch. Several villages had been severely damaged and the loss of life was already up to twenty people with a lot of people still unaccounted for. Some farms and vineyards had been badly damaged. I hadn't really appreciated until that moment how much Helen meant to me and it took me all my time to keep calm.

Then, after three more hours Worldwide phoned and said that as far as they could find out the girls hadn't stayed in the crew hotel at all but had rented a car and gone off up country somewhere. They told me that Simpson's parents had also been on the phone and I asked for their number.

It was difficult to decide what to do but I felt incapable of doing nothing. I knew instinctively that something must be seriously wrong. I rang the Simpson's and a very worried Mrs Simpson answered the phone. They knew as little as I did. They had no idea where the girls had gone. I gave them my mobile number and email address and they agreed to contact me if they had any news.

Analysing my premonitions I realised it was Helen's predilection for visiting wineries that worried me. I decided to call the police in Melbourne and after one or two side trips I finally managed to contact the department responsible for missing people and they confirmed that the two girls were on their list. The man at the other end of the phone was very helpful after I explained my interest and that I was calling from England.

"You do realize Mr Talbert that we are having to deal with some serious bush fires up towards King Valley about 130 km north east of here. We are sure they were started deliberately but the wind has been very strong and our fire fighters are working at full stretch. Matters are made worse because at this time of year it is unusual for fires to break out and some of the crews are on holiday. We're getting help from New South Wales but the problem is that we've had a very dry winter. We are doing our best to find the ladies but it is very difficult and there are a lot of other people who cannot be found. Of course we've got the registration of the car which is a great help. We've alerted the Victorian fire authority as well as our police in the area. We're communicating with the airline so I suggest you keep in touch with them."

My heart sank but I did manage to get the address of the police station and the local Worldwide office number in Melbourne. I decided to wait twenty four hours and if nothing had been heard I would fly out. I rang Helen's parents to tell them the situation which of course alarmed them and they were very relieved when I told them I was going to fly out. I decided to call Worldwide to make a booking but they only had two flights a week to Melbourne so I booked with Etihad leaving at 0910 the day after next knowing I could always cancel if we got some news. But there wasn't any news and reading *The Age* again over the internet there clearly were serious ongoing problems with the fires. They had caught three people who had allegedly started the fires but that didn't help to put out the terrible conflagrations that were currently raging. I remembered that Victoria had had some appalling fires a few years earlier with whole villages being destroyed which made me feel even more worried.

I took a taxi early in the morning to Heathrow, caught the flight to Abu Dhabi and went straight on, arriving at 1815 in Melbourne the following evening. The Worldwide desk at the airport was closed so I caught a taxi to the downtown Novotel in Collins Street. There was nothing I could do that night so I went exhausted and frustrated straight to bed. I turned the TV on and the ABC channel was broadcasting news of the fires throughout the night, giving locations, warnings and casualties. The situation sounded almost out of control in spite of the herculean efforts of the fire-fighters. In the morning I bought a pay-as-you-go mobile phone and then walked to the Worldwide offices close by. I met Frank Daly, the local manager, who couldn't have been more helpful.

"No news Peter I'm afraid. The police and the fire people are doing their best. You appreciate that if the worst has happened it may be very difficult for their bodies to be identified."

"But the car, Frank, surely they can find that?"

"Well I suppose it's good news that they haven't found the car yet."

I didn't share in that sentiment. I knew deep down that I wasn't ever going to see Helen again; she would have contacted me well before then if she had been able to. I just had to wait for the call from the police. If she was in the fire area there was nothing I could do since the roads were closed and only the fire-fighters and the police were allowed access. I rang Mike Mansell in Sydney, the insurance broker who had given me my first break and enabled me to set up as an aviation insurance advisor. He had married the Australian girl who had helped me solve the case and moved to Sydney. I told him what had happened and he did his best to cheer me up but he knew as well as I did that the chances of Helen being found alive were very slim since we hadn't heard from her.

Two days went by with the fires still burning. I listened to the news on ABC all the time filled with worry and despair. I felt so helpless. Then suddenly the weather changed, the wind eased and some significant rain came up from the coast. Frank called. "Bad news, Peter, I'm afraid. They've found the car in a winery which has been completely destroyed including the accommodation. There have been quite a few casualties. There are two bodies in the car and the forensic people are examining them. They've asked us to try to get dental records and things like that."

"Frank, Helen was wearing a diamond engagement ring. That might help. Was Beryl married? Maybe she was wearing rings. That might be easier than dental records."

"I'll tell them about your ring and try to find out about Beryl. I do know she was married but I seem to remember she was divorced. Are you prepared to drive to the winery if they'll let you?"

"You bet."

"I'll let you know."

Frank called back a few minutes later. "OK Peter. The police say you can go up there now the fires are under control. You're to report to the Mansfield police station and they'll escort you. I'll lend you a car. Do you want a driver?"

"Yes to the car, but no to the driver. I've driven out here before and I've brought my Garmin GPS navigator. Where's the car?"

I decided to check out of the hotel and in three hours I was at the police station. They examined me very thoroughly making themselves satisfied that I was who I said I was. They briefed me very carefully and then they allowed me to follow a police car through countryside which had clearly been devastated by the fires. The car was soon full of acrid smoke, despite the recent rain. There were fallen gum trees lying down everywhere and those that were left were completely black without leaves. There were a few European trees still green but not many. We reached the winery and a couple of guys in white overalls, dirty with ash came up to us. They didn't say much. They pointed to the burnt out car. The bodies were inside. "I think they tried to escape in the car but it must have been too late." One of them showed me Helen's ring. It was almost completely black but the stone and its setting were still in place. I nodded.

"Yes, that's the ring I gave her."

"Do you want to see the body? It's very badly burnt."

I forced myself to agree and they gave me an overall to put on. I went to the burnt out car and could just make out two incinerated corpses. It was unbelievable that Helen, so vibrant, alive, so wonderful could just be the lifeless charred mass in front of me. There was nothing I could do or say and I went back and stood by myself for a long time.

The senior of the two forensic experts came up to me. In spite of my utter desolation and despair I knew some decisions were required. "Would you like us to put the two bodies in separate coffins? We can arrange that." I nodded as best I could. "We've got some formalities to do but if you would sign some identification papers at the police station we can arrange for the coffins to be sent to wherever you want. Their cases and belongings are almost burnt to a cinder and not worth recovering."

I followed the police car back to the station and signed some forms and they gave me the ring which I wrapped up in my handkerchief. Beneath the black carbon, by some quirk of fate, it looked almost unmarked. I told the policeman in charge I'd let him know in the morning where the coffins should go and asked if there was anywhere local I could stay the night. Somehow I didn't feel like rushing away immediately. I wanted to be near Helen.

There was a bed and breakfast close by where the owners had somehow managed to preserve their property with stand pipes and a powerful diesel driven generator. I drove there and mooned around. As it got dark some stars somehow shone through the smoke remnants and I could just see the Southern Cross resplendent in the moonless night. I barely slept at all but decided in the middle of the night that it would be better for the girls' parents for the bodies to go back to England. First thing in the morning, back at the police station, I called Frank and he agreed to arrange things. I found it was people's sympathy that put the greatest strain on my emotions. I didn't break down but my eyes were always wet and often I had to turn away and swallow.

I filled in the addresses for the coffins and they reassured me that the coroner would sign the death certificates immediately and the coffins would soon be at the mortuary building at the airport.

I drove back to the Novotel very slowly and called Frank.

"When's your next flight to UK from Melbourne?"

"The day after to-morrow."

"If the coffins have arrived can they go? I'd like to travel as well if that's possible."

"Sure we'll give you a seat. I'll let you know what goes on."

Like an automaton I checked my email and there was one from the Department of Transport asking me to be available for interview in two days time. My initial reaction was to throw in the towel but somehow I felt Helen would not have wanted that so I sent a holding email telling them I was in Australia and would contact them when I knew my movements. I decided to send an explanatory note to Bob Furness who of course knew all about Helen, following the ditching near St Antony. It was too early to phone him so I sent an email. At eight o'clock that evening he was on the phone.

"Peter, I'm so sorry. What can I say?"

"Nothing, Bob but thanks for phoning. As I told you I've been short listed for the Chairman's job but I've told them it will have to wait."

"Don't worry about it, Peter. I'll explain."

I wasn't sure whether I wanted the interview panel to know but decided that they would be bound to hear one way or another since I had told Roger of Senior Placements that I was engaged.

I called Mike Mansell who asked if I'd like him to come over for the night and after a hesitation I agreed. He arrived at five o'clock and we went into the bar, not that I was in the mood for a drink.

"Liz sends her sympathies. She couldn't come as she's still running the dress business and we've got a one year old now." He sensibly decided to talk about other things. "I read about that business at Hong Kong a few weeks back. Hull Claims insured the plane. Are you involved?"

I explained the circumstances and how I had been to Hong Kong and that I wasn't really satisfied.

"Peter, what about the one in New York. That was Cat III as well wasn't it?"

"Mike, that's even more strange in a way. The guy should have done a missed approach but instead he took the autopilot out and tried to land. I've got some more work to do on that one. I've got some ideas but they don't make sense."

I also explained about being short listed for the Chairman's job. "That's great Peter. You'll be terrific in that job and it will help to take your mind off what's happened here."

"Yes, I think I would like the job but it will be a gamble for the civil servants. People think I'm a loner."

"Well, Bob Furness will put them right I'm sure."

I really appreciated having Mike to talk to. He was a great companion. We stayed up quite late so that I was tired and I managed to get some sleep. We met for a quick breakfast and then Mike was on his way. Meanwhile Frank Daly came on the phone and said the coffins were at the airport and would be going back that night. My ticket would be at first class check-in. He also told me he had notified both sets of parents though he knew of course that in Helen's case I was effectively next of kin. This was a great relief because I hadn't got round to sorting out the UK end. I hoped the parents would be sorting out the formalities and the funerals.

The flight left on time and twenty four hours later at 10.30am local time I arrived shattered at Gatwick. There was a message to contact Worldwide after landing. One of the ground staff said the chief pilot, Charles Hendrick, wanted to see me. Presumably Frank Daly must have told him I was on board; I knew Charles well from the aircraft ditching near St Antony. I went to the Worldwide desk and after a short wait Charles himself came down to meet me. He was wearing his normal blue pin striped suit with a plain blue tie but I thought he looked more tired than when we had first met.

"Peter, great to see you. I'm so sorry to hear about Helen. I know you were very close." I half choked. Everybody was so kind but I found it very difficult to respond without showing emotion. Charles sensed how I felt. "Have you got time for a coffee?" He turned to the girl behind the desk. "Please look after this bag for Mr Talbert. He'll be down for it later." We went up to Charles' office and I took my computer in its carry-on bag with me. He asked his secretary, still Mary Turner the one I knew, to make us some coffee.

Charles decided to carry on talking until he reckoned I felt like joining in. "It's been a bad day for us losing two pursers. They were both very good at their jobs and they will be hard to replace." He paused, changing the subject. "Are you involved with that accident at Chek Lap Kok?" I nodded. "Is it just pilot error? Have you been out?"

I managed to find my voice. "Yes, I've been out to Hong Kong. The autopilot failed at the critical moment during a Cat III approach and only one engine accelerated. The pilot had a very difficult job and, as far as I can make out, no training. Luckily no-one was hurt. There's something strange about the accident which I haven't found out yet. Goodness knows where the aircraft is now."

"I think it's still there. You know we go there on our way to Australia and one of our captains told me that the fuselage without wings is between the two runways with a temporary cover over it."

"Not sure what good it will do but I suppose it could come in useful."

I gradually relaxed and stayed with Charles for an hour or so. Then Mary led me back to the Worldwide desk where I collected my bag and a taxi took me home. As I entered the empty house pushing a stack of mail to one side I felt a terrible emptiness and despair. Somehow the fact that Helen had been pregnant seemed to make her loss much much worse. I mechanically unpacked my bags and sorted my clothes out. The mail was staring at me but I left it and went into the living room, turned the television on and watched without seeing anything. Later I woke up and went to bed and dozed through the night, waking occasionally with a hollow void remembering Helen.

***

In the morning I lay in bed wondering what to do when the phone rang. It was someone called Henry Denis from the Department of Transport. I knew I had heard the name before but could not remember when.

"Mr Talbert, forgive me for disturbing you. I was checking whether you were back from Australia. I think you know that we'd like to have a chat sometime fairly soon regarding your application to be considered for the new post of Chairman of the Transport Safety Board."

I forced myself to concentrate and hoped I did not sound too disconnected. "Mr Denis, thank you for phoning. I got back yesterday without a break and am still trying to adjust to the time change. I haven't got my diary in front of me at the moment but would early next week be alright? May I phone you back in an hour or so when I'm in my office?"

Denis agreed and I got out of bed. I remembered as I stood in the shower where I had heard his name. Bob Furness had mentioned it when I told him that Charles Simon had called me to make sure I knew of the new chairman's post. Downstairs I picked up the mail and went into my office. I suddenly realised that I had started to think and plan again. For a moment I felt guilty at not thinking of Helen all the time but I knew that though the loss was terrible my life had to carry on.

I realised that I would need to talk to Helen's parents to find out the funeral arrangements before I called Denis. I had decided that I probably wouldn't attend Beryl Simpson's funeral since I was sure that Worldwide would be represented and I had never met her. Helen's father answered the phone and I told him as best I could of the circumstances of visiting the burnt out winery. It was not an easy conversation for either of us. He told me that they were still waiting to hear from the undertaker but the funeral was almost certainly going to be at the Porchester crematorium. It could not be before the following Thursday at the earliest. He promised to let me know.

I went into the kitchen, got some bread out of the freezer and forced myself to have some toast and coffee. After a bit I went back into my office and called Henry Denis; his secretary put me straight through. "Mr Talbert, thank you for calling back so quickly. I've been looking at our diaries and wondered whether next Tuesday at 10.30 would be alright for you? I'm sure you appreciate that we've seen the other applicants and obviously we'd like to finish the selection process by seeing you. However, in all the circumstances if you feel the date is too soon please say so."

"Mr Denis, you're being very kind. I've done some checking and next Tuesday will be fine. Where will the interview be?"

He told me it would be in the main building in Marsham Street, which I was expecting, at 1030. I started going through the mail but somehow I didn't have the same enthusiasm that I normally had. I felt as if in a strange way Helen and I were both watching the way I was behaving. Bob Furness called which cheered me up a bit. I called my parents which I think surprised them since I didn't do that as often as I should. We talked about my Australia visit and they asked about the funeral. As I put the phone down it rang immediately.

"This is Bill Castleford. I've been trying to contact you. I wondered if you've had any more thoughts or ideas about the accident to Echo Victor?"

"Bill, I'm glad you called. I've been thinking quite a lot about the accident. I'd like to come out and talk to the NTSB people. What's happened to the hull. Do you know?"

"No, Peter, I don't. Do you really need to look at it? Surely it can't help."

"Yes, Bill, I would like to look at it if it hasn't been destroyed."

"Well I'll see what I can do. When could you come out if I can locate it?"

"Next week I think. I'll wait to hear how you get on with NTSB. By the way, I need to look at the modification state of your autopilot and related boxes."

"Why? Jonathan always assures me we are completely up to date."

"I know but it's worth a double check. After all, you people sub-contract the work. Anyway let me know how you get on."

It seemed odd to have two similar accidents using the same avionic supplier so close together even though they were thousands of miles apart. Landings of course were always the critical part of any flight but an aircraft with a properly equipped autopilot shouldn't have any trouble landing in fog. Having the same firm supplying the autopilot was probably a red herring since Total Avionics had an enormous market share in the commercial airplane marketplace.

As I got myself a coffee I suddenly realised that I didn't know the date of Helen's funeral and there was no way I could go out to New York before then. Reaction set in again. I felt really depressed but there was a lot of routine work I could do. I decided I'd better start working instead of thinking of Helen and the emptiness I felt. A trip to New York would probably help me to get on with my life and to my surprise I found I was quite looking forward to going to Marsham Street for my interview.

On Monday Helen's father told me the funeral was definitely going to be on the Thursday at 1530 at the Porchester Crematorium in Fareham. He asked me if I would say a few words and I hesitated, feeling the occasion might probably be too much for me. However, I knew I had to say yes. I agreed to meet at their house and we would all go together to the crematorium.

I spent the day thinking about the interview and managed to sleep well. I was at Marsham Street at 1000 and asked for Mr Denis at reception. I was clearly expected as my badge was ready. I signed in and Denis came down to escort me to his office. He was about my age, late thirties. I was glad to see that he was wearing a dark grey suit and tie; the fashion of dressing down so beloved by some politically correct advocates was a mistake in my view. Apart from anything else, as one got older a tie hid the neck which did not improve with age. As the time approached he led me into the room to be used for the interview and introduced me to the other four members of the team who were all having coffee.

The first person I met was Charles Simon who had called me originally to let me know about the new appointment. I guessed he was about fifty and he also was smartly dressed in a blue suit. He was friendly and he introduced me to John Luscombe, a politician and the Minister of State for Transport. As I had anticipated, the scientific advisor was present and the final member of the team was the senior civil servant and Permanent Secretary, Sir Philip Brown.

Some minutes later Brown looked at his watch and made it clear that we were about to start. He sat to the right of the Minister with Denis on his right. Simon was on the Minister's left with the scientific advisor on the end. Brown was clearly running the interview and made it clear that our meeting was going to be as relaxed as possible. However sitting on the other side of the table, facing them all, I didn't feel very relaxed though in fact I was rather looking forward to their questioning.

"Mr Talbert, we've had chats with three other applicants for the new post of Chairman and are delighted to meet you as our fourth and final applicant. We are particularly grateful that we are seeing you so soon after your return from Australia." It was obvious that they all knew of the reason for my trip to Australia though not, I hoped, all the details. "We are all aware of some of the aircraft accidents that you have investigated so successfully. Clearly were you to be appointed Chairman your experience would be invaluable. Perhaps you would care to tell us why you would like to be appointed to the new post?"

I was expecting this approach and it suited me well.

"I believe the idea of a Safety Board is a really excellent one and fits in well with the unrelenting march of technology." I could feel myself getting into my stride. There seemed no point in holding back. "Aircraft, ships and trains are all getting safer, whatever system is used to measure statistically the accident rates. Furthermore the tools or recorders being fitted in the vehicles to enable accidents to be investigated are becoming very similar. It seems sensible to avoid duplication of resources, like recorder examination laboratories, and we also need to consider whether nowadays accident inspectors need to be dedicated to just one element, land, sea or air."

I went on for a bit developing my thesis and then waited to be questioned. The scientific advisor had nodded agreement with some of my comments which pleased me. Simon had first go. "You've made your point very effectively about technology being the driver but we're talking about an organisation which needs administration. Forgive me for saying so but aren't you a bit of a loner?"

Instinctively I felt he was playing the devil's advocate. He wanted to get my apparently weak points out into the open. "Administration is needed of course but the first requirement for this new post is leadership and I believe that that will be my strong point. If I may so, there will be no shortage of people in this building who will ensure that the Safety Board is correctly structured and that the interface with the accident boards is correct." Brown smiled. "This Board's remit is to promote safety and that is what I would propose to do. I would not interfere with the day to day running of the accident boards though I would expect to be kept informed of the critical issues of each Board.

"Of course, organisations never stand still. Possibly it may be sensible to look at the ways in which the three accident boards are organised; if we meld the technology, is there a need to meld the organisations in some way? One thing is for sure, were I to be offered the chance of being Chairman I would not rush into making any changes."

We discussed this issue for a bit and then the politician had a go. "Peter, safety is a burning issue in this country." I did not respond in any way to John Luscombe's unfortunate turn of phrase but I could see Brown squirming with disbelief. "If and when there are terrible accidents you will be required to be interviewed by the media ad nauseam. Do you think you will be able to handle that?"

Again, thanks to John Southern, I was expecting the question. "I expect I can do with some extra coaching but I've already had the press and media at my door as a result of the earlier work that I've done. In fact in the early days of most accidents there is normally very little that can be said while the facts are being established and my main job in those cases I expect will be to restrain speculation, sympathise of course with any dependents if there have been casualties and to make certain that help is on its way to those that need it."

Luscombe tried to develop this aspect of the job but it seemed to me, and I suspect to the others, a bit off the main purpose of the discussion.

Denis then asked me a question which I had been expecting much earlier in the discussion. "Mr Talbert, do you still fly? I see you were an airline pilot at one time."

"I stopped flying some years ago because I was told I had a heart condition that would stop me flying, a systolic murmur. I think I could have challenged the decision but I had begun to realise that being an airline pilot all my life was not what I wanted. As you know I have a degree in electronic engineering and I was particularly interested in the new electronic systems coming on to the flight deck and the way pilots interacted with them. So I started a new career talking to airline pilots, but as you will be aware things started to change and I became an established aviation accident consultant.

"However, to answer your question I recently got my medical category back, I have a valid FAA ATR licence and have done some flying recently."

"What sort of flying? Commercial with the airlines?"

"No, not at all. I believe there is a future for light jet engined aircraft being used as ab initio trainers and in fact I've been flying one." I paused for a moment. "Oh, there is another interesting project I have got involved with. Vision Unlimited asked me to evaluate their latest Enhanced Vision System which they are about to try to sell to the airlines and I have done some flying in their demonstration aircraft as well." There were some blank faces and I tried to explain about HUDs.

John Luscombe immediately asked what I thought was a very good 'chaser' to my account of recent flying, though I realised later that he was putting a marker down in front of the rest of the committee. "Mr Talbert. You are obviously right up to speed in aviation matters, perhaps you would be more suited to the post of chief inspector at the AAIB."

I reacted to that question immediately. "As I mentioned earlier, new technology and improving accident rates are changing the total accident investigation scene. Whoever becomes chairman of the new Safety Board will want to consider the role of the chief inspectors in all three accident boards. I believe I would find learning about rail and marine transport regimes fairly straightforward. To give an example, in the English Channel position reporting and secondary radar monitoring of commercial shipping is now standard and the debate on what should be required for private craft is very similar to the debate on mandatory equipment on private aircraft."

There were more questions from Simon and Denis and then I realised the allotted time was coming to an end as Brown drew the interview to a close.

"Mr Talbert, is there anything you would like to add to finish our discussion?"

"I started by saying that technology is the driver that drives us all. The new Board will need a mission statement and I'm glad that there does not seem to be one already as I believe the Chairman has a role to play in the formulation of the statement. Safety of course has to be applied to all facets of our lives and I notice that the American National Transportation Safety Board has a wider remit than the proposed remit for our Safety Board. Furthermore the influence of Europe and the EU cannot be ignored. Possibly the mission statement of the Safety Board may well need changing in the years ahead.

"One final point, if I may; the composition of the Board needs to be defined. I would hope that it is the intention to have the chief inspectors of the three accident boards on the Safety Board but if the budget permits it, consideration should be given to inviting one or two UK experts to join the Board, maybe an academic and/or a statistician."

Brown looked at me and decided that now was not the time to explore the new subjects I had exposed. "Mr Talbert, this has been a very useful meeting indeed. You have clearly given a lot of time and thought to the functioning and purpose of the new Board and perhaps you've even given us food for thought." He paused and then smiled. "I expect you would like to know when you can expect to hear from us. All I can say is that it should be a matter of weeks rather than months."

Denis led me back to his office. "That went very well, Peter, if I may say so. I don't know how the others felt but I rather enjoyed some of the topics you raised." He looked around in a slightly surprised manner. "Didn't you bring any papers?"

"No. There was no point."

"You're right of course. I think some people like to hold papers to give them inspiration."

I left feeling that some of the other candidates must have brought self-briefing material. I certainly hadn't needed anything and on reflection I felt I had made a good case for being selected Chairman though it was difficult to tell what the interviewers wanted and, of course, how the other candidates had fared.

Back in the house I felt Helen was there telling me she had always known I would do well.

***

On Thursday morning when I got up there was a message from Bill Castleford saying the aircraft was in temporary store in the Bronx, New York. It was being held there by a firm called WeScrapIt Inc prior to be broken up. I decided to take the opportunity for getting away from the house with the memories of

Helen for a few days so I told Bill I would be arriving in New York on Friday and could he ask NTSB to let me see the plane, probably on the Monday; I needed his NTSB and the WeScrapIt contacts. This way I would have a week-end in New York before starting work. I booked the flight with British Airways and went back to the Courtyard Marriott web site on 40th to book accommodation.

I put on the darkest grey suit I had, found a black tie and arrived at Helen's parents' house in plenty of time. Helen's younger sister and her elder brother were both there, neither of whom I had met before. The sister Shirley, I was relieved to find, was nothing like Helen either in looks or temperament being much quieter and more heavily built. It was the brother in fact who was more like Helen; I discovered he was a maths teacher, lived locally and was married with two young children. The atmosphere was very quiet as we set out for the crematorium. I decided to follow in my car so that I could leave at any time.

There was a much larger number of people than I had expected. To my surprise I saw Charles Hendrick, the Dunstons and one or two senior members of the airline. I had a subdued chat with Tom and Elizabeth while we were waiting. We were admitted exactly on time and there was a vicar who took us through the service. After about fifteen minutes it was clearly time for me to say a few words.

I don't remember exactly what I said but I think I pointed out that it was a sad time for everyone who had known Helen, particularly her family. And, I added, for me personally as we had planned to get married in two weeks time when she came back from Australia. I told them what I'm sure they all knew, that she was an amazing girl and that she had demonstrated all her power, skill and endurance saving all those people when the aircraft in which she was flying had to ditch near St Antony. She was incredibly bright, quick and of course beautiful and a terrible loss for us all. I believe I finished by saying the obvious, that the world was a poorer place without her.

I wish I could have said more but it took me all my time to manage what I did say. Watching the coffin disappearing was a terrible moment. Talking to her parents as we filed out of the crematorium was agonising. I didn't feel I could stay but Charles

Hendrick came after me and persuaded me to go to the nearby Jolly Sailor where there were a few sandwiches with tea and coffee.

Elizabeth Dunston came up to me. “If you need any help, Peter, please let me know. I know you won’t have had a chance to think about things yet but didn’t Helen have quite a lot of gear in your place?” I nodded. “Well if you want me to help you clear it sometime don’t hesitate to call. Here’s my telephone number.”

I chatted as best I could to some of the other people who had come back to the pub and then said goodbye to the family. We all knew we were most unlikely ever to meet again. Somehow the world had slammed a door in our faces.

Chapter 7

The following morning I got a cab to take me to Heathrow and checked in with British Airways in plenty of time for a 1500 departure. We arrived on schedule at 1830 and I was soon through immigration. As I stood there waiting for my luggage I suddenly felt I recognised the back of a young woman a few yards away waiting for a bag. I couldn't be sure but it looked like Charlie, the art expert, who had worked with me finding the missing paintings when the aircraft from St Antony had disappeared on the way to Bermuda. I moved to one side without letting her see me and checked it was indeed her. She was a lovely girl but I didn't feel I could face her and have to explain about Helen.

My bag appeared and I tried to collect it so Charlie wouldn't see me and I left rapidly making my way to the cab rank. I had to wait a little while in the line until I got to the front. I glanced back as we drove away and saw Charlie also waiting but she wasn't looking my way.

In the Marriott I checked my email and Bill had sent me the telephone numbers and names I needed. It was a bit late to chase the contacts but I rang Bill. "I'm in the same Marriott as last time. Thanks for the information. I'll call them all on Monday, it's a bit late now."

"Fine, Peter. The NTSB said you'd better be quick as their final report is coming out next week and they are going to authorise scrapping what's left of Echo Victor."

"Alright Bill, I'm planning to go there Monday. By the way, I'll need a contact for Airlines Servicing at Newark when you've got a moment. You'll have to tell them that you're authorising me to look at their records."

We rang off and I lay on the bed and considered how my world had fallen apart without Helen. Maybe if I got the Safety Board job it would help a little but I knew I could never forget her. I went down to the coffee shop, had a bowl of soup and then went back to my room and tried to sleep. There was another email.

"I'm involved with the aircraft that went into the water. If that's why you're here, it would be nice to have a chat. Love Charlie. PS It would be nice to catch up anyway."

I should have known she would have seen me. I could have spoken to her but somehow I didn't feel strong enough even to chat. It was going to take me a long, long time to get over the loss of Helen. As I did my work I thought of the chance sighting of Charlie at the airport. She still looked incredibly fit, athletic and a very attractive woman. Though I had avoided her I knew I couldn't prevent her finding me if she wanted to; she only had to ask the people at Castle Harbour Airlines and I was sure someone would tell her where I was.

It took me a long time to get to sleep and then, when I did, I was walking with Helen along a beach somewhere I didn't know. There seemed to be miles and miles of white gleaming sand, the sun shining down, with the waves breaking gently on a completely deserted shore. I wanted to say something to her but when I turned she wasn't there. I didn't know what to do so I carried on walking and then suddenly I realised with relief that Helen had somehow got ahead of me and I started rushing to try to catch up. I shouted but she did not seem to hear and then as I finally got alongside, puffing and exhausted, I looked at her and it was Charlie. I tried to ask her if she had seen Helen anywhere but everything froze and all I could hear was the roar of the waves. I tried to do something to help to find Helen but instead woke up with perspiration on my forehead though it wasn't hot in the room. After that I only dozed off and on, thinking about Australia and Helen and, for some reason, the Southern Cross shining down on the burnt earth.

When I got up I felt jaded and decided I needed some exercise. There was nothing useful I could do on a Saturday so I strolled along 5th Avenue to the Frick Collection on 70th. I wandered through the amazing collection of pictures which is never allowed to leave the building. I stopped and stared at Constable's picture of Salisbury Cathedral.

"Do you like it?"

I looked towards the voice and saw Charlie smiling at me. I was silent for a moment not knowing what to say and then she squeezed my hand as if knowing there was a problem.

"Come on, Peter. It's a nice day. I'll take you for coffee in the park."

I didn't argue and followed her. We left the building and crossed 5th Avenue into Central Park. She led me across the park to the Boathouse restaurant holding my arm. "It's a bit late for coffee. Shall I buy you lunch?"

"That would be very nice, Charlie."

She was making all the decisions and chose a table on the deck overlooking the park. "Not too cold for outside?"

"Perfect. You look great, Charlie."

"Thank you." She looked at me carefully as if she knew everything I was thinking and every ache I felt. "Why not tell me all about it?"

That was the thing about Charlie. She was smart and knew intuitively that something had changed, something wasn't right. I suppose if things had been normal I wouldn't have avoided her at the airport and she had worked that out. I wanted to tell someone how I felt and I knew she really wanted to know. So I told her, slowly, painfully about what had happened, bit by bit, the lot. About the ditching, about St Antony and about Helen, our engagement and then Australia.

It took a long time but Charlie listened without saying anything until, finally, she murmured, "that must have been really terrible." I nodded agreement, my eyes full of tears. She reached up and held my right hand. "And she was pregnant?"

I looked at her in amazement, shattered, eyes wet, uncertain what to say. "How did you know? No-one else has any idea. I haven't told anyone."

She let go of my hand and took the handkerchief from my hand and wiped my eyes. Then she looked at me. "Peter, we went through a lot together looking for that aircraft and those pictures. I got to know you, what makes you tick, how you react. It's obvious. You both wanted your child to be born after you were married." She stopped for moment and we looked at one another. "You know people don't change, we just get older and possibly a bit more restrained. Wiser perhaps."

"I'm sorry, Charlie. I only avoided you the other day because I couldn't face telling you all about it." She nodded. I tried to regain my composure. I wasn't used to being so emotional. I tried to change gear, to be me, the cold unemotional insurance investigator. "Now that's quite enough about me. What have you been up to? Are you married? Boy friend?"

"No Peter. I'm not married. I tried a boy friend but it didn't work. At the moment I'm on my own in an apartment with a girl friend close by."

"Are you still a V-P in your insurance company specializing in paintings?"

"Very much so but I don't travel around as much as I used to."

"Well why were you at the airport then?"

"You have to know the reason for everything?" I smiled slowly and nodded. "I suppose that's why you always find the answers."

"But you still haven't told me. It was an international flight."

Charlie gripped my hand. "I was on the same flight as you but you didn't see me. I was economising in world traveller plus. I had been looking at some pictures which we were insuring." She relaxed her grip.

"You mentioned you had an interest in that aircraft that went into the water?"

"That's right. Our Bermudan friend Mr Morrison[7] sent a picture to the Guggenheim for some exhibition they were having. It was in the roof rack and we managed to get it back but not surprisingly it had got damaged. We've had to send the picture to a restoration specialist. It will be alright but it's going to cost a bit."

"Did he tell you he was sending it? Was the picture covered?"

"Alright, you definitely haven't changed that much. Nosey as ever. And you got it right first time. He didn't ask us. It was only a small picture being hand carried. He claimed he was allowed to move pictures for exhibitions but in our view he shouldn't have done it without asking us. We are still negotiating but meantime the picture is being restored to its original state."

"Hardly."

"You know what I mean."

---

[7] *The Final Flight* by same author

"Are you putting a claim on Castle Harbour Airlines?"

It was her turn to look at me. "That's a very good question. I'd better consult you. Would we be wasting our time?"

"Probably. It looks as if the pilot made a mistake but the airline was operating the aircraft correctly as far as I know."

"However, Peter, I get the feeling there is something you don't understand?"

"Charlie, you seem to know things I haven't told anyone else. It's a bit frightening." I looked at her. "Yes, I'm not really satisfied but I don't know why. That's why I've come back. In my view the pilot acted out of character." I thought about Morrison's picture. "That picture, surely it wouldn't be worth going to court? Probably only the lawyers would be pleased."

"That's my view. The sum of money is not really large enough."

I suddenly realised that I had ordered my meal and eaten it without consciously having paid any attention to the food at all.

"Would you like a coffee?"

"Charlie, does a long black translate into American?"

"We are in a global world now, Peter. A long black can be had almost anywhere." She smiled. "But it tastes better here."

For some reason I could not explain I decided to confide in her and told her about the Safety Board which I had applied for.

"Peter, it would be wonderful if you got the job. It would be a break from your past. Something completely new. A challenge."

The coffee came and went. Charlie looked at her watch. "I must go home. How long are you staying in New York?"

I told her about wanting to look at Echo Victor.

"But why do you need to look? Surely it's the inside that matters. It's the software you can't see, not the hardware."

"Charlie, who told you that?"

"I think you did. It's true isn't it?"

I nodded, wondering what I dare say. We had a long look at one another. "Charlie, it's been really great seeing you, again. If you ever come to the UK let me know."

I gave her a kiss on the cheek and remembered the smell of her perfume. I watched her walking away, still very athletic and still a lovely figure to watch. I decided to walk back to the hotel and tried to start thinking of Echo Victor. I had been lonely before, but now it seemed even worse.

***

Sunday morning at exactly 8am John Southern called me; I had just had a shower and was trying to decide how to spend the day. Thinking about it later I realised that he had been waiting for me to wake-up.

"Peter, sorry to worry you on a Sunday. I know you're in New York. Derek has been and come back from Taipei and says he checked all the paperwork and everything is fine."

"That's good. Did he see Fred?"

"Oh yes. He saw everybody.

"Did he establish the training procedures for CatIII?"

"You always ask the right question. Richard asked him that and he wasn't pleased when Derek didn't know the answer. However, we've got another problem. The Chinese embassy aviation man has been round to Richard and asked if we could send someone to check the paperwork. I told him that Derek had just been but apparently someone in CAAC, Shiu Liao, is not happy."

"That's the guy who met me, Bruce, the one I told you is very sharp. What's his case?"

"Peter, I don't know. Can you talk to him?"

"Not now I can't. I'll try this evening and let you know."

John rang off and I thought some more about the two accidents. I did not believe that the reason for the incidents could be the same even if the avionics and autopilot were identical. I decided to add William Roscoff to my list of calls. The day dragged a bit and not having anyone to talk to and exchange ideas with really left me feeling down. The only person I knew in New York was Charlie but I didn't feel like calling her, though I knew I could contact her with an email.

At 8pm I called Bruce since by my calculations it should be 8am the following day in Hong Kong. He answered and after a few exchanges he realised who was calling him.

"Bruce, the aviation expert in your embassy in London has told Hull Claims Insurance that you would like someone to go out to Taipei and check the aircraft and the paperwork."

"Yes Mr Talbert, that would be very helpful."

"But Derek Finborough has just been out."

"Yes, Mr Talbert. We would be very pleased if you could go."

I was nonplussed. He clearly felt that Derek hadn't done a very good job. "Bruce, I'll talk it over with Hull Claims and we'll let you know."

In the morning I called John and discussed the matter.

"Peter, my boss doesn't want to upset CAAC. We've got a lot of business coming up. It may be a waste of your time and our money but Richard wants you to go."

"John, I'm not keen. However, I'll try and go straight after leaving here but you'd better tell Fred what is happening. Please confirm by email he'll accept my visit. He's refused me once. Send him an email now and you should get a reply to-morrow morning your time. Meantime I'll investigate when I can go and timings."

After John had rung off I saw there was an email from Bill giving me the name and number of Airlines Servicing at Newark. I tried calling WeScrapIt Inc but had no success finding Bill's contact. They had a web site and I saw its location in the Bronx. I entered the place in my Garmin Navigator in case the cab I intended to take had a problem.

I phoned Total Avionics and I was put straight through to William Roscoff. "It's Peter Talbert here. We spoke before about the CC21 in Hong Kong and the modification state of the autopilot."

"Yes, Peter, I remember very clearly. You woke me up in the middle of the night. Have you made any progress? Was mod 156 done?"

"It looks like the mods were done but William, to be honest, there's something not quite right and CAAC are unhappy. I may have to go to Taipei. But that wasn't why I called. I'm in New York as Castle Harbour Airlines have asked me to help them and to look after their interests in connection with the European 630 which went into the water at Kennedy. Strangely, that was also a Cat III approach and again the autopilot disconnected and of course it was again your avionic suite. I wondered if there might be a similar modification state issue?"

"Peter, like you I thought it was strange having two similar accidents so close together. Yes, the autopilot is the same in both aircraft types so it is probably worth checking the modification state. However Airlines Services here at Newark are a first class outfit and I'd be amazed if the aircraft was not bang up to date with regard to modifications, software and hardware. Are you coming over to have a look."

"Yes I am. Is your office at Newark as well?"

"Yes. The headquarters of Total Avionics is not too far from the airport. Huge building and I'm tucked away at the back. I would buy you a coffee but you were lucky to find me in. I'm off to the West Coast for a few days. However, if there is a problem don't hesitate to call me again."

I decided it would be sensible to go to Airlines Servicing first to save wasting everybody else's time in case the modification hadn't been done. I called Bill's contact, Eddie Gonzales, and he said it would be alright if I went straight over. It was nearly twenty miles to the airport but it wasn't worth renting a car. There was a cab waiting at the front of the hotel and the driver was very pleased to take me to the airport though he had to get his book out to find Airlines Servicing at the far side of the airfield. Gonzales soon appeared at reception and took me to a small meeting room where there was a pile of documents.

"Peter, Echo Victor was very new and we did very little work on it. However here are all the relevant documents which came from European. If you're checking mod 156 on the autopilot it was done before it came out here. We had to do the other five aircraft."

"You knew what I was after?"

"Oh yes. Total Avionics had a serious problem with the Cat III installation and only solved it when they introduced the mod."

Gonzales opened the relevant folder and showed me both the aircraft and autopilot documents with 156 marked off.

"Eddie, I'm wasting your time and mine looking at these documents. Total Avionics support told me I would be. Look, I'll just have a quick scan through and I'll get out of your way."

I left after about an hour and Eddie got a car to take me to the terminal so I could get a cab to WeScrapIt in the Bronx. Unfortunately the cab driver seemed to understand only Spanish but he had a large street map. Between that and my GPS, which I had switched on, we managed to find the place.

There was a man at the entrance and there was a stream of trucks coming and leaving with mounds of mangled metal. The man at the gate directed me to an office just behind the entrance and I asked for the person that Bill had given me. The guy behind the counter grabbed some sort of mobile phone and spoke to someone who I assumed was the man I wanted. After a about five minutes a burly dark man appeared wearing a hard hat and a yellow protective suit.

I explained I wanted to look at Echo Victor. "You mean that corroded wreck that slid into the water at Kennedy." I nodded. "You'll need a hard hat and you can borrow that jacket." I dressed myself and he led the way into a long dilapidated covered building where there was a badly corroded fuselage. Outside, exposed to the weather, were a couple of badly damaged wings with the engine pylons completely wrecked. I walked to the front of the aircraft but it was badly damaged. I would have liked to look in the flight deck but there was no obvious way into the fuselage. I walked round it but I couldn't see anything unusual. Then we went outside to look at the wings but again I didn't see anything odd.

I thanked the guy who showed me round and he gave me his card. "Call me if you need further help, Mr Talbert, but I understand we're scrapping the fuselage at the end of the week."

Back in the hotel I called Bill's NTSB contact, Fabio Costello, and managed to speak to him. I explained my interest and wondered when the final report would be out. "Peter, aren't you the guy that investigated that Bermuda Triangle aircraft that crashed in Colombia with all those paintings?"

"Yes, that's right. Such bad luck on the pilots after such a nightmare journey. Still we got the paintings."

"Those FARC guys are ruthless, shooting the plane down. When Castle Harbour called me, gave me your name, and asked that you might see the wreckage I thought it might be you. How did you get on with WeScrapIt?"

"No problems. They showed me the airplane. Not in very good shape."

"You're right there. Did you find anything?"

"Nothing of interest I'm afraid. I would have liked to have gone into the flight deck but there didn't seem any obvious way in as the fuselage was so crumpled. Did you manage to get a look?"

"Yes, we supervised emptying what we could recover from the plane. Only the luggage racks escaped being covered by the river so we didn't get much out. The flight deck was a crumpled mess as you saw."

"Fabio, is the fuselage going to be destroyed at the end of the week?"

"No. In fact some professor, Corrigan I think the name was, called me from the New York State University in Albany as he wants to examine the effect of salt water corrosion on wiring and structure and so it is going to be moved there next week. Why do you ask?"

"There's something odd about the accident. I know it's a clear cut case of pilot error but it seems so out of character."

"Well we are just issuing our final report. Do you want me to send you a copy?"

"Is it on your web site?"

"Will be to-morrow after 0800."

"Well in that case, Fabio, thanks for the offer but I can always copy it down if I need to."

"Fine, Peter, keep in touch if you have any ideas."

I thanked Fabio and called Bill. "I've checked with Airlines Servicing and all the modifications seem to be in order. Didn't spot anything unusual on the aircraft at WeScrapIt but I wasn't able to get inside the fuselage. Luckily it is going to New York State University so I may try next time I'm here."

"Why bother Peter? Let's face it Trevor made a mistake."

"Maybe but I'm not satisfied and even if you don't pay me, Bill, I'm determined to find out why Trevor did what he did."

"Peter, let's be quite frank. All I'm interested in is getting the insurance from Airplane Protection."

"I'll do my best for you but we must find out the full facts in case something similar occurs again."

I put the phone down, wrote up my notes and then looked at flights to Taipei. I could go on Wednesday morning 11.15 and get in 22.00 the following evening on the Thursday, changing at Tokyo, twenty two long hours. I could work all day Friday and maybe leave Saturday on Lufthansa in the evening. It looked a gruesome trip via Bangkok, Munich, Dusseldorf and London City getting in at 5.30pm but at least I would be home. I didn't book the flights as I had not heard from John.

I tried watching the TV. I noticed that as long as I had work to do I didn't feel too bad but the moment my mind had time to wander I felt very down and missed not having Helen to talk to. I even considered talking to Charlie again but somehow, because I liked her, it didn't seem right. I went to sleep early but didn't sleep all that well.

John called me punctually at 8am. "Fred says he will be very pleased to meet you and apologises for not seeing you a few weeks back."

"Alright John I will leave here to-morrow morning unless something comes up here and will be working in Taipei on Friday. Hope to be back Sunday."

"That's fine. Maybe we can meet next week."

I booked the Taipei flight but not the onward flight to London. Then I switched on the news in the morning. The local newscasters were all analysing the NTSB report saying pilot error in every sentence. It was almost certainly true but I hated coming to that conclusion when the pilot wasn't there to explain or defend him or her self. After a quick breakfast I logged on to the NTSB web site and read the report itself. I read it through carefully so as not to miss anything. There was only one thing new which had not been mentioned on the TV. The crash recorder showed that it was a pilot disconnection and not an autopilot malfunction, unlike the Hong Kong accident; this fitted in well with the fact that all the modifications had been carried out.

The rest of the day passed very slowly and I checked in for my flight in plenty of time the following morning.

***

Twenty two long hours later I clambered out of the Airbus 340, cleared immigration and customs and caught a cab to the Towneplace Marriott. I checked in and went straight into a room which was a small suite. I rang room service for an omelette and some decaffeinated coffee and then I managed to doze.

The phone rang. It was 8.30 in the morning. "Mr Talbert, this is Fred. I'm so glad you are here. What time shall we meet?"

I started enquiring where his office was but he interrupted me. "Look, I'll send a car round now to your hotel and we can discuss things at my office."

I got dressed hurriedly, got myself organised and went down to the lobby where the driver was waiting. I wasn't sure what I was expecting because Fred's English was so good but in fact he looked like a typical Chinese business man, quite short with very dark hair and a close fitting suit.

"Mr Talbert, this is a real pleasure. Thank you so much for coming out. I'm not sure how I can help. I've spoken to the pilots and they tell me that the autopilot cut-out at a very critical moment and then one of the engines did not respond when they tried to overshoot. I've explained all this to your Mr Derek and he agreed. He is arranging settlement of our insurance claim."

"Yes, Fred, if I may call you that. We understand that but you see if all the modifications have not been done then the insurance may be invalidated. So we just want to look at the maintenance records as a routine check."

"Will that be necessary? You will be very welcome to check but everything is in order and all the modifications had been carried out. We showed everything to Derek."

"I know that Fred but I must have a look as well. Could you arrange that?"

"Of course. Let me call Oscar, our chief engineer."

Fred had a long conversation in Chinese and then he smiled at me. "Oscar is sending a car over to take you to his office."

"Fred, one more thing. As you know, for pilots to fly in Category III conditions they have to have regular training programmes." I wasn't altogether surprised to see Fred looking as if he hadn't heard me. "Your training procedures are very important.

Please talk to your chief pilot and get him to email me your training plan."

Fred nodded in very half-hearted manner. I sat in his office and waited and after thirty minutes a car arrived and took me to the airline's maintenance base at the airport. I went into reception where the girl at the counter made a telephone call and then asked me to wait. After about ten minutes a man of obvious Chinese descent appeared. "Mr Talbert, my name is Yang Jianli but you may call me Oscar. I am in charge of the airline maintenance."

"I'm Peter Talbert and the insurance company just want me to look at your avionic servicing records."

"Mr Talbert, please come with me. I shall be delighted to let you see them."

He took me into what I took to be his office and on a table there was a huge pile of documents. "Please Mr Talbert. Have a good look."

He went back to his chair and I started to look at the documents. They were servicing records and modification states of the flight system, the radios, the inertial systems, the GPS navigation systems and the Flight Management Systems. It would be necessary to check with the manufacturers support organisation that all the outstanding modifications had been incorporated but judging by the dates, which were very recent, everything looked in order.

I checked all the documents carefully. "Oscar, everything seems fine. I just need to see the autopilot servicing and modification documents and then I'm finished." I looked at Yang Jianli and he looked straight back. "Aren't they there?" I shook my head. "Mr Talbert, I'll talk to our records department and find out why they haven't been sent up."

Nothing happened and after an hour I queried Yang Jianli and he got on the phone again. "They can't find the documents. They think the Taiwanese Civil Aeronautics Authority have got them. I'm sorry I can't help you."

I considered the situation. "No problem Oscar. I'll go over there and see them there."

Just for a moment I thought Yang Jianli looked uncomfortable. He made a telephone call "Mr Talbert, my office now tells me that the documents have been sent by our CAA to the CAAC in Hong Kong."

"Oscar, perhaps you would be kind enough to arrange a car to take me to your CAA offices?"

"Mr Talbert, I told you that your Mr Derek has seen the records. There is no need for you to trouble yourself."

"Oscar. I have come out here to see all the records including the autopilot."

I got out my phone and sent a text message to John Southern. 'Can't get hold of autopilot modification documents. Please double check with Derek that he saw them and that he checked the autopilot modification state. As you know I am concerned because Total Avionics told me a few days ago that no automatic landing must take place unless all modifications up to 156 have been installed.'

I looked at Oscar.

"Can you get someone to take me back to Xie Tingxi's office?"

Oscar, I thought somewhat reluctantly, organised a car to take me back to Fred's office. He came with me, spoke to the secretary and then went in to see Fred. By now I was getting rather annoyed. After about fifteen minutes I was invited into Fred's office.

"Mr Talbert, I understand that you have been unable to see the autopilot maintenance records of B33057. Yang Jianli here has checked with our CAA and they have sent the records to Hong Kong."

"To the accident inspectorate?"

"Yes, that's right. Luckily your Mr Derek has seen the records and so he can vouch for the fact that they were up to date."

"Fred, thank you. Can you arrange for a car to take me back to the hotel."

"Of course. Can we help further in any way? We'll let you know when the records are returned."

"Yes, I intend to stay in Taipei until I have seen the records. Meanwhile I shall call Shiu Liao in Hong Kong to check when the documents are coming back and also the modification state."

I went back to the hotel and sent another message to John Southern saying that I intended to stay until I had seen the autopilot documents and gave him my room number in the TownePlace

Marriott. There was an eight hour difference to UK so I could expect to hear very quickly from him as he arrived in the office. I went to the coffee shop to have something to eat when my phone rang. "Mr Talbert, when I told you the modification sheets were in Hong Kong we were wrong about the records. We had them all the time. We will send a car out in about an hour to collect you."

The car duly arrived and I went back to Oscar's office. All the other documents had been cleared away and the autopilot record sheets were on the table. All the modifications up to 156 were marked as being completed.

"Oscar, that's a great relief. May I have a copy of the modification sheets? In colour, please."

Oscar looked at me, looked as if he was going to argue and then changed his mind. "Of course, Mr Talbert." He made a phone call and two minutes later the maintenance records were removed and ten minutes after that I had a full set of the sheets.

"Mr Talbert, would you like us to do anything else? Can we make an airline booking for you?

"Oscar, that would be very kind. Can you book me to go back to England to-night via Frankfurt?"

"Of course. If you wait here I can let you have copies of the e-tickets in a few minutes."

We chatted about the airline and the financial state of the area until my ticketing documents arrived. It was a first class ticket for that night leaving just before midnight.

"Oscar, you shouldn't have done that. Business class would have been fine."

"Mr Talbert, it is a pleasure."

Up in my room at the hotel I got an email from John Southern. 'Derek said he saw the sheets in Taipei and everything was in order. Is there a problem? John'

My reply was short and to the point. 'Have now got sheets but the ink looks too new. Not sure yet how to prove it.'

I went down to the lobby to tell them I would be checking out that evening and then got something to eat in the coffee shop. When I got back to my room and opened the door I knew there was something wrong but before I could do anything I felt a great pain in my head and passed out.

Now you see it

I came to and it was dark. I couldn't see anything and I had a splitting headache. I felt terrible but there was a glow from the digital clock. I tried to get to the clock and the phone next to it but I could not reach it. All I could manage was to knock the phone on to the floor. I must have passed out again. The next time I woke there was a noise of knocking on the door and then I felt someone looking at me. I was aware of being carried somewhere into a vehicle and passed out again.

When I came to I knew I was lying in a bed in a room which looked like a hospital ward. A nurse came in, saw I had woken up and then disappeared. Next a man who was obviously a doctor appeared and started checking me over with a stethoscope.

"Can you hear me, Mr Talbert." I tried to nod but it hurt like mad. "You were attacked in your room and robbed." I tried to nod again. "You have concussion. You must lie completely still and rest. We will need to do an MRI scan."

Sometime later I felt myself being taken on to a table and then going into some tube and out again. I was very glad to get back on to the bed. Next time I woke up the pain had eased a bit and I tried to move but a nurse came in and indicated to me that I should lie still. Since everybody I saw seemed to be Chinese and had no English except for the doctor I felt frustrated but too weak to care.

I must have slept again but this time when I woke I knew I wasn't going to die. The doctor re-appeared and checked me over again. "How do you feel, Mr Talbert?" I think I managed to mumble 'a bit better'. "Your MRI scan was good and you should be able to leave here in a few days. Would you like to talk to anyone?"

For the first time I realised that nobody knew where I was and that I ought to be planning something but I didn't feel like it. However instinctively I knew I had to try to pull myself together. All I could think of was asking to see the British Consul. The doctor nodded and left and the nurse reappeared with some pills and a bowl of soup. To my surprise I felt hungry and she helped me drink it by transferring it to a mug.

Later a British looking lady came into the room but I had no idea of time. She was carrying a case which I recognised was my travelling bag. The nurse propped me up and the visitor sat down close to the bed.

"Can you hear me? I'm Alice Browning and I work in the embassy."

I managed to find my voice though it was rather weak. "Yes thank you. I'm very glad to see you. What happened? What time is it? I know I'm in Taipei but the last thing I remember was going into my hotel room."

"Mr Talbert you were attacked and robbed sometime on Friday evening. You passed out but luckily for you the phone was off its hook. You had said you were checking out but on Saturday morning the hotel operator reported the phone was not working and that you had not checked out so they sent someone up to have a look. They got the hotel doctor in and rushed you to hospital here at the Mackay Memorial Hospital. I assume you are British?"

"Of course, didn't you check my passport?"

"Mr Talbert, there was nothing left in your room. No passports, wallet, credit cards, phone. All that was left was your clothes and your bag which I've brought."

"Netbook?"

"Nothing Mr Talbert."

"What day is it?"

"It's Tuesday, you were attacked on Friday."

I thought about the news she was giving me. "How am I going get home?"

"Well I've brought a form here and when you feel up to it you need to fill it in and I'll take a photo. We can let you have a ticket and money to get you home and a temporary passport."

"How long will it take?" I realised I must be feeling a bit better as my impatience started to show itself.

"Just a few hours but please tell me why are you here?"

I slowly explained I was visiting West Orient Airlines. An idea occurred to me. "If you ring the chief executive, Fred I call him, and tell him what happened he should give you an eticket to get me back." I had a thought. "No, on second thoughts please don't call him. I'd rather he didn't know."

Alice Browning took a photo of me and then left me saying she would collect the form to-morrow and let me have money, passport etc. With difficulty I managed to fill in the form. I was worried that I had not let my parents know where I was and I didn't remember their telephone number. Losing my phone and netbook left me in a real mess because the two devices were my memory. I suddenly remembered Helen; if only she were alive. She would have sorted things out.

I gradually recovered and on Friday the doctor said I could leave the hospital but recommended I did not travel for a few days until I got my strength back. Alice came and gave me a passport and got me to sign for some local money. "You will need to exchange this passport for a new one when you get home. There is an endorsement in this temporary passport to enable a new one to be issued. When are you flying home?"

"Don't know, but I don't fancy going back to the hotel."

"We understand that. You can stay in a house we manage near the embassy for a few days. You'll have to go to the local restaurants for food, I'm afraid, or a hotel."

"Thanks very much. Could you book me back to London on Sunday via Frankfurt, business class.

"Sunday? Pushing it a bit aren't you? By the way the doctor says you should have a wheel chair and I'll order one for you." I started to protest but she lifted her hand. "He's right. There are long distances to walk at the airports and you will find you are not fit enough. I'll come back and take you to our house where you can stay."

I thanked her though I was still not sure about the wheel chair. When she came she gave me a ticket, some more money in Taiwanese currency and UK pounds; she told me that I would get an invoice when I got home. I was very glad to reach the embassy house, luckily well located by a McDonalds and two hotels. I lay on the bed and tried to work out what I needed to do. By now I reckoned I was almost back to normal and realised I needed credit cards and a driving licence for a start. I wondered whether the thief had been using my cards.

Sunday came and I was very glad of the wheel chair, especially changing from China airlines to Lufthansa at Frankfurt. Heathrow in fact was not too bad, again thanks to the wheel chair. During the flight I realised I didn't have a key to the house but hopefully my neighbours, the Marchants would be in.

Armed with the sterling Alice had given me as I was able to get a taxi back to Kingston and home. Luckily Julia Marchant was in and managed to find my key so I didn't have to break in.

The first thing I did after sorting out the alarm was switch on my computer and to my relief all was well. I then sat down and worked out all the things I needed to do starting with ringing my parents. That done I checked the two credit cards that were missing and found that they had not been used. I cancelled them and ordered replacements. I ordered a new netbook using a credit card that I had not taken with me. I had eaten quite well on the aircraft but I drove to the local Sainsbury's to stock up with food. I also remembered to get a passport form from the post office

Back home I rested and began to think about my recent visit to Taipei. I had lost the copies of the modification documents which I wanted to examine carefully which was a nuisance. I considered ordering some more but decided to wait. It was time to call John Southern.

I told him as best I could what had happened.

"Peter, what a rotten time. Did you have a chance to review the modification situation?"

"Yes and No. The autopilot modification sheet was not available when I first looked. They produced it after a bit but it looked suspect to me so I asked for a copy which they gave me. I think I told you the ink looked very new. I had intended to show the sheet to William Roscoff of Total Avionics."

"Can't we get another copy?"

"You can try."

"But Peter, when we sent him back Derek said he saw the modification sheets."

"Pity he didn't bring back copies. Then we could have compared the sheets."

There was nothing more that I could do for the moment which was just as well as I decided that it was going to take me several days before I was properly fit again. Everywhere I looked as I wandered round the house reminded me of Helen which didn't really help my recovery.

Chapter 8

A few days later when I came back from my first day at the Farringdon Office after my return there was a message on the answer phone from Charlie. “Peter, I’m unexpectedly in London. Give me a call on my UK mobile.” I copied the number down and walked round the house wondering whether to call her or not. I realised I would like to talk to her but I felt it was wrong to get involved again. Of course it was no longer going to be difficult talking to her now she knew about Helen. However, I was definitely undecided what to do for the best. In the house I felt Helen was watching me and I couldn’t help wondering what she would have said. I tried to analyse my reservations about calling Charlie and realised that it was going to be impossible to keep a Chinese wall between us. She knew me far too well and we had been lovers once. Getting involved with Charlie was going to be like being sucked into a black hole. Once in, it would be hard to escape; not that I disliked Charlie, quite the reverse. It was just that my moral upbringing felt it was wrong even to consider another woman so soon after Helen had died.

I decided to do nothing. I started doing some work and the phone rang. I didn’t have a display of the number calling so all I could do as I picked up the phone was to hope it wasn’t Charlie.

“Peter, great to hear from you. Where have you been? I thought you were avoiding me.”

I couldn’t very well ring off so I explained where I’d been but didn’t mention the robbery. I made routine conversation “Charlie, where are you? How long are you staying?”

“I’ve been commissioned to look for some paintings for a client and if he manages to buy them at the auctions then we’ll insure them. I’ll probably be here for another week.”

“Where are you?”

“I’m staying at the University Women’s Club.”

“Sounds rather austere. Where is it?’

“In Audley Square, Mayfair somewhere.”

“That’s convenient. How on earth did you manage to find it?”

“I’m a member of a club in New York which has reciprocal rights.”

“That’s nice.”

Our conversation hesitated.

“Peter, what’s the matter? You sound as if you’re talking to a stranger.” She paused. “Alright, I know what the problem is. It’s Helen, isn’t it? You don’t think you should be talking to me. It’s being unfaithful.”

That was the thing about Charlie, there was no mincing words. With her you had to look at life head on; when she put it like that I felt stupid, but in fact I realised that was how I felt.

“Come on, you can’t shut yourself in a monastery. Where shall we meet? At your club? I’ll take you to the theatre. What do you like, Peter?”

“Anything that you fancy.” I realised I hadn’t refused. I felt the need to carry on talking and decided to tell her about the attack in Taipei.

“Will you be OK to-night?”

I pulled myself together and tried not to behave like a wimp. “Probably. I’m feeling much better, thank you. You can nudge me if I fall asleep. Why don’t we meet at the RAF Club? We can have a snack and a drink and then you can tell me where we’re going.”

“Where’s the RAF Club?”

“128 Piccadilly, near Hyde Park Corner. All the cab drivers know where it is. How about 6pm?”

“Look forward to it.”

I suddenly realised that the last time I had been there was with Helen which left me feeling uncomfortable again. I got a text message on my phone from Charlie ‘Make it 5.45 and I shall be walking.’ After dealing with my mail I showered, changed into a suit and drove to the DaVinci car park at Hyde Park Corner. Charlie arrived on time. She looked very smart and was wearing a grey suit with skirt and dark stockings. Her hair was quite short. She was wearing a gold necklace with matching earrings and a ring on her right hand.

“You look great. Where are you taking me?”

She leant forward to be kissed on the cheek and the perfume was still the same.

"To the Opera to hear Bryn Terfel in Tosca."

"Covent Garden. How on earth did you manage to get tickets?"

"By saving up."

"You know that's not what I meant. Wasn't the place fully booked?"

"I managed to get two seats in one of the boxes and we'd better get a cab straightaway as I've booked dinner in the Amphitheatre restaurant."

"Charlie, you shouldn't have done that. It must have cost you a fortune."

She looked at me steadily and I looked back. "I wanted to. You did a lot for me and I never really said thank you."

"You paid me my fees and a large bonus for finding the pictures."

"Forget it. You earned every penny."

I did what she said but it was difficult not to remember everything that we had done together in St Antony.

The restaurant was a perfect start to the evening and the box was magic. Bryn Terfel was magnificent and I felt really spoilt. As Tosca killed Scarpia Charlie grabbed my hand and held on tight. I left on a high and I could see that she was thrilled as well.

"If we rush we can get a drink in the RAF club before the bar closes and then I can drive you back to your club."

"We'll need a cab for the Club, you still are a bit under the weather and then I can walk to my Club, it's only a few yards."

We managed to get a cab and we both had the Club pinot grigio. "Charlie, that was fabulous. An evening to remember."

It was time to go but I could see Charlie wanted to talk about something else.

"Peter, you haven't told me about what went on in Taipei. What really happened? Was it pure chance you were robbed?" I realised what an asset Charlie must be to her insurance firm. She waved me to be quiet as I tried to speak. "No, now is not the time. How are you placed over the week-end?"

I was torn between wanting to refuse because of Helen and wanting to talk to Charlie which I enjoyed. As usual she sensed the hesitation.

"Come on. You need to go out. You need to talk, to unwind. You can't just work by yourself, moping."

I gave in, partly because I knew she was right. I did need to talk more. "Well in fact I've got nothing special on. What would you like to do?"

"I've always wanted to go to Tudeley and look at Chagall's stained glass windows." I must have looked shattered. "What's the matter, my dear. Have I said something?"

I was speechless for a moment and somehow the way Charlie had said 'my dear' got to me. "It's alright. Give me a moment." I swallowed and sorted myself out. "I was going to take Helen there when she got back. We had just been to the Royal Academy and seen his paintings."

Charlie touched my hand. "To tell you the truth I don't think much of his paintings. I think his glass is better."

"You're the expert but that's what we thought as well."

We didn't say much more. We walked slowly towards the car park steps and she stopped.

"What time then?"

"How about 10 o'clock? But Charlie, I'll walk you back to your club."

"There's no need. I'm a big strong lady and you're still weak."

"I'm not that poorly and there are some nasty people about."

She smiled and agreed. As we walked on I was trying to decide whether I was just being chivalrous or wanted to be with Charlie. I decided it was probably a bit of both.

We reached Audley Place and stopped at the entrance. She leant forward to be kissed on the cheek and then pressed the key pad and went into the building, leaving me with the smell of her perfume. As I drove home I realised two things; I enjoyed being with Charlie and the more I saw her, the harder it was going to be to move away.

Bob Furness called me in the morning. "Peter, I'm so sorry. I was almost certain you would get it."

"Bob, what on earth are you talking about?"

"I just happened to spot it in the *Daily Telegraph*. The Chairman of the Safety Board is going to be Lady Margaret Rogerson."

"Bob, who on earth is Lady Margaret Rogerson? This is all news to me."

"What do you mean? Hasn't anyone told you?"

"No, Bob. Nobody has told me."

"That's appalling, that it should appear in the paper first."

"Don't disagree. But who is Margaret Rogerson?"

"Apparently she has just finished five years as Chairman of the Board of Film Censors."

"Any other qualifications?"

"The paper didn't mention any."

"I'm speechless. I thought they wanted someone with relevant experience. Certainly that was the impression I gained in the interview." I paused. "Bob, I have to tell you I'm rather disappointed. The more I looked at the job the more I thought I would be able to do it and make the Safety Board really effective."

"What are you going to do about finding out if the story is true?"

"It'll be true alright. The government always tells the press first about everything. All I'm going to do is to check my mail and if there's nothing there I'll call the Department of Transport. Thanks so much, Bob, for letting me know."

I looked at my mail which had just arrived but there was nothing from the Department of Transport so I rang Henry Denis.

"Peter, I'm so sorry. I'm afraid the story in the press is true but how it leaked out we don't know. The letters to the candidates haven't been written yet."

"Henry, it seems to be the way of the world now. Government by leaks and errors. Anyway, no hard feelings."

I hadn't realised how disappointed I was going to feel at not getting the job. Subconsciously I had been preparing myself for a change and now I would have to reassess my whole life, especially without Helen. I knew that one of the reasons I had particularly wanted the job was because it would have stopped me thinking about her all the time. The interview at Marsham Street had gone so well apart from John Luscombe, the Minister, who didn't seem to be with it, that I really thought I might get the job. I suddenly realised that Luscombe's question about being better fitted to take over Bob Furness's job was very deliberate.

The week-end seemed to come quickly and it occurred to me that I was waiting to confide the news about not getting the Board job to Charlie. No letter had arrived despite what Denis had said, which I found incredible.

I collected Charlie from Audley Place and we had no difficulty finding Tudeley as I had put the church position in my GPS navigator. We were not the only people there but the church luckily was not crowded. Charlie looked at the windows in a much more careful way than I ever could but then that was her job. After an hour or so I took her to The Poacher close by for a bar lunch.

"Peter, thanks so much. Another tick in the box."

As we sat down her phone rang. "Cheryl, how's his cold?" I could not hear the reply but she carried on. "That's good but he'd better not go to school until he's really better." She got up and carried on the conversation outside.

"Sorry about that Peter." She could see I had my eyebrows raised. "Cheryl is the friend who looks after my son while I'm away." She smiled in a way I didn't understand. "Didn't I tell you I have a boy."

To my surprise I found myself being indignant. "No, you know perfectly well you didn't. You told me you had had a partner but not that you had had a child. You said you lived alone. Now I know why you don't travel as much as you used to. How old is he?"

"He's four and lovely."

She took out a picture and showed me a photo of a young boy. "Charlie, he looks great and just like you."

"Peter, tell me. How are things with you? How are you managing?"

Charlie clearly didn't want to discuss her son and how she came by him. I was glad to change the subject as it wasn't any of my business. I told her about not being selected Chairman for the Safety Board.

"That's a shame. You were looking forward to the job, weren't you?" I nodded. "You needed a new challenge."

"Well I've got my medical back and I've done a bit of flying in a small jet aircraft. In fact I've just done a trip across the North Atlantic in one from Mojave to Cambridge."

"I'd love to do that. How much room is there in the aircraft?"

"Not enough, Charlie. Two pilots in a small cabin and the cramped rear seat on an Atlantic ferry is filled with fuel."

"Do you need two pilots?"

"Legally no, but on a ferry it is much safer to have two pilots."

"Can I see the aircraft?"

"You seem very keen. There is one in the UK at Cambridge. It's the one I flew back as co-pilot."

"I've always been keen to learn to fly. Can I learn to fly on it?"

Again Charlie stopped me in my tracks. She seemed to want to do everything that Helen had wanted to do.

"Peter, is that what Helen said?" I nodded. "I thought it was. I could tell from your face. You'd never be any good at poker."

I ignored her remark. "Charlie, that's a very interesting question about learning to fly on it. Of course you can but I'm not clear whether you can get your private pilots licence. You're an American so it may be alright. You would have to find out."

"What's the problem?"

"A jet engined aircraft is considered a high performance aircraft. The regulators haven't yet faced up to the fact that you can have slow jet aircraft with very similar performance to propeller training aircraft."

Charlie was quiet for a bit. We finished our lunch and we started our drive back to London. Once again I could see she was planning something.

"The auction at Christie's is on Thursday. Why don't you take me to Cambridge on Friday and show me the aircraft you flew. I'm not booked to go back until Saturday."

I could have ducked the question and pleaded pressure of work but I knew I would enjoy the day out and I needed the distraction. All my plans for the future seemed to have collapsed and I wasn't yet ready to think things through.

"Let me call Marshalls and see if the aircraft is there."

We went back to the RAF Club and had a drink in the bar. I left Charlie and went outside to use my phone. I spoke to a salesman, Arthur Broderick, who told me that in fact the aircraft was there and it would be alright if we had a look at it. I told him we would be there about midday.

I went back in to Charlie. “I’ll pick you up from your club at 0930. By then the worst of the traffic will have gone.”

“You’re spoiling me and I like it.”

I took Charlie back to her club and was offered both cheeks as she left. The smell of the perfume seemed to permeate the car on the way home and took a long time to disappear.

She was waiting for me as I drove up to her club on the Friday so I didn’t have to park on a double yellow line. She was wearing a grey trouser suit which was very sensible since she would probably have to clamber in and out of the LightJet.

“How did you get on at Christie’s?”

“I bought two pictures though it was tricky as I had to have my client in New York on the phone and the second one was above his reserve. There was a third one and I didn’t dare move or the auctioneer might have sold it to me thinking I had bid”

“Sounds very exciting.”

“Yes, it was. In fact it’s the first time I’ve been to an auction in London.”

We arrived on time and managed to find our way through the hundreds of cars outside the Marshall’s building and into Arthur Broderick’s office.

“You were with Monty Rushmore on the ferry when he got ill weren’t you? I gather you did a great job landing at Kulusuk. Quite a trip. We’re very pleased with the aircraft, I think we’re going to be able to sell quite a few of them.”

“Yes, it behaved really well though not sure Monty enjoyed it. When are you going to get a full C of A?”

“In a couple of weeks I think. Still the lack of it is not holding us back. We’re demonstrating it all the time.”

“Will pilots be able to get their licence on the aircraft?”

“I’m sure they will. EASA are huffing and puffing but only because they hate simplifying regulations. It’s quite illogical to have different rules with aircraft that have the same field performance and a much simpler power plant to manage.”

The LightJet was outside and so we were able to walk round it and also climb in. Charlie’s phone rang, she looked at it and walked away to answer the call. Broderick had been talking to the crew chief servicing the aircraft.

"The plane has to do a quick air test to check the flight system. Would you like a ride?"

I looked around to see Charlie returning. "No thank you but I think I know a lady who would."

Slightly to my surprise Charlie looked really pleased.

"We'll have to ask the pilot. It's not a critical flight so there shouldn't be a problem."

We went back into Broderick's office. He called the pilot, Phil Lovelace, and explained the situation and apparently Phil agreed to take Charlie. Broderick produced some coffee and a sandwich while we were waiting and then Lovelace came into the office. I made the introductions and then Phil took Charlie out to the aircraft. It started up under its own power, taxied out and took off to the west. After about an hour it returned and did two touch-and-gos and a landing.

I went out to the aircraft and helped Charlie out, not that she needed it with the cabin floor being close to the ground. She looked delighted. She kept on thanking Phil and then gave her name and address to Arthur Broderick. We got into the car and drove into Cambridge and parked behind the old Garden House hotel, which had turned into a Hilton. We walked into the town and I showed her Trinity College, my old college, with its Great Court and Wren library. She was fascinated by the documents on show in the library and would have spent hours looking at them but the library was being closed. We walked back to the hotel.

"What time is your flight to-morrow?"

"5pm. Why do you ask?"

"Have you got time for meal here before we go back?"

"Absolutely."

We went over to Fitzbillies close by. It wasn't the most elaborate restaurant but it was different from a standard Hilton packaged meal in the Garden House.

"I'm enjoying my day out. Did I tell you he let me fly the plane and stall it?"

I smiled. "Yes, Charlie, several times."

"He even let me try to line it up with the runway but that wasn't so successful. I need practice."

"Well in a year or two there should be some LightJets in New York state. You can learn to fly. Or you can have a go with propellers right now."

"We'll see. I might move to California."

"Have you come into a fortune, Charlie?"

"No, but I've saved a bit and I don't want to spend the rest of my life looking at pictures and living in New York."

"But your boy. He will need educating. By the way is he OK?"

"He's fine now, thank you." She smiled. "I know you can't help yourself but you don't have to monitor my phone calls. Anyway, you're right. It's the education that worries me. That's why I want to move soon if I'm going to."

"New York's a great place. It's got everything. Theatres, Museums, Parks, Wall Street…"

She interrupted me. "and people. Lots of people, cars, noise."

"Well I'm afraid I can't help you, Charlie. But keep in touch. Let me know what you decide. Maybe you could move to Europe. Perhaps the UK but not London because it has far too many people and is growing all the time."

"But it's got good schools."

"Depends what you're looking for. Competition for schools and for Oxbridge is much keener than it was in my day."

"I'm definitely unsure."

"Well be very careful. You've got a super job, very well paid and, though I haven't been there, I'm sure you have a very nice apartment in the centre of the town. You may regret any change you make."

We finished our meal and I drove her back to the club. This time she kissed me softly on the lips and I realised afterwards I hadn't really minded. "Thank you, Peter. You've been great. Try and keep in touch and I'll contact you if there's any news to tell."

As I drove home I felt rather sad. Being with Charlie this second time around had been very pleasant but in a way I was relieved she was going. Last time in St Antony we had been drawn ever closer sexually as we had tried to find out together what happened to the aircraft and the paintings; as we made love for the first time the excitement was increased for me as I finally realised where the missing paintings must be. This time we were five years wiser and I had a great gap where Helen had been. Nevertheless I realised that of all the people I knew, Charlie was the only one I felt I could talk to without any reservations. We had an empathy which I couldn't really understand with her being an American in New York and me, a Brit living in London.

***

For the next week I settled down to my routine work. Then I got a message from Chuck Steventon telling me that he was off to Seattle that day as the weather looked as if it was going to be foggy for a few days. Would I like to join him? He was staying in the Red Lion in Bellevue which suited me as I liked staying there, even if it was next to the freeway. I knew I had to leave as soon as possible while the fog was still there but it was too late to leave that day. I checked on the weather channel that the fog was forecast to stay for the next day or so and booked with British Airways for the following day.

We left at 3.15 pm and arrived at 4.55 pm local time nine hours later. Chuck's weather forecaster proved to be very accurate as we landed in thick fog and made a perfect touch down. I was very impressed that the Captain managed to find the terminal as the visbility was very poor.

I rented a car but had a rather unpleasant drive in the fog to the hotel. As I checked in there was a message from Chuck asking me to be at the Corporate Center at 1900 hours. I had managed about three hours sleep on the plane but I certainly didn't feel I was really ready for some demanding flying. However the opportunity was clearly too good to miss so I spoke to Chuck who seemed in great form and told him to expect me when he saw me. After dumping my bags in my room I got back into the car and crawled along 405 back to the airport. I managed to find Perimeter Way but I had to call Corporate Reception to describe where I was and where I had to go. Eventually I found the facility, parked the car and went in to the operation/briefing room.

Chuck was there with a Boeing test pilot, Augustus Tull commonly know Gus. They were drinking coffee and clearly were waiting for me but had realised my problem getting there.

"Not to worry, Peter. There are not too many aircraft flying. Thanks to you we've managed to get special permission from the FAA."

"What do you mean 'Thanks to me'?"

"Well I invited the FAA pilots over as you suggested and, like you, they wanted to see the aircraft flying in fog so they arranged with air traffic for us to fly to-day below the published weather minima."

"They've flown with you, then?"

"Yes, two of them came over and were very impressed."

I wanted to ask some more questions but decided to wait until we had flown.

We went out to the aircraft. The weather was foggy, damp and most uninviting and I was glad that Gus was going to fly with Chuck and not me. The visibility was about 1000 feet so that it was just possible to taxi visually. Gus sat in the left hand seat and after starting the engines he lowered his HUD. Chuck switched the display system on to his head down vertical display so that I could see a picture of the taxiway in front of the aircraft on his display from my jump seat. Air traffic gave us permission to taxi and they were clearly watching us on their radar as we taxied out. We could have managed without the infra red and the radar sensors but having the EVS certainly made things a lot easier.

We lined up and the runway was very clear on the head down display. Gus took-off, put the autopilot in and under radar instructions manoeuvred the aircraft round for an approach. He coupled the autopilot to the ILS and though we were in fog the runway showed up very clearly ahead. As we approached the runway the visibility just cleared so that the runway lights came into view as Gus disconnected the autopilot and made a smooth landing.

Chuck raised the flap, re-trimmed the elevator, Gus opened the throttle and we went round for another approach. We had to do a very wide circuit as there was an Alaskan Airlines aircraft landing ahead of us. This time Gus flew the aircraft manually down the approach and again the fog cleared at about 150ft above the ground so that he was able to land manually. After we landed he taxied round and I got into the right hand seat with Chuck moving over to the left one.

I lowered my HUD and Chuck raised his, putting the display head down. I decided to try to do exactly what Gus had done and immediately after take-off settled the aircraft in a climb and engaged the autopilot. It felt very strange flying the aircraft on the symbology on the HUD though in fact the autopilot was doing it for me. As we turned finals the combination of the ground database, the symbology and the two sensors was very impressive so that I felt I could see the airfield and runway ahead even though there was absolutely nothing to see. However on this approach the runway lights did not appear looking through the HUD when we were down to 100ft so Chuck took over and made a go around.

He did the next approach, lowered his HUD, and left the autopilot in until below 100ft. The loom of the approach lights shone up through the cloud and then the real runway lights appeared, exactly correlating with the runway on the HUD and head down display. Chuck touched down and we taxied back to the corporate center.

We took our gear out, closed the aircraft down for the night and then I followed Chuck's car back to the hotel. Five minutes later we were sitting in the bar pondering over our flight.

We were all delighted with the performance of the total system but there was still a big question mark as far as I was concerned. Gus and Chuck were talking all the time and Chuck noticed I was very quiet.

"Chuck, did your FAA pilots tell you how the EVS would be certificated?"

"No, Peter. I did ask them but they were unsure and undertook to come back to me. I think they have to consult the legal eagles who write the regulations."

"Please let me know what they say when you hear from them."

"There's something worrying you?"

"A new piece of flight equipment which gives extra capability has to be integrated into the flight deck, particularly if it affects landing performance in bad weather. You've only got to look at the statistics to see that the most frequent phase of the flight when accidents occur is during approach and landing."

I think Chuck thought I was overly concerned with something that worked as well as their system. I was very tired and didn't feel like talking about software certification or accuracy of displayed runway headings so I made my excuses and went to bed.

In the morning I called Roger O'Kane, an avionics expert of the Independant Transport Aircraft Company who I knew and who was based in Seattle.

"Roger, what are you doing for lunch?"

"Stranger. You must want something again."

"Not really. I happened to be here doing some flying last night and thought of you."

"I'm not sure I believe you but I'll meet you at our favourite diner just before noon to beat the rush."

Flushed with success at making an appointment so quickly I tried Michael Noble, the chief Aviation Week journalist based in Seattle.

"Peter, you must be involved with that accident at Kennedy. What's happening?"

"I am but you're wrong. I'm here in Seattle and thought it would be great to meet up."

"Le Provencal, 6.30."

"Done. See you there."

I logged on to British Airways and saw there was a 21.50 flight to London but it would be very tight to have dinner with Michael Noble and catch the flight. I decided to have the next day off and made a booking for the following night. I made some notes on the flight the night before but didn't feel ready to submit a report to Harry Foster.

I was at the diner on time and saw Roger waiting outside in the damp atmosphere.

"You haven't chosen a very good time to come flying."

"Actually Roger, you're wrong. I've been flying with Vision Unlimited."

"When, last night?" I nodded. "You must have been mad. The system isn't certificated and needs integrating on to the flight deck."

"I agree. But the actual sensors, database and symbology work very well."

"Well we're looking at it for offering to our corporate customers but we're also considering some competing systems. What else are you up to?"

I told him about the aircraft at Kennedy. "Looks like a clear cut case of pilot error but I'm not sure why the guy made the mistake."

"Maybe he should have had that EVS system of Vision Unlimited."

"Possibly. It would depend on how it was certificated."

"What else is going on? How about Hong Kong?"

I smiled. "Actually I've been out there as well. Have you looked at the CC21 at all?"

"You bet. Have to watch what the competition is doing. Total Avionics do the equipment so there shouldn't be any problem there."

"Yes, you're right but, in fact, the autopilot disconnected at the critical moment during a Cat III landing and then an engine didn't accelerate as they tried to go around."

"The aircraft uses a Chinese engine?" I nodded. "Maybe a problem there." He smiled. "When are you going to settle down and stop flying the world every time something goes wrong?"

"Good question. You're right I probably do need a change, a new challenge." In fact the loss of not getting the chairman's job on the Safety Board combined with losing Helen was really making me think what I wanted to do. I did need a change but I didn't feel like discussing the Safety Board with Roger.

We chatted for a bit more and then Roger went back to work. I went back to the hotel, did some routine work and then drove up to Kirkland and Le Provencal. Michael hadn't arrived but I sat down and ordered a beer. In fact he was twenty minutes late and I was just wondering what to do when he arrived.

"Sorry I'm late but Boeing were giving us a briefing on their new airliner and they had laid on a small reception afterwards."

"Michael, you should have cancelled. I only suggested meeting for a chat."

"I know but I wanted to leave anyway as we had heard it all before. And you always have some problem I like to know about."

"Not to-day."

"I saw the other day that you people are copying our NTSB. Now that's a job that would have suited you. I see they are going to appoint an expert in classifying films. Not sure that's going to help. Did you apply?"

"Our new Safety Board will not be an exact copy. I think your NTSB has a wider remit on safety and the prevention of accidents. The Transport Safety Board will be confined to overseeing the existing accident investigation boards, for the moment anyway."

"You seem very much up to speed. You did apply?"

"Yes, Michael, I did. I felt I was in with a real chance but I didn't get it. I suspect the appointment is a political one."

"You'd have been good. A breath of fresh air. Mind you I don't see how you can have a new board. I would have thought the EU wouldn't allow it."

"I wondered about that too. But I didn't make a thing of it."

We chatted about Boeing and Independant and the way the technology was going. The situation was increasingly difficult for airlines as aircraft needed to be more and more efficient but the airframe life was so good that it was difficult to justify buying new ones.

Back in the hotel I watched the television for a bit and then went to bed. In the morning I took my time getting up and then went down to Seattle docks, parked the car and caught the Vashon ferry. I walked over the island for a bit to get some fresh air and have a think. Then I had a coffee at Café Luna, caught the ferry back and drove to the airport to catch the early flight to Heathrow.

Chapter 9

At Heathrow I fought my way through the mad scrum that seemed to be the unpleasant hallmark of the airport and bought a Times on the way to find the cab I had booked to take me home. I opened the paper to see on the front page 'Whistleblower reveals that new Chair of new Transport Safety Board was forced on selection committee by Minister.' I read on, fascinated, as the article explained that Rogerson hadn't even been on the headhunter's original list but was added on at the last moment when they had finished interviewing, apparently authorised by Luscombe. He had allegedly forced his choice onto the committee. Brief minutes of the final meeting were quoted in the article and apparently the Minister had said that it was quite clear that only Rogerson had the necessary management experience and so there was no alternative but to choose her. The article pointed out that Lady Rogerson had no experience in transport or safety matters. However her husband. Lord Rogerson, previously a senior union official had been the favoured candidate for his local parliamentary constituency. The party headquarters had then parachuted John Luscombe into the constituency and, in order to avoid a selection contest for the parliamentary candidate, Rogerson withdrew from the contest so that Luscombe was adopted unopposed. Then, in the next honours list, Rogerson was given a peerage and 'elevated' to the House of Lords.

As I read the article it occurred to me that I still had not had a letter from the Department of Transport. I looked at the mound of mail as I entered the house but I could not spot the letter. I hadn't been at home long when the phone rang. It was Bob Furness. "Peter, have you seen the Times?"

"Yes Bob, where on earth did they get all that stuff from? Do you think it's true?"

"Oh, yes. One thing is for sure. The whistleblower is going to get fired when they find him or her. Presumably the leak must have come from someone in the Permanent Under Secretary's office."

"Why? If the so called minutes were circulated it could have come from a recipient's office. More likely I would have thought."

"Well wherever it came from, this story is not going to go away for a day or so. I shall be watching the news and Newsnight this evening on BBC 2."

On the lunchtime news the newscaster explained that there had been a statement from the Prime Minister's office saying that Lady Margaret Rogerson was an excellent choice of Chair for the new Safety Board and that the Prime Minister had complete confidence in the Minister of Transport, that the Minister had done nothing wrong and that investigation was taking place to find out the source of the leak.

John Southern phoned. "I wonder if Luscombe will have to resign? What a carve up. Presumably he was under some pressure from Lord Rogerson."

I found it difficult to get on with my work, what with being tired from the flight and the breaking news. A reporter from the Mail telephoned in the afternoon, asking me something I suppose I should have anticipated. "We understand you were the leading candidate. Allegedly Lady Rogerson has had no experience of transport and accidents. Wouldn't you have expected the new chairman to be an expert in the field?"

"I have no knowledge of what you are talking about. The Government apparently has made a decision and that's an end of the matter."

"Mr Talbert as a leading candidate didn't they tell you? Have you got a letter from them explaining their decision?"

"No comment."

The journalist went away I'm sure feeling he had something, otherwise surely I would have admitted I had a letter. In fact it was incredible that the formal letter had still not arrived. However almost immediately there was a ring at the front door. It was a motor cyclist from the Department of Transport. It was the much delayed letter which Henry Denis had promised me, signed by Philip Brown, saying that I was not the successful candidate. Goodness knows what was happening in the Department and why the letter had taken so long.

Strangely this gossip in the media didn't really excite me. I had already adjusted to the fact that there was not going to be a step change in my life. I would still be rushing round the world at everyone's bidding but with no Helen to keep me sane. Meantime I was still wondering why poor Trevor Smithson had not gone round again at Kennedy.

John Southern came on the line again and we discussed my recent visit to Taipei. "John, I'm not happy that everything is as it should be. Don't be in a hurry to settle with them if you can avoid it. Derek's reports seem inconsistent."

"Peter, I feel as you do. We'll certainly hang on until the CAAC issues its report. That should delay things several months in my view."

My telephone rang as I put it down. It was Charlie.

"Guess what." I decided not to guess. "Are you still there? I'm coming to England again."

I was pleased but also slightly concerned since I had assumed that, to coin a phrase, I had seen the back of Charlie. I just wondered whether she was being kind to me and looking for trips to the UK. "Great. When are you here?"

"In two days time. I've got another commission to find some pictures and bid for them."

"Isn't that a conflict of interests if you're going to insure them?"

"Don't see why. It's more business for my firm."

"Do you get paid for these jobs?"

"You're joking. Do you think I'm a philanthropist?"

"How about an art lover."

"Maybe but I don't love for free."

"You couldn't possibly expect me to comment, my love."

I realised I hadn't called her that since I was in St Antony but I told myself I had done so only because of the way the conversation had gone.

"Peter, is it confirmed that you didn't get the job you wanted?

"'fraid so."

"Who did get it?"

"The one I told you about. A lady who has been chairman of the board of film censors."

"What does she know about safety?"

"Nothing."

"What does she know about?"

"Apparently how to pull the strings of government to get a cosy job."

"But it won't be a cosy job."

"Depends on how the Safety Board is organised."

"Sounds a crazy appointment to me."

"Would it help if I told you that her husband is in the House of Lords and knows John Luscombe, the Minister, very well?"

"Are you telling me that there's been some skulduggery?"

"I didn't know Americans knew that word."

"Nonsense. We invented it and don't change the subject. What are you going to do about it?"

"What am I going to do about it? Nothing. I don't have to. Some whistleblower has leaked the minutes of the selection committee. Allegedly they were told by the Minister that the lady concerned, Margaret Rogerson, would have to be the new Chair because clearly she was the only one with the necessary experience of administration."

"So now it's out in the open what's happening?"

"I'm not in the sleazy corridors of power. How should I know?"

"It sounds as if your system is worse than ours."

"Probably. We don't have a constitution like yours with checks and balances. Basically we have a dictatorship with an election once every five years."

"My love, it's rotten for you. You were looking forward to it and you would have done it so well." A pause. "However the news doesn't have to be all bad. I've got a suggestion to make. You can take a holiday."

I thought for a moment. "You know that's not a bad idea. Where shall I go?"

"How about Australia. You can come with me. I've got two insurance jobs coming up out there, almost the moment I finish in the UK. If we go now the weather won't have got too hot. Should be very pleasant."

"Where are you going? It's a big place."

"Not altogether sure yet. Sydney of course and probably Melbourne. How about it?"

I sensed that my answer was important. Somehow I had known all along that the phone call would not be a trivial one. A throw away remark wouldn't do. It was inconceivable that we could go away together without getting involved. My ethical nature was telling me it would be wrong to go away with Charlie when Helen had died so recently. But there was something about my relationship with Charlie that I couldn't explain. If I was going to change my job, being with her might be an opportunity. I temporised for a moment. "What about your boy. Can you leave him?"

"Oh, he'll be alright for a couple of weeks. He loves Cheryl and she has a daughter of the same age. I'll have a couple of days with him when I get back before I leave."

"Charlie, you know I think your holiday is a great idea but it doesn't seem right." I forced the words out. "Like being unfaithful. You know what I mean."

"Of course I do, my dear, but I really meant what I said to you before. You can't keep thinking of Helen. You need to stop agonising and carry on with your life."

"Charlie, it seems only a few days ago. It seems so heartless for me to go on holiday and enjoy myself."

There was a long pause but I knew that there was going to be only one answer even though I felt extremely uncomfortable. It was decision time. "Alright Charlie, you're on. But Melbourne worries me a bit."

"I know, my dear. We need to talk about it."

"Alright. Let me know when you'll be in the UK and we can see if it's possible to arrange something."

She rang off. Thinking about it I wondered if she had thought through the whole thing. She knew I hadn't got the job from her last visit. It was her way of helping me get over not being selected. She knew I had really wanted it and that not having Helen made matters much worse. My problem was that I knew I would be uncomfortable meeting people who knew about Helen and who wouldn't understand that Charlie was special, something from the past.

I was glad I hadn't offered to let her stay in my house; I wasn't sure either of us wanted that. Apart from anything else it was full of Helen's things. I was going to have to move sometime. What on earth was I going to do with Helen's things. It needed to go on my difficult decisions list but then I decided to ring Elizabeth Dunston. Tom answered the phone.

"She's away. Can I help, Peter?"

I explained the problem to him. "Elizabeth offered to help and I would like to take her up on her offer."

"I'll get her to call you when she gets back."

My mind drifted back to going away with Charlie. I realised that I didn't know what was going to happen about staying in hotels. We had slept together once before but that was several years ago. She now had a son and I had had Helen. Probably twin beds seemed to be the way forward, it would be cheaper than two rooms. Anyway I didn't have to worry. Charlie was making the arrangements and she would be sure to know the correct solution.

Her idea of Australia suited me very well. Their air traffic control system seemed to be leading the world, probably driven by the vast distances it needed to cover and the relatively small budget available. It always surprised me that the population of the whole continent was less than greater London. It seemed a great country for private flying with thousands of private landing strips.

Apart from my terrible last visit, my times out there had always been in connection with airline accidents or brief talks to the airlines about the new avionic systems and the problems associated with the modern flight decks. Perhaps this time I would have a chance to look around. Charlie only had two weeks but I could probably manage a bit longer. CASA, the Civil Aviation Safety Authority, was based in Canberra so I could go there either before or after her visit.

I settled down to reading the technical magazines. Enhanced vision systems were clearly becoming big business; Total Avionics were advertising a system for commercial airliners as well as for business jets. I went to their web site to read the specification and their claims for the system, not surprisingly, were very similar to Vision Unlimited. I ran the videos which showed landings in fog and it struck me that the actual pictures were almost identical to the approaches I had experienced in Seattle with the VU system.

In the middle of watching the approaches the BBC rang asking me to take part in Newsnight as they were running an item on the recent appointment of Lady Rogerson as Chair of the new Transport Safety Board. They knew I was an expert in these matters and they would value my opinion. No mention was made that I was possibly the preferred candidate but I was damn certain that if the Daily Mail knew that then the BBC knew it as well and they were hoping to pop the question and catch me by surprise. I declined to take part.

However, in the evening I decided I might as well watch Newsnight on BBC 2. The producer had decided to make a cause célèbre out of the appointment. Predictably, neither the Minister, Lady Rogerson or Lord Rogerson would agree to be interviewed. A sycophantic member of parliament, who clearly was looking for promotion, said how ridiculous it was to suggest that there could be anything wrong in the selection of Lady Rogerson. However there was an opposition MP who was interviewed immediately afterwards who pointed out that the selection of Luscombe as a parliamentary candidate had caused great controversy, since Rogerson at the time was the announced choice of the local constituency party and Luscombe was forced on the local party's headquarters. A secret ballot of the constituency was ordered as a compromise to be overseen by the Electoral Reform Society and then, very unexpectedly, Rogerson withdrew saying he had complete confidence in Luscombe. Then, surprise surprise, when the next batch of life peers was announced, Rogerson was on the list and a year or two later his wife, a school teacher, was appointed to be Chair of the British Board of Film Censors.

Next a BBC reporter was interviewed who said he had spoken to a member of the selection committee who had confirmed that Luscombe had forced Rogerson through against the advice of the committee. A statement was read out from the Prime Minister's Office saying that a detailed investigation was being carried out to find the source of the leak.

In the morning I picked up the Telegraph from my front door and read that some web site had published an email from Lord

Rogerson to Luscombe thanking him for agreeing to appoint his wife as Chairman of the Safety Board. The Prime Minster's Office said that the police were being called in to find out how this email got into the public domain. A leading article said that Luscombe should resign and Lady Rogerson's appointment should be stopped.

I tried to get on with some work at lunch time but Bob Furness called again. "Peter, she's not going to take the job."

"Bob, what's happening then?"

"Don't you ever watch the TV or listen to the radio? Lady Rogerson. She's just issued a statement saying that she's changed her mind and wants to stay on the Board of Film Censors. "

"I suppose it was either her or the Minister. I'm glad, regardless of the politics, that she decided to quit. It's going to be an important appointment and I can't help feeling she wouldn't have been up to it."

Two days later I was in my office in Farringdon Street when my phone rang. It was Charlie. "Just got in. I'm in the University Women's Club again. Are you very busy? I've got to look at some pictures in Christie's at 2pm. It would be good for you."

"I am not sure I need to have good done to me. Anyway I seem to remember I had to straighten you out on real pictures as distinct from fakes a few years ago."

"I'll ignore that very rude remark. There are no fakes at Christies."

"How about certificates of ownership?"

"Peter," she sounded serious for a moment "has there been something in the paper then?"

I realised that my shot in the dark was getting me out of my depth. "Where shall we meet?"

"How about the Ritz?"

"Charlie, you really are a big spender. I was going to suggest next door, The Wolseley. Do you think you'll be able to find it?"

"Drop dead. 1pm."

I caught the tube to Kings Cross and the Piccadilly line to Green Park. I was a bit early which was just as well as the place was very popular. I had barely sat down when Charlie arrived. "Did you really come in this morning? You don't look tired at all."

"I got quite a lot of sleep. I ate before I got on the plane instead of wasting time eating the meal." A pause. "What was that you said about ownership?"

"Charlie, I wasn't serious. There hasn't been anything recently in the papers on disputed ownership. I only though of it when I was reminding you about fakes. One reads of all sorts of scams. I imagine if one is buying a valuable painting it's necessary to be very careful indeed on authentication, fakes and the history of the painting."

"You bet." Charlie relaxed but lowered her voice. "Peter, there are a couple of paintings I've been asked to buy but I'm a bit worried about them. There is a German who is claiming that certainly one of the pictures being sold is really his because the Russians took the picture from his grandfather's house in Berlin during the war and he is the only descendant left."

"Surely all those claims were settled years ago? Anyway, I thought the British Government had passed a law about giving immunity to imported paintings."

"Only from one museum to another. Privately owned paintings are something else."

"Who is selling the paintings?"

"A Russian."

"Surely Christie's wouldn't sell the painting if there was any doubt on ownership."

"You're right but I'm afraid that if I buy the paintings on behalf of my client, the German will start a court case to try to prevent the paintings being exported."

"Then you'd better not buy the dodgy one, Charlie. Surely if there's any doubt on ownership nobody will buy the painting?"

"You'd be surprised. Mind you the price won't be as high. That's why my client is tempted."

"Rather you than me. When's the auction?"

"In three days time, but I've got to try and learn a bit more about both paintings. Would you like to see them? You can come with me."

We went into King Street and entered the shop front to reception. The girl made a phone call and a very smart lady appeared, introduced herself to Charlie and was clearly bending over backwards to be helpful. I was impressed with the stature that Charlie clearly had in the art world. As an afterthought I was introduced and then we had to go through a security search before we entered a room full of pictures which I assumed were going to be in the sale. Charlie knew exactly which pictures she wanted to look at and spent the next half hour examining them. I wandered round the room looking at all the pictures and went back to Charlie.

The pictures were in frames. “Are you going to look at the back of the pictures, Charlie?”

“Relax, Peter. This isn’t an accident investigation. I’m looking at the paintings. They are going to show me the back of the pictures to-morrow morning. This must be boring as hell for you. Why don’t you go back to your office and we can talk later. I shall be going to bed early to-night to try and get some sleep.”

I accepted her suggestion and went back to Farringdon Street. Henry Denis called me. “You have been selected to be the chairman of the new Safety Board. Congratulations Peter, when can you come and see us?”

I was almost speechless and perhaps stupidly I replied. “The substitute? Second best?”

“Peter, don’t even think like that. You can guess what’s been going on in our place. I’ll be fired if I even discuss the matter.”

I decided to chance my arm. “You’re not the whistleblower then?”

“No, Peter I’m not. However, as you can imagine, there’s an intensive search going on.”

I was more than a bit shattered because though I wanted the job I never really believed it would come my way because of my lack of experience in government environments, though I knew I was being seriously considered.

“We need to go through contractual matters and terms of employment and then we need to talk with you and hear your views on how we should proceed in setting up the Board and who is going to be on it.”

“Absolutely, though I’m sure Charles Simon has a few ideas.”

“Peter, I knew you’d understand the situation. When do you think you could come and see us?”

“The day after to-morrow, probably.”

"Peter, the committee agreed that we should get your appointment signed, sealed and delivered before there's any more nonsense but we don't want to advertise your appointment for a few weeks so please don't discuss the matter with anyone, and I mean anyone, but at least you can start planning."

I wondered what I was getting myself into. The new post would definitely mean an end to my current method of working and entail learning all sorts of new skills but I realised that amazingly I was looking forward to it. I remembered that Denis had told me not to discuss it with anyone but I was beginning to realise that I was treating Charlie as special.

There was message from Harry Foster asking me to ring him.

"Peter, thank you for calling me. Have you seen the advertisements for EVS from Total Avionics?"

"Yes, Harry. You've got some competition by the look of it."

"You're right there but I'm very worried because I think they've got hold of some design information from us. I don't believe they could have done what we've done so quickly. I know they only started the programme about nine months ago."

"Maybe, Harry, they are just winging it, hoping to prevent potential customers buying your EVS. Anybody can make a video."

"I don't think so. We haven't been showing videos but we can tell looking at their videos that they are using our technology. They've integrated microwave radar with the infra red sensor and they just couldn't have done it in the time without getting information from us."

"Can't you just go for a patent infringement?"

"No, Peter. That sort of approach is very long winded and difficult to prove. Meantime the competitor sells the product. I'm ringing you because I think this requires someone of your experience to find out if there was a leak and if so who did it."

"I would have to come out to have any chance of doing that, Harry. And really I would need to talk to Total Avionics. Have you spoken to them at all."

"Yes I have. I spoke to Matt Watkins, the CEO of the whole company based in New Jersey, saying I suspected that his firm had been stealing our designs. He vehemently denied stealing anything and invited me to send someone to discuss the matter and I'd like you to be the man."

"Harry, are you sure your system is so different from that of everybody else?"

"Yes I am. There must be someone in my firm who is selling our secrets to TA for them to have a system like the one they are showing. That's why I want you to come out."

"But Harry, I'm not an expert in your subject. I'm just a general avionics engineer."

"Maybe, but I think you have an instinct for knowing when people aren't telling you the truth. Will you do it?"

"Harry, if I'm going to do it I will have to come and see you first and it's not going to be cheap for you. And one other thing, I'm only going to be available for a few days because I'm going on holiday."

"Then when can you come out? The sooner the better, particularly if there is an end date. "

"I'm not sure. I'll let you know in the next day or so."

We rang off and I suddenly realised that I was letting Charlie's visit to London affect my decision. In fact, Harry's request was obviously very urgent from his viewpoint but I was now trying to fit in a holiday before I became a government employee. Actually I wasn't too keen to think of myself as a civil servant but I reassured myself that I was on contract.

In the morning I decided I had better work out my diary very quickly until the end of the year but I couldn't do it without knowing Charlie's plans. I drove into London and parked in the DaVinci car park, then took a cab to Farringdon Street. I didn't want to interrupt Charlie's work so I sent her a text message asking her to call. Meantime I gave some thought to Vision Unlimited's problems and the suspicion that Total Avionics had stolen some design information. It clearly was going to be difficult proving anything. The firm had several facilities in the United States and also had facilities in the UK and Germany.

Elizabeth Dunston called me and we discussed how we should deal with Helen's things. We agreed there was no point in giving any of it to her parents as it was just clothes. There was nothing else that I knew of except some personal effects which I wanted to keep.

"Peter, do you think it will all go into my car? We've got a station wagon."

"Yes, I'm sure it would."

"OK. Then I'll come round and collect it all. I'm home for a few days. I thought I might take anything that's worth having to a charity shop."

"That would be perfect. Stand by." I looked at my diary. "I'll have to call you, if that's alright. Probably in a couple of days."

Charlie finally called me at the end of the day. "I'll buy you dinner and we can plan our Australia trip."

"Why don't we have an early bird special and go to Rules in Maiden Lane? Where are you?"

"Sotheby's in New Bond Street."

"You get around. Can't you make your mind up?"

"I've just got another job to look at a picture here and possibly insure it."

"Are you buying it as well?"

"Not this one. Can I walk to Rules?"

"No. Cab, fifteen minutes. I've got something to tell you."

"Tell me now."

"Too difficult."

"See you at six."

Charlie arrived before me and already had a pinot grigio. I asked for a bottle of champagne and two glasses.

"What's going on?"

"I've got the job but you're not allowed to tell anyone. I'm not sure why I'm telling you." I looked at her and realised I really liked being with her. Without Helen, I needed someone and Charlie was very sympathetic and caring and I liked the way she looked at me. "Lady Rogerson retired hurt, as we say in cricket. Presumably she was told that as her husband had sent a stupid 'thank you' email to the Minister who he had pressurised into choosing her, they didn't dare give her the job."

"That's wonderful, my dear. What shall I do with the Pinot Grigio?"

"Drink it quickly and then get stuck in to the champagne."

"You'll be sorry."

"Don't you mean 'I'll be sorry'?"

"That's what I said."

She finished the pinot grigio, tasted the champagne and then produced a calendar sheet for October and November. "I've marked when I need to be in Sydney and Melbourne. What do you think we should aim to do?"

I looked at her dates, last week of October in Sydney and first week of November in Melbourne. "It's all very close." I told her about Harry and Total Avionics. "I'm not sure I can fit it all in before you want to go. And I don't know the dates for the new job."

"Peter, why don't you go out to LA now? Then you won't have to buy a round the world ticket. You can do your thing with Vision Unlimited and then we can fly out together to Sydney. I'll have to stage through LA anyway. We can rent a car and drive to Melbourne. Then you can fly home from there with Qantas.""

"But I'm planning to go to Canberra to see the aviation safety people after you've left."

"Why can't I see Canberra?"

"Alright we'll include Canberra on the way. We'll have to allow at least two extra days."

"Peter, you're right. We must leave enough time at Sydney and Melbourne. I'll see if I can't slip my Melbourne date by a couple of days. There isn't an auction involved like here."

"Charlie, it's going to be tight at the beginning of the trip but I'll risk it."

We looked at our diaries and fixed the outbound and return dates and I said I would need to advise her on the Canberra dates in the middle.

"Charlie, I must check the Opera House to see what's on. It would be rude not to go there."

"And I'll fix the accommodation. Will you fix the car?"

"Fine. It all sounds great but I don't really know how long it's going to take with Vision Unlimited."

"If you go to-morrow then if you have any time left over you can go flying in Mojave."

"You're very kind organising things for me. However I'm not sure I can get everything in one bag. It'll be cold in the desert and getting warm in Australia."

"Take two bags and store one in LA. It's got to be possible."

"Alright I'll see what I can do. When are you leaving here?"

"In two days time after the auction. Text me after you've spoken to your Harry guy and I'll call you."

"I'm going to call him the moment I get home. I'll call you in the morning. I was thinking of trying to get into the Sondheim musical to-night but that might make things a bit late."

"Let's go for it. We've finished our meal. How far is the theatre?"

"Three hundred yards."

I was fully recovered from Taipei and we moved smartly to St Martins Lane and managed to get two stalls not too far back. The show was well done and Charlie had a drink in the interval which made we wonder if she had hollow legs. I must have been near the limit anyway and kept to water. We took a cab to the RAF Club and Charlie was very close, considering the width of the taxi but I found I didn't mind. We managed a coffee before they shut the bar. I walked her back to her club but this time she didn't argue. We kissed good night which definitely took a bit longer than the previous ones; I detected a warmth and pleasure on her part which I found I really enjoyed. On the way back to the car I realised that Charlie seemed to be taking over my life and that I wasn't fighting her off, which worried me in a way because I wasn't sure it was right. In reality it didn't really matter but to anyone who knew me and had known Helen it would look very unfeeling, which wasn't really the case at all. Thinking about it yet again I supposed that it was because I knew Charlie so well from the past that everything seemed to be happening so quickly.

Back home I rang Harry. "How about if I came out in three days time? By the way which bit of Total Avionics is doing the EVS?"

"Not absolutely certain. Now that I know you're coming I'll call Matt Watkins and find out. I'll also tell him to expect a visit. Let me know your flight details and I'll book the same hotel as last time?"

"That'll be fine.

I logged on to British Airways and booked a flight three days ahead. I was just going to sleep when Harry came back to me. "The facility doing the EVS is in the UK, Peter, near Basingstoke. Matt is going to fax you the details of the place and the person to contact."

"Do you think I'll be able to do any good without being briefed at your place first?"

"There's nothing to prevent you going back again."

I agreed but didn't confide in Harry that there was likely to be a three week gap between visits, if it proved necessary for a return visit. I dropped off to sleep thinking of Charlie and Australia, my previous visit to Melbourne and remembering I hadn't looked at the Sydney Opera house web site.

Chapter 10

In the morning there was an email from Matt Watkins telling me to contact Chris Henderson, Managing Director of Total Avionics, Basingstoke. I waited until 9.15 and called the number Matt had sent me. It was a direct line to Chris Henderson's secretary. She must have read some emails from Watkins because, instead of asking me who I was and what did I want, she put me straight through. Chris understandably sounded on his guard. "How can we help you? I understand Matt Watkins has agreed that you can visit and talk to my team producing the EVS." I nodded involuntarily and then agreed. "Well Tommy Tucker is your man in charge of the project. In fact the project is so important that he is on our local board of directors. What would you like to do?"

"Can I come over and have a chat to-morrow?"

"You can come this afternoon, if you like. We've got nothing to hide."

"Actually that would suit me much better. How about 2.30pm?"

Chris agreed and I logged on to British Airways and made the LA trip three days later since I needed time to get organised, work as well as packing, before disappearing for nearly a month; the ticket cost more than usual as it was an open return. I rang Henry Denis at the Department and confirmed my appointment to look at the contract and discuss the job in more detail.

I decided to take a long player recorder with me inside my brief case to Total Avionics at Basingstoke. It was quite a convenient device as I could plug in another microphone and I had one fixed to the inside of the brief case itself. This arrangement was quite useful since I had found that some people didn't like knowingly talking into a microphone. I found the location of the division very easily since it was part of the facility that Smiths Industries used to use before they sold out to General Electric. Presumably GE must have sold the facility on to Total Avionics.

I sorted out the papers and my netbook and then carried them separately from the briefcase; on an impulse I switched the recorder on before leaving the car. Reception signed me in and Henderson's secretary took me to his office.

"Peter, I don't know why Harry Foster thinks we've got hold of his secrets. We've been working on EVS for a long time now. In fact, as you probably know, some of the people at Vision Unlimited actually came from Total Avionics."

"Yes, Chris, that's true. That's why they know that you weren't working on EVS at the time."

He looked embarrassed. "It was before my time so I can't comment. Let me call in Tommy Tucker and he will show you around the plant where the EVS work is going on."

Tucker arrived, medium height, blonde hair, slightly overweight and wearing an immaculate blue suit. He led me down a long corridor and then into his office, which had a large window overlooking an extensive area full of computers and, I noticed, some infra red sensors and microwave radars.

"I operate from this office and I supervise everything that happens in the project." Tucker had a strong American accent that sounded as if it came from the southern states. "I've got a chief engineer who has both a hardware and a software team working under him. My job is to make sure that the program is on time and on budget. In addition, I have a continual dialogue with our marketing people and also I make sure that production know what will be required as we make sales.

"As you are clearly aware, we are in competition with Vision Unlimited and I think we are slightly ahead of them, judging by the reaction of our potential customers."

"Tommy, is there any chance of your letting me have a timeline of your technical achievements? I believe that should be enough to convince Harry Foster "

"I'll let you have our latest progress charts. That should give you all the details you need. Now what can I show you?"

He led me outside and I met his chief engineer, Jimmy Brown, who took me over to a rig with a HUD and head down display. "We have a terabyte hard drive with airfield data for most of the world. In fact we have a huge advantage over Vision Unlimited in this area since we have been using the information for our Ground Proximity Warning equipment for many years. Vision Unlimited are just developing one product whereas our EVS is just part of our total flight deck capability. Our infrared capability uses standard sensors and then our autopilot people have been driving head up displays for years with what is really standard symbology."

"You make it sound very easy, Jimmy. How about the microwave radar?"

"We buy that in and then mix the output with the infra red information. We haven't had any problems in the interface."

I looked at him, made no comment but raised my eyebrows. He didn't respond in any way.

"How long have you been working on the project?"

Tommy produced a booklet full of charts. "Maybe this will help. It was a bit of a rush but I've just managed to get this booklet produced for you, Peter, so you can show Harry Foster." He showed me the relevant chart with the build up of man hours on the project starting four year previously.

"How about the software, integrating the various components, the database, the infra red, the radar and the symbology?"

Tommy produced another chart with the build up of imaging software code for driving both the HUD and head down displays.

"May I talk to your leaders of hardware and software?"

"Of course."

I talked to the two engineers and everything seemed quite normal as far as I could see. Tommy asked if I had finished and I agreed but asked to go round looking at the various rigs. As I wandered round Tommy pointed out that they were upgrading their equipment to make their development more efficient.

The final stop was at a simulator and they showed me several simulated approaches as I looked through the HUD. The whole effect was very similar to the development rig at Vision Unlimited which is what I would have expected, whether there had been any stealing of design or not. I looked for Tommy to look at his booklet to check on some details on the interface between the systems but he had disappeared so I asked Jimmy if I could look at his booklet. He told me he had been on the project for just over six months. I took the opportunity to copy some numbers and then we did some more simulations.

Tommy took me back into Chris Henderson's office and I told him how very impressed I was with the equipment. Tommy sent me away with a fistful of pamphlets including the booklets.

I texted Charlie when I got home to ask her to ring me and I explained the change of plan.

"Peter, that's great. I've booked both our flight from LA to Sydney and from Melbourne back to LA and emailed you the details. The bookings are etickets in my name. I'll start a joint account and you can pay all the joint expenses in Australia to help equalise things."

"If you've booked business class then the hotels are going to have to be five star if I don't have to pay you any extra at the end of our trip."

"I have booked business class but the hotel rooms are suites which will probably make your eyes water when you pay the bills."

Trust Charlie to have sorted out the hotel arrangements very elegantly. There clearly was going to be no shortage of beds. I was reminded of one of Helen's favourite remarks 'always remember you have a choice', but I was beginning to wonder who was going to make the choice.

"Peter, are you still there?"

"Yes, Charlie I'm still here and thinking about the arrangements and what more needs to be done. I've got the car and the Opera to do."

"How did you get on to-day?"

"Fine. Not sure yet what the answer is until I've been to Palmdale. How about you?"

"Yes, everything went well."

"All well in New York?"

"How do you mean? I don't have to report back every few minutes."

"Charlie, if we are going on a holiday together you will need to talk to your boy every day so please don't evade the issue. I'm looking forward to meeting him one day."

"Well since you ask so nicely, he's fine thank you."

"See you in LA. Keep in touch."

I called Elizabeth and she agreed to come to the house the next day to take Helen's things.

I didn't feel like talking to Harry as it would be bound to develop into a long conversation so I reconfirmed my flight by email and closed my telephone and computer down. As I lay in bed I was glad I had dealt with Charlie's boy. It was pointless her trying to minimise the importance of the child to her whenever she was with me. I smiled at my earlier concern on the hotel arrangements; I should have know Charlie would have the whole thing sewn up.

The next day I was at Marsham Street in plenty of time for my 1030 appointment with Henry Denis. He took me down to a solicitor in the legal department who had my contract prepared. I scanned through it and saw that my salary was considerably greater than the one in the advertisement.

"We take into account not only age, qualification and experience but our new scale also ties salaries to the salaries in the business world. We feel we have to match them." No comment was clearly expected from me but I found it amazing that people in government employment could imagine that they deserved to have comparable salaries to the business sector when, in reality, they were in featherbed employment without taking any risks. "The annual increase is a general one for people in your pay bracket, determined year by year. These days it is not overly generous. The pension is still a final salary one so there shouldn't be a problem there and you can make additional voluntary contributions if you wish. You don't have to decide now."

"Holidays?"

"I was coming to that. You get six weeks plus an extra month allocated to learn about the latest developments both in technology and in the market place. This is regarded as very important so that you are completely aware of the industries in which you are involved. In fact you can have more time if you judge it necessary."

"What about termination?"

"The contract is valid for seven years and can be extended year by year. The Department has to tell you at the beginning of the final year whether they will be extending you for a further year."

"What happens if they wish to terminate my employment before the seven years?"

"In that case you will receive three years salary for the first two years on termination and two years salary after that. In view of the generous termination amount, you only have to be given one month's notice of termination."

"Are these terms standard within the Department?"

He looked at me and smiled. "No. this a new procedure we are adopting to fit in with modern attitudes on rewards."

"What about bonuses?"

"There are no bonus rewards set out in advance but every year you can suggest special targets which, if approved, will each qualify for a bonus."

The financial package was greater than I was expecting and in fact it definitely was a relief to me since I had been getting concerned that I might be losing money if I was to get the job.

"Do you expect me to sign now?"

"Not at all. We suggest you take the contract away with you and show it to your solicitor or any advisor you might have. If there are any problems let us know so that we can discuss them. Come back to see us as soon as you can so that the agreement can be signed."

I felt very comfortable with this arrangement and went back up to Henry Denis.

"I've been given the financial side but I need to see what I'm expected to do."

Henry smiled and produced a document labelled 'Draft terms of reference for Chairman of Transport Safety Board.'

"Why don't you sit down in the next office and have a read. The document is double spaced so you can make alterations and suggestions. If you want I can give you a file to put in the netbook I see you've got there and then you can alter it as you go along."

I felt that I needed to read and try to assimilate the terms of reference before starting to type any definite suggestions of change so I refused the offer of the file. In the empty office I started to read the document and I could see that generally I was not going to have any problems. However I felt that the suggestion of monthly meetings with the heads of the three accident boards, air, sea and rail would be too heavy a load on the existing boards. My view was that there should only be two a year though I anticipated having special meetings on particular agenda items. I also needed to define the Board membership.

Charles Simon appeared and suggested that we went out to lunch. He had booked a table at Shepherds close by. I had been there a few times previously when discussing with key decision makers some of the issues resulting from accidents I had been investigating. It certainly wasn't the cheapest restaurant in the area but well suited for business discussions.

"Let me apologise straightaway for what happened over the selection process. You've clearly read what the press managed to get hold of. We've had our security people looking for the leak, so far without success." He lowered his voice. "I don't really mind if they don't find out but of course we might have a more serious leak sometime so we need to get rid of any moles." He raised his voice again. "Peter I'm really delighted that you were selected to be Chairman. I was afraid that some of the other members of the selection committee might have preferred someone more used to government organisations but I wanted someone like you who would look at what we have and decide what needs changing. It is no use in my view introducing a new committee like the Transport Safety Board unless we make alterations to make sense of the change. Some of the points you made during our meeting were key to your selection." He grinned. "Mind you I thought you chanced your arm when you mentioned the wider remit that the NTSB has and the possible interference of the EU in your final remarks."

It was my turn to smile. "I don't think I used the word 'interference'. I think 'influence' sounds cosier. However, I wanted to put a marker down because I believe these are key issues which will need addressing."

"I agree but presumably you will want to get the Board running smoothly first with the three existing accident boards."

"Well yes, but from day one I want everyone to realise that the new Board means changes. There will be no point in having the Board unless we take advantage of the new organisation. I think I mentioned that technology drives change and one of the first moves I want to make is to have a common accident recorder system, both in the equipment on the vehicles and in the analysis procedures. We don't need three labs, particularly as there are so few accidents, thank goodness."

"Peter, what about the accident boards themselves?"

"Well we are not nearly as big as the NTSB. I wonder if we couldn't just have accident investigators who could be used for rail, sea and air? Otherwise I think we are going to have a lot of inspectors with not a lot to do. The introduction of the Safety Board is forcing a reassessment of what we've got now."

"I agree completely. I'm not sure everybody realised when the design or agenda of the Board was being formulated what was going to happen. I was pretty certain there were going to be upheavals and I was convinced it needed a fresh mind on the job. I've looked at the way you investigate accidents and I think the reason why you sometimes get to the answer first is that you are not constrained by conventional views. I used to be surprised how well you got on with Bob Furness bearing in mind the way you operate until I realised that one of Bob's strengths was that he was always open to new ideas."

"What about the draft Terms of Reference that Henry has given me?"

"You'd better introduce some of the ideas that you are contemplating but wrap them up. I'm not sure my boss is ready for any big changes immediately."

"I'd like to list the board Members as well but at the moment I'm not sure who the outside members should be. However, I may have some ideas."

"Yes, please. We'll have a think as well."

We had a very pleasant lunch. Half way through I couldn't resist asking Charles what were the chances of the whistleblower being found.

"No idea. As you can imagine, Luscombe was spitting blood and the Permanent Secretary got a good ear bashing I think." He paused and looked at me. "However perhaps it was a blessing in disguise, though we don't like whistleblowers."

"It seems to have been done very cleverly so that no-one was able to see the actual document and deduce who had done the leak. Of course the connection between Margaret Rogerson's husband and Luscombe made everyone assume that nepotism or whatever you call it was being applied. In fact from the tone of the leaked email, perhaps even pressure in some form. Luckily it is not my business except that I want the Transport Safety Board to be a success. Anyway it was convenient that she decided to stand down."

Charles smiled. "Yes, Peter, you could say that."

I refused any alcohol during the meal and I was pleased to see that Charles did as well. He turned to me as we separated. "Let us have an amended Terms of Reference or Mission Statement a few days before you plan to come back and maybe we can then get the show on the road."

I spent the rest of the afternoon going through the paperwork that Henry had given me, making a lot of notes and then using the memory stick which he had given me to load the Draft Terms of Reference into my netbook. I worked on them and sent my proposals including Board membership back to Simon explaining that I would be away for the best part of three weeks.

The thing that amazed me the most was the salary that I was being offered. It matched quite well what I was currently earning but that included the bonuses I had received for the successful investigations I had completed. With my new job I would be able to work nine to five and get paid whether I was doing a good job or not. In addition there were bonuses for self declared targets and a gold plated pension benefit which there was no way I could afford as a self employed person. Government employment had definitely changed in the last ten or twelve years; maybe it was due to copying what was going on in the EU at Brussels.

Elizabeth came round the next day. I showed her the bedroom where Helen kept her clothes; she could see I looked uncomfortable. "Look, let me move all the clothes to the car and then we can see if there's anything else." I didn't argue but stayed out of the way in my office. She came in after a bit.

"All done. Here's some jewellery and bits and pieces." She gave me an assorted box full. "What about downstairs?"

"No, thanks. I'll deal with the rest. There may be stuff for her parents."

I made some coffee, we chatted a bit and then she was on her way. I looked around and I could see photos and all sorts of things which reminded me of Helen but I didn't feel able to remove them.

***

I packed two bags, one for LA and one for Australia as Charlie had suggested. She had sent me full details of the flights as promised plus the hotels. The Sydney Opera House on the day I earmarked for our visit had a choice of a concert or an opera, The Bartered Bride. The concert was the Sydney Symphony Orchestra playing a Wagner's overture The Flying Dutchman, Beethoven's Pastoral Symphony, Elgar's cello concerto and Tchaikovsky's 5th Symphony after the interval. I decided not to ask Charlie since I loved the Elgar and chose central stalls.

I first booked the car in the States to sort out my visit to Palmdale. Then I chose a Hertz car in Sydney but picking it up at the Hotel since the last thing we needed was to drive in to central Sydney after a long flight. We were going to drop the car off at Melbourne airport and I was pleased to see that the actual drop off charge at Melbourne airport was very reasonable compared with the UK or the States.

The next day I got a cab to collect me and take me to Heathrow. It was Terminal Five and not too bad for once. British Airways had finally got their A380s and I was forced to admit the flight was absolutely splendid. I took the opportunity on the flight to look in some detail at all the papers I had got from Total Avionics at Basingstoke. After landing, the customs and immigration were very quick and I was checked in at the Hampton Inn by 6pm. There was a note from Harry saying he was expecting me in the morning at eight.

As usual after a flight across the Atlantic I woke early but managed to doze until 6am when I got up and had a short swim followed by breakfast in the coffee shop. The weather was fine but the temperature at 2,500 ft was only 41°F. I drove over to Vision Unlimited and was at reception at five minutes to eight. Pat, of course, was already there and came along to take me to Harry's office. Harry arrived as we got there and I sat outside for a few minutes while he got organised.

"Peter, great to see you. Good flight?"

We got through all the pleasantries and the order for coffee. Then we sat on a large sofa and he started quizzing me about my visit to Total Avionics in Basingstoke. "Did you learn anything?"

"Harry it looked a really professional organisation."

"Well it would, wouldn't it? They're a great firm. But their EVS came out of left field as far as I'm concerned."

"They gave me this booklet with their project development costs as well as the design of their system."

Harry looked at the numbers. "I just don't believe it. They never started four years ago, nine months is my information."

"They did have their global ground database, Harry, which they use with their warning system."

"I know but the interface software to make the system reliable is a monster. Their software size isn't big enough unless they got a short cut from us."

"There's just one thing, Harry." I paused and I felt he knew something was coming. "I was lucky and managed to get a look at the chief engineer's booklet. It wasn't as new as mine and I copied a few numbers down." I passed him a few rudimentary graphs I had managed to sketch on the plane.

Harry stared at the man hours for the software development. "Luck, Peter? You were more than lucky. You're a genius. These are what I would expect. They could never have got where they are to-day with those man hours and the start date is two years later than in your book." He thought for a bit. "Did you talk to the chief engineer?"

"No, not by himself. It was a miracle that I saw his booklet. Tommy Tucker, their project manager, must have gone to the toilet. By the way, Tucker is an American not a Brit." It was my turn to pause. "You know I don't think the engineer realised that the booklet Tommy was showing to me was different from his."

"But the engineer must know if they got a package from us."

"Not necessarily, Harry. He may have been told it was a subcontracted job. I didn't have a chance to find out how long the engineer had been with the firm; he told me had been on the project six months."

"The radar, Peter. Where did they get that from?"

"They said they got it from the same people you do. You told me that you don't have an exclusive with them."

"No we don't, except that they can't sell some of the special features we got them to add."

"Surely it's the interfacing that is the trick, not the raw radar?"

"You are quite right but the bells and whistles on the radar are important as well." He thought for a moment. "Tommy Tucker." Harry mused over the name. "But his boss must know the situation?"

"Chris Henderson. I would imagine so but I suspect head office, Matt Watkins, doesn't know. He probably thinks the sun shines out of Chris Henderson's rear."

Harry grinned. "You've made my day."

"Hardly, there isn't evidence yet to take them to court. You don't know how the trick was done. You need a lot more, surely. There must be an information conduit between someone in your lot and either Tommy Tucker or someone else."

"Peter, do you think you can find out?"

"I've no idea. Tell me, how many people here know that you suspect Total Avionics of being given a helping hand?"

"Oh, I expect everybody knows. Their jobs depend on the firm being successful."

"Have you tried 'Tommy Tucker' on Google?"

Harry turned sideways to the machine next to him. "He's not listed except with Total Avionics. I wonder if he was involved in some doubtful situation elsewhere and he's got a different name now. I see he was in marketing on the West Coast based in San Francisco. A man of his seniority ought to show more on Google."

"Harry, it's strange that he's working in the UK unless he was placed there by someone in Total Avionics. Maybe there is someone in the Total Avionic US team who is involved. What do you think was actually given to Total Avionics to enable them to accelerate their programme?"

"There were two things in my opinion. First there must have been a set of interconnection diagrams showing the flow of the various pieces of information. One of the tricks of our EVS is the way we do this to ensure perfect line up between the symbology, the ground database, the infra red and the radar. The other piece of information which matches the flow diagram is the software design and the modules which would save the people writing the actual code months of work."

"Would it need a software expert to pass the information over or could anyone do it?"

"Anyone could pass the information on but obviously it would need experts to actual write the software in detail. However, if the top level design was given to them it would save months or even years of work."

"Harry, that's going to make finding the person very difficult. It's very hard to know where to start."

"I know. Any idea where you would like to start?"

"Yes, I'd like to start with your chief engineer, Patrick Williams and then talk to Chuck Steventon, your chief pilot."

Harry called Patrick and established he would be free in about an hour. "Peter, wait in the next office and Patrick will come and collect you. What are you doing this evening? I'd like to take you out somewhere."

It seemed to me I was on an impossible assignment. There were so many interconnects between the employees of the world's avionics companies. There were industry meetings of engineers all the time under the auspices of the Society of Automotive Engineers and similar societies. Engineers were always giving talks advertising their products and the competition was always there, listening and making notes. The pilots also had their meetings such as the US Society of Experimental Test Pilots. From what Harry had told me it would be easy to pass stuff over or at least start making an arrangement. And though Harry didn't like to admit it, with high capacity memory sticks it was very difficult to prevent a really determined employee downloading information, including actual software code.

Patrick arrived and I went to his office. He told me that he was the one who broke the bad news to Harry that Total Avionics had probably got some inside information. He showed me some of the diagrams that would be invaluable to Total Avionics. He gave me a list of three people who had access to the critical information. After a couple of hours I had had enough and asked Patrick to set up meetings with his three engineers in the afternoon. He called Chuck and I went over to his office.

We went out to lunch and discussed the problem. "What about Jean Spencer, is she reliable?"

"You two didn't get on too well, did you" He grinned. "She is completely reliable, Peter. She'd kill anyone who leaked information."

"Is she married?"

"Yes, he's a captain with American."

"Do you have anyone else?"

"Not development pilots."

"Chuck, have you ever given talks about your EVS? To SETP for example."

"Yes, I gave a talk last year to the annual symposium. I don't have a list of attendees but I'm sure there were people there from Total Avionics. As you know they must have had the information well before then."

"What about Jean?"

"She's been to various meetings where the opposition has been, but you know the leaking didn't have to take place at meetings."

"I know but it can start there."

I made no progress and went back to Patrick. With his help I spoke to his three engineers, all of whom seemed absolutely first class and were very enthusiastic for the work they were doing.

I went back to the hotel feeling I was wasting my time. Harry came round and collected me at 6.30pm and took me to Eduardo's Restaurant. "Peter, Italian alright with you?"

"No problem."

We went straight to our table and Harry ordered some very acceptable white wine. He asked me how I'd got on and I had to admit I had really made very little progress. "Harry, obviously it's good that we know Total Avionics have been cheating but as we said it won't do any good in Court. No-one will believe my evidence since you're the one who is employing me."

"Peter, if I can't stop them offering a system against ours to the airlines I think we will have to close down. I'm not prepared to borrow and borrow until we go bankrupt."

"How long have you got?"

"About six months. I'm not sure if any airlines have actually ordered the new EVS systems yet. We're quite close with a couple but if Total Avionics start announcing sales we shall be in trouble since they can offer a completely integrated flight deck system. We can only offer the EVS."

"Well I don't want to waste your money. What I'd like to do to-morrow is to talk to your personnel department and look at the key engineers and pilots previous employments plus their references. After that I'll see if I can come up with any more ideas. I'm off on holiday in Australia in a couple of days but you can always get hold of me and of course I can always get hold of you."

"Alright Peter, in the morning come over and I'll alert my human resources chief to expect you. Come and see me before you leave." He thought of something. "Did you say you might be changing your job fairly soon?"

I explained I had applied for the Chairman's job of the new Safety Board which he understood because of the United States having an equivalent NTSB. However I didn't tell him I had got the job.

There was not much more we could explore on the EVS problem and we chatted about the avionics industry and the airlines. Henry dropped me back at the hotel and I went straight to bed.

I spent the next day with the human resources executive getting details of all the people I had spoken to with their education, employment and noted any unusual points. I also checked their married status and children. I managed to find a record of recent meetings they had attended by looking at their expense claims, which I found very revealing because some people claimed a lot more entertainment of prospective customers than others. However there was nothing particularly significant that I could notice. I felt very frustrated and very worried for Harry.

In the afternoon I went back to the people I had chatted to the previous day to see if they had had any more ideas but I drew a blank. Then I went to see Harry to explain that for the moment I had made no progress. I promised to keep in touch and asked him to feed me any significant moves by Total Avionics like marketing advertising.

As I left Harry I realised that I had a bag to get rid of so I asked Pat to look after it and she came up trumps. Because of the flight timings, Charlie had planned to book a room in LA for both of us before she went on to New York and I returned to London. I told Pat I would let her know the name of the hotel in plenty of time.

Back in the hotel I realised I had two clear days before going down to LA and on to Australia. I called George Straker at MurrayJet and he invited me up but didn't promise anything. Charlie sent me an email telling me she was now in New York and would be staying overnight in the Los Angeles airport Marriott before going to catch the plane. I logged on and booked a room in the same hotel.

In the morning I called the Best Western to make certain they had a room before leaving for Mojave. George asked me about the ferry to UK and then showed me the demonstrator test aircraft which was now back from SBAC. "Peter, I've checked with the Chief Pilot, Adrian Wallace. He's flying the aircraft to-day and he'll take you along. It'll be about midday. If you wait in the ops room he'll collect you."

I sat down in the ops room and got out my Vision Unlimited papers. Clearly the Total Avionics facility at Basingstoke had some explaining to do but it would probably be unwise to accuse them of anything without having proof. Harry could approach Matt Watkins and tell him of his suspicions but however good a guy Matt might be, he would be very loathe to admit to the fraud even assuming that he established that there was one. We needed more evidence and there was nothing that I could see that was going to help.

Adrian appeared on time wearing a flying suit. He was about five feet eight inches, very slim, fortyish with a small neat moustache. We introduced ourselves. "Peter, there's a changing room through there," he pointed to the back of the room, "with some flying suits. You'll be more comfortable with one on and it won't spoil your clothes."

We went out to the aircraft and to my surprise he put me in the left hand seat. "We're only doing some routine cruise performance measurements and George told me you flew the Marshall's aircraft to Cambridge."

"I helped Monty Rushmore. Actually he was very good to me as he let me fly alternate legs after the first few flights."

"You're being very modest. Monty has told me the whole story, how he was taken ill, couldn't move and you had to land at Kulusuk because you couldn't make Iceland."

The flight deck was not nearly as complete as the aircraft that I flew across the Atlantic but the controls were the same. I started up and Adrian sorted out the VHF radio. After we got airborne we climbed up to 25,000ft and he told me the area for the tests. As on my flights with Monty we were under the control of FAA Joshua radar which simplified things. There were three runs to do and then another three at 29,000ft. The aircraft didn't have an autopilot and Adrian did the first run. He let me do the second one and I found I had to work quite hard to maintain altitude smoothly because the air was more turbulent than I wanted.

"Peter, what licence do you have? ATR?" I nodded. "I'm an examiner, would you like a type rating?"

"You bet."

"Well let's do some stalling, spinning and a few aerobatics when we've finished these runs."

Adrian took me through all the necessary manoeuvres and emergencies finishing up in the circuit. I wasn't used to doing spinning on a type check but I'd never had a rating on a jet aircraft that was purported to be an initial trainer. I did a couple of landings, one without any flaps and then a full stop. We taxied back in. "Well there's no problem there. Let's go in and complete the paperwork and I can sign you off."

We sorted out the forms and then had a quick sandwich. I couldn't believe my good luck. I went back to the hotel and tried to do some other jobs I had outstanding. I tried calling Charlie but she wasn't in her office. I called her home number which she had given me. A boy's voice answered the phone. "I'll get my Mom." And Charlie came on line. "Charlie Simpson here."

"Peter Talbert here. Charlie, he sounded great."

"Yes, though I'm not sure I like him answering my calls."

"Everything on track?"

"Yes all OK. I'm just going to spend the afternoon in the office trying to catch up. I'll probably go in again in the morning. My flight's not until mid afternoon. What time are you going to the check-in?"

"That's up to you. I'm staying in the Marriott as well tomorrow night."

"That's great. I shall look forward to that."

"Just as well as we are having the best part of three weeks together."

"Who's complaining? See you soon."

She rang off and I sorted out my two cases and then watched some television before going to sleep. In the morning I took my time and drove back to Palmdale where I left my bag with Pat. Then I drove down to 405 and stopped off at the Getty again. As I wandered around looking at all the magnificent paintings I thought of Helen. We should have been going round together but fate had intervened. It seemed so unfair.

As I drove down to the airport and dropped the car off I idly wondered what sort of guy Charlie's partner had been and why they had separated. Maybe Charlie had just wanted a child as so many single women seemed to these days. Seemed a bit hard on the boy but I was prejudiced. I was sure Helen and I wouldn't have stopped at one.

I caught the courtesy car to the hotel but Charlie hadn't arrived. It was 7pm and I was wondering what to do when my phone rang. "Made it. What room are you in?"

"734"

"We're on the same floor, 712. I'll knock on your door when I'm ready to go down. Fifteen minutes."

There was a knock after twenty minutes and Charlie was there looking in very good shape wearing a green suit. I'd forgotten how slim and elegant she could look and her bra, which I could just make out through a thin blouse, didn't do her figure any harm. It was difficult to believe she was a mother with a four year old child but I remembered from St Antony how athletic she was.

"What are you looking at?"

"You, of course. You look great" I kissed her cheek. "It's a great perfume. What is it?"

"Never you mind."

"But I can't buy you any if I don't know what it is."

"Well we'll make it a challenge while we are in Australia. See if you can discover what it is. Where are we going? Restaurant or coffee shop?"

"Latitude 33 or whatever it's called these days unless you want the full romantic dinner treatment."

"There's no answer to that that I'm prepared to give. Lead on."

We went to Latitude 33. Charlie ordered a small filet steak and a Cabernet Sauvignon; I settled for salmon and a French Chablis. which I was able to have by the glass which surprised me.

"Peter, we'd better start a kitty to keep our finances straight." She got a diary out of the small evening bag she was carrying, extracted a pencil from the diary, grabbed the bill which had appeared and entered the amount. "Fine. I've entered that you've paid."

We went back up to the seventh floor. Charlie offered me a cheek and went to her room and I turned and went to mine. I realised, a little shamefacedly, that I wouldn't have really minded going with her but I couldn't forget Helen. Perhaps the holiday was going to be a strain on both of us.

Chapter 11

In the morning we met for breakfast. Our flight wasn't until the evening. It occurred to me that we could have travelled the previous night but Charlie obviously had decided not to go straight on. She looked at me. "By the way I've checked us both in with the airline. I know we could have gone last night but we're on holiday and I need to look at some of the Getty paintings. I thought I would have to go alone but now it's really great. We can go together."

We decided we'd not rent a car but take a cab. Charlie grinned. "I know it will cost more but Kitty is paying." I didn't tell her I'd spent most of the day there yesterday.

We checked out, left the bags with the bell captain and we were on our way. Charlie knew exactly what she wanted to look at and where all the pictures were. It was an education just watching her. "You've been before, Charlie."

"Once or twice. Have you?"

"Once or twice and yesterday."

She jumped back. "Why didn't you say so? I didn't mean to bore you."

"You're not. Watching you look at pictures is something else. I'm really enjoying it. And I'm even learning a thing or two."

"Peter, I meant to tell you. I only bought one of those pictures we saw in Christie's. When I looked at the back I wasn't satisfied. I think it may have been a superb fake. Anyway I told my client not to touch it."

We had a sandwich and Charlie spent another couple of hours in the galleries. I wandered round the rest of the buildings for a bit and then we met up in the café. There was no hurry as we only had to go back to the Marriott to pick up our bags and then drop them off at check-in. Everything went to plan and we went straight to the business lounge. The flight left on time and we got out of the aircraft to a lovely Sydney dawn two days later. "I don't feel as if I've lost a day, it's more like we've spent two days in the plane."

"Well Charlie, we are now properly on holiday. What are we going to do?"

"I don't know about you but I'm going to bed if I can remember which hotel."

"You booked at the Marriott on Circular Quay. No worries."

She smiled. "I'm not sure I like your Australian accent but I'm glad we're not driving."

We got through customs and immigration quite quickly and a cab took us to the hotel. I gave my credit card as surety since I knew I was paying. "Don't worry, Peter. I've put the airline tickets into Kitty as well so it will all be very easy to settle up when we separate."

The suite was magnificent, on the 10th floor with a splendid view of Circular Quay, the Bridge and the Opera House. Charlie chose the room with the en suite bathroom. We unpacked and I looked at her. "Have you worked out your timings? What time does your lad go to bed? What's his name anyway?

""Peter is his name. You'll be able to remember that. I like to call him before he goes to bed. 6pm, what time is that here?"

"I make that 10 o'clock so you can call him in a moment."

"You're very solicitous for him."

"I suppose I feel sorry for the lad, left without his mother and no father."

Charlie came over and hugged me. "You really are a love. I'll call him now."

"Hang on. I'll dial the number for you on my machine, it'll be cheaper than any other way."

I launched SkypeOut and we heard the phone ringing. Cheryl must have answered the phone. "They're in the bath so I managed to beat him to answering it. All well?"

I left them to it and sorted out my bags, had a shower and put on some lightweight clothes. It was only spring but the weather was pleasantly warm. When I had finished Charlie had ended the telephone call and was in her room. I checked the rest of my email but there was nothing else urgent. Then I called Mike Mansell.

"Peter, great to hear from you. Where are you?"

"In Sydney on holiday before I change jobs but don't tell anyone."

"What's happening? It sounds great. When can we meet? Come round to dinner."

"We'd love to."

"Who is we?"

Charlie appeared wearing some short shorts, a sweater which accentuated her figure and some smart casual shoes.

"An art insurance expert who helped me find the pictures from that plane which disappeared flying to Bermuda and who is working out here."

"Do I know him? Where is he based?"

"She is based in New York. Can I call you back when we've worked out our schedule for the next few days?"

I put the phone down and looked at Charlie.

"You look fantastic, Charlie." I could feel myself stirring, while feeling vaguely ashamed.

"Thank you, Peter," and she came over and kissed me softly on the lips which didn't help. "Not bad for a middle aged Mum."

"I'm not arguing."

"Just as well."

I decided to get on safer ground. "And how is Peter?"

"Full of the joys of Spring, even though it is Autumn. He told me to take him a kangaroo back. I must buy some cards to send him."

"I thought you were going to bed."

"I've got a second wind. Let's try and keep awake and go to bed early."

We went down to Circular Quay which as usual was full of a mixture of holiday makers and ferry passengers. There were the usual players on didgeridoos, which I found rather noisy, and some other entertainers but we went straight by and walked to the Opera House. Charlie looked at it with its amazing sail like roof "It's fantastic. This is one place I haven't been to."

"Well to-morrow night you can break your duck."

"That doesn't translate well into American. What on earth does it mean?"

"You obviously haven't played cricket."

"No, I haven't. It's must be the only sport I haven't played."

"Well going to the Opera House for the first time to-morrow night will break your duck. If you score nought in cricket you have a duck."

"I thought we were going to a concert."

"Alright but you know what I mean. Do you want to go on a tour. They take place every hour or so."

"Not to-day. Maybe some other time when I'm fresh."

We wandered back and had a coffee right by the water looking at the Queen Victoria moored on the other side of Circular Quay.

"Peter, I can't get over this place. I've been to Sydney before but always rushing round. It's all here, the ship, the Quay, the Bridge and the Opera House in perfect weather. And our hotel, it's so convenient." She paused. "I'd better phone the art establishment about the picture I need to look at so that I can advise my client."

She took out her phone but I stopped her. "Always use this phone while you're here. It's a pay as you go Australian one. Our regular phones will be very expensive."

"When did you buy this, Peter?"

She saw at once that I really didn't wish to be reminded and she held my hand. I felt I had to tell her, though I felt she already knew. "I bought it when I came out to find Helen. The Australians are very sensible about pay as you go mobiles. If you want to, you can just buy the SIM card and put it into your regular phone. I find it easier and not a lot more expensive to have two phones. Not like your country where you have to sign your life away to have a phone."

We were silent for a bit and then she phoned her art contact in Sydney. I heard her making an appointment for the day after to-morrow. When she had finished I suggested we went over to the Queen Victoria to find out what time she was leaving. We were in luck as it was going in another hour.

We sat down on the quay for a bit and then went up in the elevator to the viewing platform. The ship was huge and we could see everything being prepared for departure. Clearly the passengers had been ashore because there seemed to be an unending stream going aboard. Finally they stopped coming, the gangway was raised from the ship and retracted. We watched the huge hawsers connecting the boat to the quay being undone and brought aboard. The radar antenna by the wheelhouse started to rotate, there were three loud blasts from the ship and slowly, imperceptibly the boat started to move astern and leave the quay. The gap widened between the boat and shore and then we could see that she was going astern right across the harbour without the aid of tugs. The bow started to turn away from us towards our hotel, then towards where we had been having coffee and then pointing at the Opera House. As the stern of the boat neared the other side of the harbour the bow was able to point towards the harbour mouth and then the liner steamed ahead going right past the Opera House.

Charlie turned, held me tight and kissed me.

"What was that for?"

"Because I felt like it and because that was absolutely fantastic."

"There's another one coming in tonight."

"Well it'll have to manage without us. Let's go and have a rest. I'm exhausted."

We went back up to our rooms and I lay down and dropped off. Charlie lent over me, kissed me and woke me up. "Don't sleep too long or you won't sleep to-night.

"How long have I been asleep?"

"Couple of hours. Kitty is going to buy you a drink and something to eat in the bar overlooking the harbour."

I sorted myself out. Charlie had already changed into a sensible length skirt and not a mini, which I was forced to admit to myself would be exciting but not ideal for an evening drink in the Marriott bar, but then I knew I was very conservative. Charlie had a chardonnay and ordered some fried jumbo shrimps. I followed her example and when we had finished we went to our rooms.

In the morning Charlie woke me. She was fully dressed in quite long shorts and a very thin white sweater with a white bra underneath. "You've slept well. I thought you'd have been tossing and turning all night."

"So did I."

"Let's go down to breakfast and we can discuss things."

I didn't know what there was to discuss but it would be good to rake over it. I had a quick shower and put on shorts and sandals to celebrate the Sydney weather. "Peter, I'm having the full breakfast. How about you?"

"I'm not all that hungry but I'll give it a go."

Charlie wanted to go back to the Opera House for a tour and I went round with her. I always found the whole story of the building was unbelievable. The design by Jorn Utzon was incredible but it had to be modified because it was not possible to construct the building. Now, finished, it had to be one of the most recognisable buildings in the World along with the Eiffel Tower, Big Ben and Tower Bridge. Charlie was on a high when we left, obviously very impressed. We took the ferry to Manley and had lunch overlooking the Ocean. Then we went to the Northern Head to look across the harbour entrance, a magnificent and unforgettable sight. After we got back on the ferry to Circular Quay we went up to our suite to get changed for the concert.

We had a quick drink and a sandwich before walking back to the Opera House and going into the Concert Hall. The Flying Dutchman overture was played superbly as was the Pastoral Symphony but it was the Cello concerto that held me. For some reason it made me think of Helen and I felt my eyes filling with tears. When it was over I didn't move and Charlie realised that I was upset. She held my hand for a bit and then we got up to wander slowly round the building during the interval.

Tchaikovsky's 5th Symphony cheered me up and we walked back to the hotel. We went to the bar and had a couple of drinks. Charlie was great and tried to make me laugh. Up in our suite she held me very close and kissed me. Then she left me and disappeared into her room. I went in to my room and got into bed. A few minutes later I heard the door open and as Charlie slowly got into my bed she whispered "I just couldn't let you lie on your own feeling miserable."

She wasn't wearing anything at all and we held each other very close. Then slowly we made love, not erotically but because we cared for each other and it seemed the right thing to do.

In the morning she rolled over, threw the bedclothes back and I looked at her. "Well, my love, what happens next?"

"It depends what time your appointment is."

"Yes, that's been worrying me."

"Why not delay it for an hour?"

She got out of bed and found my phone. I heard her delaying the appointment for ninety minutes. She put the phone down, pulled off the rest of the bed clothes and looked down on me. This time I knew what happened next.

***

We got up slowly, showered together and went down to breakfast. “Peter my love, I’ve been thinking. We could save a bit of money on this trip.”

“How?”

“I’m not convinced we need full suites at the hotels. Why don’t we just go for superior twins?”

“Sounds good to me. Kitty will definitely like that.”

“To hell with Kitty. How about you?”

“You wouldn’t possibly expect me to comment.”

“Oh yes I jolly well would and quickly.”

“Charlie, it will be lovely.”

“I hope so.”

“Kitty thinks it might be cheaper to have superior doubles.”

“She’s infallible.”

I reached for her arm and then her hand.

“Darling, I’ve got a question to ask you.”

“Go on.”

“Was it chance we met at the Frick?”

Charlie didn’t look at all abashed. “Of course not. I know Ricardo Gemelli quite well because I’m always going backwards and forward to see Morrison and all his paintings in Bermuda. I told him I had seen you and he told me where you were staying. I went round to the hotel to see you and I saw you coming out and going north. I decided to follow you and the rest is history.”

“But you didn’t know anything? About Helen?”

“No, how could I? When I saw that you were ignoring me I wanted to know what was going on.”

I mused for a bit and looked at my watch. “You’d better get moving.”

“What are you going to do?”

“I’ll manage to pass the time. Don’t you worry.”

I went into Charlie’s room and saw a copy of the print out of the hotels she had booked for us and sent to me. I called them all in turn and downgraded the rooms to superior doubles. I made a note of addresses for entering them in my navigator. Then I wrote 'done' against each hotel as I did them. However as I came to Melbourne I felt very uncomfortable. The hotel Charlie had booked was the Westin; it was almost opposite the Novotel where I stayed while I was waiting for news of Helen and it brought back terrible memories as I had wandered up and down for hours at a time. I felt a deep sense of guilt returning because I was travelling and living with Charlie so soon after Helen had died. From being on a high, enjoying my holiday I began to wonder what I should do. For about an hour I just sat and thought things over. Then I realised regardless of how I felt I'd better call Mike since we were committed anyway.

"Mike, how about to-morrow night for a meal? Let me take you out. The Tower in George Street. Will you be able to find a baby sitter?"

"No worries. Thanks very much. Looking forward to it and hearing about your new job."

I went back to my EVS papers and tried to put my doubts about what I should be doing with Charlie to one side. Looking again at the partners of the VU engineers I suddenly remembered something Harry had said to me. I looked at my watch, he'd be at home so I called him.

"Harry, forgive me for asking but do I remember your saying that your wife had left you?"

"Yes, Peter. About two years ago. I suppose it was partly my fault. I was working too hard and neglecting her."

"Harry, do you and did you go to a lot of conferences?"

"Yes I have to. I learn quite a lot and I also like to tell people what we are doing, particularly airlines."

"Forgive me for asking but did your wife go with you?"

"Yes, of course. What are you getting at?"

"Harry, this is very difficult but I have to exclude everyone from my investigations. Do you mind if I ask you some personal questions."

"Go ahead, if you must."

"Look Harry I don't want to pry into your private life but I have to explore all possible avenues. Do you take your work home?"

"Of course."

"On occasions would you have taken the critical diagrams home."

"Yes."

"Would your wife have recognised what you brought home?"

"Of course, her first degree was in electrical engineering before she got into human resources. What are you suggesting?"

"Harry, I'm compiling a list of suspects. Did you and your wife separate on bad terms?" There was a long pause. "Harry, I'm really sorry but I have to know."

"Yes, our relations deteriorated badly before she left me."

"Was there another man?"

"I don't like this Peter. Yes, she had met the chief engineer of an airline we were hoping would buy our equipment." There was a long pause. "Peter, are you suggesting my wife could have given the information to this guy?"

"Harry, it clearly must be a possibility."

Another very very long pause.

"Are you still there, Harry?"

"Yes, I am. Peter, if you're right I'm absolutely horrified. How can we find out if you are right?"

"I'm not sure. Is this guy still with the airline?"

"Don't know. Obviously I got someone else to deal with them."

"Do you have any contact with your wife? Children?"

"We didn't have any children. No, we have no communication at all."

I asked Harry for all his wife's details and then decided that it was time to stop. "Harry, let me think about what you've just told me and I'll call you to-morrow if that's alright."

Charlie came back full of what she had been doing and I tried to respond. "It's a really great Degas. It's genuine alright but not very well known. I'll call my client after we've had a drink. What have you been up to?"

"Well I've been into your bedroom and got the list of hotels you booked. Not sure where my list is at the moment."

Charlie looked concerned. “My love, what’s wrong. You look as if you’ve seen a ghost?” She looked at my face. “What have you done?”

“It’s alright really, Charlie, I just rang all the hotels and downgraded the rooms.”

“Well you could have fooled me.”

I couldn’t bring myself to tell her how my sense of guilt had returned so I tried to change the subject.

“I had an idea last night.” I told Charlie about my conversation with Harry.

“Without wishing to be indelicate, Mr Talbert, I seem to remember the last time you slept with me you had one of your ideas.”

I responded automatically. “Yes, we must keep it up.”

She grinned and so did I, perhaps a little ruefully as I hadn’t intended making a joke. “I’m not arguing with that.” and then she carried on. “What are you going to do?”

“I’m not sure. I’ll talk to Harry again to-morrow morning first thing our time.”

We went down to the restaurant and had a meal. Up in the bedroom we sat down on the sofa in the living room between the two bedrooms and I held her in my arms.

“Charlie, you’re lovely. You understand me so well but I can’t help feeling very guilty. Forgive me, I must say it. Helen only died a few weeks ago. And the Hotel in Melbourne is just opposite where I stayed when I came out to find her. It all seems wrong.”

“I understand, but you can’t control what happens in life. You’ve got to move on.”

I didn’t say anything but realised that what was happening was probably irreversible. I started to head for my room.

“Peter, don’t sleep alone feeling awful and my bed’s bigger than yours.”

She left me and I decided to follow her sometime later.

In the morning we had a slow breakfast. “Charlie, have you finished with that picture you were looking at? Have you any more work to do?”

“Yes, I’ve got to go the Art Museum and talk to some people there.”

"We'd better go up then and here's my phone."

She went into the bedroom to call her son. She was soon roaring with laughter and it was clearly a great success. Fifteen minutes later she came back and returned my phone. "I had to stop. There was no money left."

"No worries. Kitty will top it up. Off you go."

My UK phone rang. It was Harry. "Peter, I'm sorry if I was being difficult last night. You really shattered me but thinking about things you could well be right. Terrible thought that my wife has ruined my business."

"We don't know that, Harry."

"Peter, the more I think about it, the more certain I am that you're right. I don't know what to do."

"Give me the man's name and airline." There was silence. "Harry I must know if we are going to sort this thing out."

"Pietro Greco and West Shore Airlines based in San Francisco. Our sales campaign with them was going very well up to a couple of years ago and now they barely talk to us. My chief salesman says he's heard there is going to be a sweetheart deal with Total Avionics. Now I realise what must have happened."

"Harry, I'm due back in LA from Sydney in a couple of weeks. I propose to call Greco and make an appointment."

"But what will you say to him?"

"Harry, you hired me to find out what's going on. Trust me. Best you don't know."

I looked at my watch. Greco with any luck would still be in his office.

I logged on and found West Shore Airlines straightaway in the online Yellow Pages and rang them. The operator put me through to Greco's number and his secretary. "Who shall I say is calling and the reason for the call?"

"Peter Talbert. It's a personal matter."

There was a pause and she came back. "He says he only discusses personal matters on his home number or would you write."

"Ask him if he wants me to tell you the reason for my call. He may not want that."

Another pause and Greco came on line. “Mr Tallboy or whatever your name is, you’ve got a cheek threatening my secretary. What do you want.”

“I want to talk to you about your relationship with Total Avionics.”

“What the hell has that got to do with you?”

“I’m in Sydney at the moment. I don’t think it is advisable for us to discuss the matter over the phone. I’m sure when I’ve told you the problem you will agree meeting is the best solution. Your secretary might be listening on the phone.”

There was a pause. “Who do you represent? I’m very busy.”

“Mr Greco, I’m an insurance agent. Hull Claims.”

“We don’t use them.”

“Well Mr Greco if you want me to write down exactly the reason why we should meet and post the letter to you that will be fine by me. I’ll be in Australia for just over two weeks. I can ring you when I get in to LA and then decide how we should proceed. You should have got my letter by then.”

“Alright. What did you say your name was?”

“Peter Talbert. I’ll give you my mobile number if you need to contact me.”

“Let me look in my diary.” There was a pause and then he gave me a date just over two weeks ahead which fitted in well with our schedule.

“Thank you Mr Greco. That’s perfect.”

“I can manage 1100.”

“That will be fine. I’ll call you to reconfirm when I’m back in the States.”

I gave him my contact details, rang off and called Harry. “I’ve spoken to him. He’s seeing me in two weeks time.”

“Does he know what the subject is?”

“Yes. I asked what was his relationship with Total Avionics. He was clearly on the defensive from then on. I threatened to post a letter to him explaining the reason for requesting a meeting and he caved in and gave me the appointment.”

“I’d like to be a fly on the wall at your meeting.”

“Harry, we don’t know for sure yet but I agree the way he acted looked suspicious.”

Charlie came back very tired. “I’ve been looking through all their pictures. My mind’s bursting”

“Hope you took plenty of notes and that you’re not too tired. I’ve arranged for us to go out to dinner with an old friend and colleague of mine and his wife. It’s only a few minutes walk from here. 7pm”

She nodded. “I’ll rest on the bed for bit.”

“Well while you’re resting we need to make some bookings. We‘ve got three days before we go to Canberra and you’ve left a gap in the hotels. What had you planned?”

“Wasn’t sure.”

“Why don’t we go up into the Blue Mountains and stay in Megalong Valley? I’ve only done it once before and all I remember is the stars. There were so many because the sky was so clear and no light pollution.”

“Which of your girl friends were you with?”

“I was on my year out and we didn’t have any girls. Come on. Shall we do it? Mike Mansell, the guy we’re dining with to-night, recommended a place near Blackheath.”

I looked at the place Mike had recommended on the web, Woolshed Cabins. It looked fabulous but I decided to phone. The girl at the other end confirmed the cabin I had chosen was available for three nights and gave me instructions how to find her house to get the key.

We got changed and walked to the Emporis building in George Street. The Australia Square Tower restaurant was on the 47th floor and I was glad I had booked a table as the place was jumping.

“Peter, the place is moving. It’s revolving. How super, we’ll be able to see the whole of Sydney.” She squeezed my hand with pleasure. “You bring me to some lovely places. Thank you.”

“It was your idea to take a holiday.”

I stood up as Mike and Liz appeared and made the introductions. We sat down and the two girls sat down next to one another. I started to protest but Liz would have none of it. “Peter, I know you’ll be talking shop with Mike so it makes much more sense for me to talk to Charlie.”

“But I won’t know what you’ll be saying.”

“You can be very quick, sometimes.”

They seemed very happy with the arrangement so there was no point in arguing. Liz sat next to me. "I'm so sorry about Helen, Peter. Mike told me."

"Thanks." There was nothing more I could say and it was difficult to explain about Charlie. It seemed so callous but it wasn't really like that at all. I didn't believe in fate but meeting Charlie out of the blue couldn't have been just chance.

"And Mike tells me you're getting a new job."

"Yes, Liz. I was very lucky. It's a UK Government job but it doesn't start for some time and you mustn't tell anyone. "

Charlie butted in. "Liz, it wasn't luck at all. Peter spent a long time working out what the job was and how he was going to run it. He had to prepare for and have two gruelling interviews and now he has to think how he is going to deal with all his existing clients."

I looked surprised. "Charlie, you're right. Thank you."

Liz looked at us both. "Peter, you're very lucky."

I nodded as I was beginning to realise just how lucky I really was. We had a great evening. Whilst I was talking to Mike it was clear that Liz and Charlie were getting on like old friends.

Charlie and I watched them catch a cab back to their house at Darling Point and we chatted as we walked back to the hotel.

"Liz tells me it was thanks to you she became a dressmaker."

"Yes, I took her out to dinner as a thank you for helping me and she was wearing a fantastic suit. I asked where she got it and she told me she had made it. When she came over to the UK to give evidence at the Inquiry I took her to Harrods to meet the buyer and the rest is history."

"But she didn't work for Harrods did she?"

"Oh no. She started making clothes back in Australia and then started her own store. I think she's doing well but, like anything else that is successful, it's hard work."

"How's Mike doing?"

"Very well, I think. We didn't really discuss it too much."

We started packing our clothes before we went to bed. Charlie suggested we reorganised our two bags so that we could leave one closed until we reached Canberra. It seemed a sensible idea, particularly as she seemed to be in charge of the packing.

***

In the morning we checked out and made our way into the Blue Mountains along Highway 32 to Blackheath. We bought some wine and some staple foods and then turned left on to Megalong Road where the road rapidly became dirt. We found the house with the keys and the lady showed us the cottage, miles from anywhere in a field but with electrics, water and sewerage. She left us and we looked at one another before we went in. There was absolute silence. It was amazing. We took our few things into the house but we didn't like to disturb the peace. Finally Charlie said "This must be heaven," and I just nodded and embraced her.

We poured ourselves some wine and sat outside watching some sheep in the distance and the skyline gradually disappearing as it got dark. Then the stars appeared, more and more and more. "You were right, my love. It's wonderful. There's Orion's Belt low down in the northern sky but its barely visible because of all the other stars."

It began to get cold and we went in, had something to eat and went to bed. In the morning we walked to the top of a nearby crest and saw the valley stretching for miles out of sight. Then we had breakfast and went into Blackheath. We chatted in the paper shop and were advised to go to Blackheath look-out. There we saw the Kanimbla Valley stretching below us and we thought we could see our cottage. We spent the rest of the day going to other look-out points and in Blackheath my mobile started to work again so she called her boy. Her face was a picture as she chatted with Peter and it was delightful to watch. We spoilt ourselves by having dinner in Blackheath.

It was eerie driving back to the cottage, not a sight or sound of anything else. Charlie got as close as she could with her hand on my thigh. As we got out we again revelled in the silence and almost tiptoed into the house. We lit the stove and made love on the sofa when the room was warm but then it got cold and we went upstairs.

In the morning we got up late, luxuriating with the sun shining through the window directly onto the bed and our bodies. Then we went for a walk round the farm, drove into Blackheath for a sandwich and then back to the look-out. Finally we had supper and lit the fire again but didn't bother to go upstairs though I had to fetch a duvet down.

Next day we packed up, handed over the key and started back towards Sydney and then took the M7 motorway down to the Hume Highway and onwards to Canberra. We had booked at the Rydges Hotel in City for convenience for the meetings I had arranged with people from CASA, Air Services Australia and the Australian Transport Safety Bureau.

"Peter, how much work have you got to do here?" We were sitting in the restaurant looking at the lake. "What am I going to do while you're working?"

"Well you've got to go to the War Memorial. It's fantastic. There are quite a few pictures there but also watch the videos. There is one about the way Australians and New Zealanders helped the UK in bombing Germany in the second world war, G for George. It is fantastic and reminds us all how many lives they lost. It should be compulsory viewing for all British Members of Parliament."

"You'd better not say that if you're going to be working for the UK Government. You might be unpopular."

"Only with the politicians."

"Alright, we'd better not go down that route. What else can I do?"

"Would you believe the National Art Gallery? And if you're desperate you can look at the Mall."

"Not without you."

"Incidentally did you arrange to call your lad earlier tomorrow? I'll have to start at 8.45."

"Yes, I told Cheryl to make sure he's back from school quickly. They finish in the first year at 3pm and so I'll be able to call him just before we have breakfast."

We slept well after the long drive and Charlie took my phone to make her call while I was checking my email. I didn't listen but school was clearly one subject.

Luckily I was in the lobby early waiting for Vince Masella, General Manager Air Transport Operating Group of CASA as he arrived ahead of schedule. "Peter, if it's alright with you I've arranged a room for us to talk in the Australian Transport Safety

Bureau in Mort Street. It will save driving to Phillip. We can walk so I've parked the car opposite here."

"Suits me as I'm meeting Ted Gaillard from Air Services Australia this afternoon."

We walked over to the Bureau, signed in and went to a meeting room. "Peter, we've all been reading about the selection process for your new Transport Safety Board. I gather the woman who was selected decided to back out."

"That's one way of putting it."

"Did you apply?"

There was no point in hiding the situation and I explained that I had applied but I decided not to tell him I'd got the job.

"Yes I did and presumably there will be a new selection."

"Well if you don't get it, the chief executive here retires in about four years. You could apply for that job."

"You mean the Australian Transport Safety Bureau?" He nodded. "That's very interesting but they'll never give the job to a Pom."

"You're probably right but you can always read the required qualifications when the job is advertised. If you managed to get on the short list in the UK you must stand a good chance over here."

"Not at all sure. Anyway don't let's talk about me. What's news over here?"

We discussed the latest issues being driven by new aircraft and technology. The A350 and the Boeing 787 were flying into Australia but they were no problem since the much larger A380 had sorted out the aerodrome issues some years earlier. I raised the subject of VVLJs and licences but Vince dealt mainly with the airlines. Synthetic vision was a certification issue but the Australian airlines had not yet specified the latest equipment. He guessed CASA would follow the FAA procedures. Vince had to leave at midday.

"Peter, it's great seeing you again. Think about the job here. If you qualify it might suit you."

"Vince, thanks so much for coming to see me. Hope to see you again soon."

I called Charlie. "Where are you?"

"I'm just about to leave the War Memorial."

"Well grab a cab and ask for Koko Black. We won't eat there but it's a good meeting place."

She arrived in ten minutes and we went to a café just up the street for a quick sandwich.

"Where are you going next, my love?"

"The National Gallery. How did you get on?"

I told her about the job coming up at the Australian Transport Safety Bureau but she felt as I did that it would have to be an Australian. She went to the cab rank and I walked to Air Services Australia and checked in. Ted came down to meet me and he brought me up to date on the issues facing the authority. Like Vince he asked me about the UK Transport Safety Board and I had to go through the whole thing again but unlike Vince he didn't mention the ATSB job coming up.

When I got back to Rydges there was no sign of Charlie so I went up to our room and showered. She came in and took over in the shower and then we went to the bar for a drink. I could see she had some news. "I really enjoyed the Gallery. I asked for the curator and she gave me a royal tour."

"That's because you're so well know in the art scene."

"Not as well known as you are in aerospace."

"Absolute nonsense. I saw the way they treated you in Christie's"

"Well what I wanted to tell you is that there is a post coming up. They're looking for a director of procurement and it's going to be advertised world wide. She thinks I would be qualified for it if I was interested."

"And are you?"

She looked at me, smiled and held my hand. "We'll just have to see what happens, won't we. There may be jobs in England, who knows." We both knew that our holiday was drawing us closer together and it was not going to be just a fling in the southern hemisphere.

In the morning my mobile phone rang as we were going down to breakfast. It was Pietro Greco.

"Mr Talbert, we need to talk."

"But we're going to talk in a week or so when I get back to the States."

"I can't make that meeting now. There's a Board meeting of the airline and I have to attend. If I travel to-day we can meet in Australia wherever you are and then I can get back."

"But we could talk on the phone now though I'm not sure it would be wise."

"But I've got something to show you which will explain what happened. Where will you be in the next day or so?"

"Well it seems stupid but if you really want to fly out I will be in Melbourne."

"What hotel?"

"The Westin in Collins Street."

"Fine. I'll call you when I get in."

Charlie had been impatiently listening. "What was all that about?"

"It's that guy who gave the VU papers to Total Avionics in Basingstoke. He wants to talk to me in Melbourne. I'm not sure I should have agreed."

"Well as long as it doesn't interfere with our trip down the Great Ocean Road it's alright by me."

After breakfast I kept my appointment with the Director, Aviation Safety Investigation at the ATSB and once again I had to go through the routine of explaining how a new chairman would need to be appointed. Interestingly the subject of the retirement of the Chief Executive wasn't mentioned but I suspected that the Director was going to apply for the job and regarded me as possible competition, not knowing that I already had a job.

I left at midday and called Charlie on her mobile. She had gone back to the National Gallery and I agreed to meet her there. We went to the café and she introduced me to the curator she had met the day before. From the conversation, the curator clearly wasn't going to apply for the job and she had given Charlie an envelope with the details and the application forms.

After lunch Charlie showed me briefly round the Gallery and then we went over to the Mall and through some of the stores. She wasn't really interested and we went back to the hotel. We had a spare day ahead of us and we decided we ought to look at a vineyard. There were at least thirty five near Canberra and the hotel barman advised us to go to Greystones, emphasising his choice by selling us a bottle of red wine to go with our dinner.

We took our time in the morning and after the regulation phone call to New York we managed to get to the winery by about eleven, just in time to taste some wine and have lunch. In the afternoon we went back to Canberra and went for a trip on lake Burley Griffin.

We had a meal in a nearby café which had been recommended to us and then sorted our things out ready for Melbourne.

In the morning we left early and stopped at Gundagai for breakfast. From there we drove all the way along the Hume Highway and then downtown to Collins Street where we passed the Novotel before arriving at the Westin. Charlie could see me remembering again and took over checking in. They only had a double room suite but agreed that they would charge us at the superior twin rate. Our meal was rather quiet and when we went up to the suite I went into the spare room but Charlie came in. She didn't say anything but held me close and we went to sleep.

Charlie had to visit an auction room and two galleries, both in Flinders street and it was going to take two days. On the second day I was waiting with a crowd to cross the road. I felt a huge push in the back and a car knocked me to the ground as I fell forward. I felt an agonising pain in my left upper arm and I lay on the ground wondering what to do. The car had stopped and the driver came over very shaken exclaiming it was impossible to stop. Two policeman arrived almost immediately and listened to his explanation of what had happened. There was no way I could get up; the pain even prevented me from speaking coherently or doing anything else. An ambulance arrived very quickly and two paramedics took me to a hospital. A doctor appeared and I was given a pain killer which left me feeling rather detached as I was taken to a ward, undressed, put in a bed and then taken to have my left arm x-rayed. Some efficient nurse starting taking my details down and somehow I managed to tell them to call the hotel and leave a message for Charlie.

The same doctor who had first examined me re-appeared and told me what I had guessed already, that my upper left arm was broken. Another doctor, who turned out to be an orthopaedic surgeon, arrived and after looking at the x-rays gave me the news that I would need an operation to repair the bone by attaching a metal plate or rod screwed to the bone. Apparently I was very fortunate as they would be able to start the operation in two hours. The doctors disappeared and two nurses got me ready for the theatre. I must have dropped off to sleep and awoke to find Charlie looking at me with great concern.

"What happened, my love?"

"I fell onto a moving car. Bloody lucky it wasn't a lot worse."

"But how?"

"Somebody pushed me."

"What do you mean pushed you? Were there a lot of people?"

"Quite a lot but I think it was deliberate."

Charlie looked at me in disbelief. "You're not serious?"

"I'm not in a joking mood, my love. Look at my arm."

"Have you told the police?"

"I expect they think it was an accident." I paused. "What time is it?"

"Four o'clock. But…"

"Not now, Charlie. They're about to operate. I'll be alright, my love. Go back to the hotel and have a good rest. Carry on with your work and come and see me to-morrow. I'll be full of drugs after the op and probably won't know you but don't worry."

The nurse came back with a form I had to sign agreeing to the operation and the consequences, whatever they might be. Charlie looked at it. "You're signing your life away."

"I'll be signing my life away if I don't sign it. Give me a pen."

With great pain and difficulty I scrawled what was meant to be a signature and the nurse took it away. Charlie stayed until I was being given a knock-out injection for the operation and left looking very worried.

The next thing I knew I was back in the ward still with a pain in my arm. I realised I was being given pain killers and dropped off to sleep. It was all most uncomfortable but the nurses were superb. I was taken for some more x-rays at what I guessed was the following morning which proved to be very painful despite the pain killers. Later the surgeon appeared and told me he had looked at the x-rays and the operation had been a complete success.

He explained, and I tried to listen carefully, that I now had a metal plate in parallel with my upper arm bone, called apparently the humerus. The flesh on the arm had been put back and sewed with absorbable stitches and the wound dressing would be removed after two weeks if it hadn't fallen off first. If all went well I'd be allowed to leave the hospital in about four days but I'd need a sling for six weeks plus regular strong pain killing drugs for about a week and then ibuprofen for another three weeks probably. The arm would need x-raying after the six weeks before the sling was removed and then I'd almost certainly need some physiotherapy.

Despite my discomfort and being drugged I was able to follow what he was saying and my mind was, if not exactly racing, trying to think out all the implications.

"But the plate. When does that come off?"

"Why do you want it off?"

"Surely it can't be a good thing to leave it there. Must get in the way."

"Depends. Shouldn't inconvenience you but removing it traditionally is quite a big operation. However at your age it should be possibly to do it and it may be possible to remove it arthroscopically without having to do a full operation. Still that decision is at least six months away, probably a year, depending on the knitting of the fracture."

Having pronounced my future he left feeling very satisfied with himself. Luckily I dozed off to awake seeing Charlie looking wonderful in a short pullover and fairly short shorts. She had a bag in which I guessed were some of my clothes. She saw I was awake and bent down to kiss me.

"How do you feel?"

"You look great."

"Only politicians answer a question with a question."

"It wasn't a question. It was a statement of fact."

"You must be feeling a bit better. You're arguing with me. How do you feel?"

"Not too good, but I could be worse I suppose. But I'm going to have to have a sling for six weeks."

"Better than a coffin forever."

"But a sling?"

"What colour would you like?"

I reached for her hand. "You're great. What on earth are we going to do, now I'm in this mess?"

"You're going to get better and then we're going on the Great Ocean Road, you, me and the slings."

"Slings?"

"You'll never keep one clean for six weeks."

"How did you know I was alright?"

"How do you think? I called in the evening after the op and again this morning."

The nurse came in to give me another pain killer and Charlie got up ready to go. "I've finished my work and told Wendy, you remember, my boss," I nodded, " that I'll be delayed a week. She's seeing if she can get me some work out here. I'll come and see you in the morning. Sleep well, my love."

Time drifted by and though my arm hurt a bit the pain killers did a good job and I managed to get some sleep. Charlie appeared at about 10am and she looked even better than the day before. She saw me looking at her. "I think you're on the mend. Have you tried walking?"

"Only to the loo."

"Well that's a good start."

"What about Greco?"

"What about Greco?"

"Did he call? He said he was coming here to talk."

"No-one has tried to call you."

I thought about that for a bit and then changed the subject. "I haven't told my travel insurance people. I think my wallet and the rest of my things are in the cupboard here." I tried to point down to the left of my bedside.

Charlie found the wallet and my insurance card. "Well, darling, I'll bring your netbook in to-morrow. Do you need anything to read? The moment you feel better you're going to be impossible and trying to get out before you're ready."

"I don't suppose they have wifi here. Could you download Aviation Week for me at the hotel?"

"Only if you give me your username and password."

As she left a policeman appeared together with a man in plain clothes who seemed to be in charge and who I judged to be a detective. He asked if I felt able to talk and I nodded.

"Mr Talbert, can you remember what happened?"

"I was waiting to cross the road to the tramway with a lot of other people. There was a stream of cars and just as a grey one was coming along I felt a push in the back and I couldn't stop myself going forward."

"Do you really think you were pushed?"

"I was pushed alright."

"Was it deliberate?"

I was expecting the question but I didn't feel able to share my suspicions with them. "It felt like it but it's going to be impossible to find the culprit."

"Why would anyone want to hurt you?"

"Kill me. It was miracle I got away with just a broken bone."

The detective looked at me. "I've been looking you up, Mr Talbert. You're a global aviation insurance investigator. It seems to me that you might well have people who might want to do you harm. Have you?" I hesitated. "What are you working on at the moment Mr Talbert?"

"Look Mr." He gave me his name. "Mr Fisher, I might have my suspicions but I can't prove anything."

"We have a first class computer based visa system. If your suspects are foreign nationals we can soon find out if they were over here."

I hesitated and asked for a pen and a paper. I wrote down some names and gave them to Fisher. "But even if one of them did try to kill me they may have hired a local here."

"Mr Talbert, no doubt you are a super detective in your business. Let us do the detective work in ours."

Fisher shook hands with me very carefully and they left. I realised that I had given away a lot more than I intended.

A special nurse came in and gave me instructions on how to use the sling and how to clean myself without washing off the dressing. I was being encouraged to start walking and I realised that this was vital if I was going to escape from the hospital. Armed with my sling I started exploring the place though the arm was still very painful.

The following morning I felt a lot better and was up and dressed by the time Charlie arrived. “Great to see you up but don’t overdo it. When are they going to allow you out?”

“Not sure. The surgeon is coming to see me this afternoon after some more x-rays. Probably the day after to-morrow if all is well.”

“Good. Your insurance is under control. If your credit card can stand it, pay the bills and the firm will repay you. However if you can persuade the surgeon to bill the insurance company direct that would be much better.”

“How are you managing?”

“Very well. I’m seeing some paintings here this afternoon on behalf of the Nation Gallery in Canberra. The curator called me via New York.”

“That’s very good. Off you go.”

The surgeon came, still very pleased and it was agreed I could leave in two days. He prescribed special pain killers on a reducing dose and then change to ibuprofen. We talked about fees and we agreed that he would send me his invoice to Charlie in New York.

“By the way there’s something I forgot to mention. You’ll set off the security screens at the airports. We can give you a bit of paper if you like but you might just as well get used to it and it will be a lot quicker if you let the guys scan you.”

“Well that’s a good reason for having the plate removed.”

“Your choice.”

The following morning someone from the hospital accounting section came to see me and again we agreed that the bill should be sent to New York. Charlie came to see me and was obviously delighted to see that I was improving fast. We arranged that I would spend the following night in the hotel and then we would be on our way.

Next day I said good bye to all the nurses who had looked after me and Charlie watched over me as I walked slowly but steadily to the entrance with my arm in a sling. Back in the hotel she put me in the coffee shop and went up to our room to dump my gear.

She came back looking concerned. “Peter, were you really pushed? Who on earth would want to do that?”

“Pietro Greco for one. He didn’t want the fact that he gave the papers to Tommy Tucker to come out. Remember, he called me in Canberra and checked where we were staying? He said he would call when he got to Melbourne but he hasn’t called. He could have waited until I came out of the hotel and then pushed me when the opportunity arose. I’ve not met him so I wouldn’t recognise him.”

“Was he trying to kill you?”

“Presumably or put me out of action. Just as well we weren’t waiting for a tram. I got away very lightly.”

Charlie thought for a moment. “Do you think he’s still here.”

“No. He would have run out of time if he was here.”

“Did you tell the police?”

“Yes, I was forced to. There was a detective who came to see me and who caught me off guard. Bit weak I suppose.”

“Are you sure it’s alright to go on tour. We could fly home and you can rest there.”

“I’m not sure resting would be a good idea. I’d go mad. I’m alright but you may have to help me dress and cut up my food. See how we go. Oh, wash me as well so I don’t get the dressing wet.”

“That could be fun.” Charlie smiled and kissed me. “No worries. It will be a pleasure. Thank goodness you’re safe but this is the second attack in a few weeks.”

“I know. Perhaps it’s just as well I’m changing my job.”

***

In the morning Charlie helped me get up. Sleeping hadn’t been easy since I had to lie on my back and it was difficult to move. I couldn’t shower but had to hand wash myself with Charlie helping. We checked out of the hotel and loaded the car but it took a lot longer than usual.

We had about five days left of our holiday and we decided to do a circular tour down to Philip Island to look at the penguins, the seals and the Koalas. When we got to the cottage where we were staying I called Pietro Greco’s secretary. I explained I had been ill, suggested a new date in five days time and asked her to confirm the meeting by text message.

We spent the next day going round the Island and then went across the Queenscliff-Sorrento ferry to the Great Ocean Road. After a day or so I managed to do more and more by myself but getting a shirt on was not easy. On the Sunday we stayed in a cottage at Aireys Inlet and drove to the lighthouse. As we walked down the path to the look-out point I felt a strange premonition. It was weird. My heart started to beat faster as I looked down and saw the long empty beach with its white gleaming sands stretching for miles and the sea breaking on the shore with its incredibly bright foam.

I knew immediately it was the one I had seen in my dreams with Helen and Charlie walking along the sand. I held Charlie as close as I could as we looked down on the beach. She looked at me but didn't say anything; she could see I was feeling very emotional. I felt almost afraid.

I whispered in her ear just above the roar of the surf. "Charlie, I've been here before, in my dreams." She didn't move. "I was with you both. It's unbelievable."

I looked down and saw that further, in the distance, it looked as if it might be possible to get down to the beach and Charlie agreed to take me there without arguing. She helped me to stand on the sand, just the two of us, alone on the deserted sand with just the roar of the surf. It was uncanny, almost unreal.

Instinctively I knew that Helen was leaving me forever and would remain just an unforgettable memory. The time had come to look forward and not back. I took Charlie's hand again and we went to the restaurant just across the road from the cottage, ordered our meal and I ordered champagne without asking.

"I'm not sure, my love, you should be drinking alcohol with the pills you're taking."

"It's a special occasion." I looked at her steadily. "Charlie, I've got a proposal to make."

"Go ahead."

"I've just made it."

I thought she looked surprised but very pleased at the same time. "Did you forget something?"

"Oh. I love you. I thought that was obvious.

"You're amazing."

"Do I take that as a yes?"

"Tell me about your dream, darling. Had you really never been there before?"

"Never. It's my first time on the Great Ocean Road."

"It's amazing."

"Perhaps there really are more things in heaven and earth, Charlie, than are dreamt of in our philosophy.

She looked at me and smiled. "You really are lovely and I think I really do love you but, my darling, I seem to remember you saying to me in St Antony after we'd found the paintings 'I'm afraid we've got to climb our own separate ladders now.'"

"Well I was wrong, Charlie."

"Peter, you're gorgeous and kind and thoughtful but you live in England and I live in New York with a boy you haven't even seen. He may not like you and then where would we be?"

"Of course he'll like me. There's nothing to dislike. What are you smiling for?"

"Look my love, we're having a lovely holiday together in more ways than one, and one way is super, but we've got to find a modus vivendi or it won't make sense. If we get married it's got to be for better and not worse, if that's possible." I suppose I looked a bit disappointed, rebuffed and surprised but she added, smiling. "But don't give up asking. I might give you a definite answer one day." She emptied her glass, got up and we went back to the cottage.

As was now standard practice Charlie helped me get into bed. She looked down at me carefully. "How are you going to be able to manage? Aren't you meant to be going to San Francisco to meet Greco or whatever his name is?"

"That's been worrying me. However, he told me he wouldn't be there. Not that I believe him. When do you have to be back?"

"In about four days but I expect I could negotiate. Would you like me to come with you to San Francisco?"

"I'd love you to if he's there. Putting it another way, I can't go without you." She stroked my face and I looked at her again. "I think you'd better move and get into bed or I might hurt my arm. I'm definitely getting better"

***

We left early and drove to Melbourne airport like a comfortably married couple. I suddenly realised our bags were all mixed up but luckily it wouldn't matter since I was relying on Charlie for the next few weeks. I suppose I had thought of going back to UK but that was clearly a non-starter for the moment. We checked in, comfortably on time, and Charlie had to work hard dealing with the bags by herself. There was only a short delay getting through security, dealing with my arm. In the lounge I managed to text Pat at VU asking her to send my bag to the LA Marriott and re-confirm the Greco meeting.

The flight left on time and we arrived the same morning due to the date change. Neither of us got much sleep because it was difficult to rest comfortably with my arm even though the seat reclined fully and Charlie was determined to look after me.

At LA Charlie again worked very hard dealing with the bags by herself. However she had insisted on requesting a cart to take us along the interminable walkways since I was only moving at half speed. She got us to the taxi line and after that things got easier. While we were waiting she chatted to Peter before he went off to school.

In the apartment I lay on the bed and considered what to do next. I called Greco's secretary and she put me through. "Mr Greco, I thought you told me you were not going to be able to meet me because you would be away?"

Greco sounded strange but I couldn't decide what was the matter. "But we're now meeting a week later."

"Alright then I'll be up to have a chat in the morning."

"I thought you wouldn't be able to come"

"Why shouldn't I be able to come? What made you think that, Mr Greco? We clearly have a lot to discuss."

"I think we should cancel the meeting."

"Mr Greco, I'm sure you realise that the matter we need to discuss is best not done in a court room."

"Whose talking about a court room?"

"I am and so will everybody else in the aircraft industry. If you take my advice you had better meet me."

Greco was clearly undecided but gave in. “Alright, eleven o’clock to-morrow.”

With the meeting with Greco confirmed there was a lot to be done. I was still able to use my netbook, mostly with one finger and I started by getting Charlie on the same flight as mine to San Francisco.

She was watching me. “How long are we going to be there?”

“Not more than a day. Maybe we can fly overnight to New York to-morrow. Tell you what. Let’s call Luggage Forwarding now and get rid of at least two bags. We’ll be in New York by the time they arrive and if we’re held up in won’t matter.”

“Let’s get rid of all the bags and we’ll be able to manage with just your roller which I can handle. Give me half an hour before you call them and I’ll sort everything out.”

She was as good as her word and the bags were picked up in the middle of the afternoon. We had a quiet day and ate in the coffee shop; as a matter of regular routine I tried to arrange my diet so that Charlie didn’t have to cut things up for me.

Lying in bed thinking things over, I felt pretty sure now that Greco had passed the papers over to Total Avionics though somewhat apprehensive if he had indeed pushed me into the car, trying to kill me.

All of a sudden I remembered what Roger O’Kane had said in Seattle. I made a note that I needed to have another look at Echo Victor.

Chapter 12

We had to get up early in the morning to catch our flight because of the time it took to get me washed, shaved, and dressed. At the airport I called Pat to speak to Harry but he wasn't in the plant. She told me as far as she knew nothing had changed in the three weeks I had been away. The flight left on time for San Francisco and without any bags to claim we were soon out of the airport. We managed to find a cab to get us to West Shore Airlines maintenance, but understandably the driver we found was not very pleased as it was only on the other side of the airport by North Field Road. We went to reception and the girl checked with Greco's office that I was expected. Charlie disappeared to the restrooms and I sat in the lobby; to my surprise Greco himself appeared and indicated that we should sit in a corner at a table by the window.

He was dark, well built, about forty fiveish and I guessed probably quite attractive to the ladies. He had obviously spent some time and money at the dentist since some gold dental work was visible when he smiled, not that that happened very often during our meeting.

I could see he was looking at my arm in the sling. "How did you get that?"

"Don't you know?"

"Of course I don't know. Why should I?'

"Do you want me to tell you?" He looked very uncomfortable.

"Mr Greco. Since we spoke some one attacked me from behind and tried to kill me in Melbourne and I was very lucky to escape as you can see."

"That's terrible. Did you catch the person?"

"Mr Greco, when I asked to talk to you the first time I was just going to talk about the papers you gave to Total Avionics. Now of course things are much more serious. You wanted to come and see me in Melbourne and asked me where I was staying. I think you did come and see me and tried to kill me pushing me in front of a car."

Greco looked terrible and very frightened. "This is absolute nonsense. I never went to Australia. And I don't know what you're talking about giving papers to Total Avionics."

"We'll come to that in minute. May I check with your secretary that you haven't been to Australia? That you haven't been away anywhere? That you really did have a Board meeting?"

Greco realised that he was caught. He clearly didn't want me to talk to his secretary. "No you can't talk to my secretary. I changed my mind and decided not to see you in Australia."

"But you didn't tell me that the meeting we're having to-day could still take place. You knew how to contact me. Tell me, were you ever alerted to attend a Board meeting?"

"I told you. Of course I was."

"Well Mr Greco, the situation is that I've told the Australian police that you knew my movements and that I suspected you were the one that pushed me. I must warn you that they are thinking of coming to visit you so you'd better get your story straight. Even if you won't tell me the truth you'll have to tell them."

"I've told you the truth."

"Which bit? That you didn't go to Australia or that you were going to a Board meeting?"

"Alright you can ask my secretary if you like. I've been here all the time and there wasn't a Board meeting. I was just trying to put you off coming here."

"Before I talk to your secretary let's discuss the original reason why I've come to see you." Greco looked as if he knew he was in more trouble as I changed tack. "I've been doing some work with Vision Unlimited looking at their latest EVS system. I gather you saw the early version of the system while it was being developed a couple of years ago."

Greco started to look very uncomfortable and I guessed that he wouldn't be able to brazen things out if he indeed had given stolen information to Total Avionics. He tried to say something but I interrupted. "Why don't you let me finish? You might say something you wish you hadn't." He started to bluster but I held my hand up. "Look if you take my advice and don't want to get in even more serious trouble you'd better let me finish. I've visited the Total Avionics facility in Basingstoke, England, saw Tommy Tucker and looked at their EVS system and it struck me that they couldn't have got to the technical situation they are in to-day with their system unless they had got some help. Their architecture is almost identical with Vision Unlimited."

Greco tried to rally. "Well it would be, Mr Talbert, since both firms are trying to do the same thing."

"True but bearing in mind when Total Avionics started the project, the development time is impossible."

"How do you know when they started. Tucker told me they have been working at the system longer than Vision Unlimited."

"Oh, so you know Mr Tucker?"

Greco realised he had already spoken unwisely and he tried to recover. "Of course I do. Our airline is considering buying their system."

"What made you change your plan of buying from Vision Unlimited?"

"Oh, we never intended to buy from Vision Unlimited, we just wanted to see where they were up to."

"Well the problem I have with this situation is that the chief project engineer allowed me to see the project start date and the actual development hours spent on the project which were very different from the figures in the booklet that Tommy Tucker showed me. The figures were minuscule compared with the Tucker booklet. They had obviously been given key design information."

"Who did you say you worked for? Hull Claims?"

"No Mr Greco, I have been retained by Vision Unlimited to find out how Total Avionics got their information and of course it wasn't very difficult to find out, was it?"

Greco started to perspire. "You can't prove anything."

"It wouldn't look too good in court while the lawyers were interrogating you as a witness, would it?"

Greco said nothing and was clearly wondering what to do and say. "What are you suggesting Mr Talbert."

"If you sign a document admitting that you gave Total Avionics the documents you got from your wife, then you may be lucky and not called into the witness box. It will all depend on Total Avionics, but my guess is that the Chief Executive of the whole company won't want their reputation ruined because the people in Basingstoke broke the law. Remember, the stuff you handed over covered quite a few patents."

Greco was very quiet for about ten minutes and looked at his watch. “I guess I don’t have much alternative do I?” I made no comment. “Do you have a form of wording?”

I produced four copies of a form I had prepared in Melbourne while on the first day while Charlie had been working, before I had been attacked. “Mr Greco, if you sign this form I will certainly try to prevent this matter going to court. Apart from anything else if lawyers get involved they will bleed us all white and Vision Unlimited can’t afford it.”

Greco signed the form. “Mr Greco, we’ll have to have it witnessed. I don’t think we should use your receptionist.”

I went over to an airline captain who was just leaving, showed him my card and asked if he would do us a favour and witness the document. I was in luck as the guy recognised my name and knew the story of the aircraft that had disappeared a few years back flying to Bermuda. Greco listened as the captain started talking about it all and I saw him staring at me in new light. The captain witnessed the signatures and left obviously delighted at meeting me.

I gave Greco a copy of the form he had signed. “Now about the attack on me in Melbourne you’d better get your story right about Australia.”

“I told you I didn’t go. I’ll take you up to my secretary now.”

I looked at my watch. “I’m pressed for time right now. I’m happy to leave it to the police. As he turned to leave he stared at me. “Tucker told me to be careful of you. He must have known who you were.”

As he disappeared into the elevator Charlie appeared from somewhere. “I wouldn’t like to get on your wrong side, even with a bad arm.”

“Where were you watching from? Anyway he was a cheat.”

“And a potential murderer.”

“I’m not sure. I think I believe him when he said he didn’t go to Australia but I suppose he might have hired someone. Mind you I don’t think he has the balls. Anyway I think he’s very frightened. I told him the Australian police were coming to see him.”

“Are they?”

“I don’t know. All’s fair in love and war.”

"Nonsense and you'd better be very careful if that's what you think. What happens now?"

"I ring Harry."

I called Pat and this time Harry was in. I explained about the document I had.

"Peter I bless the day I decided to call you. What can I say and do?"

"The first thing Harry is don't tell anyone what is happening. I'll explain why when I see you." He muttered agreement. "The second thing is have you got an aircraft free to collect us so I can give you the papers and discuss what you want to do next?"

"Who is us?"

"My partner who currently has to travel with me as I've got a broken bone in my arm."

Harry said he'd call me back and he did almost immediately. "We're going to spoil you. Chuck is coming up with the Raytheon 800. Go to the fixed base operator on the north side of the field and wait in the pilots' lounge. We'll get a message to you. He reckons he can be there in two hours from a standing start."

The girl at the desk organised a car to take us to the FBO and we grabbed a couple of sandwiches and looked at the TV. Chuck was better than his estimate and I was paged to meet the aircraft. He kept the engines running but he had moved over so I could sit in the left hand seat. I showed him my arm and he got back into the left hand seat. I motioned for Charlie to go in the front and he agreed. She got comfortable in the right hand seat and I sat behind watching. We were soon on our way and an hour later we taxied in and Chuck shut the engines down. "I don't know what's going on but Harry seemed very excited. Do you think you know how the information was leaked?"

"I believe so but we need to try to settle the matter without anything becoming public. The fewer people who know the better."

We walked into the pilots' lounge. He asked about my arm but I wasn't about to give him any real details. Chuck left us and I went to see Harry who rushed out and welcomed us into his office. I introduced Charlie who went to talk to Pat, full of herself and the flight she'd just had. Harry wanted to know how I damaged my arm but I decided not to tell him my suspicions. Instead I opened my bag, found my leather document case and took out the forms that Greco had signed. Harry read one and beamed. "Peter, fantastic. That should satisfy any judge."

"Harry, surely that's not what we want to do? In my view the last thing you need to do is to go to Court. How well do you know Matt Watkins?"

"Fairly well. We often meet at conferences."

"Well as I told you, my theory is that he doesn't know what Basingstoke has done. I think you should go along and see him and show him this document that Greco has signed and try to come to an agreement."

"For money you mean?"

"Not at all. You don't need money. What you need is for them to stop working and selling their version of your EVS."

"They'll never do that."

"Don't bet on it."

Harry thought about all this. "Peter, I need you to come with me."

"Wouldn't you prefer a lawyer?"

"Let's keep them out of it. You'll be better than any lawyer I can think of. You know the technology as well as the deviousness of human nature."

"Where does Matt work? Presumably it is the head office?"

"New Jersey. Actually Newark."

"Alright here's the deal. If you buy me a cab we'll take a red eye special to New York to-night and I'll stay in New York until you come over and then we'll both go to see Matt. I'll charge you of course for to-day, the extra day in Melbourne I had working for you and for any days I work for you in the future."

"Peter, you're on. Financially you are being incredibly honest. Most people would rip me off or demand a huge bonus."

"Well I really should have negotiated a bonus on this job. To be honest I feel I should have one but I'm aware you haven't sold anything yet. Here's another deal. You pay me a bonus when you make your second sale."

"Peter, you'll never be a success in business. You're too fair."

"Harry I'm delighted to help but the delayed payment doesn't apply to my expenses which will include a half a trip to New York, business class."

"Why only half a trip?"

"Because I was going there anyway Harry, unexpectedly, with Charlie and my original return ticket is from here to Heathrow not via New York. You'll have to pay that ticket, of course, as well as the extra segment."

"Whatever you say, Peter. I'll pay by return. When do you need a cab to LA?"

"I'll let you know when we've got a flight. Maybe Pat could do that for us since you're going to pay half."

"We'll pay full fare and stop quibbling."

"Charlie's already got a ticket providing it's the right airline. Pat can ask her."

Pat sorted it out and booked us on an American Airlines flight leaving at 10pm getting in at 6.30 in the morning at JFK. Harry insisted we had an early bird special and Pat organised a cab to take us to the airport from the restaurant. He promised to let me know when Matt Watkins could see us.

Everything worked like clockwork. We got a cab straightaway to Charlie's apartment though the traffic was heavy early in the morning going into New York.

"We need some sleep. Neither us slept too well on the flight. Can we rest together? What sort of beds do you have?"

"I have a very large double, King size."

"In UK that's not very large."

She looked at me as if sizing me up. "It's big enough for me, well over six foot wide. There probably will be room for you as well but my advice to you is not to get too excited or sleepy for that matter, until Peter has gone to school."

"With my arm there is no point in getting excited, in case you hadn't noticed."

"Abstinence makes the heart grow fonder."

"I'm not sure you've got the quotation quite right."

We arrived on East 73rd Street to a very upmarket looking block. We went up to the third floor and the moment we got in Charlie called Cheryl. A few minutes later there was a knock on the door and a lady appeared who I assumed rightly to be Cheryl plus a young girl called Sonia and a very enthusiastic boy who almost knocked Charlie over in his excitement. Cheryl and I shook hands and started chatting while Peter quietened down and, as he talked to Charlie, I could see he was eyeing me, trying to make up his mind where I fitted in.

Cheryl looked at her watch, Charlie nodded. "Thanks Cheryl for taking him to school. Off you go. See you this evening. Not sure what time as I don't know what we're going to be doing to-day."

Cheryl left with the two children and as they went out she turned to me. "That wasn't quite true was it? I'd better help you get ready for bed. Pity you can't help me in your condition."

But I wasn't listening. "He's a great little lad, Charlie. You're doing a great job."

"Yes. I am very lucky."

"Does the father help with the maintenance?"

"Peter, don't let's go down that road. What's over is over. You have to love us, warts and all. I do what I have to do with regard to Peter."

"But it must cost you a bomb."

"Peter, in case you hadn't noticed I'm a well paid executive and I can manage. The trouble with you is that you are old fashioned and don't believe in single mothers."

"No I don't. It's not fair on the children."

"Is that why you proposed to me?"

I look aghast. "Charlie, you don't think that do you."

She grinned and undid her skirt in a very provocative way and let it drop to the floor, showing her black stockings, suspenders and tiny black underpants. She turned her back to me and slowly bent down to pick up the skirt.

"It's not fair your doing that. Do you want me to break my arm again?"

"Just testing."

***

"What time does Peter come home?"

"3.30pm. What time is it?"

"Time we got up. It's 2pm. I don't know about you but I slept like a log."

"So did I. Look I've put your things in the closet there. You can use that part in the corner and those shelves."

I felt like saying 'is that where he put his clothes' but decided anything to do with the other guy was off limits if our relationship was going to prosper. I managed to wash myself though I had to be very careful not to get the arm and its wrappings wet.

Cheryl, Sonia and Peter arrived shortly after 3.45pm and the children had our undivided attention for a couple of hours while they had tea and told us about school. Charlie took them off for a bath and then read to both of them for a bit. Then Cheryl took Sonia off and Charlie put Peter to bed.

"Where does Cheryl live?"

"Down the corridor in another apartment. Her husband went off with another woman and as he is very well off she got a fantastic settlement. She probably won't have to work again but she loves helping me with Peter, the two children get on so well together."

"You're very lucky but it's a rotten life for her. Doesn't she want to get married again?"

"Only if Mr Right comes along but how Mr Right is going to find her I don't know."

"We need to take her out a bit. Do you have baby sitter?"

"I use an agency but insist on the same girls, Susan, or Babs as a back up. If they're not available then I don't go out." She stopped and carried on. "I love the way you think about Peter and me and Cheryl and Sonia. In spite of everything I think you're very kind at heart."

"Not sure I like the caveat 'in spite of everything'. Seriously, let's take her out. Somewhere where she can be seen. I think she would scrub up very nicely."

"I agree but don't get too enthusiastic or you're on your own."

"We can't go out to-night. What are we going to do about food?"

"I thought I'd cook for you."

"Great. Are you going to ask Cheryl to join us?"

"I hadn't planned to but I will if you like."

"Well she's worked hard for you while you've been away. It might be rather nice."

Charlie kissed me. "You really are lovely but don't get any ideas."

She called Cheryl who was delighted. She brought Sonia with her and put her in the other bed in Peter's room. I guessed this was a fairly standard routine. "Why don't I ring for some pizzas. That way we can talk and we don't all have to stand in the kitchen."

Charlie took our orders and then rang the restaurant. "Peter, wine is in the fridge or over there in the rack. I'll have red." I looked at Cheryl and we all had red.

"Not sure I can do it even though it's a screw top."

Charlie helped and then lifted her glass. "Here's to us, all five of us." We echoed her toast and then Charlie kissed me, as if to make sure. We told Cheryl about our trip and she told us what the children had been up to.

Cheryl looked at my arm. "How did you do that?"

"I was run over by a car."

Charlie joined in. "Somebody tried to kill him."

Cheryl looked alarmed. "Why? How?"

"Somebody pushed me hard when I was in the front of a crowd trying to cross the road."

"Do you know who? Did you get him?"

"No, I was lying on the ground unable to move. I was very lucky. An ambulance arrived very quickly and the hospital was superb." I decided to change the conversation and to push my luck. "Isn't a bit dull here? I suppose you manage to get away by yourself occasionally."

"Why should I go on holiday by myself?"

"Surely you need a change from children once in a while? Do you need help with Sonia? I'm sure it must be possible to sort something out between us."

Understandably Cheryl looked surprised but Charlie joined in. "You know, he's right. It's one of his worst faults. Why not go on a cruise, first class somewhere, and find a toy boy?"

She grinned. "Charlie, you know it's not a bad idea but I'd prefer a real man, not a toy boy. Where shall I go?"

I butted in. "Fly to Fiji and then go to New Zealand and Oz."

"Why and when?"

"The Caribbean and Hawaii are cruised out, in my opinion. You don't get so ripped off when you go ashore down there. And you must go to Sydney and Circular Quay." Charlie nodded. "Get a travel agent to find a boat for you. But don't economise too much. Take your best clothes and dazzle them."

Cheryl looked at Charlie. "Do you know what you've got hold of here?" She looked me up and down. "He's full of ideas."

Charlie nodded. "Yes, I know. I'm not sure what to do about it."

Cheryl smiled at her and grinned at me. "Well you'd better not be too long deciding."

The pizzas arrived and we had a nice evening, shifting two bottles of wine. I was getting tired in spite of our rest during the day. Cheryl left leaving Sonia with us. "I'll be round early to get her up and get her ready for school."

My parting shot was "Don't forget the cruise."

As I nearly dropped off to sleep Charlie dug me in the ribs. "That was very nice of you to offer my services to look after Sonia while you'll be in London."

"How do you know I won't still be here? It depends when she goes, what I'm doing and whether you're going to accept my oft repeated offer. Anyway, if there's a problem I might come over specially."

"All right. I'm holding you to that."

"I know but I've thought of something else."

"Not now."

"I can't stop myself thinking."

"You should be thinking what I'm thinking."

"Well I've remembered that I need to call New York State University in the morning."

"Well that's not what I'm thinking."

In the morning everything was different. Cheryl and Charlie swung into action getting Sonia and Peter up, washing them, dressing them, feeding them and getting them off the school just in time. Charlie put on her working suit, kissed me goodbye and was gone.

"Will you be able to manage?"

"I've got all day to try."

I got washed and dressed after a struggle but I was definitely getting more adept at doing it. Just as I finished the phone rang; the bags had arrived from Luggage Forwarding. I didn't know the telephone code to let the man into the building so I collected the door key which Charlie had given me and went down in the elevator to let him in. I could see our bags through the glass entrance and so I operated the door. The courier was a large dark lady and she soon got the three bags into the elevator and then into the apartment. I got her to put the bags on the floor so I could open them.

The only bag I could open was mine and I decided to take my clothes and put them on the shelves that Charlie had indicated to me. Then I sat down and started to think about my relationship with Charlie and how we could make a go of it. My deliberations were interrupted by Harry coming on line.

"Peter, I've spoken to Matt and explained the situation as best I could. He was very cool but agreed that we should meet to discuss things. However he's away in China for the next week."

"When can he manage?"

"Eight days time."

"Alright Harry, I'll be around."

When he rang off I called New York State University in Albany and got put through to Professor John Corrigan in the Material Sciences faculty. I explained my interest in the Castle Harbour Airlines European 630 wreckage and asked if I could visit on Monday.

"Peter, we'd be delighted to help you. You're in luck in two ways; first we got a good deal and we saved transportation costs by putting the fuselage near Union City, New Jersey and, secondly, we've sawn off the back end of the fuselage so you can clamber along the inside. We've got it under cover but it will be an obstacle course to get to the front."

"John, I've got a damaged arm at the moment. Is there any way I can look in the flight deck or what remains of it from the outside?"

"Well we've cut a few holes in the fuselage to examine the skin so you may be lucky."

"Fine. Where should I tell the cab to take me?"

"Peter, I'm spending the week-end in Manhattan. I'll take you to the site. Where can I collect you?"

We finalised the arrangements and rang off just as Cheryl came in with Peter and told me Charlie wasn't going to be back until sixish. "Can you look after him and put him down? I've got something I need to do." And she was gone.

Peter wasn't the least put out and produced a book for me to read to him about animals. Charlie came back in the middle of the session which caused it to end prematurely. She finally got him to settle down and shut the door.

"Charlie, you look as if you could use a drink."

"Only a triple G&T."

I wondered if she was joking as I gingerly started the operation though opening the tonic bottle was a challenge. I decided that doubles were the order of the day though she clearly was not intending to stop me. We sat down.

"Peter, I'm not sure I like going away. There's so much to do when you get back."

"Any good pictures been stolen while you've been away?"

"No, thank goodness, but we've got a lot of new business and it's necessary to be so careful that we're not being used for an 'insurance job'." I raised my eyebrows. "You know, being asked to insure pictures which are not genuine, or not owned by the client or similar scams. What have you been doing?"

"Talking to Harry and sorting my calendar out. I'll have to go back to England to sort out my contract and the new job. They've got my proposals but the deal has got to be consummated. Problem is that I daren't go by myself as I'm frightened of damaging my arm before it has set properly."

"How long would we be away if I come with you?"

"Well in UK probably two days."

"My love, you know I'll come. I'm sure Wendy will understand and maybe I can find a job to do. When do we go?"

"Well I've got to be back in time to go with Harry to Total Avionics. How about Tuesday night?"

Charlie checked her diary. “I’ll have to work Tuesday but that’s no big deal. You’re on. Why not Monday as a matter of interest?”

“I told you. I’m going to Union City New Jersey to look at the wreckage again.”

“You never give up.”

“You’re right. Will you marry me?”

“A definite maybe.”

“In that case I’ll check in the morning that Henry Denis will be available.”

“Make certain they pay you properly. I know you. You’ll take on the job because you want to do it.” I looked at her and stopped for a moment. She noticed straight away. “What have I just said that upset you?”

“Nothing really. It’s just that your remark was so like Helen. Forgive me for mentioning it.” She squeezed my hand. “Don’t worry. It takes a long time to get over things. You need to be doing something else. When will the job start?”

“I’m not sure yet. It won’t be for a couple of months, I think. Probably on 1st January. There’s something else I haven’t told you. They’re paying me a lot more than the advertised salary plus I suspect good bonuses. It’ll probably match what I’m getting at the moment but I won’t have to work so hard. And of course the pension is fantastic, gold plated.”

“That’s great. I can stop work.” I shook my head.

I told her of my deal with Harry. “You’ve done well, Peter, and you’re very fair. You wouldn’t last a minute in the art world.”

“We don’t have a deal yet. By the way what happened to that picture of Morrison’s on the flight that ditched?”

“It’s being done but has to take its place in the line. The guy doing it has more work than he can handle.”

“Is there a leak in your glass? It’s empty.”

“Well try filling it up again and see what happens.”

“I’m not sure I’m strong enough.”

“It will be fun trying.”

“Not in my condition. Have you eaten anything at all to-day?”

“Had an egg sandwich.”

I got up and had a look in the freezer part of the fridge. There were some lamb chops and some frozen vegetables.

"Can I get you something? If I'm careful I think I can manage this electric wok and the steamer."

We carried on chatting while I produced the food. "I can't find mint sauce."

"Where do you think you are, UK? You can see Cranberry."

"Is that Kosher?"

"It is to-night."

We sat down at the table in the large part of the room clearly designated for eating. "Darling, I can stand any amount of this. You've got hidden talents."

"Charlie, I only do simple cooking. You'll have to do the haute cuisine."

We went over to the sofa. "I'm ready for my coffee now, thank you Peter."

I found some coffee in the freezer and a cafetière. "Better and better. Turn on the TV and see what's been happening in the world."

When Charlie left to get ready for bed I sent a message to Henry Denis asking if it would be alright to come in on the Wednesday afternoon

We had a quiet week-end which suited me as I had been wondering whether I been doing too much with my arm.

On the Monday morning John Corrigan arrived at 9am and we drove straight off to Union City. We parked near a small hangar type building which looked very new.

"Peter, as you can see we got some significant funding for our research project. We think it's very important to check on the aging processes of all materials, particularly when used in aircraft. Wiring for example is absolutely critical. Aircraft metal skins as well of course though the emphasis is transferring to composite structures and the method of attachment."

We went inside the building and the fuselage was surrounded by temporary platforms for accessing the structure and there were lots of tables loaded with material taken from the inside of the fuselage. I walked round the front and fortuitously a hole had been cut in a position which I guessed must be just behind the first officer's seat. John pushed a wheeled platform into position and helped me climb up the step so I could peer inside. Because of the buckling of the nose it was difficult to see the instrument panels but I did manage to find what I suspected might be attached to the roof above the pilot's head, a damaged but still recognisable HUD.

"John, if you have no use for it, could you sometime remove the HUD, officially certificate where you found it and then send it to me?"

"No problem. NTSB has given the fuselage to us and declared no interest in it so we can do what we like with the bits. Why do you need the HUD?" I explained about the accident. "That explains something, Peter. I noticed some equipment had been taken from the nose of the fuselage. There are signs of recent damage but I didn't know what might have been taken. Presumably the HUD doesn't work by itself?"

"You're absolutely right. There was probably an infra red sensor and a microwave radar antenna fitted on the aircraft. I wasn't able to see that something had been taken when I was at WeScrapIt. I should have looked harder, perhaps."

He showed me the two areas where the skin damage seemed more recent than the accident itself. "Peter, who would have removed the sensors?"

"That is the 64,000 dollar question. Thank so much for your help. If you don't mind I think I'll get a cab back as I'm off to UK in the morning."

When I got home I started some telephoning beginning with Bill Castleford in Bermuda. "Bill, I'm back from my holiday in Australia and I've had another look at Echo Victor's fuselage and flight deck."

"You haven't been sitting on your hands. Did you learn anything, Peter?"

"Yes Bill, I did. Why didn't any of you tell me that the aircraft had an EVS system?"

There was a long pause. I could tell from the background that we were still connected. "Bill, it's all over now. If there's anything to come out, it will come out."

"Peter, I was hoping you would find out what happened to the aircraft without your knowing about the EVS. European gave us the equipment free of charge as long as we didn't advertise we had it; they wanted to be able to show pilots the system, very occasionally. European arranged the aircraft FAA certification but we realised after we got the plane that the EVS wasn't included."

"What did you do? Surely you should have told the FAA in New York?"

"We spoke to European and they told us everything was safe and that the equipment wouldn't work on an autopilot approach. If we'd told the FAA they would have stopped us flying and we needed the aircraft to fulfil our schedule so we did nothing."

"I see. I think I'd better stop acting for you right now, Bill. I can go back to UK and no-one will be any the wiser. The NTSB man has not mentioned the EVS in the accident report, presumably because he thinks, like you, that it's irrelevant. A clear cut case of pilot error the report said, which it probably was."

"Peter, I apologise. I should have trusted you. You had better carry on until you're satisfied."

"Alright then, is my memory correct? Martin told me Trevor was on the delivery flight?"

"Yes that's quite right. He went with Martin."

"Was he ever in command?"

"No, there was a European pilot with them checking them out."

"And had Trevor flown the aircraft since then?"

"I've no idea."

"Well could you find out and let me know? It might be relevant. Trevor did something out of character and I'd like to find out why. I want to make sure it couldn't happen again. I'm going to talk to Martin and Barbara again if I may."

"Yes, you go ahead and please keep me in the picture if there are any developments."

My next call was to Martin Spencer. I could tell straightaway that Bill had already been talking to him. "Martin I think you know I've discovered that Echo Victor had an EVS. Why didn't you tell me?"

"Peter, it wasn't relevant. It didn't work on the approach and we didn't want to get into trouble with the NTSB."

"Well you probably are in trouble but anyhow, as I told Bill, NTSB are classifying the accident as pilot error. They haven't mentioned the EVS in their accident report, I don't know why since it shouldn't have been possible for European to deliver the aircraft with the EVS on the aircraft and not certificated. Anyway I'm calling you to find out how the EVS actually worked, how it was installed."

"Well Peter as you know the EVS was only displayed on the HUD if we were not doing an autopilot approach. So we only could use the EVS if we were going into airfields which were not equipped with ILS. Since this was very rare most of us never bothered with it at all."

"Couldn't you use the HUD with just the simple parameters displayed like ILS deviation, speed and radio altitude?"

"No, Peter, the way European had given the installation to us it wasn't possible to get the symbology by itself. If the EVS was on then we got everything, steering commands, speed, height, deviation, the output from the infra red sensors and the microwave radar."

"Martin, what was the background to European giving you the system. It would have cost a bomb if you'd bought it."

"Well European had been doing tests on an aircraft fitted with the very latest EVS and for the moment they had come to the end of their trials. They needed to sell an aircraft from a financial viewpoint. They offered us their test aircraft at the basic price without charging us for the EVS. It was a no brainer."

"What was the system like? Did you try it? Did you get any training?"

"At the factory Trevor and I spent three hours each in the simulator and we looked at it during our acceptance flights. It worked incredibly well. However as I told you it didn't work when making an autopilot approach. Because of this we didn't use the EVS. However as part of the deal they wanted to be able to show potential customers our aircraft and asked us to register the aircraft Echo Victor, Enhanced Vision."

"Martin, I'm an idiot. I should have realised. When Jonathan told me your tail registrations I wondered why Echo Victor was different. I didn't ask him. By the way who provided the system on Enhanced Vision."

"Not sure. I think it was a French company. I assumed it was Thales."

"Another thing. I gather you and Trevor were on the delivery flight?"

"Yes, the European chief pilot, Ludwig Teifel was in command. We needed to get our type rating validated with the FAA. We had to fly across the North Atlantic, Reykjavik, Frobisher Bay, Montreal. We did two legs each in the left hand seat."

"How much flying had Trevor done on the aircraft once you were back in Bermuda?"

"Apart from the type rating he hadn't done any. It was his first flight. As you know we had only had the aircraft a month and Trevor went on leave after the delivery."

"Martin, thanks for all that. If I find anything more I'll call you."

The other thing I had to do was to talk to Barbara again. I tried the mobile number she had given me but her phone wasn't switched on. I left a message asking her to call me which she did almost immediately.

"Peter, I've got the news. Martin called me."

"Barbara, you should have told me."

"Martin asked me not to, Peter. He said it was nothing to do with the accident."

"Alright. What's done is done. But tell me this, did Trevor have the HUD down?"

"I don't know. I've been agonising for days trying to remember. I was so busy listening to the ATIS visibility and watching the speed, the deviation from centre lines and keeping an eye out through the windscreen that I didn't notice. He certainly didn't have it down at the beginning of the approach."

"OK Barbara, I just wanted to check."

There was an email saying that the meeting on the Wednesday would be alright so I booked two tickets on the earlier flight the following night to Heathrow and a cab to meet us. I sent an email to Charlie confirming it was all fixed.

There was one more phone call I needed to make. It was to the foreman at WeScrapIt asking him if there had been any other visitors to the site before me.

"Mr Talbert, yes there was. I remember him clearly. He was very smartly dressed with a pronounced southern drawl. He said he was from the insurance company and he asked me to take a couple of pieces of electronic boxes off the fuselage nose. It didn't worry me as the fuselage was being scrapped and he gave me $500 to do the work."

"Do you remember his name?"

"No, not at all. The way the guy looked I don't think I would have believed it anyway."

There was nothing else I could do for the moment except routine work. Peter arrived followed by Charlie and we had a quiet evening.

In the morning I got out the papers I had emailed to Henry Denis and got myself up to speed again. Charlie arrived back in plenty of time and packed a small bag for our things plus my roller cabin bag.

We decided to use a cab rather than getting her car out and we left on time after eating some snacks in the business class lounge. We got in at dawn and this time I did manage some sleep in spite of my arm. The cab was waiting and we were home in about forty five minutes, just ahead of the worst of the rush hour.

Charlie took the bags in as I cancelled the alarm. I shovelled the mail into my office.

Charlie looked round. "Peter, are you insured for me to drive the car." I nodded. "Good. I'm now in full practice driving on the left after Oz so we're going out to somewhere nice for breakfast. There's nothing here except nostalgia."

"Good idea. Let's go to the Cannizaro hotel. It's a nice place and you won't have too much trouble with the traffic."

I opened the garage door and the gates with the remote openers and Charlie backed out. As I predicted there was no problem with the traffic and we drove up to the hotel. Charlie clearly approved and we had a good breakfast though I still needed some help with the bacon and sausage. We did some shopping on the way home and then we sat down in the living room. She looked around, got up and went into the kitchen and then upstairs.

"Well the place would have to be completely redone before we could live here."

"Do I take that as a yes to my proposal of marriage?"

"You're rushing things. The house needs doing anyway. It's dated. But it can wait. What do you need to be doing now?"

"I want to think about my meeting to-morrow with Henry Denis and check all my mail. What do you want to do?"

"I'd like to go to Christie's and the National Gallery while I'm over here."

"Well you could go to Christie's to-day and the National Gallery to-morrow while I'm working."

"Will you be able to manage?"

"I'll be fine using taxis but I'm not going out to-day."

Charlie went out and I worked for a bit though I began to get tired. She came back about 4pm and we went to bed early. In the morning we had a light breakfast and I did a bit more work. Then we had an early lunch at the Wolseley. I caught a taxi to Marsham Street for 2pm and Charlie said she'd walk to the National Gallery to get some exercise.

I signed in and Denis's secretary escorted me to his office. He looked at my arm in the sling and I told him I had been hit by a car. He had read my suggested changes and told me that Charles Simon had agreed them. Simon in fact was away for a couple of weeks but wanted things to proceed. However he didn't want me actually to start work in my office until 1st January which was about two months away which suited me fine. I wrote in the date and signed four copies of the contract which had already been signed by the Finance Director. Henry gave me my copy which I put carefully away after making three copies.

"You are now Chairman of the Board, Peter. You'll get paid from to-day's date. You need to be thinking of how you are going to operate, the outside board members and looking at the three accident branches. I've got a large envelope here of the information you need and if you need anything else just let me know. Charles has asked that we don't announce the appointment just yet as he wants to tell Brussels first as a courtesy. In addition he wants the fiasco of the Rogerson appointment to be forgotten. Probably 1st December is a realistic date for publicity. Suggest that we don't tell anybody until then."

"Henry, that's fine by me but people like Bob Furness are bound to ask you and me what's going on. We'll have to agree that no decision has been made."

"Yes, that's what I thought as well. Will you have any difficulty with your clients?"

"I don't think so. I've got some open matters I'm still dealing with but hopefully they will be done by year end."

I went home finally realising I could start making plans but knowing it was going to be difficult. The obvious solution would be for Charlie to get a job in the UK and then Peter could have a settled education. She arrived half an hour after me and we went out to the George for a drink and a pizza.

The following day we caught the early flight to New York and were back in the apartment by 12.30. Charlie dashed off to work and then later appeared unexpectedly with both children. The kids were delighted to see me and she was able to dash back to work and leave me in charge. Even though everything was under control I was glad when Charlie arrived to apply the finishing touches and turn out the light.

"Now we're back we can take Peter to the Bronx Zoo on Saturday. He's been wanting to go for ages. He seems to be fascinated by wild animals."

Harry called. "I've booked in the airport Sheraton. Where are you staying?"

"I'm in New York. I'll get a cab and be at the hotel for about 11.30. I expect you'll be resting. I'll be in the bar or somewhere. You can always call me on my mobile.

We didn't stay up late and in the morning the gang got the children off to school as usual and I was on my own. I decided to leave early for the Sheraton, called on my phone for a cab and was at the hotel soon after 11 o'clock. Harry joined me and I had to explain about the arm; we had a light meal and discussed the situation ad nauseam. Then we caught a cab to Total Avionics.

We were clearly expected as our badges were all made out and, after signing in, Matt's secretary took us up to his office on the sixth floor. After a very short wait Matt came out and said hello to Harry who introduced me.

"Mr Talbert. I know your name of course from some of the accidents you've been involved with. However, I didn't expect to meet you." He stared at my arm. "Are you OK sitting in that chair? Can we make you more comfortable? What happened if I may ask?"

"No problem thank you. A car hit me as I was waiting to cross the road."

"How did your visit to our facility at Basingstoke go?"

"Well Mr Watkins, I was given a very good tour by the project director Tommy Tucker but I'm afraid there was a large inconsistency between the working man hours which he showed me and the actual man hours which had been spent on the project."

Watkins looked genuinely surprised. "How do you mean? How do you know?"

"The chief engineer let me see his papers while Tucker was away. I don't think he could have been on the project very long. He clearly didn't know what Tucker had given me for the man hours and the start date."

"What did Tucker say or Chris Henderson for that matter?"

"I didn't discuss it with them as I needed time to think what must have happened."

"And what conclusion did you come to?"

"I think Tucker had a special booklet printed for my benefit which was clearly different from the real one. It meant that Harry's feeling that copyright data had changed hands seemed very likely."

"Mr Talbert, I respect the way you investigate things but don't you think all this is a bit fanciful?"

"Mr Watkins, I had a feeling that something was wrong so I interviewed all Harry's staff to understand what might have been passed over and to try to find out who could have done it."

Harry, looking very uncomfortable, joined in. "Matt, this is all very difficult for me. You probably don't know but I had a very nasty divorce about two years ago and my wife left me and went off with the chief engineer of West Shore Airlines, who had been negotiating to buy our new EVS the moment it became available. Peter pointed out to me that she could have copied my papers when I was at home and given them to the engineer."

Matt looked concerned. I was rapidly coming to the conclusion that my guess that he didn't know what the people at Basingstoke had been up to was right. "If Peter's right that's terrible." He looked at me. "What did you do?"

"I had a chat with the chief engineer. He clearly never expected to be interrogated and he admitted he knew Tommy Tucker. He realised he was caught and agreed to sign a form admitting he had handed over the papers he had got from his wife to Tucker."

"Why on earth did he agree to sign?"

"Because I pointed out that if he signed the whole matter might not come to court."

Harry produced a copy and gave it to Matt who read it carefully and looked at us both and then said to me. "Peter, why did he do it? Money?"

"Possibly. Tucker was clearly after money. He sold himself and the documents to Chris Henderson. Maybe Tucker promised money to the engineer, Greco, but I wonder if Greco agreed to do it just because Harry's wife was so very vindictive."

A long pause. Matt turned to Harry. "Well what do you want? We're clearly infringing a lot of your patents. Money?"

He looked at Harry but Harry looked at me.

"Matt, I take it nobody wants to go to Court?" He nodded. "Money is irrelevant to Vision Unlimited. What Harry wants is for Total Avionics to stop making the product altogether."

"Peter," We had come to first name terms, I suspected, because we respected one another. "We can't do that."

"Why not. Surely you can do a deal with Harry so that you can offer a whole flight deck system and Vision Unlimited can supply the EVS.

Harry looked startled for a moment and then slowly nodded his head.

"What if we don't agree to stop making our EVS?"

"Look we don't want to go down that route. Since money is not the issue, Vision Unlimited would have to take you to court. The publicity would be appalling and you might have to stop anyway. There would be an injunction preventing you from selling while the case was on, anyway, because Greco's statement says it all."

Matt thought for a moment and then rapidly made his mind up. "Peter, Harry, I'm sure you don't expect me to give a decision right now. I've got to talk to Henderson and find out what has been going on." He looked at us both. "Believe me I had no idea at all of any of this. However, between you and me, I had been very impressed if not surprised with the speed of the EVS development at Basingstoke. When you called me, Harry, I had a nasty feeling something might be wrong but I didn't do anything. Maybe I should have, but," he looked at me and smiled grimly, "I'd never have found out the source of the information transfer."

I looked at Matt. "Unfortunately there's a bit more to this than I've said. You asked me about my arm. Well in fact I was pushed into the car in Melbourne. It wasn't an accident."

"Why would anyone want to do that?" They both looked at me in amazement.

"Matt, I think whoever it was didn't want me to find out what had actually happened on the EVS project. What I didn't tell you was that Greco had called me in Canberra and asked that we meet in Melbourne because he would be away when I got back for our pre-arranged meeting. He said he would be at a Board meeting. Unwisely as it turned out I told him my hotel. If he was there he could easily have pushed me."

"Did he call you in Melbourne?"

"No he didn't."

"Was he there?"

"Good question. Having met him and spoken to him I don't think he was. I don't think he has the guts to do anything like that."

"But you said somebody had pushed you into a car."

"I think you need to check on Tommy Tucker's movements."

Matt looked at me in disbelief. "How would he be involved?"

"I think Greco called him after my first conversation with him from Sydney and Tucker realised I had worked out that Greco had given him the data, patented information, call it what you will. He knew his job would be up if you ever found out the truth. He persuaded Greco to call me and find where I was staying in Australia. He was probably on the West Coast already, maybe with Greco talking about installing EVS on his aircraft. I don't know that he wanted to kill me but he certainly wanted me out of the action."

"Peter, what a terrible story if it's true. It would be a police matter."

"Matt, I was forced to give both their names to the Australian police. However, I've no intention of raising it again. Of course it will be easy enough for the police to check on Tucker's movements. I'd be surprised if Chris Henderson knew what Tucker was up to. If Tucker went to Australia then clearly he was the one who pushed me. Unlike Greco he knew what I looked like."

There was silence for a bit while Matt thought things over. Understandably Harry wanted a plan and a timetable. "Well how shall we leave it? When can we expect to hear? I've been thinking and Peter has probably come up with the perfect solution of working together. We'd still want to sell our complete system to other flight deck avionic vendors."

"Alright you two. Here's what we'll do. Give me a few days to get Henderson over here, sort things out and then I'll call you. Henderson will have to sort out Tucker's movements, not that it affects EVS, but it might affect the way we deal with him."

We left and gave our badges in down at the lobby. I had an idea. "Harry when are you going back?"

"To-morrow. I'm staying at the Crowne Plaza, JFK. Why?"

"Come and have a meal with us to-night."

"Sounds a great idea."

"Sit down for a moment while I call Charlie."

I called her office and my luck was in. "My love, have you any plans for to-night?"

"No, why? Break it to me gently."

"How about going out to dinner, the four of us."

"Hold on, my love. Who are the four?"

"You, me, Cheryl and Harry Foster."

"Maybe Cheryl doesn't want to come out dinner. She may be washing her hair."

"I don't think Cheryl has washed her hair for many years. She might have a headache if that translates across the Atlantic."

"Oh yes. That translates OK. I think I'm getting one. Only joking. I think it's a great idea. I'll check with Cheryl and then the baby sitters. If not I'll have to cook you all a meal."

"You're wonderful. May we go straight to the apartment?"

"Make yourself at home. Your treating it like one."

"I want it to be our home."

The phone went dead. I turned to Harry. "All fixed I think. Charlie's sorting it out. We'll get a cab back to the apartment."

The cab was very slow as the traffic was building up. Luckily Charlie was dealing with Peter as I made the introductions. "Hello again. Your Peter has been superb. I think he's saved my company."

Charlie smiled. "Yes he can be quite useful. Like getting drinks and booking tables for dinner. Cheryl can join us Peter and we've got a baby sitter. I'll have a drink when Peter's settled. Pinot Grigio, please."

"What time can we go out?"

"Seven. Where are we going?"

"Don't know yet?"

I joined Harry with a Scotch, having noticed that Charlie's drinks cupboard had most things. I rang the Algonquin and got a table at 7.30pm.

Charlie shut the door and asked where we were eating. I told her. "I'll just get changed and you'd better warn Cheryl where we're going."

"Why?"

"My love, just do it. The number is by the phone."

I did as directed "Cheryl. We're eating at the Algonquin."

"Great. It won't be slacks then. Is Harry nice?"

"You ask some impossible questions. He's lovely and not a toy boy. And he's single."

"What took you so long?"

The phone went dead and I joined Harry. "Peter, what are your movements?"

"Not sure. Not planning anything for the moment. Should be here in New York."

"Good. I may need you here."

"Let's wait and see what happens. I don't see how Matt can call us before next week."

Charlie appeared looking absolutely fantastic. Her skirt was short but not too short and as usual her bra was doing an absolutely splendid job. I could see Harry was impressed. There was a knock on the door and Cheryl and Sonia appeared. Cheryl put Sonia straight down with Peter and announced she also wanted a Pinot Grigio. I mentally congratulated myself on my view of Cheryl. She had scrubbed up beautifully and also looked terrific. If I'd been judging a beauty contest I would have chosen Charlie but an independent judge might have been hard pressed for a decision. I looked at Harry who seemed very appreciative.

After a bit the phone rang and Charlie let the baby sitter in downstairs. Shortly afterwards there was a knock on the door and Susan appeared, a middle aged lady who definitely looked the ideal babysitter. We drank up, went down and caught a cab to the Algonquin.

We sat down in the Oak Room with Charlie next to me instead of opposite so that she could help me if necessary not, I noticed, that Harry minded.

I looked at Charlie. "I thought you'd all like it. Something special."

Harry chipped in. "Peter, it's a great choice and I insist that we split the check. You've saved my life."

"Thanks for the offer, Harry. It isn't necessary but I'll accept. I'll choose the white if you'll do the red."

I ordered a bottle of Chablis which I liked and there was silence as we all studied the menu. By common consent we went for the fixed price menu. There were four choices for the starter and four for the entrée as well and we all chose something different.

Harry and Cheryl seemed to be getting on well and I could see that Charlie was loving it all. She put her hand on my knee and I stroked her hand for a moment. "Peter, what made you think of it?"

"Darling, it suddenly occurred to me that it might be nice. We had a good meeting and hopefully it might be sorted next week."

"Cheryl's really enjoying it. Harry's very nice."

The food came and went and we never stopped talking. Charlie and I decided to share the fruit, mousse and ice cream mixture notwithstanding the menu was fixed. Harry and Cheryl debated the situation and followed our example but chose the cheesecake. We all finished with decaffeinated coffee.

Harry looked at his watch and decided it was time to go as he had an early start back to the West Coast. I noticed he had given his card to Cheryl and she had written on the back of another one. We all went out together, Harry got a cab to Kennedy and then we got one back to the apartment. Charlie asked Cheryl in and I took Susan down and put her in a cab. When I got back they were into the liqueurs and I found a Drambuie.

"Peter," I looked at Cheryl, "thanks for the meal. I really enjoyed it."

"I didn't give you a meal. Harry did."

"It was your idea and you organised everything. And Harry was very nice."

"Are you coming with us to the Zoo to-morrow?"

"No, thank you. Sonia goes dancing on Saturday mornings." She looked at Charlie. "May I leave Sonia here to-night?"

She left and we were alone. Charlie beckoned me to the sofa. "That was a great evening. You did well."

"Have you changed your mind yet?"

She looked at me. "We've got to work out where we would work, where we would live. Otherwise it will only end in tears. The Atlantic is too wide, my love."

"Why can't you get a job in London? And we can get Peter's education sorted out."

"Possibly. Come on, we need some sleep. We've got a busy day to-morrow."

As I lay in bed I suddenly had an idea which I hoped wasn't too far fetched. I grabbed Charlie. "No, not now. I need to sleep. I've got a headache."

"I've just thought of what might have happened in Hong Kong."

"Wonderful. Will it be different in the morning?"

I realised I shouldn't have disturbed Charlie but I felt rather ashamed that I had not thought of my idea earlier and wanted to tell someone. It was a long shot but worth investigating. My immediate concern was the whereabouts of the fuselage of the CC21. I crept out of bed and sent Bruce an email 'Please advise by return the location of CC21 B33057.' I crept back to bed by Charlie who didn't stir.

In the morning I checked my email while Charlie was dealing with Peter. There was a reply from Bruce. 'CC21 has been cut up but the fuselage and wings are still intact. Aircraft in shed near airport. Bruce.' My reply was short and to the point. 'Will almost certainly need to inspect fuselage. Peter.' It was Saturday so I sent another email to William Roscoff asking him to call me as soon as possible. There was nothing more I could do except wait.

We went to the zoo wearing plenty of warm clothes and Peter had a great time. I noticed he loved the kangaroos jumping. "Charlie, do you think it is significant?"

"What do you mean?"

"Kangaroos and that job at the National Gallery?"

"Not really."

"It could have been an English Carthorse."

We gave Peter something to eat at the zoo and then took him to the aquarium in the afternoon. He was exhausted when we got home and we packed him off to bed very early.

We sat down and Charlie held me close. "Why did you wake me as I was going to sleep last night?"

"Sorry about that but I had an idea."

"So you said but I was washing my hair."

"You said you had a headache. Anyway it wasn't that sort of an idea. It was about what happened in Hong Kong."

"Did it still seem a good idea this morning?"

"Yes but it needs testing. I'm waiting for a telephone call."

"Well I had an idea as well after you woke me. It occurred to me that I rather liked having you next to me in bed, even if your arm restricts you. It seems a pity for it to stop."

I looked at her and thought about kneeling.

"Don't even try. But the answer's yes."

"But I haven't proposed yet."

"I'll forgive you."

As we embraced her eyes filled with tears.

"Why are you crying. It won't be that bad."

I went to my brief case and then, when she came over to sit down on the sofa, I reached out and grabbed her left hand.

"Charlie, I've got a very special ring here." I took the ring which Helen had had and I slipped it on her finger. I'd had it cleaned but it obviously wasn't absolutely new.

Charlie looked at it. "It's really lovely. It's stupid of me but somehow I don't mind that it's the one you gave to Helen. In fact you did it because it was so special. I feel I shall treasure it even more."

It was my turn to fill with emotion. "How on earth did you know?"

"I didn't know but somehow I did. It's the sort of thing that only you would do. It's actually very lovely."

Charlie poured me a beer and I looked at my phone. I had missed a call when we were in the aquarium. I called the number back. It was William Roscoff. "It's Peter Talbert again. I'm in New York. According to the airline the aircraft that crashed in Hong Kong had all mods up to 156 according to the records. Just out of curiosity what was so special about the mods that made autolanding without them prohibited?"

"Peter, we had to introduce an additional box with extra electronics to make certain that all the cross monitoring was carried out correctly. We found that we were getting spurious disconnects due to inaccurate signal monitoring."

"But that's what happened to that CC21 that crashed in Hong Kong."

"I know. That's why I told your man Derek and you to check the mod state of the equipment."

"I sort of guessed the modification wasn't just software. I noticed that Airlines Servicing showed me an aircraft mod state form as well as an autopilot one at Newark. In fact I think you mentioned hardware as well as software. William, do you have an engineer in Hong Kong?"

"Peter, we have a large office and six engineers in Hong Kong."

"If I can get CAAC to agree, can you send an engineer to look at the wreckage of the CC21 to see if the new avionic box had been fitted? The aircraft is in a shed by the airport, so the CAAC man tells me."

William laughed. "So that's what you think happened? It's not the first time that mods have been entered and not carried out. We'd be delighted to look."

"William, leave it with me. I'll talk to CAAC."

I found Bruce's card and telephoned him in Hong Kong. I explained that we needed to check whether a modification had been carried out correctly and was it possible for an engineer from Total Avionics to inspect the wreckage. He agreed straightaway and I said that I would get the engineer to phone him.

Next I phoned William Roscoff again and asked him to get the aircraft inspected and gave him Bruce's number.

In the morning I heard Charlie calling Liz in Sydney and though I tried not to listen I heard her mentioning the job at the National Gallery and, I was slightly surprised to hear, that I had proposed to her and she had accepted.

I phoned John Southern, even though it was a Sunday. "John, an idea occurred to me yesterday and I've thought of a way of checking if the mods were really done on that aircraft. I've discovered there's a hardware element of the mod, not just software. I've arrange for a Total Avionics engineer in Hong Kong to look at the wreckage."

"Peter, I knew I was doing the right thing asking you to go out."

"John, you're jumping the gun. The mod may have been done. But there was just one thing I hadn't told you which made me suspicious. I think I told you, the ink didn't look old enough even though the page had been crumpled. And I now realise that they should have shown me the aircraft modification state as well as the autopilot."

"Are you thinking what I'm thinking? About Derek?"

"Yes. I think the airline may have got at him "

"Peter, I hope you don't get that job in DfT. We'll miss you."

"John, the jury is still out on the mod."

"Look Peter, let me know as soon as you can."

At 8pm my phone rang and to my surprise it was Bruce from Hong Kong. "Mr Talbert, the engineer has looked where the new hardware box should be and it is not there. He tells me that the aircraft should not have been doing an automatic landing. It would be very helpful if you could let me have a copy of your report to the insurance company."

"Of course, Bruce. But I will need a formal statement from the Total Avionics engineer as I am sure will you. I will contact Total Avionics."

"Thank you, Mr Talbert."

I called Roscoff again. "Have you heard, William?"

"Yes, Hong Kong called me straight away."

"Will you let me have a copy of the inspection report as soon as you can? Hull Claims has got to deal with the airline. Email will be fine."

"No problem."

"By the way, I'd appreciate it if your people didn't discuss what they found with anyone. Actually I'm still in New York and will be for the next day or so. I must have been near you the other day. We visited Matt Watkins."

"It is near us but out of my league. How did you get in there?"

"It's a long story which I'll be glad to tell you if we ever meet up."

Charlie took the phone from me. "Another problem solved in Peter Talbert's casebook"

"Solved but not finished, Mrs Talbert."

"You're getting ahead of the game, Mr Talbert. That's something else we'll have to work out."

"What are you going to say to Peter?"

"Don't worry about it."

"I need to call John Southern but it will have to wait until the morning now so let's try and get some sleep."

"Done."

Chapter 13

In the morning the normal whirlwind took place. While it was going on I checked my emails and there was an email from Sir Philip Brown, the Permanent Secretary of the Department of Transport, asking me to call as soon as possible.

"Peter, what on earth can he want?"

"Don't know but it must be urgent, as he's the most senior man in the Department. Very strange."

Charlie and Peter left and I decided to call Sir Philip straightaway. His secretary put me straight through.

"Peter, thanks for calling back. Where are you? In Australia?"

"No, Sir Philip, I'm in New York."

"I've called you because I'm afraid we are in a very difficult position with regard to the Safety Board. The EU Commission have been on to us saying that they don't want us to create this new Board because they have plans to have a Europe wide Safety Board overseeing all the national accident investigation boards."

"Can they stop us creating this Board?"

"That's a good question Peter. No, they can't and for my money I'd go ahead. But it is a political decision whether or not to tell the EU to mind its own business and the Minister feels we must cooperate with the EU."

"Sir Philip, if I understand you correctly you are saying the whole idea of the UK Safety Board is scrapped, terminally."

"Yes, Peter, I'm afraid so. Obviously the conditions stated in your contract stand. You will get the agreed termination pay. I'm sorry it had to end like this and all I can do is to wish you every success in the future. I will of course be writing to you confirming this conversation."

I was silent.

"Are you still there, Peter?"

"Yes, Sir Philip. Obviously I'm very disappointed as I was looking forward enormously to doing the job." I hesitated. "If I may say so, it's strange how things work out. That leak wasn't necessary after all."

There was a pause at his end then "I'm not sure I want to understand you but I'm beginning to realise why you have been so successful in your investigations."

"Never mind, Sir Philip. You're quite right. It's probably better that way."

There was no reply. I was absolutcly shattered. One moment my future seemed secure including a married life with Charlie. Now I was just left with my existing job which somehow didn't seem as attractive as it had been. I clearly needed to talk to Charlie to see how she saw things but the conversation would have to wait until the evening. I called John Southern who was in his office.

"John, the mods weren't done, and you tell me that Derek said they were."

"I know what you're saying, Peter, but that's a relatively minor matter. Apparently Richard had realised some time back that Derek may have been a bad choice and that was why he encouraged me to get you to go out again. Apparently Derek was a bad engineer and had poor judgement. Richard almost apologised to me for choosing him."

"What happens next?"

"Well the important thing is to work out how we deal with Fred and his airline now we know the truth. Are you at home or in the office?"

"I'm still in New York. It suited me to come back here and I wondered whether you wanted me to go out or whether you were going to talk to Fred or get him to come and see you."

"I need to think about that and talk to my boss. I'll call you back. By the way, Peter, did you get that job in DfT. I know it's selfish but I hope you didn't."

"John, unfortunately your wish is granted. The EU has vetoed the Safety Board."

"You're joking. Surely they can't tell us what to do?"

"No they can't, but our politicians are weak as water. Not like the French who would tell them to jump in a lake or words to that effect. There's bound to be an announcement hidden away somewhere in the near future if it hasn't occurred already saying that the need for a Safety Board is being re-evaluated or something like that. They won't dare say the EU has stopped it. Incidentally I did get the job but that won't be mentioned."

"Peter, that's appalling. They go through the whole selection process, choose someone and then cancel the post."

"Actually John it was worse than that. I actually signed the contract and was in post."

"Hope they have to pay you off."

"That was the only good thing. They are going to, handsomely, which gives me time to think what I'm going to do now."

"Well at least you got something out of it, Peter. I'll let you know about what we're going to do about West Orient Airlines."

When we had finished I considered yet again how Charlie and I were going to manage. In fact just because the job was cancelled it shouldn't really make any difference since I still had my insurance practice and any job Charlie got in London would be completely independent of mine. However it occurred to me that perhaps I was sufficiently well known that I could operate from New York, but then I would need a green card which would let me work in the States and we certainly couldn't manage in the apartment; it was too small for me to be able to work there. I would need a proper office though perhaps it could be in a new house or large apartment. Everything really depended on how central the location was. The decision process was of course complicated by the fact that Charlie was thinking of applying for the job in Australia. I wondered what would happen then if she got it. We would have to move there and stay there because Peter would need a proper base for schooling. Again if I could work from New York there was no reason to suppose I couldn't work from Australia, though Canberra didn't have any international flights which was a pain.

Charlie called. "Are you doing anything? I'm going to let my fiancé buy me lunch. Actually a sandwich and it'll have to be quick. Give me a call as you are approaching reception."

She came out of the building as I approached and we went down a back street to a small diner. "What have you being doing, mastermind? What did your UK government official want?"

I told her.

"You're joking. Peter, is that it? What cheek. Can they just turn it off without so much as an apology."

"Charlie, he was very apologetic."

"Which pocket can you put that in? Surely you must have signed a contract?"

"Yes, in fact I was already on their payroll."

"Well wasn't there a severance clause?"

"Yes. They'll have to pay me three times my salary as a lump sum."

She looked at me and then grinned, in spite of herself. "Isn't that quite good?"

I smiled. "Actually it's quite a large sum. I suppose it could be worse. I'm not sure how the tax people will handle it."

"Well we won't need Kitty after all. I can be a kept woman."

"I don't think that would suit either of us Charlie. I know that the payoff is quite good but it's not the same as having the job. I am definitely disappointed. However the money gives me time to think. For some reason it has unsettled me. What I have been doing for the last few years now seems tame, over, finished."

I was silent for a bit realising I was very disappointed. I hadn't realised how much I was looking forward to the new job. Charlie was quiet as well as she ate her sandwich. Then I decided to explore the situation.

"I've been thinking about us. Do you still want to marry me?"

"You're crazy. It's you I'm marrying. Not the Department of Transport or whatever you people call it." She thought for a bit. "It's not a big deal not getting that job. We live in a global world and you can work from anywhere."

"Australia?"

"Why not, Peter, if that's the way the cookie crumbles."

"Well that's the conclusion I came to, my love."

"Now that's settled when are we going to get married?"

"You're sure?"

She looked at me, concerned. "Are you sure? Do you want to change your mind?"

"Don't be stupid, my darling. You know I love you. I just wanted to give you the chance of backing out because I'm unemployed."

"Now you're being stupid, Peter. We're both able, capable people and can work anywhere. What are you doing this afternoon?"

"Are the two questions related?"

"In a way. We can't get married without a licence and it only lasts for sixty days."

"That's interesting. You people in New York have some funny rules. What's the validity of the marriage certificate then? Do you have a sticker for your rear car fender 'a marriage is for life and not for Christmas'?" I took the precaution of ducking. "Seriously, darling, how do we get a licence in New York?"

"We need to go City Hall in Worth Street before 3.45pm but we can apply on line first."

"Surely we have to be there?"

"I mean, lovely one, that you can go home now, download the form, fill it in, we can sign it this evening and together we can present it at the Clerk's office to-morrow."

"What about a blood test? I thought some States needed them."

"Not if you're white Caucasian."

"I thought all men are created equal. We'd never be allowed a distinction like that in UK."

She ignored my remark and looked at her watch. "Thank you for my lunch."

Back in the apartment I logged on and I saw just enough to know that Charlie had to be with me dealing with the application. Then John Southern called me, upsetting my concentration.

"How about another trip to Taipei?"

"Fair enough but it's going to cost you. And won't I need some paperwork?"

"You bet. We're going to get Fred to sign a document with revised premiums as a result of what they tried to do to us. It will take our lawyers a day or so to draw up the forms. Where shall I send them, your office or to you in New York?"

"Will they be signed by you people?"

"Yes, they will."

"Well in that case please send them to my fiancée's office in New York."

"Peter, congratulations. Do I know the girl?"

"You certainly know of her. Charlie was the art insurer helping me find the pictures."

"Yes, Peter. I think I did meet her once. A beautiful tall athletic girl if I remember correctly."

"Yes, John you do remember correctly."

"This trip is going to be expensive for you. My arm's in a sling and I can't travel by myself. I hope Charlie will agree to come with me."

I explained about the accident but I decided not to tell him my suspicions since he wasn't involved.

"Where are you going to live?"

"Don't know yet."

"Well Peter, you don't have to be in England to do your job."

"Yes John, we've come to that conclusion but we'll have to make a decision soon as her son needs a proper education."

"I understand." He clearly didn't know what to say. "I'll let you know when we post the forms."

"Fine. I'll email the exact address and addressee."

I sent the email off with the despatch details for the documents and then went for a walk in Central Park. I got home as Cheryl arrived with Sonia and Peter, who was by now regarding me as part of the furniture. However, Cheryl seeing me there decided to give the children their tea in the apartment so she could chat.

"Have you heard from Harry?"

"Yes, thank you Peter. He really is lovely and he sent me some flowers. You were brilliant organising the Algonquin."

"To be honest it was pure luck but I did know he was divorced because his wife left him and incredibly she gave some of his firm's secrets away which could well have bankrupted the firm. I can understand couples separating but to be that vindictive is unforgivable. We were chasing up that problem when we were together in New Jersey the other day."

"Well I've been promising myself a trip to the West Coast for some time so I think I'll take it and go and see Harry in Palmdale."

"Will you take Sonia?"

"I don't think so. Charlie and I will plan how to look after her. It's wonderful having her here so close and now you," she added beaming at me. "You're a definite bonus."

"I'm not sure about looking after little girls. I'm better with the older ones."

She laughed. "So Charlie tells me."

I turned round as we heard the apartment door close. "Talk of the devil, Cheryl."

Charlie had arrived quietly with brief case, looking every inch the professional woman, which of course she was."

"What did I tell you, Cheryl?"

"That Peter's better with older girls than little girls."

"I know. It worries me sometimes."

She came up to me and gave me an affectionate kiss. "Did he tell you we're engaged."

"No, he didn't." She looked at Charlie's hand. "What a lovely ring."

"Yes, It's great. It's special and I really treasure it."

Cheryl gave Charlie a kiss and then came over and gave me one.

"Cheryl, watch it. Don't excite him."

Charlie got changed into casual clothes and took the kids off for a bath.

Cheryl was clearly thinking. "Peter, where are you going to live?"

"Not sure. If it's here I'll need a green card, but maybe UK, or could be Australia if that's what Charlie wants. We've got to sort out Peter's education fairly soon."

"If you three go we will both miss you terribly."

Charlie came back and the children went off to read in Peter's room. "Charlie, we can't download the form. We have to fill it in on line, we get a reference number and then we go to the Clerk's office to sign it and pick it up.

We spent the next half hour filling the form in, trying to remember details of our past lives, like my ex-wife's maiden name and what her middle name was.

Charlie hugged me when we'd done it all. "Fine, if we leave at eight o'clock to-morrow we can be at the Clerk's office when it opens at 8.30. We can get the licence and then we can decide what to do next." She looked at Cheryl. "OK for school?"

"Fine. I'll take them both back now with me, if you like. It will be easier in the morning and you two can celebrate."

She left us and we had a quiet drink. "Peter, your parents? Won't they want to be there when we're married?"

"They don't like travelling and they would be terribly nervous here. What about your parents?"

"They rather disapprove of me because of Peter."

"But everybody knows about the art world's licentious living."

"Not my parents in up-state New York."

"Why don't we just get married here and go and see your parents when we can? And mine for that matter."

"You seem very keen."

"My darling, I don't want to lose you." I didn't add 'like I lost Helen' but then I didn't have to with Charlie. "You have to have twenty four hours between getting the license and filling in the actual marriage form. Apparently we can go to the Clerk's office the next day, stand in line, and get the marriage certificate certified so that it's on record. Cheryl can meet us and be the witness"

"Well to-day's still Monday. We can get married on Wednesday."

"Like Solomon Grundy, Charlie."

"Hope not. Didn't he get taken ill Thursday, grew worse on Friday, died on Saturday, buried on Sunday, that was the end of Solomon Grundy?"

I ignored her. "It's a pity that the kids won't be there."

"They can be if we don't send them to school. However I think it will be a lot easier if they go to school as usual. There won't be much room where we actually get married."

"Yes, you're right."

"Don't worry, darling. Peter will soon get used to it. He regards you as part of the family already."

"I know. It's amazing and rather nice. By the way I suppose you will be able to get some time off to get married?"

"Hope so. I'll ask Wendy to-morrow."

In the morning we didn't see Cheryl at all as we left well before 8 o'clock. We were at the office before it opened and we were registered as first in line to get our licence. We identified ourselves to the official's satisfaction, signed the licence, got it approved, checked we could come back to get the certificate the following day and walked off with the licence. Charlie dashed off to work and I slowly went back to the apartment.

Charlie called me. “Just one problem, Wendy wants to be there as well. She thinks you’re lovely.”

“That’s nice. Clearly a woman of distinction. We’d better have lunch somewhere. How about the Boathouse where we started our lives again?”

“Great idea but Wendy says Tavern on the Green in the Park would be better.”

“A woman of discernment as well. What else does she say.”

“You’d better make a reservation.”

“A woman of experience.”

I did as I was told and was wondering my next move when Harry Foster called. “Matt has called. He’s fired Henderson.”

“What about Tucker?”

“He’s had to resign. Apparently the Australian police checked his visa and movements. He was in Australia when you were pushed. Matt thinks the police will be contacting you any day now. He’s furious with himself for not realising something was wrong.”

“What deal did you make?”

“Matt doesn’t want to stop selling the product so we will have an exclusive deal with him. He’ll buy everything from us except the ground database.”

“You know Harry, you ought to buy his database, it’s not really your speciality and it will need updating all the time.”

Harry laughed. “For once I’m ahead of you. Matt’s going to see what he can do.”

“When are you coming over to negotiate the deal?”

“How did you know? Thursday for Friday.”

“That’s convenient. You won’t have to go back until Monday morning.”

“Peter, you can read the future.”

“No I can’t. I’m just good at making obvious deductions and I’m delighted you’re getting some time off. Are we going to see you?”

“Don’t know yet but I expect so. Do you want to come with me to see Matt and his team?”

"Thanks for the offer but I don't think I can contribute anything. Come to think of it I may have to go to Taipei though now I know you're coming I'll try and put it off until Monday."

I did some work giving advice on some routine insurance claims when an email arrived from John Southern. He was sending the forms special delivery which should arrive on the Friday. He had told Fred to expect a call from me giving my arrival details.

Cheryl brought Peter in and left me in charge. Charlie came back from work, disappeared to get out of her working clothes and reappeared as Peter was getting into bed.

"You're doing superbly, darling. I'll take over now. I want to have a chat with him."

I grabbed a beer and some time later she appeared looking pleased. "I just told him that you were going to live with both of us from now on."

"What did he say?"

"Nothing really. He seemed to assume that it had already happened."

"Is he going to stop calling me Peter?"

"Shouldn't think so." She looked at me in a speculative way. "Do you want him to?"

"Well it's all going to be very confusing when you call 'Peter'. You should have called him something else 'John' or 'James'."

"There's no problem. You're 'darling' and he's 'Peter'. Anyway it's too late now. Stop yattering and get me a drink. I need it. In a way I wouldn't mind getting the Australian job as I won't have to be so polite to customers who don't know the back of a picture from the front. Mind you it won't solve anything will it?"

"I thought we had decided it wouldn't matter. And I'll tell you something. It will be easier to get a house and a decent school in Canberra than here in New York, or in UK for that matter."

"Not sure about that, but how about some rain?"

"They've got plenty of rain in Queensland and lots of sun for desalination in Sydney, Melbourne, Adelaide and Perth. In addition the country has got lots of minerals. Nowhere in the world is perfect, my love. Life's a compromise, you know that."

"I agree. When are we going to do the Canberra application form?"

"Not to-night. We need to celebrate our last night of freedom."

"H'm. Not sure I like the sound of that."

I gave her a pinot grigio. "We have a problem, your cellar is disappearing fast for some reason."

"It won't matter as our cellar is going to increase with effect from to-morrow."

"Which reminds me Miss Simpson, when you become Mrs Talbert what are you going to call yourself? And an associated question how am I going to get a US bank account quickly as a poor limey."

"Well what I thought we'd do for a start, maybe to-morrow afternoon, is to go in to my bank and open a new joint account which effectively can be yours only. You'll need that for all your bills and payments and transfers from UK. As for the Mrs Talbert, forget it. I shall carry on being Charlie Simpson, art expert."

I remembered I hadn't told Charlie about Harry coming to New York. She was amused and said we should tell Cheryl.

"You're joking. I bet Cheryl knew long before I did."

The phone rang and I watched Charlie answering it. It was clearly Cheryl telling Charlie about Harry. I felt Charlie would be more comfortable if I wasn't listening to every word so I went into the spare bedroom and switched on the television. She collected me about ten minutes later. "You can come out now. I'm glad you warned me about Harry."

"Are we going to see them?"

"Possibly. She says she'll let us know to-morrow at the wedding."

I couldn't help grinning. "That's a fine turn of phrase. What are you going to wear my love. I'm a bit surprised you haven't been rushing round buying something."

"You will have to wait and see. Are you going to go with Cheryl to the clerk's office and wait for the bride?"

"No I'm not. I thought we'd all go down in a yellow cab. You might change your mind."

"You're just not romantic, but I agree. What are you going to wear?"

"The only suit I've got here."

"A good decision. What colour is it?"

"Dark grey. By the way there's something else I haven't told you. How do you feel about going to Taipei on a honeymoon?"

"The same way as I would feel having a hamburger in Super Sam's down the street for a wedding breakfast. When are you off?"

"I thought I might go Monday 1115 and get in 2200 on Tuesday."

"But you can't go on your own. You might damage your arm. And you still can't cut up all your food. And it sounds like a long trip, my love."

" 'fraid so. Change in Tokyo, about 22 hours. Gruesome."

"Hope you're getting well paid. When will we back?"

"Are you sure you can get away?"

"I'll double check but a honeymoon is a good excuse."

"Well I think we should be back Friday, if we can get away first thing Friday morning we can be back after lunch, same day via Tokyo. Only takes just over 17 hours coming back."

"Great. Come on, we've got a lot to do to-morrow. Cheryl's dealing with Peter in the morning while we get dressed."

In the morning we got up early, saw Cheryl get Peter away and then we got dressed. I put on my suit early and got out of the way which was just as well as John Southern phoned and started going through the insurance options with me. I told him to write it all out very carefully and be prepared for phone calls in the middle of the night.

Charlie appeared in a super light yellow suit which she filled beautifully and I produced an orchid which I'd had the forethought to buy the previous day on the way back from getting the licence. Cheryl appeared on time and we went down to Worth Street in a cab. I saw Wendy waiting in the lobby and we agreed it was a long time since we'd last met. "Peter, I'm not surprised you're getting married. I could see you two were very close when we were trying to find those paintings a few years ago."

We went in to the 'marriage' room, the licence was inspected as were our identification documents. The official got Cheryl to sign the form and the certificate was stamped. It all seemed very correct. We were told that a formal notice would be sent to us confirming that our marriage was in the New York City records. There was no marriage ceremony and nor were the words used 'Do you Charlie Simpson take this man Peter Talbert to be your lawful wedded husband' or what ever was the equivalent in the States. We left clutching the marriage certificate, knowing we were married but feeling we were missing something. Wendy sensed the situation. "What we need now is a celebratory drink," and she hailed a cab.

At the Tavern on the Green we were shown to our table and I ordered champagne. Things rapidly improved after the second bottle and Wendy decided her office would be a better place if she didn't turn up that afternoon. Cheryl left to get Peter and Sonia and at about 3.30pm Wendy decided she'd better go home and try to sober up before her husband came back from work. We thought in the circumstances it might be better if we caught a cab and were delighted to find that Cheryl had Peter with her and had left a note, 'see you to-morrow.' Charlie thoughtfully started helping me undress even though I could do it by myself now.

Later we sat on the sofa and I idly considered the situation. "Mrs Talbert, what happens next?"

She got up and went over to her desk. I looked at her. "Charlie, my love, do you think you will do yourself justice trying to fill in the form in your condition."

"What's wrong with my condition?"

"Depends what you're trying to achieve."

"I don't have to be dressed to fill in a form. You're altogether too conventional. You can come over here and help."

"I'm not sure if I come over it's going to help."

"Well we'll just have to see but be careful with your arm."

***

In the morning I gave Charlie the National Gallery application form before she left. "I'll be far too busy to look at it," was her parting remark.

Cheryl came in later and sorted out Peter's clothes. "Are you free Saturday night? We thought we might go out for a meal."

"Great. We'll sort out the details later."

Understandably Charlie hadn't taken me to her bank yesterday but I definitely needed an account. I decided I'd better try to do my accounts but it was difficult without being in my office in London. I checked my bank statement on line and I was glad to see that the three times my salary was already in my current account. I moved the payment into my web saver fixed interest account and made a note to get some financial advice. I sent a text message to Charlie to remind her and she told me to meet her at the Chase Bank in the same street as the apartment at 5.15pm. She opened a new account with me as a signatory and we went home.

I told her about Cheryl and Saturday night and I heard them making the arrangements. Then she called Liz in Sydney telling her we were now married. She also mentioned that my Safety Board job had not materialised. That evening I called Fred in Taipei and told him when I planned to arrive.

"Mr Talbert, I don't understand why you are coming all this way to see me."

"Fred, I'm afraid we need to discuss the maintenance of the CC21 that had an accident in Hong Kong. We have made some more investigations. I have discovered the whole truth of the autopilot modifications and the arrangement with Mr Derek."

"Mr Talbert. I still don't understand what you are saying but I'm sure we will be able to explain everything."

"Good. Please collect me at 0900 from the Towneplace Marriott on Wednesday morning."

Charlie, who had been listening, commented "He didn't seem too pleased."

"I think he will be getting very worried. I'd better make sure I can book the flight we need and the hotel. I should really have done that first but I wanted to be certain he wasn't going to run away or make some excuse why we shouldn't go."

I made the necessary reservations and then Mike Mansell called me. "Peter, Liz tells me your job has fallen through. I thought it was all settled."

"Yes, Mike it was. I should have told you. Would you believe after signing the contract the job itself was cancelled?" I explained how the EU had in fact vetoed the whole concept.

"Peter, that's ridiculous. Surely your government doesn't allow itself to be pushed around like that? I bet the French wouldn't, EU or no EU."

"Mike, I can't argue. It's just what I said. For some reason at the moment our politicians and our senior civil servants seem to love the EU. Sometimes I think it's just for the money. As you can guess I'm not an EU lover."

"Are they paying you any compensation?"

"Three times salary."

"I suppose from their point of view it's very generous bearing in mind you hadn't done anything."

"It's no substitute for having a job, Mike. I was gradually disengaging and I suppose now I'll have to start looking for work again. Anyway I'd better stop complaining. Hope we'll be seeing you and Liz again soon."

I rang off and we went to bed. On Friday both Charlie and I worked, she in her office while I worked in the apartment. Saturday we took Peter swimming and then he went to visit friends. Charlie decided she would try to complete the forms for the job at the National Gallery, Canberra.

"What about referees, my love?"

"I've got the Director of the Guggenheim and the Managing Director of Christies in London."

"That sounds fantastic. How do you know them."

"Well we insure some of the Guggenheim pictures when they are in transit and I've done quite a bit of work at Christie's one way and another."

"Have you written why you want the job?"

"I'm in the middle of doing that now. If you leave me alone you can check it all in about an hour."

"Don't forget to mention you're married and have a dependent spouse. If you don't do that they may not let me in."

"Relax. You can check everything when I've finished."

Later on we went through the pages together and Charlie typed in the final changes. Then she emailed the whole thing to the firm in Sydney that the Gallery had commissioned to produce a short list.

We got changed and Susan arrived to look after Peter and Sonia. We went to Cheryl's apartment to find Harry already there. After a drink we walked round to a restaurant near by and had a very pleasant evening. Harry told me he had come to an agreement with Matt and final details were currently being worked out.

On Sunday we did very little. Charlie decided we could manage with a carry on bag, my netbook and one bag to be checked. The next morning we left at 7.30 to go to Kennedy and the aircraft was pushed back spot on time at 1100. After a change in Tokyo we arrived Tuesday evening and went straight to the hotel. I managed a few hours sleep before we got up and had breakfast. I called the embassy and spoke to Alice.

"I'm back here in the same hotel. I'm seeing the boss of the airline who I think may have planned the attack on me last time I was here."

"Is that wise, Mr Talbert?"

"My wife is a judo expert and is with me. I just wanted you to know we're here."

"Be very careful, Mr Talbert."

I rang off and Fred called.

"Mr Talbert, I shall be at your hotel at nine o'clock."

It didn't seem worth arguing so I didn't and twenty minutes later he was at the hotel. Charlie wanted to go downstairs but I persuaded her to stay; I felt very weak with the sling and I knew she was very strong. I asked him up to my suite. He looked a bit shaken when he saw Charlie but I explained how I needed help with my arm and couldn't travel by myself. In fact Charlie disappeared into the bedroom.

He started checking all round my apartment, presumably looking for hidden microphones.

"Fred, don't worry I don't have a tape recorder and as far as I know the room is not bugged. Incidentally my wife never repeats anything she hears and there are no secrets between us."

Fred still looked carefully at the walls before starting. "Mr Talbert, I told you over the phone I did not understand what you were saying about the autopilot modifications."

"Fred, its quite simple. The necessary modifications were not done to the autopilot, the modification sheet you showed me was filled in after the accident and Mr Derek conspired with you so that he would say nothing in return for an agreed payment. What you hadn't realised was that there was a hardware modification that went with the software modification and that was not carried out."

Fred hesitated for a moment and then looked horrified. "Are you sure, Mr Talbert? This is all news to me. Oscar told me everything was correct. What shall we do?"

Clearly Fred was going to pretend it was nothing to do with him and he didn't know anything.

"I don't what you're going to do, Fred, but I've made a full report to Hull Claims. I'm not a lawyer but I understand that deception will probably invalidate the whole insurance claim."

For the first time Fred looked a little unsure of the situation. I felt he was sizing me up. "Mr Talbert, surely we can come to some arrangement."

"Like the one you came to with Derek, Fred?"

I got the feeling he then gave up trying to bribe me and was trying another approach. "Mr Talbert, I am deeply offended that you think I knew about this mistake and was trying to ask Derek not to tell his firm."

"Well that's one way of putting it."

"Clearly Yang Jianli has done something very wrong and I will investigate what really happened. I would not want to have a dispute with Hull Claims."

"Fred, I've done my job. I have found out why the accident happened due to faulty maintenance and, of course, incorrect briefing to the flight crews who should have known that the autopilot was not cleared for automatic landing. Furthermore the pilots were not getting regular training on the simulator for Cat III landings. Had they been trained they might have been able to deal with the autopilot and engine failure. Now what happens financially is between you and Hull Claims. By the way, Derek has now admitted he knew the aircraft wasn't modified."

Fred looked unsure what to say but remarked, unwisely in my opinion, "I knew nothing about it."

"Hull Claims have asked me to get you to sign these papers which set out the insurance arrangements for all your aircraft from now on. In addition there is a form saying that Hull Claims will not be paying the full insurance for the CC21."

"Mr Talbert, they have to pay half whatever happens."

"Fred, not if the airline has made a fraudulent claim."

Fred looked very worried indeed. I made it clear that the conversation was over for the moment and Fred left. The time in UK was 8 o'clock in the morning so I called John Southern and told him about my conversation with Fred. "John, I think that Fred will pretend he knew nothing about the deal. He looks like a survivor. What are you going to tell your boss?"

"The facts as we know them. He can deal with Derek."

"Fire him, you mean I hope."

"You bet."

"What about the insurance? Not that it's anything to do with me. I told Fred you didn't have to pay for the CC21 as there had been a fraudulent claim. He looked very unhappy."

"I shall call him and tell him that he will have to sign the revised insurance conditions which you've got with you or we shall be suspending his whole insurance."

"When are you going to do that?"

"I'll call him after midnight to-night my time, your to-morrow morning first thing so that he can meet you during the day and sign the forms."

"Great. That means we should be able to get away Friday and be back Saturday in New York."

Charlie and I had a meal in the restaurant and we discussed my interview with Fred which she had listened to with interest with her door partly open.

In the morning Fred called at 9.30 when I was just beginning to get worried. He wouldn't let me come to his office but he came to the hotel at 11 o'clock. I showed him the forms.

"Mr Talbert, I'm not sure I can sign these forms. It will cost our airline a lot of extra money and we won't have been paid in full for the loss of our CC21."

"I understand your problem Fred but if you don't sign by the end of the day then I believe none of your aircraft will be covered. Fraudulent insurance claims cannot be tolerated."

"But I had no idea."

"So you keep on saying." I stopped and looked at him. "And I suppose you had no idea that I was attacked in my hotel room after I left you last time I was here and had to go to hospital?"

He looked suitably concerned.

“No. I had no idea. What happened?”

“Someone entered my room when I was in the coffee shop and hit me when I got back, nearly killed me.”

“That’s terrible. How long were you in hospital?”

“Several days.”

“Did you get your things back?”

I looked at him steadily. “Fred, how do you know I lost anything?”

He realised he had made a terrible mistake but tried to recover. “I assumed it was a robbery.”

“You were right. You wanted to get the copies of the autopilot sheets back which Oscar had given me because you knew that there should have been a reference to an associated aircraft modification introducing a terminal box for the cabling.” Fred looked at me wondering what I was going to do or, it suddenly occurred to me, how he was going to get me silenced. “I haven’t told the police yet of what you did and I won’t if you sign these forms now. However I have told the UK embassy.”

I saw Charlie emerge quietly from the bedroom looking very threatening standing next to Fred. He looked very unsure of himself whilst obviously calculating what to do.

“You can’t prove anything.”

“I don’t think you would welcome being investigated. Fred, I have no desire to tell the police so this is what we’ll do. Listen very carefully. Give my wife your mobile phone right now. We are going to pack up, check out and go to the airport. You are going to come with us. We will give you your phone back at the airport.”

Fred hesitated and I picked up the phone to call the police. He reluctantly produced his phone and Charlie took it and stood between Fred and the door. I started packing up all our things at high speed though my arm made me rather slow. I could see Fred thinking and so was I. Fred still hadn’t signed the forms. “It makes no difference to me whether you sign the forms or not but your aircraft will be uninsured if you don’t sign.”

He hesitated, took out his pen and signed the forms. I gave him his copies but I could see he was eyeing the door.

"If you leave us before we get to the airport then I will make sure that the police know what really happened that Friday evening."

"But you have to check-out."

"No we don't. They will bill me but thank you for being so concerned."

The irony was lost on him. We left and Fred had clearly decided to do what I wanted. At the airport Charlie gave him his phone and we left him to pay for the cab. We didn't wait for our planned flight but managed to get on the 1840 to Los Angeles and we were very glad when we had actually taken off.

"Charlie, you were marvellous with Fred."

"Don't' sound so surprised. I think you forget sometimes that I'm an athlete and very strong. They didn't give me my job as an investigator because I adorn the place."

"But you do."

"Thank you, Sir, she said. By the way you were pretty good yourself. I kept the door ajar and heard every word. You certainly know some very nasty people what with him and Greco."

"Not to mention Tommy Tucker. The fact is that we are both in risky businesses when it comes to illegal goings on."

At Los Angeles we had a short wait in the lounge before catching the first daylight flight to New York. While waiting I saw a headline in the locally printed Financial Times. Apparently there was going to be a UK General Election brought on by arguments within the Government's Members of Parliament and Ministers.

We were back in the apartment by 5pm and Peter came rushing in from Cheryl's apartment. We both tried to stay awake but decided to go to bed soon after Peter.

***

In the morning I called John Southern and told him that Fred had signed the forms.

"You did well, Peter. I didn't think he'd sign so quickly."

"He didn't have much alternative. I told him I would go to the police and tell them."

"Tell them? Tell them what? Peter, you're not making sense."

"About the hit man he sent round to the hotel and nearly killed me. I told you all about it."

"No you didn't. You told me you'd been knocked down and robbed. Is this anything to do with the your arm being broken?"

"No, John. That was something else. I thought the robbery was all too convenient for Fred and Oscar. My suspicions were aroused when my cards hadn't been used."

"Peter, I'm not sure we ought to be doing business with them."

"Well wait and see if Fred stays on as MD."

As I put the phone down it started to ring again. It was Harry just as Charlie was producing breakfast. "The FAA have been looking at our system with a view to certificating it, Peter. I'm so glad you advised us to get them to look."

"Harry, where are you? Can't you sleep? It must be 5.30 in the morning Pacific Daylight Time."

"You're quite right but I took a red eye special to JFK and I'm just down the corridor. Cheryl invited me over for the week-end."

"Harry, are you sure she wants to be involved with EVS on a Saturday morning?"

"It's OK. She's just taken Sonia to dancing lessons."

"Great. Well I don't wish to be unsympathetic but it's half term and we're having breakfast at our end of the corridor and Charlie is indicating that we need to close the hangar doors if that translate into American."

"Understood, Peter. Talk to you later."

Charlie looked at me and grinned. "You're a Yenta."

"I can't be a Yenta because she's a female matchmaker. Is there a word for a male one, not of course that I am one? Surely you've been here long enough to speak Yiddish."

"I don't know the word but I'm sure there is one. Anyway you know what I mean. You've known Cheryl five minutes and you've as good as married her off."

"Charlie, it would be nice if it worked out. They've both had a rotten time." She nodded. "Are we seeing them this week-end?"

"No idea. I don't like to worry her when Harry's here. If she wants to see us she'll call."

I nodded but part of me wanted to know what the FAA people had said to Vision Unlimited. Charlie went out with Peter and I went into the spare bedroom to look at my email. They returned at about 4pm but my phone rang as I was about to join them. It was Harry.

"Peter, have you finished your breakfast? Why don't we all have lunch together to-morrow?"

"Good idea but I'll have to check with the management." Charlie had worked out what Harry was saying, dug me in the ribs and nodded. "I've checked and we'd love to."

"Good. Can you spare a moment?"

"I expect so but we'd better be quick."

"The FAA said the EVS with the radar is great but for an automatic landing the system must be switched off. I believe that's their standard ruling on business jets as well as airliners. They are frightened of a conflict between the visual and automatic systems."

"Harry, that seems absolutely right. Airlines are buying your system to land at airfields which are not equipped for automatic landings, and/or have inadequate airfield lighting and/or have ILS not to the full standard. You don't have a problem with that do you?"

"I suppose not. I thought pilots would like to be able to see the airfield while the aircraft was doing an automatic landing. However we've discussed it and we're making the necessary provisions for switching."

"Harry, the risk assessment of the automatic landing system has been done without EVS. Having the pilot watching could actually reduce the safety factor. It depends on the software standard of the EVS and also on the integration software. Another thing, the directional accuracy of the EVS must be virtually perfect so that it lines up with the ILS and the runway itself. If both systems are on together there has to be a perfect match or the pilot won't know which system to trust."

"Anyway, Peter, whatever I think doesn't matter. As I said we're making a small alteration to our design to provide an interlink with the autopilot so that when automatic landing is selected the EVS cannot be selected to the displays until the approach is finished and the aircraft has landed. It's no big deal."

"That's first class. When do you get your first customer?"

"Very soon. On an ITAC airplane, which is convenient being on the West Coast."

Charlie was still listening and pushing me to stop. "See you tomorrow, Harry."

We put Peter to bed and sat down. "Darling, how are you managing to carry on your business living here?"

"I've been thinking about that. At the moment all my telephones are being diverted to my UK mobile but it's a bit inconvenient. How about having another line here and having an answering machine?"

"That won't be a problem but we've got to decide sometime where we're going to live. This apartment isn't big enough for us if we're going to live in New York. If we go to London then you've got your house so that's OK except that it needs a complete going over. Actually I'd prefer that we had a new house together; I don't like sharing it with all your wives and girl friends."

"What about Australia, Charlie?"

"Look we both know that Australia isn't really an option. I think you'd go mad living and working in Canberra while I work at the Gallery. Anyway I haven't been short listed yet. When push comes to shove they'll want a local."

"Not sure you're right and from my point of view CASA, Air Services Australia and the Australian Transport Safety Bureau are all headquartered there." She raised her eyebrows. "The Australian safety people, the air traffic headquarters and the accident investigation people are all based in Canberra."

"But your business is worldwide. Australia is only a very small part of the world aviation scene."

"I know but their aviation expertise is second to none."

"Alright, good. Anyway we don't have to decide now. You can get me a drink and we can watch an old British TV programme on PBS."

Chapter 14

Charlie called me from the office late Monday afternoon. "I've arranged the second telephone line. A guy is coming in to-morrow morning to swap the single outlet to a double. By the way, the head hunters want to talk to me. I didn't want to do it from the office so they are calling me this evening."

"I thought they might short list you without an interview in view of your experience, qualifications etc."

"Apparently not. I expect they have to justify the money they charge the Gallery. By the way I think you're on duty with both kids after school. Harry hasn't gone back yet."

"Tell me about it. They are both racing round at the moment. Cheryl was in and out like a flash. Surely Harry should get some practice in?"

"I'm not sure I'd trust him with Peter."

Charlie arrived as the children were drying themselves. She changed out of her working clothes, read to them and put them to bed. She then had time to sit down and read her notes and her application form before the phone rang and she was talking to the recruiters. The interview seemed fairly routine but then, at the end, it seemed rather familiar. I recognised that they were checking whether Charlie had any hidden domestic problems that would only become apparent when the media started investigating her. "I am very happily married and have one boy, nearly six years old."

There was a pause while the interviewer responded. "My husband is English, a recognised expert on aviation insurance matters."

Another pause. "This is a global world. He can work from anywhere and I'm sure Canberra would be perfect with CASA, Air Services Australia and the Australian Transport Safety Bureau all headquartered there." A pause. "Surely you know, the Civil Air Safety Agency, the headquarters of the Australian air traffic system and the accident investigation people?"

Another pause. "I wouldn't be interested in the job if he couldn't get an unrestricted visa and be able to work in Australia."

The interview came to a close. I grinned. “You didn’t say how long you’d been married and that the boy was an add-on if you know what I mean. They probably thought he was ours.”

“Well he is from now on.”

“It sounded as if you were going to say ‘Don’t call me. I’ll call you’.”

“I thought I’d spell it out. There are lots of jobs going.”

“I was very impressed with your knowledge of what was in Canberra.”

“Well we had only just discussed it the other night.” She looked at me with some concern. “I suppose you will be able to get the right sort of visa?”

“I don’t know. I imagine so, though they have a points system which I imagine I would need to satisfy.”

“Surely if I’m working in Canberra and you’re my husband you’ll have all the points you need.”

“I’ve always assumed so but it will be worth checking if I’m allowed to work. The only problem might be that I won’t be working for an Australian organisation. Anyway no point in worrying about it. If you are short listed and called for interview you can make it clear what is required. I’m sure they have human resources people who can find the answer very quickly. I suppose I could download the information pamphlets which have the rules but they look very difficult to interpret and I’d rather not.”

“Well it’s all over now. I’ve probably blown it.”

“Nonsense. Did they tell you when you might hear?”

“Very soon, they said, whatever that means and I’d like a gin and tonic, thank you.”

I joined her and we went to bed early. In the middle of the night I suddenly had an impossible thought about Trevor and the crashed aircraft VP-BEV. I wanted to wake Charlie up and tell her my wild idea but I remembered that last time I had done that I hadn’t been the flavour of the month, even though the idea turned out to be a winner. I tried not to wake her but she moved. I heard a sort of mumble. “What is it this time?” She rolled over and held me tight.

“How did you know that I’ve had an idea? And that’s not helping.”

“Are you sure?”

***

But I still remembered my idea in the morning. Cheryl came in to collect Peter and Sonia. She told me that Harry was on his way to Palmdale and gave me his mobile number as I was very keen to contact him in case he didn’t go straight to his office. I sent him a text message asking him to call but I had to wait until 5pm before he rang.

“What’s the problem, Peter? I’ve just driven up the freeway and got home. It’s a long flight.”

“Harry, have you ever delivered a system to an airliner?”

“Certainly not. Why do you ask?”

“That aircraft that crashed at Kennedy. It had some sort of EVS system?”

“Are you sure? Who supplied it?”

“Not certain yet. The Castle Harbour chief pilot thinks it was a European Aerospace system. Presumably from an avionic firm in Europe, Smiths, or whatever they’re called now or maybe a French firm like Thales.”

“Peter, whoever supplied it is irrelevant because it was doing an automatic landing. It must have been certificated. According to FAA the system would have been locked out. The FAA had made us interlink the system with the landing gear so that it couldn’t work again until after the aircraft had touched down.”

“Good point. However I would like to know where the system came from and what the safety interlinks were. I had better talk to EASA and see what their rules are. They should be the same as the FAAs.”

I rang off and decided I’d try Bill Castleford. He was still in the office. “Bill, Peter Talbert here. The accident to Echo Victor.”

“Peter, have you got any news?”

“No. But I’ve got some questions. Your chief pilot didn’t seem to know who made the EVS when I asked him some time back. How well briefed is your chief of maintenance?”

"Jonathan Stable? He'll know a bit but we didn't give the system any priority since it never worked when the autopilot was working."

"Can you transfer me?"

Jonathan hadn't left and came on line. "Can't tell you much about the system, Peter. European provided it. I saw it work in their simulator and it was amazingly realistic but EASA hadn't given it a full release so the pilots were not allowed to use it in the circuit. Anyway it was locked out when making an autopilot approach."

Before going to bed I sent Monty Rushmore an email asking for a contact to discuss the EVS on the Castle Harbour European 630. My mobile rang at 6.30am just as Charlie was getting up.

It was Monty. "Peter, hope I didn't wake you. Great to talk to you. I did the certification on Echo Victor. The Castle Harbour 630 had been used by European for preliminary test work on an EVS system. It was actually a very good system with passive infra red, a synthetic ground display and I think it had a some sort of radar as well. They hadn't certificated the software and hardware installation with EASA and so we wanted to prohibit its use altogether but someone in European pulled some strings with EASA and we were prevailed upon to let it work but prohibit its use in the circuit."

"Do you know how they did it?"

"No. They should have put an interlink with the autopilot and the landing gear operation."

"Did you fly the aircraft after the EVS had been prevented from operating during a landing?"

"No. It was such an easy thing to do."

"I thought the FAA certificated the Bermuda aircraft."

"Yes, that's right. But they rely on EASA once they've agreed the basic aircraft certification."

"Monty, do you have any idea who was responsible for the EVS design?"

"'fraid not. You'd better ask them. Now you come to mention it they were rather coy about the whole system. I know it sounds silly but they were almost embarrassed that the system worked so well."

"Monty, I think I know why they were so coy. Thanks for the information."

"Do you think the EVS had anything to do with the accident?"

"I don't know. Let me ask you a question. Did the EVS work with the autopilot?"

"Certainly not. It was locked out."

"But it did work flying around."

"Yes."

"From what you've said you must have tried it in the circuit even if you wouldn't let Castle Harbour use it"

"Absolutely."

"Thanks a lot. I'll call European. Do you have a contact?"

"Try Ludwig Teifel, their chief pilot."

We had breakfast and the moment Charlie left, the phone man arrived and installed the second telephone line with broadband. After he had finished I found the number in Munich for European Aerospace and called Ludwig Teifel. I explained I was involved with Echo Victor and wanted some information on the EVS. "Peter, good to hear from you. I think we have met. I'm afraid I can't help you. I don't know anything about the EVS. You must talk to our publicity people."

Somehow I sensed that Ludwig should have said 'I won't help' you rather than 'I can't help you." I decided not to waste any more time but to call Harry.

"Peter, what are you saying? That Total Avionics had installed a complete system infra red, radar, synthetic vision on Echo Victor?"

"That's what I believe."

"Are you sure?"

"It is the only thing that makes sense. Tommy Tucker must have done a deal with European to use one of their EVS trial systems on a test aircraft. Echo Victor was new to Castle Harbour airlines but it clearly had done a lot of flying with European. CHA obviously got the aircraft at a favourable price as it was not brand new."

"Peter, European must be very embarrassed. Presumably they know that Chris Henderson and Tommy Tucker have gone and I bet the grape vine has told them why."

"How are we going to prove what happened?"

"I'll call Matt and tell him what we suspect and get his new man at Basingstoke to investigate."

"Sounds good."

"By the way I think Tommy Tucker removed the infra red sensor and the radar antenna when the fuselage was in the WeScrapIt facility."

"Why would he want to that?"

"Not sure. Presumably he didn't want anybody to know where the equipment came from."

No sooner had I put the phone down than Charlie called from her office. "I'm on the short list."

"Surprise. When are we going?"

"Surely you don't want to go to Australia again?"

"Why not. We've got to decide where we're going to live."

"Canberra, of course, if I get the job."

"You didn't answer my question."

"How does next Monday grab you?"

"Badly. I'll have to stay to look after Peter."

"I was going to ask Cheryl."

"I think you may find that Cheryl is busier than she used to be."

"I'd forgotten about the Harry dimension." She laughed. "And it's all your fault. I'll try to see if Susan will live in while we're away. She did it while I was in UK the first time. We shouldn't be away more than five days." She was obviously thinking. "Are you sure you want to come? It would be nice but I'll be so busy and not thinking about us at all."

"Let's talk it over this evening."

I called my phone provider and asked them to arrange call forwarding so that if the phone was not answered in the UK after five rings the call would be transferred to my new phone number in Charlie's apartment. I was very impressed as about an hour later the calls started coming. An answer phone would clearly be required as Charlie wouldn't be over the moon if UK calls started coming in at 4 o'clock in the morning.

I thought about Australia and came to the conclusion it was silly for me to go with Charlie, but then I realised that after losing

Helen I was scared of losing Charlie. While I was musing over the problem she arrived, quite early for a change. "I've checked the flight and we're going to have to leave on Friday to arrive Sunday morning and get some rest before the interview. I'm about to book, OK? With Qantas business. Shall we stay in the Rydges again?"

I nodded and noticed she had assumed that I was going with her and, despite what she had said earlier, she was treating my trip as a fait accompli.

She came over, gave me the FT and we sat down. She held me tight. "All done. But you didn't have to worry. I wouldn't have gone to any vineyards." I looked at her with my eyes going moist and she kissed me. "It didn't make any real sense when you said you wanted to come with me just for the interview and then I worked out what the problem was."

"You make it very hard for me to have secrets."

"Good. I don't like secrets. What have you been doing to-day?"

I explained about Echo Victor.

"What happens next?"

"I'm waiting to hear from Harry after he's spoken to Matt Watkins at Total Avionics. I want to talk to someone in European engineering but I've got to pick my moment. I got a brush off from the Chief Pilot but I think he was only following orders."

"New subject. Did you see the paper?"

"How could I? You've only just given it to me."

I looked at it and it was full of the forthcoming UK election and the endless political promises that were likely to be forgotten once the election was over. It all seemed so stupid.

Harry didn't call me until midday EST the following day. "Matt said you were right. He spoke to the new guy in charge at Basingstoke and apparently it was their test system which European had agreed to fly. But because it used so much of our technology they wanted to keep the systems under wraps. Then European needed to make a sale for their year end results and apparently Tommy Tucker was a bit concerned that it still had the EVS gear on."

"So where does that leave Castle Harbour?"

"Can't answer that but you might like to know that European have been on to our marketing people asking us to quote for an

EVS system. I think they've worked out that the system was basically ours. They want to offer it as a standard modification."

"Well done. It's your first sale."

"Listen. Are you going to be around next week-end?"

"Not this week-end. Charlie's going for an interview in Canberra and I'm going to carry her bag."

"What's happening to the boy? Can we help?"

"Thanks a lot Harry. Really appreciate that but Charlie's arranged for her regular sitter to live in while we're away and take Peter to school etc."

Friday came at great speed and we left at 1840. There was a two hour refuelling stop in Los Angeles and we were on our way again getting in 0920 on Sunday morning. We had both managed to get some sleep and as usual I was able to catch up with some work and magazines. Charlie had kept herself up to speed for her interview. Somehow we found our way to the domestic terminal and arrived at Canberra ready to lie down. We checked in at Rydges, had a shower and went to bed.

Charlie woke me and dragged me down to the restaurant. "If we sleep all evening we'll wake up in the middle of the night and then what will we do?" I didn't have a chance to reply. "That was a rhetorical question. I'm glad we decided to have a day off tomorrow. I think I'll need a day relaxing."

"What shall we do?"

"Rest, walk and eat."

We went back to our room and followed Charlie's instructions for the Monday. On Tuesday she caught a cab at nine fifteen for her ten o'clock interview. I found I couldn't concentrate during the morning but she finally appeared at 1pm on a high. She clearly had enjoyed herself. "Peter, I've no idea how I did but I had a lovely time talking to people who understood the art world."

"When will you hear?"

"In a few days."

"Did you explain your marital situation."

"They asked me and I pointed out there might be a difficulty with your coming out straightaway. I told them what you did and that you intended to work from Australia and that if there was a problem to include me out."

"That must have gone down well."

"Actually they looked concerned and said they would get their human resources people to look at the situation."

"That's good. They must be taking your application seriously." She nodded. "I've had an idea while you were away. Why don't we go to Sydney and see Mike and Liz if they're free? And if they're not we'll go out on the Town."

"To McDonalds on Circular Quay?"

"I rather like that revolving restaurant."

"Yes, it was great but perhaps we should try something else."

"OK. But let me try Mike."

I sent him a text message asking him to call and he came back almost immediately. I explained our situation and he suggested that we met at our hotel and then have dinner on a boat in the harbour. "It's not haute cuisine but the scenery is great. We will both have to come from our offices so it suits us. I'll book for a 6pm departure."

"Mike, why don't we meet at the boat at 1745 and we can use our mobiles if things are going pear shaped?"

I brought forward our flight with Qantas to a 10 o'clock departure the next morning and booked the Marriott again. Everything went according to plan and after checking in we walked in the Botanical Gardens. We were at the Quay in plenty of time. Mike and Liz arrived within a few minutes of each other and we went aboard. I had to explain my sling but I did not go into the full details. As Mike predicted the menu was not remarkable but the trip out to the Heads and back was very enjoyable. Charlie explained why she had come over and I noticed that Mike and Liz seemed very interested. Liz looked at us. "Where would you live? Canberra?"

Charlie laughed. "You say that as if Canberra is the end of the World and not the capital of Australia."

"Well Sydney is lot more exciting, even Melbourne would be."

Mike had been listening to the exchange. "When will you know, Charlie?"

"Very soon."

He looked at me. "Will you be able to come out? Where will you work?"

"Good point. Charlie said she wouldn't take the job without me. Apparently they are finding out the situation."

"Peter, I may have a solution if Charlie gets the job. My business is growing rapidly as I have just got a big job arranging the insurance of a lot of the new Qantas aircraft. I need help and it occurred to me you might like to join me as an equal partner." I was lost for words for a moment. "Peter, what do you think?"

"Mike, it is taking me a little time to comprehend what you are offering me and thinking out all the angles. It sounds incredibly generous and a great opportunity."

"Not sure about the generous bit, Peter. Even though we would be equal partners in the firm, the agreement obviously would have to recognise all the years I've spent building up the business. As for opportunity, if Charlie was offered the job it might suit you both."

"But we'd have to be in Canberra."

"It's a lot closer than London or New York."

"Are you sure you know what you're offering, Mike?"

"You bet. I'll be a lot happier checking the airlines out if you're there confirming correct maintenance and operation. And if anything goes wrong I won't have to pay someone else to protect our interests during the accident investigation."

"When do you need an answer?"

"As soon as possible but obviously you'll want to know about Charlie. Why don't you call me the moment you know if she's offered the job or not."

"Mike, we'll talk it over. We've always assumed that I would carry on as a one man band, a world wide consultant. I never considered a job like the one you're offering me.:

"Tell you what, Peter. You could still investigate accidents but it would be as a member of our firm."

"Sounds a good deal." I looked at Charlie who nodded.

The boat returned to Circular Quay and we said our farewells. In the morning our flight left at midday Thursday and we arrived still on Thursday twenty one hours later to be greeted by Peter and hear all his news. Charlie put him to bed and we immediately followed though we both woke up in the middle of the night feeling hungry.

"Charlie, six weeks are up. I need to see a specialist to confirm all is well with my arm and then start some therapy."

"We'll deal with it to-morrow." There was a pause. "Peter, what do you really think of Mike's offer?"

"My darling, I'm not sure. It's a great offer but it depends on you, obviously. If you don't get the job then we wouldn't want to live in Australia, would we?"

"If I didn't get the job we could live in Sydney if that's what you want. Mike said you could still do accident investigation."

"True, it's not as if you wouldn't have plenty to do for the first few months."

There was a long silence.

"Darling, are you asleep or is this a pregnant pause?"

She rolled over towards me. "Peter, how long have you known?"

"Well I sort of guessed. How long have you known?"

"For sure this evening when I checked the mail and saw the result of the blood test."

"Did they tell you whether Peter will have a brother or a sister?"

There was another very long pause.

"Out with it, darling. I bet you know."

"Don't you mean step brother or step sister."

"No, my love. I know what I mean."

She reached out and held my arm

"How long have you known?"

"Well it occurred to me that Peter was very advanced physically and mentally for the four years old you told me he was. You seemed a bit inconsistent talking about his age. If he was five my calculations told me that you must have been having it fast and loose with someone else while we were in St Antony. And I didn't believe that so Peter had to be ours."

"But we only made love once."

"So. It was a proper job, as they say in the west country."

"You can be very coarse sometimes." She thought some more. "When I accused you of marrying me because Peter didn't have a father, did you know then?"

"Well I certainly suspected but I was horrified that you thought I might be marrying you because of that."

"But when did you know for sure."

"When I was tidying up our clothes in the bedroom I saw something like a marriage certificate but it was Peter's birth certificate. The date of birth gave the game away and then I noticed you'd put my name on it as well, just to make sure, not that that would have counted because I hadn't signed the certificate."

"Why didn't you say something?"

"I asked you to marry me for the umpteenth time."

"But if I had known you knew I would have said yes."

"Exactly. That's why I tried to keep Peter out of the decision making process."

"You're too clever by half."

"Life's strange. What would have happened if there hadn't been that accident and I hadn't see you in New York?"

"You mean if I hadn't seen you. Peter would have grown up without a father."

"You might have met someone else."

"Maybe, I'm not sure. I'd already decided in St Antony that I wanted a child before I got any older. Though I would never have admitted it, I rather fancied you as the father though I resigned myself that we could never get married. So I stopped taking the pill while we were in St Antony and we had that one night stand though I haven't forgotten you rushed off and left me."

"Whose being coarse now?"

She ignored me. "When I saw you again I couldn't resist finding out what you'd been doing, particularly as you were avoiding me."

"So what happens next? Do we tell Peter?"

"About having a sister?"

"No, Charlie. About my being his father."

"Oh he worked that one out ages ago."

"Did you tell him?"

"Only when he asked."

"Well why does he call me Peter?"

"Because he likes it and for the moment it amuses him."

I got up and managed to grill a bacon sandwich with two cups of tea and returned with it all on a tray.

"I've married a treasure."

"But not an art treasure. Eat up, sup up and then shut up."

"That's very rude."

"We need some sleep. I don't know about you but I've got a mountain of mail and messages to deal with."

We turned the lights out. I poked her. "Did you mean sister?"

"What do you think?"

In the morning Peter was despatched to school by Cheryl, Charlie went to work and I settled down to work in the apartment.

***

Bill called me on my mobile. "Airline Protection have just told me that they've discovered that Echo Victor had a HUD which wasn't certificated properly and that they are not going to pay us in full."

"Yes, Bill, I was afraid they might."

"What do you mean, Peter?"

"Well I'll tell you what I think happened on the approach. For some reason best know to himself Trevor pulled his HUD down. When Trevor took the autopilot out to go round again the EVS appeared."

"But Peter, it was locked out on the approach."

"It should have been, but the interface modification hadn't been carried out properly. The EVS should be locked out on the approach but in fact it was only locked out when the autopilot was engaged. The correct interface would have prevented the EVS coming on again until the undercarriage had been selected up and down again."

"You're saying, if I understand you correctly, that the moment Trevor took the autopilot out the EVS reappeared. What do you think happened then?

"Well I know from my own experience at Vision Unlimited what a superb system they have. Because Trevor had his HUD glass down when the EVS appeared I'm sure he felt he could 'see' the runway. Unfortunately the fog cleared at that moment and so he was even more confident that everything was 'go' for landing. He throttled back and tried to carry on the approach. However the fog came back and of course he now had no automatic throttle. He had to fly the aircraft and control the airspeed and it wasn't as easy as he thought. He'd only flown the HUD once in the simulator when they collected the aircraft. We know the speed got too fast and, in trying to correct the speed, the aircraft went to the right of the centre line of the runway and it got too high. He must have thought that he would still be able to land using the EVS and he tried to correct by applying left bank but he was too low, the wing tip hit the ground, the aircraft was far too far down the runway and it was all over. "

Bill was quiet for bit "But Trevor died."

"I know Bill. You knew Trevor, I didn't. However as everything came to pieces around him he probably realised he had made a terrible mistake. He knew he shouldn't have pulled the HUD down and that he should have abandoned the approach. He lived for his flying and he knew that his career would be over. Barbara said he didn't move from his seat. The icy water was pouring in and I think he just gave up."

"But it wasn't really his fault. The EVS shouldn't have appeared. If it had been installed properly he would have done a normal missed approach."

"But that's exactly how accidents happen. It's always a combinations of things that you don't want to happen all occurring at the same time."

"You don't know for sure do you, Peter, about the EVS?"

"No I don't, but it should be possible to find out from European Aerospace or from the Basingstoke facility of Total Avionics."

"How do they come into it? I thought it was a French system."

"No, Bill. It was a system that Total Avionics had developed using unauthorised information from Vision Unlimited."

"Well where does that leave us financially?"

"I'm not a lawyer, Bill. However, you must have some sort of a claim against European Aerospace. They are certainly liable in part. As I explained, the installation should have been arranged so that once the EVS had been locked out then it couldn't come back again until either power had been removed from the aircraft or the undercarriage had been selected and locked up. It just shows that it is important not to try to cut corners. Monty, the EASA pilot, told me they were unhappy with EVS being left on the aircraft but their advice was ignored and I don't think they flew the aircraft again before delivery."

"Peter, thanks for telling me all this. I'll talk to our legal people and I'll get them to call you for advice. Can you check on how the EVS was actually installed?"

"Bill I think the correct procedure would be for your people to talk to European and try to find out exactly what they did. However I could check with NTSB and see what the instrumentation said."

"Peter, I'd appreciate that. Please let me know how you get on."

I put the phone down and decided I would talk to Jane Roberts in the FAA Office before talking to Fabio Costello. She wasn't in but she called me in the middle of the afternoon and I told her the whole story as I saw it and asked for her advice and what I should do. "Peter, thanks for calling me. Two things strike me. Both the FAA in Europe and EASA have screwed up and NTSB won't be over the moon if the news gets out before they say anything. You clearly have no axe to grind. Why don't you tell NTSB what you think happened so that if they want to they can immediately issue a bulletin in effect telling the certification authorities, that's us and EASA, to make sure that the interlink between an EVS system and an autoland system must be very carefully checked."

"Jane, sounds good. Presumably you people relied on EASA for the issuance of the airworthiness certificate?"

"Absolutely. We check on the basic aircraft but we tend to rely completely on EASA for a non-standard piece of equipment like EVS going onto an aircraft, in effect a one off"

I took her advice and called Fabio Costello just as he was leaving the office. I told him what I thought had happened on the approach. I could hear from the long silence that he wasn't at all pleased as he learnt about the situation. "But Peter, the accident was still pilot error, it doesn't change anything. He should have gone round again or diverted. I don't think we need do anything."

"Fabio, my only thought is that if the airline starts legal proceedings with European, some people may wonder why your report didn't mention the EVS. I wasn't suggesting for a moment that you should issue another report but you may want to send out a special bulletin telling the certification authorities that extra care is needed with EVS systems."

There was a long pause while Fabio was clearly thinking round the problem.

"Fabio, another thing. The crash recorder has a signal which tells you whether the HUD glass is up or down. Did you look to see where the HUD was?"

There was an even longer pause. "Peter, thanks very much for calling me."

He didn't give me any clues of what he intended to do but then, in his position, I think I would have kept my cards close to my chest. If I had been a betting man I would have bet on a bulletin coming out in a couple of days.

Charlie came in and left me Peter to deal with. When she reappeared wearing a jumper and skirt she handed me the New York Times and a letter she had obviously printed out on her computer and then took Peter into his room. It was a formal letter from the National Gallery of Australia offering Charlie the job of Procurement Director. As Charlie reappeared I produced two gin and tonics.

"Peter, read all the letter, right to the end." I did what she said. The last paragraph said 'it is anticipated that your husband will have sufficient points to be able to get an unrestricted visa to live in Australia.'

"All settled then? When do we leave?"

She looked at me. "Are you sure? It's a huge step for me to leave New York and for you to leave the UK. And I haven't told them I'm expecting."

"If we go out straightaway you'll be able to do quite a few months work before you have to stop."

"They may not want me now I'm pregnant."

"Nonsense. But you'd better tell them and check."

"Good thinking. And you'd better tell Mike what you're going to do."

"I won't know until your job is confirmed. Of course I could join Mike anyway, whether you are appointed or not but that wouldn't be fair on you."

"Who says? I loved Sydney."

"You only saw the centre. Living in a large city on the edge is not much fun. You like living here but it's virtually downtown."

"Well we could do the same in Sydney."

"Not sure we could afford it if you weren't working. Why don't you phone someone in Canberra and then we'll have to wait while they discuss the situation. Meantime, as usual, we are definitely undecided."

I went into the third bedroom, which was now virtually my office and picked up the Times. The UK election was over and the Government had been swept out of office. I noticed that Luscombe had lost his seat which didn't cause me any pain.

Charlie came in. "Well that's done. I've broken the news to the Director who didn't seem too worried."

"I'm sure the law prevents someone being fired for being pregnant."

"But I'm not on their staff yet."

"They've made you an offer."

"They could claim I knew I was pregnant when I was being interviewed and didn't tell them."

"But you didn't know. You only knew for sure when you got back."

"That's very true, my darling. You can represent me."

"I've been thinking. Mike's a great chap but we'll be living in Canberra. If I carry on working for myself I'm sure we can manage and, who knows, I might apply for the Safety Board job when it becomes vacant."

"Peter, I came to that conclusion as well. We'll have a lot more flexibility in being able to do whatever comes along." She paused. "Did you see the UK elections are over." I nodded. "I meant to ask you. Did they ever find the whistle blower?"

"No. But since it was Sir Philip himself they weren't likely to."

"Sir Philip? The head civil servant?"

"Yes. The permanent secretary no less. I think he was furious that Rogerson, who wasn't on the headhunters' list was interviewed and 'selected'."

"How do you know it was him?"

"When he broke the news to me about the EU veto I as good as told him I knew he had organised the leak and he didn't argue."

"How did you know?"

"Well the information was well filtered but from the way it was done it was untraceable so I felt it had to come from him. Of course it was the email leak from Lord Rogerson to Luscombe which became public knowledge that actually settled the issue. I've no idea who leaked that. Someone in the Government who didn't like Luscombe or Rogerson."

"Why did the knowledge of the email make you certain it was Sir Philip?"

"Well I noticed one day a long time ago when I was communicating with my MP, not sure you have an exact equivalent, that he was using an email address hosted on a Government provided server. I was horrified and told my MP not to use the system because it almost certainly wasn't secure but he ignored me. I'm afraid I'm a cynic. Clearly it must be very easy for all the emails in and out of that server to be monitored."

"What would happen if anyone found out that the government was monitoring all the oppositions emails?"

"Good point. I think the excuse would almost certainly be that it had to be done 'on the grounds of National Security.'"

"I hope they don't do things like that in the States or in Australia for that matter."

I grinned. "I'm afraid that most governments are the same. They convince themselves that everything they do is alright for the sake of their country."

***

Four weeks later we were ready to go to Canberra. Charlie had put her furniture into store and prepared the apartment for renting. I had seen a specialist and was doing physiotherapy so that my arm was virtually back to normal though a little fatter than it was before.

We had moved out and were staying in my favourite Marriott just prior to departure. I had decided to keep my house in Kingston for the moment as I anticipated visiting the UK quite frequently. Charlie was just beginning to notice our daughter to be and wondering whether we were doing the right thing. Peter was very excited at the thought of going to see real kangaroos and I was looking at an email from Sir Philip Brown 'Peter, the new Minister of Transport has decided that, notwithstanding the reservations of the EU, the UK should proceed with the formation of the Transport Safety Board. She has reviewed all the papers and the original selection process and she hopes very much that you will agree to be the first Chairman of the new Board.'

Epilogue

They could see Long Island clearly ahead as they made their approach to New York's Kennedy Airport. The weather had been fine from Bermuda but the airport weather information, ATIS, was giving thick fog, visibility 200 ft on 22 Left, the runway they were going to have to use for an automatic landing using the autopilot. It was early in the morning, only 8 o'clock, and Trevor knew that the fog would soon burn off but not in time for their landing.

Air Traffic had told them to approach the airport using a Kennebunk Four arrival procedure and they were being routed a long way to the east of the airport so that air traffic radar could separate the landing aircraft. They were cleared down to 10,000ft and looking ahead he could see the low cloud blanketing the ground.

As they got nearer the airport he could see the Manhattan skyscrapers sticking up through the cloud so Trevor knew that the fog would not be very thick but listening to the airport weather the cloud clearly was going right down to the ground. He reduced speed as they were cleared down to 3,000ft and Barbara selected the first flap settings. As they got closer, the airport approach radar gave them headings to line the aircraft up with the runway and then they were cleared to start the approach. Barbara set the approach flap and selected the landing gear down. Trevor coupled the autopilot to the ILS and then, after making the final landing checks and getting clearance from air traffic control, he selected the autopilot to make an automatic landing.

At 700ft they went into the fog and Trevor pulled the head-up display glass screen down in front of him as he had done in the simulator even though he knew there would be nothing on the display because he had selected an automatic landing. Everything looked perfect on the aircraft electronic displays as the aircraft descended on the glide path. He could see on the screen that the speed of the aircraft was being controlled correctly by the automatic throttle and that they were lined up with the runway and on the glide slope.

As they descended to 300 feet above the ground Barbara called out "Captain, the visibility has just dropped to 100 feet." Trevor realised the airline regulations did not permit him to land in such poor visibility but as he disconnected the autopilot and started to open the throttles to execute a missed approach he saw to his surprise that the head-up display was now showing the full infra red and microwave radar synthetic picture of the runway and airport ahead.

The fog cleared momentarily and he could see not only the synthetic runway on the head-up display but also the approach lights directly beneath the aircraft through the windscreen. He made an instant decision to land the aircraft manually as he had done on the European Aerospace simulator in Germany. However, as he flew the aircraft following the display and the command bar on the HUD he realised that on the simulator the automatic throttle had been working; this time in the real world, he was having to control the airspeed of the aircraft manually with the throttles and the work load of flying the aircraft was very high. He saw to his horror that he had allowed the aircraft to build up airspeed so that it was way above the target approach speed. His display showed the runway clearly but he could see that he was too high. Worse still, the aircraft had gone back into the fog. However he reckoned he could still land using the display and he throttled back and banked left to try to line the aircraft with the runway.

He heard Barbara warning him the aircraft was going right as the radio altimeter called "One hundred feet".

As he tried to follow the display Barbara was yelling at him to stop trying to land and go around, but he still thought he could correct the situation.

The radio altimeter called "Fifty feet".

Suddenly, he realised it was now too late. In desperation he opened the throttles and tried to level the aircraft but there was a terrible jolt as the left wing tip hit the ground, the aircraft veered to the left and then hit the ground very hard going far too fast, a long way up the airfield. He selected full reverse on the engines and full braking but the aircraft was heading remorselessly for the end of the airfield and the river. Despite all his efforts with the brakes, the rudder and the nosewheel steering he could not bring the aircraft back to the runway He felt powerless to do anything. He should have told Barbara to stop the engines but thank goodness she had done it anyway and operated the fire extinguishers. In complete despair he knew a crash was inevitable as the aircraft slid down the bank into the water, the landing gear got bogged down, then collapsed and the aircraft was half submerged in the river Hudson.

For a moment he was frozen with horror and then automatically he grasped the cabin address microphone. "Evacuate the aircraft into the liferafts. There is no danger. "

He saw Barbara unstrapping herself from the seat and then get up, ashen faced. She opened the cabin door and water poured into the flight deck and started to rise up his legs, numbing him with cold. As she rushed back to get her life jacket he looked back through the door and saw that the cabin crew had responded incredibly quickly and that the passengers were leaving steadily through the emergency exits into the liferafts. Barbara was heading for the starboard front exit. He reached down to get his life jacket but the icy water was upto to his knees and rising fast. He stopped and didn't bother to move. He knew that he had made a terrible mistake. He only cared about flying and he realised his flying career was now finished. He felt the cold water rise further, paralysing his body.

Epilogue

Lightning Source UK Ltd.
Milton Keynes UK
UKOW052108150512

192641UK00002B/209/P